EMBER AND ASH

Fire was her enemy, a killer, a bully, despoiler and blackmailer, and she would never worship Him.

'I thought it was getting cold, and it was a shame we couldn't have a fire,' she said, and the years of life at the warlord's fort came to her aid now, when she had to put on a show for the people she was responsible for. It kept her voice light and calm, and let her put a tinge of humour into her tone. 'I won't do *that* again.'

Ash was looking at her strangely.

'So He came when you called Him,' he said. 'And He has given you a gift.' She was surprised by how harsh his voice sounded. 'He is wooing you.'

A shudder went through her, uncontrollable, and she turned away from the fire to Ash's solid strength, feeling sick and cold. He gathered her in and patted her back.

'He won't hurt you,' he said. 'He wants you to serve Him.'

Never. Never.

There, inside her, was the core of ice, like the ice-earth of the flatlands. She was the warlord's daughter, and she would not barter her people's safety for the heat in her blood and the promise of ecstasy. She knew that was what He was offering, and she rejected it. Holdfast came to stand by her side and Ember buried her fingers in the fur of her neck. The living, breathing dog reminded her of where she belonged.

'Never,' she said aloud. She half-expected the fire to die away on her words, but it continued to blaze happily.

'Well,' Ash said, considering, 'we might as well make use of this gift.'

By Pamela Freeman

The Castings Trilogy
Blood Ties
Deep Water
Full Circle

The Castings Trilogy Omnibus

EMBER AND ASH

Pamela Freeman

www.orbitbooks.net

ORBIT

First published in Great Britain in 2011 by Orbit

Copyright © 2011 by Pamela Freeman

Excerpt from *Blood Ties* by Pamela Freeman
Copyright © 2007 by Pamela Freeman

The moral right of the author has been asserted.

A CIP catalogue record for this book
is available from the British Library.

ISBN 978-1-84149-827-0

Typeset in Sabon by M Rules
Printed in the UK by CPI Mackays, Chatham ME5 8TD

Orbit
An imprint of
Little, Brown Book Group
100 Victoria Embankment
London EC4Y 0DY

An Hachette UK Company
www.hachette.co.uk

www.orbitbooks.net

To Ron

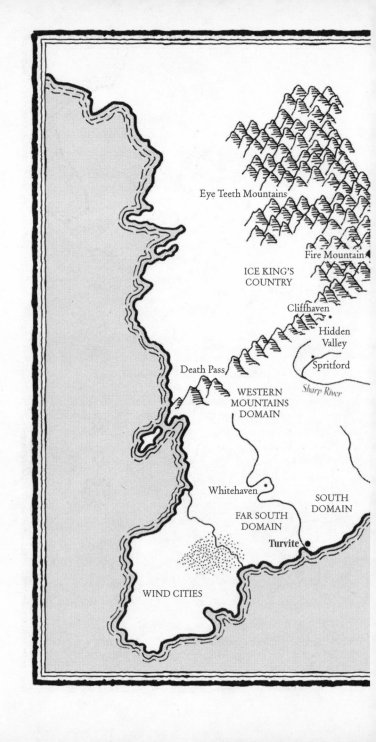

THE ELEVEN DOMAINS

THE DEEP

'This is the oath we ask of you,' the Prowman said. 'Will you give it? To be silent to death of what you see, of what you hear, of what you do?'

Ash blinked slowly. Could he give that oath? What if whatever he saw was treasonous? Or dangerous to others? But the Prowman was his uncle, in all but blood, and everyone Ash trusted, trusted him. So he nodded, and when the Prowman spat on his hand and held it out, Ash spat on his and clasped it.

'You must speak,' the Prowman prodded.

'I swear,' Ash said, his deep voice echoing off the high canyon walls.

'Do you swear upon pain of shunning, never to speak of this place outside of this place?'

'I swear.'

'Do you swear upon pain of death never to guide another to this place who has not the blood right?'

Ash had no idea what the blood right was, but no doubt he'd find out – if he swore. His curiosity was roused.

'I swear,' he said.

'Do you swear upon pain beyond death, the pain of never being reborn, to keep the secrets of this place with your honour, with your strength, with your life?'

What in the cold hells was this about? Ash wondered. But trust was trust.

'I swear,' he said, his voice coming a little hoarsely.

The Prowman smiled, his dark eyes lighting up with relief and pleasure. Then he stood back and gestured, inviting Ash to walk through.

Ash took a long breath. Before him was a narrow crack in the blood-red wall of the canyon. It was just after dusk, and the shadows were growing towards him. He and the Prowman had journeyed all day through the network of red sandstone canyons and streams and fissures that made up the wilds of Gabriston. It was a place with a bad reputation – those who went in alone, they said, never came out. Eaten by demons. Wind wailing through the canyons caused those stories, Ash reckoned. Or the many waters, falling and dripping and calling. The streams all drained eventually to the Hidden River, the fast, turbulent watercourse that fell headlong from the lake to their west.

It was a long way from the cold, clean Western Mountains, where his home was. Here the air was damp and heavy. He felt as though he were choking on it. Even the red walls oozed water like blood.

'What would have happened if I hadn't sworn?' he asked, turning his head to look his uncle in the eye.

'We would have gone home,' the Prowman said, shrugging.

Oddly enough, that was disturbing. He wanted to find out what all this palaver was about. So he walked through the opening, and waited. The Prowman went past him and, smiling reassuringly, said, 'Not far now.' It was the tone an adult uses to a child, but Ash let it pass. Although the Prowman looked only a few years older than his own twenty-one years, Ash knew he had to be far older than that – at least as old as Ash's parents. He had seen Ash born, after all – the Prowman's real name, they said, was also Ash, and he had been named after him. No doubt he still thought of Ash as the baby he'd once known. Ash was used to that. He had aunts.

So he shrugged and followed the Prowman around a turn, with the constant noise of wind wailing through rocks making his ears buzz.

There was another canyon, and beyond that another, and for an hour more they threaded their way through increasingly narrow passageways, while the night grew dark above them. Glow-worms studded the walls, giving a meagre light once their eyes had adjusted.

The further they went, the more Ash wondered why he'd come. The Prowman had just appeared one day, after an absence of years, and said he had something important to take Ash to. His mother, her pale eyes bright, had urged him to go, even though he would miss his cousin Ember's wedding. His father had shrugged. Whatever the Prowman wanted, he should have. A hero was a hero, and the Prowman was the most famous living hero, although Ash's grandmother, Martine, ran close. So Ash had agreed to go.

But this winding, closed-in path was as alien to him as the sea. He'd been raised in the mountains, where every vista was long and capped with snow; where the sky seemed so high above you that there was unlimited breathing space. He didn't like the feeling of being hemmed in. Imprisoned by the blood-red sandstone walls of the Deep.

Then they came to a violent stream, with a rocky waterfall, and the Prowman made him give blood and gave some himself and declared that they had the blood right. Ash, son of Elva, the

Prowman called him, because it was by his mother's blood that he had the right to be here. The old blood.

As the blood touched the stream, the waters calmed. It startled him: there was power here, then, of some kind. He was accustomed to power – his mother was a mouthpiece for the local gods, a kind of prophet – but he had never seen power affect a physical substance like water before. It made him more alert. There were spells operating, maybe. He'd heard so many stories of spells that as a child he'd longed to see one cast, but right now he'd do without. They went further into the maze of fissures.

Demons howled.

Ash started – that was no wind in the rocks, that was a flesh-and-blood throat making those noises. He glanced at the Prowman and saw the small smile on his face, so he bit back his questions and ignored the sound, although all the hairs on the back of his neck were upright, and his arms were furred with goosebumps.

They emerged into what seemed like bright light – an open space lit by a big fire. The canyon walls rose up all around, enclosing them securely. A good, defensible hiding spot, Ash thought, and wondered if he had been brought here to meet rebels. There were some, they said, who had been dissatisfied with the Resettlement, twenty or so years ago. Those forced from land their fathers had farmed so that Travellers could have land of their own, and live safe. They resented it, even though they were tenants of the warlords and farmed only at their pleasure. Some of them, the stories said, had taken to the wild places and raided warlords' supplies to stay alive. But surely the Prowman, whose hair was as black as any Traveller's could be, wouldn't support dissatisfied blondies?

He had only a moment to think this through. Then, from a

cave mouth on the other side of the fire, a stream of shapes came pouring out.

Demons. Demons with the bodies of men and the heads of animals. They leapt, naked, in the firelight, shrieking and howling and ululating. His throat clenched; his bowels tightened with fear. They surrounded him, their hands angling flints, sharp as knives, at his throat. Through the fear he felt a flicker of irritation with his uncle. He could have warned me, he thought. Ash planted his feet and stood still, sure that the Prowman wouldn't have brought him into a nest of demons if it were really dangerous.

'He is a member of the blood,' the Prowman called to the demons. He nudged Ash. 'Tell them who you are,' he said.

'I am Ash, son of – son of Elva,' Ash said.

'Whose blood has calmed the waters,' the Prowman prompted.

'Whose blood has calmed the waters,' he repeated.

The demons shrieked again and their hands dropped. They stood, panting as animals do, their eyes bright with interest.

'He is a bowyer,' the Prowman added. 'Will you teach him what he needs to know?' And they howled again, with approval.

Two of them, a wolf and a deer, came forward and tried to strip away his clothes. He stepped back and fended them off.

'It's all right,' the Prowman said reassuringly. 'In the Deep, we show our true shapes.' But he made no move to undress.

'You don't,' Ash said.

'This *is* my true shape,' the Prowman said. 'You are here to learn yours, as all these have done.' He gestured to the demons waiting, and Ash suddenly understood. They were men. Human men, who had come here to be transformed. Who had *deliberately* come here to be transformed. His stomach turned a little. Why would anyone choose to make himself into a monster?

'If you hold still and show no fear, you will not be harmed,' the Prowman said. 'This is the first test.'

'What happens if I pass?' Ash demanded.

'Then there are others. And eventually, if you pass them all, you will be allowed to discover your true self. To know who you really are. This is the River's gift to those of Traveller blood.'

The ground felt solid enough beneath his feet, even if the rest of the world had gone awry. The gleaming naked skins, the sharp animal scents around him, the fire leaping high and something else, some sense that he was being watched by whatever power had calmed the stream, made him dizzy. This was an invitation to journey into a place he'd never imagined; in ways that he could only dimly make out. To find – what? Himself? He planted his feet more firmly.

'I know who I really am,' he said.

The demons hissed disapproval.

'And I'm not a Traveller,' he added.

The hands with their flint knives came up again and the demons – the *men* – turned to the Prowman with anger.

'His blood calmed the waters,' he said hastily. 'His mother was a Traveller.'

'Not for long,' Ash said. 'Before that, her people farmed Cliffhaven for thousands of years. And my people have been rooted at High Fields in Hidden Valley since just after Acton came over the mountains. I have the old blood, yes, but I'm not a Traveller.'

Travellers had been despised and mistreated in the Eleven Domains for a thousand years, until the Resettlement. Even now, there were those who distrusted them. They were known by their dark hair, a sign that the old blood, the blood of the people who had first inhabited this country, flowed in their veins. The later incomers, the invaders, his father's people, were blue-eyed and blond, or red-headed.

They inspected him. His light brown hair, his hazel eyes, his big, muscular build, so unlike the rangy Prowman next to him. Unlike them – all of them were dark-haired and slightly built. Ash looked like one of Acton's people, all right, but he wasn't that either, he thought. He wasn't dark or blond – he was the two combined, and he belonged in Hidden Valley, on the land that his ancestors had claimed from the wilderness. There had been no one of the old blood living in Hidden Valley when his ancestors arrived. They had displaced no one.

'The River will show you the shape of your soul,' the Prowman said gently, as though Ash didn't understand what he was being offered.

Ash didn't want to give offence, but this primitive ritual stirred nothing in him but a vague distaste. Pity, even, for those who needed it. No doubt a secret society had been important, in the days when every man's hand had been turned against Travellers. But times had changed. Besides—

'I know the shape of my soul,' he answered calmly. 'It's an arrow in flight.'

The image in his mind was as clear as a star: fletched with grey goose feathers, his arrow soaring into the bright sky, the clean whistling it made cutting through the air like a benediction on him. That was who he was. What he did. What he wanted.

'I thank you,' he said gently. 'But I think this path is not for me.'

A bough broke and the fire shot upwards, throwing sparks. The wind caught them so that their glow seemed to dance in front of his eyes and he and the Prowman were surrounded by flying shards of light.

The demons turned away, and filed back slowly, disappointed, into the cave. The Prowman stood still, as though listening to someone speak a long way off.

'There is only one chance,' he said. 'Turn away, and She won't have you back.'

'She?' Ash asked. The River's gift, he'd said before.

'You haven't earned the right to know more.'

That was fair. But there was something else, an unasked question in the way the Prowman stood, on the balls of his feet, ready for – what?

'My oaths stand,' Ash said mildly. 'I will keep silence.'

A certain tension went out of the Prowman's shoulders, although he was disappointed, no doubt about that.

'Would you have killed me if I'd said otherwise?' Ash asked.

'Me? I wouldn't have had to. You wouldn't have made it across the stream,' the Prowman said simply. 'Come on. No sense staying here.' He nodded towards the cave. 'They won't be happy with you in the morning.'

They retraced their steps, the Prowman saying nothing, lost in thought.

'I brought you here too late,' he said. 'You're supposed to come when your voice first breaks, but I was – elsewhere – then.'

Ash shrugged.

'I don't think it would have made any difference,' he said.

As they threaded their way back through the canyons, the wind swirled around them, lifting the oppressive heat and seeming to sing through the rocks. Ash found it soothing now, even joyful, but he was still glad when they came out into the wide spaces of the Gabriston vineyards, near where they had left their horses. It was still dark, but the sky had begun to pale.

He hesitated, but he might as well say it. He hadn't wanted

to come on this trip in the first place. It was only his mother's insistence that had convinced him. There was somewhere else he would much rather be. His cousin Ember had promised it would be a party to remember.

'Since we're leaving so quickly,' he said, 'do you think we could still be in time for Ember's wedding?'

The Prowman began to laugh, as though acknowledging that his own disappointment was unimportant.

'Aye,' he said. 'If we ride at daybreak.'

PALISADE FORT, THE LAST DOMAIN

Today North and South would be unified.

Ember felt exalted by the thought. Even separated, as they were, by half a continent, the Far South Domain and the Last Domain in the north would today become a single political entity, to be ruled eventually by her husband. She and Osfrid, providing a sheltering roof from one end of the Domains to the other, two islands of justice and equality; two examples of how the Domains could be, *should* be run. Having two large domains under his control would give Osfrid a strong voice in the Warlords' Council, and the alliance with the Lady Sorn of the Central Domain made that even stronger.

She looked out the window, trying to find Osfrid in the crowd below.

The muster yard was full of almost everyone she'd ever known. All of her father's officers had come in from their estates, complete with wives and daughters and sons. Some of the sons were off on the border, in case the Ice King attacked, of course. Most of her mother's family had come, too, although her adopted sister, Elva, was still inside, her pale eyes and skin unable to bear the glare of the warm sunshine. But Elva's daughters, Poppy and Saffron, were sitting on a bench; Saffron was flirting with an officer's son while her brother, Cedar, looked on with his customary cynical smile, his dogs at his side lolling in the sun. Elva was so much older than Ember that she always thought of her nieces and nephews as cousins; they were much of an age. The eldest, Ash, was only a year older than her and her cousin Clary was a year younger, yet Clary was at home in the Western Mountains Domain, almost ready to give birth. Ember spread a hand across her own belly, smiling; maybe by this time next year she would have a baby, too.

All the people of the fort had made a circle around the wedding fire. It was an important day, the marriage of the domain's heir, but she hoped that some of them were there because they wished her well, not just because she was the warlord's daughter.

Her cousin-nephew Ash came into view, covered in dust and accompanied by a tall, dark-haired man who moved like a dancer. She was glad Ash had come in time. It set the seal on this fine day.

Springtree, the day when all the ice had melted and the may was in full flower, was the luckiest day for a wedding, everyone agreed, but here in the Last Domain it was later than in other places – only half a moon before the Solstice – and it had been known to keep cold until then. The weather was so uncertain that the stonecasters always got the Chaos stone if they tried to predict it, and the blank stone, too, which meant that anything could happen. Today, although there were still small patches of snow melting in the shade, the sun was bright and the air warm enough for her to cast aside her coat and wear only her wedding outfit.

She smoothed the delicate silk skirt down over her trousers and danced a little, just to hear it rustle. Green for Springtree, of course, but mid-green with a soft shimmer of reddish-gold somehow woven into it, the very red of her own hair appearing and disappearing as she twirled.

There he was! Below her, in the muster yard, Osfrid looked up, his eyes caught by her movement, and he smiled at her. She waved to him. He was handsome, the image of what a warlord should be.

He turned back to oversee the building of the fire they would jump over together, as he should, and she turned away, too, to rejoin her mother and his as they set the last stitches in her wedding sash.

Dark purple, this, of the finest silk, it had been brought from far beyond the Wind Cities by eastern traders, and all winter she had embroidered it with their names: Ember and Osfrid, entwined traditionally with flowers; irises in pale purple, their green stems crossed like spears below the names. She loved to embroider anyway, but making this had been a delight: at least an hour each day, when the light was brightest, when she could simply sit and daydream about how wonderful her life was going to be. She and Osfrid, loving each other, living in the warm, fertile Far South Domain, where it hardly ever snowed, where their children would run around barefoot in summer, where she would, after Osfrid's father died, become the warlord's lady: respected, rich, happy.

It was traditional that the two mothers set the final stitches in the sash, to bind the two families closer together, but Ember had to suppress a laugh. Her mother, Martine, hated embroidery – sewing of any kind, in fact, and most of the 'womanly' arts expected of a warlord's lady. She was struggling with the needle, her face set firmly in that expression Ember knew well – determination not to let her family down in any duty expected of a warlord's wife, overlying a deep, deep contempt for everything a warlord stood for.

'Done!' Martine said with relief. Osfrid's mother, Sigurd, smiled at her with a hint of reproof. Sigurd was so much a warlord's lady that Ember was a little in awe of her. Not beautiful, but stately, reserved, calm. Yet she smiled with real affection as she tied the sash around Ember's waist and stood back to let Martine tuck the ends in at the back.

'There,' Martine said. 'You're ready.' Her expression was a mixture of pride, love and anxiety – and anxiety was so alien to her mother that Ember felt a flash of fear.

'What's the matter?' she asked. 'Have you Seen something? Have you cast the stones for me?'

Although her mother was one of the best stonecasters in the Domains, seeing the future in the choosing and fall of the stones in her pouch, she had never before been able to see Ember's future in the stones, but perhaps now – Martine shook her head.

'The stones won't speak to me of you, you know that. I – I'm just unsure about all this,' she murmured, flicking a glance at Sigurd who was chatting with a couple of officers' wives at the door to Ember's chamber. 'It feels wrong to me.'

Ember sighed.

'Mam. You just don't want me to be a warlord's wife!'

Martine's mouth twisted wryly.

'Perhaps I don't,' she admitted. She tucked a strand of Ember's hair up into the elaborate knot on the top of her head. 'It's not an easy life.'

Thank the gods she herself had been bred to the job, Ember thought, instead of having it forced on her as it had been forced on her mother when she had fallen in love with her father. Where *was* Arvid? Ember looked out and yes, there her father was with Osfrid and his father, Lord Merroc, supervising the fire, laughing and chatting, at ease as he always was, in any company. The Springtree had been raised behind them, its branches adorned with long ribbons, ready for the dance which would follow the wedding. The dance she and Osfrid would lead.

'It's time to go down,' she said. She couldn't help beaming at her mother. 'It will suit me, Mam, you know it will.'

Martine laughed.

'Aye, it will that,' she said, a catch in her voice. 'You're perfect for it, and may the gods bless you both.'

For a moment, Ember was conscious of the grey in Martine's black hair, of the lines around her green eyes, and of her own maturity. She might soon be a mother herself; would she feel the same anxiety when her child married? No doubt she would.

They went down to the men as they should, the bride arm in arm with her mother and future mother-in-law. As they came out of the hall Osfrid turned and saw her and his face lit up. How lucky she was that her father had let her choose her husband – out of the six young warlords' sons who had come to woo her, Osfrid was by far the handsomest, with fine broad shoulders and chest and long, lean legs. Her heart fluttered with excitement. Tonight was her wedding night. They had kissed and touched a little, but of course that was all. She was a warlord's daughter, and her worth lay in her husband's surety of her loyalty. One man, and one man only, so that the bloodlines would be secure.

Her mother had tried to talk her out of that.

'Try him out before you buy him,' she'd advised coolly, when Ember had first chosen Osfrid. 'You learn a lot about a man in bed.'

Ember had wanted to retort that she wasn't a Traveller whore, lying down with anyone who took her fancy, but of course she didn't. Not when her mother was Traveller born and bred.

She knew her duty, and Osfrid knew his. He hadn't even tried to seduce her. Not once.

Besides, she thought now, pushing aside that slight

disappointment, her mother didn't understand the – the *beauty* of coming to a man as a virgin, offering him everything she was, for the rest of her life. How could Martine understand?

Outside the door the people of the fort were gathered, and the guests, all dressed in their best finery, all smiling, nodding, laughing. Somewhere music was playing: flute and harp and drum, a light tingling sort of melody. A few people cheered when she appeared.

Ember went forward. It struck her that she was arm in arm with the two cultures, the two peoples, of the Domains: Acton's people and Travellers, Sigurd and Martine, new blood and old, and she herself in between like a bridge.

Osfrid moved to meet her, arm in arm with her father and his, smiling as though his heart would burst.

The two mothers took her hands, the two fathers took his, and they were joined together and stood for a moment, looking into each other's eyes. Ember had never been so happy.

Arvid, as the warlord of this domain, performed the ceremony. He produced the red string that symbolised heart's blood, and bound her right hand to Osfrid's left. She would take it after, and keep it safe, and the midwife would use it to tie the cords when her babies were born.

'Heart to heart, blood to blood, family to family,' he said solemnly, his eyes suspiciously bright. He would miss her, she knew. 'Long life, long love, and death far distant.'

He stood back and gestured to where the fire had burned down to glowing coals.

'Be purified by this fire; be reborn into a new life together.'

Handfasted, they smiled at each other, and together took two steps towards the fire. They were in perfect unison. A good omen, Ember thought, as she bent her legs and leapt as he leapt, over the coals.

As they reached the highest point, buoyed up by happiness, Ember felt the air change around her. It was suddenly hot; impossibly hot. Osfrid began to turn his face towards her questioningly. He seemed to move slowly, so slowly.

A roar hit her ears like high wind, like someone enormous shouting.

The sleeping fire reared up, flames huge and impossibly high. She was surrounded by flames, a column of fire around her; the heat on her skin was unbearable but she wasn't burning.

Panic struck at her and she clutched Osfrid's hand and screamed in pain. It was alight – *he* was alight, Osfrid, Osfrid … The flames licked around her wrist, consuming the red cord, cutting her free of him and she fell, tumbling, on the other side of the fire, alone, with the flames towering over her, so *loud*, gold and orange and red and white-hot at the centre.

Osfrid was suspended in the fire, his body turning black, skin cracking open, blood, oh gods, his blood was boiling, his mouth opened in a scream he had no time to voice, his beautiful blond hair a halo of flame.

Then the fire flared even more, covering him in a sheath of white. There was nothing but flame.

There was a face.

A man's face in the fire. Not Osfrid. Not *human*. The face of the fire itself, wild and sulky and unpredictable and full of desire. For her. Despite her shock, she felt heat run through her like hot mead.

'You are mine,' the fire said, a voice half honey and half rough wood. 'Your mother should have known that. And you will come to me.'

The flames disappeared. The fire was coals again, just coals, and Osfrid had gone as if he'd never been. There weren't even any bones. Just ash. Ember knelt, cradling her burnt wrist, staring numbly at the ashes and only then heard the shouts and cries and Osfrid's mother, screaming.

'A judgement on us,' Sigurd moaned, later, in Martine's room, lying on the bed with her waiting women in close attendance. 'A judgement on us for marrying our son to a Traveller's whelp!'

Martine, passing a cold cloth to one of the women, didn't even flinch. She'd warned Ember before the betrothal that those in the south didn't think the same about Travellers; that there would be some in Merroc's court who would look down on her because her mother had dark hair, but she'd laughed it away. Times had changed, she'd said. People didn't think like that any more.

'When times are good,' Martine had said, smoothing back a strand of Ember's unruly hair, 'people are happy. But when things go bad, they look for someone to blame. Usually that's Travellers.'

So. There was Sigurd, who this morning had been so kind, so happy, now calling her a Traveller's whelp for all to hear. Her world was fragmenting around her. Everything she had relied on was falling apart. Everything she had planned was smashed beyond repair. She felt numb and cold, but underneath there was anger, and she knew that sooner or later the anger would warm her enough to let her speak. But she didn't know what she would say.

Ember got up from the chair where she had been huddled, and went downstairs. Martine followed her.

Her father and Merroc were standing by the fireplace in the hall, but the fire was out for the first time in Ember's memory. It had been put out, she saw, with a bucket of water, and smelt of wet ash, acrid and unpleasant. The men were drinking apple-jack. Merroc, ten years older than her father, looked double that, the long lines of his face dragged into furrows and his skin pale against his still-red hair. His hand shook as he raised his mug.

Another man was with them – the tall, slender man who had come in the gate with her cousin Ash. Ash himself, she noticed, was sitting quietly in the corner, with his brother Cedar. They nodded at her, but didn't smile, and she was grateful. She couldn't pretend to be all right.

The men turned as they came in and her father put out his arms to her. She walked into them but as they closed around her she felt none of the usual safety, nothing of her habitual comfort from his presence. She returned his embrace for his sake, not for hers.

She pulled herself away and turned to Merroc, hesitating. His eyes searched hers.

'Why?' he asked. 'Why did it happen?'

She had to find enough voice to answer him, but it was hard, as though she had forgotten how to speak.

'I don't know,' she said slowly. Tears started in her eyes, hot and burning as the fire had been on her wrist. They rose and fell, rose and fell, and she could do nothing but stand there and let them, because she couldn't say what she felt. The tears would have to speak for her.

'I know you loved him,' Merroc said, as though trying to puzzle it out. 'So why? And *how*?' With the last word, his free hand smacked into his thigh. 'Some enchanter. Has to be. Some enchanter with a grudge against us ...'

He turned and looked at Martine, and at the other man with dark hair. His thoughts were plain. Enchanters tended to be of the old blood. The last enchanter who had caused trouble for the Domains had been a Traveller. The odds were that if an enchanter had cast a fire spell, he would be a Traveller too.

Ember could see, in that moment, all the gains of the Resettlement being lost, vanishing like autumn mist at noon. No matter what, she couldn't let Merroc believe that. It was clear he hadn't seen what she had – the face in the fire.

'Not an enchanter,' she said, forcing the words out, having to form them carefully as though she spoke in another language. 'The fire spoke to me. That was no spell.'

Merroc and Arvid exclaimed, but her mother and the other man drew in their breaths, as though she had confirmed their fears. She turned to her mother.

'It said – *He* said, that I belonged to Him. That you should have known that.'

Martine began to sink to the ground, her legs shaking, and the other man went to support her. She turned to him gratefully and the two dark heads together sparked a memory in Ember, of being very young and seeing this man laughing with her mother. Fifteen years ago? At least. He had been visiting from the south. 'You may call him the Prowman,' Martine had said. 'Or Uncle Ash, whichever you prefer.' The man had laughed. 'Are you sure you want to saddle her with an uncle like me?' he'd asked. That was all she remembered, but now, as an adult, she realised that this was Ash the Songmaker, the Prowman of the Lake, the great hero of the Resettlement.

She would think about that later.

'Mam? What did it – *He* – mean?'

Martine stood straighter and faced the Prowman, not her.

'He's shown Himself,' she said to him. 'You knew about Him?'

'I knew some,' he said. His voice was mellow and rich, comforting. 'I knew He existed.'

'Do you think I can talk about Him now?'

'I think you have to,' the Prowman said. 'Or there will be

retribution on the old blood across the Domains, and we know what that looks like.'

Her mother shuddered and finally turned to look Ember in the eye.

'There are ... powers,' she said. 'Call them gods, if you like. We know of five, at least, but there are probably more. Fire is one.'

'But why *Osfrid*? Why me?'

Inside, she was raging. No, no, no! She didn't want anything to do with powers or gods or anything unchancy. She wanted a simple, happy life with her husband and her children and the duties of a warlord's lady.

Merroc took a step forward.

'Yes,' he said. 'Why Osfrid?'

'Fire was there when you were born,' Martine said to her. 'That's why I called you Ember. He was in the grate, looking at you, the moment after you were born, and He used up all the fuel so only a breath later all that was left was embers. It was only a heartbeat. I wasn't even sure if I'd imagined it ...'

But there was a story here her mother wasn't telling, and the anger inside her swelled larger.

'Why?' she demanded. The words were coming more easily now. 'Why me?'

'I angered Him, once,' Martine said, very softly. 'I ... supported someone He wanted, and she refused Him.'

'So He wants me instead?' Her voice was shrill, she could hear it climbing into hysteria, but she didn't care. 'Because *you* made Him angry? That's not fair!'

'My son died because you angered a god,' Merroc said, almost thoughtfully, as though weighing an argument in council.

Arvid gestured and then drew his hand back, as if afraid of making things worse.

'The Powers of this land do as they please, and they always

have,' the Prowman said. 'Believe me, I know. There is no predicting them, and no stopping them. Martine is not to blame.'

Merroc turned on him. 'Then who *is*?' he demanded. 'On whom do I take revenge?'

'Will you turn against the land itself?' the Prowman asked.

'If I have to!' Merroc snarled, and flung out of the room, up the stairs to his wife.

Feeling her legs shake, Ember moved to a chair and sat down.

'He said I belonged to Him,' she whispered. 'That I would come to Him.'

'Come to Him?' Martine asked, her voice sharp.

'"You are mine",' Ember quoted. '"Your mother should have known that. And you will come to me."'

'That's not … right,' Ash said. 'That's not how it works. The lover has to choose.'

'The *lover*?' Ember tried to keep her voice from shaking. 'He wants me—' She couldn't finish. Her mother was shaking her head, over and over.

'That's not how He is. It's *not*!'

'Martine?' Arvid said, his voice hard. 'You have never mentioned this to me.'

The Prowman put a hand on his arm. 'It's forbidden for women to talk about it to men,' he said.

'But *you* knew,' Arvid said, his eyes still stone.

'Because I—' the Prowman looked at Martine as if for guidance, and then stood for a moment, eyes unfocused, as Ember had seen her mother stand when the Sight hit her. He shivered a little, and shrugged. 'I am the Prowman of the Lake, which is one of the faces of Water, another of the Powers of this land. I have some little knowledge of the others.'

'Five, Martine said.' Arvid's voice held the warlord's tone of command, the voice he used when training his officers.

Oh gods, this was about more than her! Ember thought. This changed everything they thought they knew about the world.

The Prowman nodded.

'Five we are sure of: Fire, Water, Earth, Air and the Great Forest. There may be others. We know very little of the Sea, for example. The Foreverfroze people talk of the Sealmother. And in the deserts, the Hungry Wind is spoken of.'

Arvid waved that aside. His eyes were fixed on Martine.

'So for all the time we have been together, you have known of these powers and not told me?' His voice was full of betrayal, and Ember shared that feeling.

'You should have told *me*,' she said. 'I'm a woman.'

Martine spread her hands, which shook.

'I was trying to keep you safe from Him,' she said. 'I never took you to the fire altar. I thought, if you didn't go to Him, He couldn't hurt you – He's never done anything *like* this before!' Her voice was a cry, and it shook Ember. Her mother had always kept calm, no matter what, before.

'Yes, He has,' Ash said. 'Once before, at least, He took a woman from her own home because she had neglected Him. One of the Bynum girls.'

The anger that had been building inside Ember was too great to contain any more. Its heat was overwhelming. She clenched her fists against the soft silk of her wedding skirt and cried, 'I *will not* be owned! I will not be commanded! Lady Death will take me to the cold hells before I will bow to Him.' She meant it as a shout, but it came out flat and cold and even.

For the first time, her cousin Ash came forward and put his arm around her shoulders.

'Shagging right,' he said. He looked at the Prowman, and something passed between them. 'We don't belong to any old gods. Times have changed.'

The Prowman and Martine looked at them with identical expressions of love and concern and exasperation.

'Could be you'll have some trouble explaining that to Him,' the Prowman said.

'I will not be owned!' Ember shouted, the rage turning hot.

The cold, wet, dead fire in the grate sprang to life. Ember felt her breath catch in her throat; saw the others suspended in movement as they all turned to the hearth; and in that moment, her sister Elva came through the doorway from her father's workroom, her white hair and pale skin seeming to shine in the dimness. Something in the way she walked made a shiver run down Ember's spine. When she opened her mouth, it was not Elva's gentle voice which came out: it was deep, dark, rough, as though another being spoke through her.

'He is here,' Elva said.

Ember began to shiver. Her sister Elva was a prophet, a mouthpiece for the local gods of the black rock altars, but Ember had never seen her possessed before. She lived a long way away, in Hidden Valley, and the gods had been quiet every time they had visited there. It was *wrong*, horrible, to hear another voice come from her sister's mouth.

Ash and Cedar, Elva's sons, didn't even blink, and her mother took it in her stride.

'Give us guidance,' she asked. 'We entreat you.'

Elva turned to the hearth, her movements unsteady, as though the gods weren't used to commanding a moving body.

'Show yourself,' the deep voice said.

The fire grew, swelled, spread out into the room itself, into a tree of flame. He was there; the face, just as she had seen it. The others saw it too, and that was a comfort of sorts, that she wasn't just imagining it, wasn't going mad ... The dark, blazing, male face stared at her, eyes not red but black.

'You are mine,' it said. He said. 'You will come to me.'

Her anger flared up as fast as His flames. Oh, she'd fought against her temper since the day she was born, but not this time. This was righteous anger and He deserved it.

'I will *not* be owned!' she shouted.

He laughed, the flames dancing at His feet in rhythm.

'I don't *own*,' He chuckled. 'I *possess*.' His tone made it explicit; heat ran through her, from her nipples, her belly. How dare He! Even Osfrid had never made her feel like this.

'Not me,' she hissed.

His eyes narrowed and He turned His head to glare at Elva as though she – the gods – were responsible.

'She has the right to refuse you,' the gods said. 'You may not compel worship.'

Ember felt supported, at last. All those dawn services at the black rock altar had been worthwhile, it seemed. Fire seemed to shrug, and turned back to stare at her. Her father moved to stand in front of her, but she sidestepped him. It was dangerous, she felt, to let Him out of her sight.

'Then I must make you come,' He said. 'If you wish to relight the fires, you must steal fire from me.' He looked at Arvid, standing helpless beside her. 'If you must protect her, use the old blood. I will consume anyone else.' His gaze went past her and He paused, considering. Ash and Cedar, she realised, had come forward as well and were standing right behind her. 'Those two will do,' Fire said. He smiled, as if at a private joke.

With a great *thwump* of air sucked up the chimney, the flames were gone. He was gone. The fire was out in the hearth again, as if it had never been alight, leaving behind a scent of woodsmoke and something else, something acrid which seared Ember's throat. No one spoke. Cautiously, Ember came forward and, crouching, touched the ashes. Cold. As though the fire had died a lifetime ago.

She stood up slowly, confused. What had He meant?

Behind the wall, in the kitchen, shouts and accusations were flying.

Her mother frowned and went through the connecting door, saying, 'What's toward here?' in her best lady's voice. She came back a moment later, her face pale.

'The fire's gone out in the kitchen,' she said, looking at Elva.

Ember blinked. Why was her mother's voice so shaky? A kitchen fire …

Martine crossed the room and put her hand on Arvid's arm. They were the same height, and at the moment wore the same expression of worry, giving them a strange resemblance.

'They can't relight it,' Martine said.

'Try again,' Arvid replied.

'It will not avail,' the gods' deep voice said. Elva blinked and coughed, clearing her throat. 'This isn't good,' she added, in her own light tones.

Ember turned back to the fireplace and grabbed for the tinderbox which lay on the mantelpiece above it. Tinder on the ashes, kindling from the basket next to the hearth, flint, striker … the flint was struck and sparked, but although the sparks fell onto the tinder, they didn't catch, just charred and died. She tried again, and again, in a nightmare where everything was familiar but nothing acted as it should.

She had made fire like this since she was a small girl. Children were taught fire-making early in the Last Domain in case they were caught by nightfall in a forest, or became lost. Fire was all that would save them, then.

Her father came to kneel beside her.

'Let me try,' he said. 'Maybe a man …'

She blew on the sparks as they fell from her father's hand, but the tinder stayed sullenly unwilling to catch, and finally they gave up. Martine had her hand under her breasts, as though holding her heart firm.

People were crowding the doorways. Arvid turned to them and beckoned one forward. Holly, the woman who led his guard.

'How bad is it?' he asked.

'All the fires in the fort,' she answered. 'Except one. The bonfire – the wedding fire. That's still burning.'

'Take a brand from it –' Arvid began, but Holly interrupted.

'No, my lord. We've tried to light sticks from it, torches, tinder – it will burn whatever wood we put on it, but as soon as you take the wood from it, the fire goes out.'

All the fires in the fort, Ember thought numbly. It was spring. They could survive spring and summer without fires indoors. Cook on the bonfire. But this was the Last Domain, and when summer ended and the snow came ...

A man ran into the room and fell on his knees in front of Arvid, panting.

'My lord, our fires ...'

'Where are you from?' Arvid asked.

'Two Springs, my lord.' It was the nearest village.

'Are there any fires alight there?'

The man shook his head.

'No, my lord. Except there's a candle Mayflower keeps burning always in remembrance of her daughter, you know, the one who died so hard of the canker. That's still alight. But we can't take a light from it. And – and there's a flame, but the candle's not burning down.'

Arvid looked despairingly at Martine, and cold settled into Ember's bones. If this was the story throughout the domain, their people were dead when the first snow fell.

PALISADE FORT, THE LAST DOMAIN

S end messengers,' Arvid said to Holly. 'I want to know how far this has spread. Find out what we're facing.'

Her father wanted to collect facts, but Ember knew what he would find. Fire had taken Himself away, to force her to come to Him. To be His slave, His – what? If He'd wanted to kill her, she would be dead already, like Osfrid. She began to shake, again, as she had after the fire had killed him.

Ash came up behind her and led her to a chair, sitting her down firmly. He handed her a mug of applejack.

'Drink,' he said, his hand on her shoulder. The human warmth, so mild in comparison to the searing heat of fire, comforted her, and she drank. She stared at the mug in her hands, barely listening as reports began to come in from nearby farms and villages.

She couldn't go to Him. Over and over, she relived that moment when she had been surrounded by flames. Was that what He wanted? To have her like that forever? Shudders ran through her. She couldn't do it.

The door banged open and a woman ran in to throw herself at Arvid's feet.

'My lord, my lord, the fires—' she was gasping, tears of sheer panic in her eyes. 'The world has gone mad, my lord!'

Arvid crouched down to lift her to her feet, but Ember could see that he didn't know what to say. The world *had* gone mad. The woman's face reflected her own fear. Without fire, their people were doomed . . .

Her fault. Was this her fault? If she hadn't defied Him, let her temper get the better of her, He would not have punished her people like this. Wouldn't have needed to blackmail her . . . She shuddered at the thought of going to Him, abasing herself. Of a prison made of flame if she failed. But what else could she do? If that was the only way to get the hearths relit, she had no choice.

'I have to go,' Ember said. 'I'll leave straight away. I can be back by first snow.'

Arvid stared at her as though she were speaking a foreign language.

'You are not going anywhere,' he said. It was the warlord speaking.

She felt a moment of relief. Her father had forbidden her. It wasn't her fault; she'd offered, and been refused.

But the woman at Arvid's side, face still distorted by fear and distress – what could she say to her? When the snow came back, in winter, and this woman died of cold, or had to leave her home and everything she had in order to survive . . . would 'My da told me not to do it' feel like enough excuse then? She wasn't a child.

Her mother had pulled out the casting stones and sat right down on the floor to cast, as if she'd never been a warlord's lady, never sat at the glass table with the officers and their wives. Her father was staring as if he'd never seen Martine before.

'Fire Mountain,' she said, looking up from the stones. 'In the old stories, that's His home. The stones say she must go there.'

Arvid spun on her, his face incredulous.

'You can't seriously mean that!' he said.

Martine spread her hand wide, indicating the stones lying across the square of blue linen she used for casting.

'You'd send our only child out into the wilderness because the stones tell you to?'

Arvid's voice was oddly flat and Martine sent him a quick look, then stared down at the stones again, her fingers touching them lightly, one by one, as Ember had seen her do so many times.

'Do you want your people to die?' she asked quietly. 'Do you want them to be forced onto the roads like Travellers?'

He flinched.

'There must be another way. Some spell that can create fire without – without *Him*.'

Ash the Prowman stepped forward.

'No,' he said simply. 'The Powers are the Powers, and they control their element completely, when they wish to. Not every spark struck catches flame at His command, normally, but He controls each spark if He wishes.' He hesitated and moved to the table, where there was a water jug. 'Just as my Lady controls water, no matter where it is.'

He held his hand over the jug. There was a gurgle and the water rose up out of the jug in a straight column. Ember gasped – it was an impossible thing, impossible. Water hung in mid-air. It brought back the nightmare of Osfrid, screaming in the middle of an impossible column of fire. Cold sweat broke out all over Ember's body. She swallowed her gorge, forcing herself to get up and walk over to face her father, who watched the water with a grey, expressionless face. The Prowman took his hand away and the water fell back into the jug, a few drops splashing out onto the tabletop.

'You will not light a fire without Him,' the Prowman said. 'And He will not relent. Ember must go.'

The woman who had cried at Arvid's feet timidly put her hand on his arm.

'My lord ...'

'Get out!' he snapped. She ran for the kitchen door and a moment later he looked ashamed of himself, and spoke more quietly, to the Prowman, ignoring Martine.

'Fire Mountain is on the border with the Ice King's people! She's a child! She can't—'

'If it weren't for Fire,' Ember said clearly, 'I'd have been a married woman by now and no longer your subject.'

He stared at her, his head lowered a little, like a bull facing enemies.

'You'll all die, unless you leave this place,' she said. 'Unless you go somewhere He hasn't cursed. Or ... unless I bring back a piece of the Fire Mountain, to light the fires again.'

'You're not old enough to go out on the Roads ...' he protested.

'I was four years younger, the first time I did,' Martine said quietly, standing up, her stones tucked neatly back into her belt.

'In the south!'

Her father was right. There was a world of difference between the mild, gentle southlands and their fierce northern country. But she had no choice.

'I'm not planning on going alone,' she said.

Ash and Cedar stood there like two sides of a gatepost, although Ash was a head taller and much broader across the shoulders. But both of them were solid. Dependable. Capable.

'You heard what Fire said. We'll take her,' Ash stated.

Martine turned to Elva, looking uncertain.

'Sweetheart? Did the gods tell you anything else?'

Slowly, Elva came forward. She placed a hand on Ash's cheek, the other hand on Cedar's.

'They told me,' she said in a voice full of grief, 'that I must send my sons.'

The brothers shared a look of satisfaction, but Elva's head drooped, and they crowded around her, arms around her shoulders, trying to reassure her.

Ember went to her father and took his hand, as she had when she was a small girl. 'The gods and the stones both say I must go,' she said.

Arvid hesitated, then turned with relief as Holly came back into the room.

'Holly has some old blood, don't you?'

Looking puzzled, Holly nodded. 'My grandam was a Traveller,' she confirmed.

'So Holly will lead you,' he said. 'A full squad, all with old blood.' He looked severely at Ember. 'And no arguments.'

'Not from me,' she said. He looked at the boys, and Ash shrugged. 'The more, the safer,' he said.

'Maps,' Martine said. 'Do we have detailed maps of the mountains?'

'If we don't,' Arvid said, 'I've been paying my scouts too much for too long.'

As they found the maps, as they hurriedly packed whatever food they could find that didn't need cooking, as they unearthed the heaviest winter gear from its summer storage in the loft, as they strapped snowshoes and tent frames to the pack horses, reports came in from across the domain. No fires anywhere, with small, odd exceptions: a child's play fire, a branch of candles which had been used in a bedroom while a couple made love, another wedding bonfire in a distant village, a lamp burning in the sick-room of a dying Traveller woman.

But none of these would share their flame.

MOUNTAINSIDE,
THE ICE KING'S COUNTRY

'We take what we need!' the Hárugur King shouted, his cheeks showing red with rage under his beard. 'We do not ask!'

'Trading is not asking, Father Sire,' Nyr said, a little less patiently than the last three times he'd said it. He took a breath to calm himself and tried not to cough when the smoke hit his lungs. His father refused to have a chimney installed in the Council Cave – no breaking with tradition, even in the cause of fresh air. Tradition. Maybe that was an argument he could use. 'Our ancestors traded,' he said.

His father paused and shot a quick glance towards the circle of grey-haired men sitting cross-legged, each on the skin of a wolf he had killed himself. The Hárugur King's council had no power to gainsay the king, but they did have influence. Particularly Bren, his father's best friend and closest adviser. Bren lifted one shoulder, as if to say, 'Hear the boy out,' so his father nodded at Nyr to go on.

'The old songs often talk about trading. Taking the

Dragon's Road to the Wind Cities, for example,' Nyr reminded them.

The old men were nodding.

'That's true,' Garn said. He was the songkeeper, who taught the boys all the traditions. 'And not just the Wind Cities. Over the mountains, one song says. That one about the big blond warrior from the south who led his people out through Death Pass. We traded with them for a long time before they closed the passes.'

That caused a deep silence. Nyr felt his heart beating strongly. Over the mountains – the land of plenty, where ice came only in winter! The land of sun and green grass all year round, they said. Where a child – a *child* – could go for a walk quite safely, with no fear of wolf or wolverine or even storm. And they said that the wind and water spirits had *never* been in that country. The soul-eating monsters had disappeared from his own land twenty or so years ago, but he could remember them, just, remember the fear as the wind wraiths had chased him and his big brother Andur once, long claws out and hungry teeth gnashing. Nyr shivered with fear and revulsion. They had only just made it to the shelter of the stable in time. The greatest fear anyone in Mountainside had was that the wraiths would return as mysteriously as they had disappeared. But the southerners, it was said, did not need to fear them at all.

He had been to the country over the mountains, twice now, with raiding parties, and he had seen the green fields and the rich farms, but that had been high in the mountains, which was enough like his own country in summer to be disappointingly ordinary. But if they traded ... he might actually get to a place where it didn't snow. Or see the real ocean. The free ocean, where waves slapped the shore, as they did in the sagas.

The silence in the cave stretched on. No one was prepared to comment before the Hárugur King spoke.

'The easterners cannot be trusted,' his father said eventually. 'They are selfish, and greedy, caring not for others. If you go there, they will take your trade goods and kill you, and we will be left with nothing but grief.'

Tears stood in his father's eyes, and there was a murmur of sympathy from the council. They had all lost sons or nephews in the raiding parties. Nyr's brother, Andur, had been killed only two years before. His father had grieved thoroughly, as a man should, to put the pain behind him, but the thought of losing another son was perhaps too hard, Nyr thought. Particularly him. He had always been his father's favourite, much to Andur's disgust.

'Will you keep me home forever, to keep me safe?' Nyr asked gently, matching tears standing in his own eyes. 'Like a young maid, waiting for a lover who never comes?'

His father scratched vigorously at his beard, a sign that he was trying to avoid answering.

'I will consider it, and ask the King's guidance,' he barked, and rose, so that all the council had to stand up too. Nyr covered his eyes with his hand, the mark of respect due to a king, and kept them covered until his father strode from the cave.

Members of the council milled around a little, talking in low voices. Bren came up to Nyr and pulled a sympathetic face.

'He'll let you go,' Sami said. 'He knows it's his duty, but he won't like it.'

Nyr sighed.

'We need this,' he said. 'It's the first time ever we have a surplus of skins and tusks. We could lay the foundation for a decade's prosperity.'

'What will you ask in return?' There was a gleam in Bren's eye that Nyr knew.

'Whatever the council directs,' Nyr replied promptly, too old to be caught out. Bren laughed and patted him on the arm.

'Right answer,' he said. 'But make sure it includes some of those new bows they're making. The mountain valley archers are getting amazing range with them.'

Nyr made a face.

'You think they'd trade us weapons? I doubt it. Not the first time, anyway.'

'Then try to get a look at the bows, at least. We know that they're not using one single piece of wood, as we do. Figure out how they bind the pieces together. That's the secret.'

Bren could talk about bows all day. Nyr nodded before he could get properly started on his favourite subject and slid away to the curtained arch which led to the main hall.

The hall was full of women and children, as usual, and the old people sitting by the big central fire. No need for a chimney here – the hall had been chosen a thousand years ago because it had a natural chimney, a high crack of rock which sucked all the smoke – and the warm air, too – out the top. It was always chilly in the hall, but never cold, and there was always the sensation of air moving across your face, which was the most reassuring feeling in the world to a cave dweller. It meant the passageways were open; there had been no rockfalls.

The hall was full of smells, too, as it always was: sweat and newly tanned leather, a faint smell of stale urine from the sleeping old ones by the fire, the rich scent of roasting meat, babies and baby vomit turned a little sour, and underneath, always, the smell of rock, the rock of home.

On a scaffold made of lashed bones, high up on the eastern wall, Urno was still painting the new scene he'd started at the beginning of winter. The lower walls were all covered with scenes painted by earlier artists – ancestral treasures, his father called them. Urno's work was of the highest strata, and Nyr could trace the slow development of pigment and technique merely by running his eyes up one column of paintings. The long tradition had changed mostly in small steps, but Urno's work – bold splashes of colour, strong lines, distant perspectives – broke sharply with that tradition. He liked to hold forth about how the detailed, intricate drawings of the past were based on the carvings ancient peoples had done on narwhal tusks, and how paint did not have to follow the restrictions of line and cross-shading.

He had lost that argument a hundred times before his master, Grilsen, had died and left him in undisputed possession of the craft. So now he was painting a vibrant, swirling scene of the butterfly migration, great curls and curves of wings against a summer blue sky.

'Say what you like,' his mother's voice came from behind him, 'it cheers the place up.'

Nyr grinned and turned to kiss her thin cheek. Halda, his mother, was always wistful in winter. She was a creature of the open air, and by the end of the dark season she had fretted herself to skin and bone. The first clear day saw her tramping off into the wilderness, desperate for solitude. As a child, Nyr had thought she was trying to get away from him because he had been naughty (in winter, it seemed he was always being naughty, even when he didn't mean to be). Now he knew that she had the spirit of a wild bird, and should have been able to migrate with the flocks of geese and ducks which flew overhead each spring and autumn.

He wondered, often, what had brought his loud, belligerent father and his subtle mother together. There was no doubt they loved each other, even if his mother was more reticent about showing that in public. His father, of course, bellowed how wonderful she was, and threw his arms around her on the slightest excuse. Half his grief for Andur had been the knowledge of her deep, distracted sorrow. But she was better now.

As if to prove it, she said, 'Dalle has been talking to me.'

Dalle was the mother of Larra, a slender girl who'd been making eyes at Nyr since she was four years old. He'd have been more impressed if it hadn't started the day someone explained to her that he was the king's son. Even at four, Larra had liked the idea of being a princess. She still did, especially since Andur's death meant that Nyr was likely to be elected king after his father's death. He had cousins who would be eligible for the election, but they weren't likely to oppose him. He made a face at his mother.

'I hope you told her I'd taken a vow of celibacy.'

Halda laughed. 'As if she'd believe that!' He was known to have dallied more than once – but only with girls who would never be accepted as a wife; the daughters of craftsmen or hunters. Girls who would understand it was just for fun.

'You should think about a wife,' Halda said. 'Your father has no heirs but you. Even if one of your strawbacks had a son, he'd be out of the election.'

'I know,' he said soberly. 'But – who?'

'One of the chief's daughters from a tribute tribe, as I was,' his mother said firmly. 'The Hot Pool People, or maybe the Wolf Fold. It would be good to bind them more closely to us.'

He made a face and she slapped his arm lightly.

'You've got your other girls for pleasure,' she said. 'Marriage is about duty.'

'Was it for you?' he asked, genuinely curious.

A shadow painted her face with darkness for a moment.

'I hated your father,' she whispered. 'Until Andur was born. When I saw how much he loved his son ... I began to know him.'

The idea made him profoundly uncomfortable. Halda put her hand on his arm, her hazel eyes serious.

'Before you go on this trading trip, talk it over with your father. Start negotiations. Trust him to choose you a good girl, someone you'll be comfortable with.'

Nyr sighed. He'd always known it would happen, sooner or later.

'All right,' he said. 'If the Hárugur King approves the trip, I will agree to a marriage.'

Halda smiled. 'Did you think he wouldn't?'

'He's gone to ask counsel of the king,' Nyr said, reluctantly, knowing it would frighten her.

Shivering, Halda rubbed her hands along her arms under her sleeves, and looked back up to where Urno's butterflies cavorted across the high wall, as if seeking hope in their pictured freedom.

'Father will be back soon,' he comforted her.

'If it pleases Him,' she said. 'And then, you'll be gone. Who knows if *you'll* ever come back?'

'I'll be back, Ma,' he said, hugging her. 'Like a hungry wolverine after a food cache. You can't get rid of me that easily.'

But her face stayed troubled as she moved away to help prepare the evening meal. Nyr wondered what the king would say to his father. That was something he was not looking forward to doing when he became Hárugur King. Asking counsel of the Ice King was always risky, and sometimes, in winter when he was at his most vicious, it was deadly. The end of winter was worst ... Nyr waited for his father to return, more troubled than he wanted to admit. What if his father was struck down by the Ice King for suggesting something which went against tradition? It would be his fault.

PALISADE FORT, THE LAST DOMAIN

Holly, the senior sergeant, supervised as the full squad of twenty guards assembled, sword hilts gleaming in the afternoon sun, their horses restless with the excitement of setting out. Each guard, man or woman, had darkish hair or eyes, except for one – Tern, a youngling as blond as Osfrid himself had been. Ember blinked back the tears that thought brought and said goodbye to Merroc.

'My lord,' she said, bowing formally, as she had been taught by the southern-born wife of one of her father's officers. She had demanded it, in the face of her mother's objections. Etiquette school, an hour a day for the past six months, to make sure her manners would be up to the rigorous level expected of a southern warlord's lady. Things were more relaxed in the north, and she had had nightmares of being laughed at by the sophisticated southerners. 'I bid you farewell, and send my regards to the Lady Sigurd, with great respect.'

Merroc scowled, but not at her. His eyes were as red as his hair, and she thought he had to scowl, to stop himself crying.

'Good luck, lass,' he said.

She bowed again and turned to her parents. Martine was stony-faced out here in the yard. This was the part of being a war-lord's lady she hated most: the public scrutiny, the right of every inhabitant to inspect her and her doings. She was not someone who showed what she felt easily; in front of strangers she retreated even further. Just once, Ember thought, I'd like her to hug me, or kiss me, even if people are watching. There were plenty of hugs in private, but somehow that wasn't enough ... Arvid looked both angry and upset, but she couldn't comfort him.

'I bid you farewell, father,' she said to Arvid, and hugged him. He held her hard.

'Be careful,' he said softly.

'Mam,' Ember said, turning to Martine. Astonishingly, her mother's lips trembled and Martine stepped forward and embraced her, holding her tightly. Ember clung to her for a long moment, and then stepped back, still holding her hands.

'I'll be all right,' she said. Her mother tried to smile.

'Do you have the bone?'

Ember slid her hand into her pocket and brought out a length of cow thighbone plugged with clay. The Prowman had told them the story of Mim the Firestealer, who had gone up to the Fire Mountain and stolen fire for her people. And carried it home in a bone holder. Her mother nodded approval.

'Wind at your back,' she said. The Travellers' goodbye. A kind of blessing.

Next to them, Elva was saying her own goodbyes to Ash and Cedar, and Martine went to join her.

Curlew, Holly's offsider, brought her mare Merry up and Ember mounted. Ash had been given Thatch, one of her father's favourite geldings, and Cedar was on Snail, a chestnut who was the fastest of them all. Their elkhounds, Grip and Holdfast, snuffled around the horses' hooves, delighting in the excitement.

She couldn't look back. Riding out the gate was hard, but it would have broken her heart if Martine had been crying. Behind them, another muster was happening, as the messengers who were being dispatched to the outlying villages gathered for Arvid's instructions. Her other cousins, Poppy and Saffron, were in those parties. The fort would be almost empty, she thought, and somehow that image, of emptiness without fire, reminded her of the stories of the cold hells.

Osfrid, she thought bleakly. Go on swiftly to rebirth. Then she realised – if he does, we will not meet in our next life. Unless I die soon, too.

'Wind at your back,' Grammer Martine said to the assembled women, and they and their accompanying guards turned their horses towards the fort gates.

'Wind at your back,' Poppy's younger sister Saffron parroted happily, as she urged her horse to take the southern road. She twisted easily in the saddle to wave Poppy goodbye. As she in turn guided her chestnut through the gates, Poppy breathed a prayer to the local gods for all their safety, if safety could be found in these extraordinary times.

The chestnut, Starling, was a good horse, with easy paces. Lord Arvid had chosen him specially for her, because he knew she was not entirely comfortable with horses.

Learning to ride had been horrible, Poppy remembered. She had been six, small for her age, and the pony had seemed huge. Had *felt* huge, too, when her little legs had been stretched across its back. It had danced a little, from sheer mischief. She had cried; begged her father to be lifted off. Saffron had laughed at her, but then Saffron had their mother's knack with animals and had gaily leaped upon the pony and ridden off.

Ash had lifted her down and then persuaded her to ride in

front of him on his big bay, Sun. The big horse, so much gentler and calmer than the pony, ambled down the track to the gods' field and back again so smoothly that she demanded to be taught on him. And Ash did teach her, even though it took him away from his friends for hours that spring. He was such a good brother.

Poppy blinked back tears and concentrated on controlling the far more energetic gelding Starling. It was no good worrying about Ash and Cedar. The gods had told them to go with Ember, and that was that. She and Saffron had a job to do, and she would do it. She was half-glad that her older sister, Clary, was at home in Hidden Valley, heavily pregnant and in an acid mood thanks to the extended morning sickness which had prevented her coming to Ember's wedding. Clary had a habit of assuming that her younger sisters were useless at everything, and that would be trying, right now. She was competent. Grammer Martine believed that. Competent and capable.

But as they approached the narrow track which led through the edge of the Great Forest to the more northerly towns, she was very glad that Arvid had also sent a guard messenger with her. Or the other way around.

'You'll have to send Traveller women with your messengers,' her grandmother Martine had told the warlord.

He had been surprised.

'Why?'

'You have Travellers everywhere in this domain. If a man shows up talking about Fire there'll be trouble. Some of the older women are very ... serious ... about their worship. The punishments for sacrilege are extreme, and they'll carry them out, I promise you.'

Arvid had scowled. He hadn't liked finding out about secret Traveller worship, and he liked this even less.

Poppy shivered, thinking about the last Spring Equinox – her mother, her sisters and a couple of Traveller women who had come to Hidden Valley in the Resettlement had gone to the altar, struck fire from new flint, and as usual the fire had flared and seared them with desire. It always felt so good ... better than Vannar's lovemaking in the water meadow later that spring.

It was hard to imagine Fire's intimate, warm touch as evil. Yet she had *seen* Osfrid burn. Vanish into ash that floated away on the wind. Not even bones left behind.

And then the fires had gone out.

'How far to Salmonton?' she asked her guard, a young woman named Larch.

'Only an hour,' Larch said shyly. She was a tall, broad-shouldered girl who wore her yellow hair almost as short as a man, but she was buxom, too, so if she were trying to look like a boy she had failed completely. A few years older than herself, Poppy thought, but a country girl, not used to talking to strangers.

So that made two of them.

'Let's get there as fast as we can,' Poppy said, and Larch nodded agreement and kicked her piebald mare into a canter.

The track skirted the edge of the Great Forest, for which Poppy was grateful. They had enough to deal with already. But it was fun to ride along on this beautiful spring day, on a good horse, with another girl. She felt a little guilty about enjoying it, when everyone was in so much trouble.

She should plan exactly what to say when they got to Salmonton. And practise saying it.

'You worry too much,' her mother had told her, time and again, but *someone* had to look after things, or anything could go wrong.

*

Salmonton was a smallish town on the River Brash, a place of wooden houses and steep roofs, with boardwalks across the spring mud, and big vegetable gardens around each house. There were very few flowers growing here, except the ones which could be eaten, like marigolds and dandelions.

'Salmonton went through some difficult times in the early days,' Arvid had told her before she set out. 'They're a very, um, *practical* people up there.'

She had nodded. Good, she'd thought. I like practical people.

The open space in the centre of town was filled with people and a huge pile of kindling and logs. A bonfire without a fire. Her heart sank. So Martine had been right, and He had taken *all* the fires away, everywhere. The people were staring at a man who was kneeling by the pile, trying uselessly to strike a spark from a flintstone.

'That won't work,' she called out.

As one, everyone there spun to look at her, and she flushed. She wasn't comfortable with being the centre of attention. Not like Saffron. Perhaps she should pretend she *was* Saffron, and do what Saffron would do.

No. No, that was cowardice.

She dismounted and Larch took her reins so she could walk over to the people, who moved back to let her through to the man. The Voice, she thought, Cloud. He matched Arvid's description: tall, sandy hair, a scar along one cheek where a bear had almost killed him.

'I am Poppy, granddaughter of Lady Martine. I come from Lord Arvid with an explanation,' she said.

'Spit it out, girl,' Cloud said.

Now was the time for her rehearsed words. But almost every head there was crowned with blond or red or sandy hair, and she was suddenly conscious of her own darker brown.

Would they think she was a Traveller, and blame her for His actions?

'This morning,' she said carefully, pitching her voice as loud as she could without shouting, so the people in the back could hear, 'at the wedding of Ember and Osfrid, the Great Power Fire appeared to everyone.'

Perhaps there were more Travellers than she'd thought – several women let out exclamations and began to edge forward, to come closer to her. She swallowed a lump in her throat and went on, 'He killed Osfrid, son of Merroc.'

That caused a buzz and more exclamations. Cloud stared at her as if she were mad.

'What shagging Great Power Fire?' he demanded.

She knew this bit. Grammer Martine had been very clear about what to say.

'The local gods are local,' she said. 'But there are other Powers, five we know of, which govern this land at a deeper level. Fire, Water, Air, Earth and the Great Forest.'

'Who says?' Cloud snapped.

'I say,' a woman near him said firmly. She was old – *very* old, with hair completely white and face so wrinkled Poppy could hardly see her eyes. 'He *showed* Himself? To blondies?' she asked. There were nasty looks cast at her for using that word.

'Yes,' Poppy answered. 'I saw Him. He roared up out of the wedding fire and burned Osfrid into ash.'

A shiver went through the old woman and she groped for support from the girl standing next to her. A granddaughter, maybe, who was looking troubled.

'You'd better explain yourself, Pansy,' Cloud said to the woman.

'There is Fire,' Pansy replied firmly. 'I've ... seen Him. Others here have, too. He's only ever shown Himself to women of the old blood before this ...' She fell quiet for a moment, and then said softly, 'The world is changing.'

'Why won't the fire light?' Cloud demanded.

'He has taken all fires except the marriage fire Ember jumped over,' Poppy explained. 'To force Ember to go to Him, at the Fire Mountain. She must take fire from there and bring it back, and then we will be able to relight all our fires from that one.'

Cloud stared at her while the people around them shifted and muttered to one another. 'You expect me to *believe* that?'

Larch spoke up. 'Can you get your fire lit?' she asked. The horses stood at her shoulder, waiting patiently. Once again, murmurs rippled through the crowd. 'He has stolen all our warmth,' Larch said.

'And Lord Arvid has sent me as messenger, to tell you that he has sent Ember to the Fire Mountain.'

That caused a huge stir.

'She's only a chit of a girl!' Cloud protested.

Poppy knew what he meant. Ember was a lovely person, merry and pretty and good to be around, but she wasn't the most serious person in the world, or the most practical. Perhaps that was why Fire wanted her. Poppy felt a flick of envy. It must be terrible to have your husband murdered in front of you, but to know that Fire wanted *you*, only you ... at least you would feel special.

'Lord Arvid has sent a trusted group of guards with her,' she reassured Cloud. 'In the meantime, he suggests that all women with young babies go to the fort, as that is the only place where food can be cooked.'

The people around her frowned with puzzlement, and then began to look worried or horrified or appalled as the implications began to sink in.

'How will we survive?' one man asked.

'Ember will be back before autumn,' Poppy said firmly. Arvid had given clear instructions about this. 'In the meantime, the people of the Last Domain are renowned for courage and resourcefulness, and your lord is confident that you will find ways to thrive, even without fire.'

'We can dry meat and fish in the sun,' a woman suggested.

'Aye,' Cloud said. 'And that compost heap of yours, Bellflower, it gets pretty warm. Might be we could cook in that.'

They broke into groups, animatedly discussing what needed to be done next. Poppy was full of admiration. But one woman stood to the side, with a face so full of despair that Poppy had to go over and talk to her.

'Are you all right?' she asked.

'I'm a *potter*,' the woman said. 'How can I fire my pots? How can I earn a living if I can't fire my *pots*?' Her voice rose into hysteria and some other women hurried over, took her by the shoulders and arms, tutting and tching.

'Now, now, Columbine, don't take on so,' Bellflower said. 'No one will starve, will they, girl?'

Her tone was sharp, and conversations stopped to hear her answer. Poppy hastened to reassure everyone.

'Lord Arvid has grain and other stores put aside for emergencies,' she said, word for word as Arvid had said to her. 'He will give freely to anyone whose livelihood has been disrupted, and will ask no return.'

'He'll beggar himself,' Cloud observed.

Poppy bristled a little at his tone of slight contempt.

'My Lord Arvid would rather be a beggar than see *one* of his people starve,' she snapped. She paused as a few people in the crowd nodded sagely. 'My Lady Martine says to remind you that fish can be cured in vinegar instead of smoking. She is hoping that Salmonton will be a source of food for the rest of the domain. So you see, your trade will not suffer at all – it may even increase!'

'Where are we going to get that much vinegar?' a man demanded querulously.

'Doesn't have to be vinegar,' someone else replied. 'Lemon will do it. Or we can just pickle the fillets in brine. You need less salt that way than laying it down in barrels.'

'Brandy'll cure it, too,' another woman offered.

'Expensive shagging fish if you cure it in brandy!' Cloud said.

'What about beer?' a man asked.

It was time to go, Poppy thought. They had another town to reach before nightfall, and she really did not want to be out in the dark near the Great Forest. But Cloud stopped her as she turned to take her reins from Larch.

'We have some food, fresh cooked this morning,' he said gruffly. 'Take a bite before you go on.'

Poppy smiled at him, satisfaction blooming in her. She must have done her job properly, for him to offer that.

'Thank you,' she said. 'We will.'

THE LAST DOMAIN

An hour before sunset, Holly called a halt by a stream in spring pelt, in a clearing under tall white spruces. The forest floor was covered with a mixture of lichen and moss, luxuriating in the spray flying from the stream as it flipped and bounced over the rocks in its path.

Ember breathed in deeply as she dismounted and handed her reins to Tern.

This was the smell of spring, she thought. Water, moss, spruce gum. It was the first time since Osfrid died that she had gotten the stench of burning out of her nostrils. She stood for a moment, just watching the stream churn and splash, letting the familiar spring sound of fast-running water fill her with hope.

'What are you doing?' Ash asked.

She blinked her eyes open.

'I—'

'Horses get watered before anything else,' he said reprovingly.

'I know that. I gave Merry to Tern,' she protested.

Ash looked at her impassively. She knew that look. He'd

turned it on her often enough in the past. It was the 'You're acting like a warlord's daughter' look. Cedar came to join him, resting his elbow on Ash's shoulder and smiling sardonically at her.

'Gave her horse to the *servant*, did she?' he asked.

'No servants *here*, brer,' Ash answered in the same tone. 'We're *Valuers* in the Last Domain! We believe everyone is worth the same!'

Ember flushed. She didn't care what Cedar said or thought – he was just a mayfly, biting whatever he could. But Ash's opinion mattered, for some reason she could never pin down. It wasn't as though he were important. He was just family.

'My father has a groom!' she countered. She was aware of Holly and the others listening and flicked a look across to them. Holly and Curlew were smiling faintly. Tern looked shocked that Ash would question her, and that made her feel worse. The other soldiers pretended to ignore the interchange, but she was aware of their sidelong glances.

Ash took a step closer and bent down to her. He was near enough that she could see the deep green flecks in his brown eyes, and feel his breath on her cheek. She felt warmth creep up her face; it was ridiculous, *stupid*, but she had never been aware of him before as a man. He *smelled* male. Her breath quickened and she felt cross with herself.

'Your *father*,' he said, 'works his arse off for the people of this domain, and he has better things to do than curry down a horse. What about you, princess?'

It was an old nickname, from childhood, from a day when she'd tried to order him around and he'd wrestled her down into the mud. Princess was the name given to the Wind Cities' kings' daughters, poor things, who were married off in much the same way as warlords' daughters in the Domains, but who were also a byword for jewellery, silks and pride. She had hated that name in childhood and she hated it still.

'I am *not* a princess!' she said. She jerked herself around and went to where Tern was grooming Merry, her face flushed. Ash always made her feel so *young*, even though he was only a year older. It was something about the way he stood, solidly anchored like a great tree. As though his roots stretched down to the centre of the world. They should have called him Oak, she thought, dandy-brushing Merry from nose to tail as she had been taught, flicking the dust off competently and quickly, falling into the rhythm that Merry liked best. He spoke as if she'd never curried a horse before! Hah.

Ash brought his own bay, Thatch, over to stand by Merry and they worked side by side. Wordlessly he handed her the hoof pick when she was ready for it and she took it silently, glancing up to meet his eyes. He was half-smiling, and she smiled back, just a little, a warmth in her belly making her again aware of him as a man rather than a cousin. It was a shame he wasn't handsome. He had such nice eyes, but few girls would look past that rugged face. She wondered if she should try to find him a suitable girl to marry, and then realised she was thinking like a warlord's daughter. Or a warlord's wife, which she might never be, now. She flushed and turned away from him, sliding around to Merry's offside and brushing vigorously.

By the time she had finished Merry's mane she was thankful to hand the gear back to Tern, who took it with a shamefaced air, as if he should have stopped her doing the work. She smiled at him reassuringly.

'We're in this together,' she said softly, not wanting Cedar to hear and make fun of her again. 'Sharing equally, as Valuers should.'

He ducked his head once and slipped away to repack the

gear, but his shoulders were straighter as he went. She wondered again why her father had sent such a youngling on this trip. Tern couldn't be more than sixteen, and he wasn't the best of his age group at fighting. He was a good tracker, though, and came from the far north of the domain, where the trees petered out into the flatland, where even in summer you couldn't dig more than a foot deep without hitting hard ice-earth. That might be useful later. Who knew where they would end up?

At least the work had warmed her up a little. As the sun set, the chill struck up from the ground and she shivered as she sat on a mossy log and took the evening rations from Holly. The log was cold under her thighs so she was glad when Ash sent Holdfast and Grip to sit beside her, their warmth on her legs a bulwark against the evening breeze.

There was fallen wood everywhere, residue of the heavy snowfall two winters ago, which had brought many trees and branches down. Ember stared at one tangled heap of dead spruce boughs longingly. At any other time they would have made that the base for their campfire. She imagined the flames licking higher, spreading their warmth, and then shuddered. Fire and death would be linked forever in her memories.

'Ember,' Ash said quietly. 'Can you see that?'

She followed his gaze back to the pile of spruce boughs. They were lit from underneath with an orange glow. Flickering, yellow and gold.

Ember jumped to her feet and pushed Ash backwards as he got up too.

'Get away, get away!' she cried. 'It won't hurt me! Get behind me!'

All the others jumped and ran to the edge of the clearing before turning back, but Ash stayed at her back, feet planted.

The dogs stared at the fire with interest. Holdfast lay down with a sigh as though glad of the warmth.

'I think it's all right,' Ash said.

The fire had grown, but slowly, as a fire should, gradually taking twig after twig, branch after branch, until it had built into a normal campfire, burning merrily, hissing a little as it met damp moss, sparking as spruce gum caught and burned blue for a moment, releasing its fragrance.

He moved forward cautiously, but she put out a hand.

'Let me,' she said, and he stopped.

Ember picked up a dry branch from behind the log and advanced slowly. The fire continued to burn gently. She leaned to place the branch on the fire, and the branch settled and caught as branches should, with no more than a little creak and sigh as the flames took it.

Straightening, she was aware of her heart beating hard, her breath coming short, and the burn on her wrist was like a brand, not quite hurting, but hot, hot as a lover's mouth. She was caught, watching the flames flicker and leap; caught by the colour and the warmth and the sense of Him, there somewhere, waiting. Watching.

Ash came up beside her with another branch and crouched to lay it on the fire. But as he reached out the flames bent backwards, away from the branch, like frightened children cowering from a bully. Ash stilled, hand outstretched. Holdfast was on her feet, now, growling low in her throat, her teeth bared to the fire. Grip had backed away a little, whining, but he was still holding himself ready to leap.

'No,' Ember heard herself say. 'Not you. He wants me to tend it.'

She took the branch from Ash's hand, feeling his dry, human skin as she did, and put it on the fire. The flames reached back immediately, hungrily kissing the branch she had given them.

'Apparently,' she said, and knew that her voice was high and thready with something very like fear, 'apparently there are servants in the Last Domain, and I am one of them.'

Holly spoke gruffly.

'Service to a greater good is no shame, my lady.'

Tern had crept closer to the fire, his eyes wide.

'There are colours there I've never seen before,' he whispered, and he was right. The orange and red and gold of the flames was deeper than any fire she had seen; the spruce gum blue was bluer; the haze above the flames danced with green and silver and amethyst.

Cedar regarded her thoughtfully.

'He can't come just like that, I shouldn't think,' he said. 'Did you call Him?'

Her hands were shaking, and she stuffed them into her pockets. There were ripples of fear running through her, and something else that was not fear, but was more dangerous. Some sense of excitement, of arousal. She would kill that now, once and forever. He would have no part of her heart or her body, no matter how many fires He sent her. Fire was her enemy, a killer, a bully, despoiler and blackmailer, and she would never worship Him.

'I thought it was getting cold, and it was a shame we couldn't have a fire,' she said, and the years of life at the warlord's fort came to her aid now, when she had to put on a show for the people she was responsible for. It kept her voice light and calm, and let her put a tinge of humour into her tone. 'I won't do *that* again.'

Ash was looking at her strangely.

'So He came when you called Him,' he said. 'And He has

given you a gift.' She was surprised by how harsh his voice sounded. 'He is wooing you.'

A shudder went through her, uncontrollable, and she turned away from the fire to Ash's solid strength, feeling sick and cold. He gathered her in and patted her back.

'He won't hurt you,' he said. 'He wants you to serve Him.'

Never. Never.

There, inside her, was the core of ice, like the ice-earth of the flatlands. She was the warlord's daughter, and she would not barter her people's safety for the heat in her blood and the promise of ecstasy. She knew that was what He was offering, and she rejected it. Holdfast came to stand by her side and Ember buried her fingers in the fur of her neck. The living, breathing dog reminded her of where she belonged.

'Never,' she said aloud. She half-expected the fire to die away on her words, but it continued to blaze happily.

'Well,' Ash said, considering, 'we might as well make use of this gift.'

He sat down and toasted his bread on a long forked stick, and then spread it with thinly cut cheese so that the cheese softened and melted. Ember watched him, marvelling at his courage. He had seen Osfrid taken, and still he sat on his log as if by his own hearth.

He looked up at her and grinned, handing her a piece of cheese toast. 'Have something warm,' he said. 'It'll do you good.'

She sat next to him and nibbled at the toast, then ate it quickly as saliva flooded her mouth and she realised how hungry she was. Tern, greatly daring, had set a pot of water to heat in the fringes of the fire. Cha, that was what she needed. Nice hot cha, and be damned to where it came from. She would take his fire and use it to care for her people, but she would give nothing but dry branches and kindling in return.

She could feel heat inside her, in her belly, lower, running through her blood. She was aware of Ash as she had never been; the warmth she had felt earlier was nothing in comparison. Fire, she thought angrily. He's trying to lure me in with desire, and He's using Ash to do it. Bastard. She turned her back on the flames and watched the clear night sky instead, although her palms sweated and she was aware of every breath Ash took as if he used her own lungs.

For the rest of the night the fire behaved as a fire usually did. Ember banked it with stones and left it to burn low as they pulled out their sleeping pockets and settled down. Holly, Tern and Curlew shared the guard.

'I can guard,' Ember said. 'You don't have to do it all.'

'Tonight, we do,' Holly said. 'Tomorrow another three can take it. You'll get your turn. It's better to have three, then each can get enough sleep. More and you're changing over too often. Everyone wakes, no one is rested the next day.'

Her long experience quelled any disagreements. Ash simply nodded. Cedar and the others had already slid themselves into sleeping pockets. Martine had issued them all winter pockets, fur lined, because they were heading to the mountains, where the snow lay all year round. Ember was sure it would be too hot on this spring night, but as the fire died away she was glad of the warmth. She had not felt truly warm since the fires had gone out, except when she had laid branches on the campfire. The scar around her wrist ached with a shadow of burning, and she laid that hand outside the pocket, to cool it, and put her head on that arm as a pillow.

In the morning, when she opened her eyes, there was a small bright rounded shape in the centre of her palm. Its clear curve reflected the trees around her, the sky, the long streaks of rose cloud above, the whole world inverted and shrunk to fit her hand. She thought for a moment that someone had placed a scrying jewel in her hand. Then, as she breathed in with surprise, the shape wobbled a little, the reflection wavering, and she realised it was a tiny pool of dew. She had lain so still it had gathered there overnight.

Carefully, she sat up, cradling the bright circle of water. It had come like a blessing, and she didn't know what to do with it.

'Drink it,' Holly said from over her shoulder. 'It's good luck.'

So she sipped the cold mouthful down, feeling as if she were drinking the essence of the world around her.

The dew had fallen on her arm too, and it seemed to have eased the burning in her wrist, but their sleeping pockets were waterlogged.

She and Tern hung them over spruce boughs to dry off as much as they could while they breakfasted, groomed the horses and saddled up. The fire was dead and she kept her mind from thoughts of how pleasant a hot mug of cha would be right now, concentrating on the sights and sounds of the morning: the chattering of red squirrels in the trees to the left, the song of a spruce grouse in the distance, woodpeckers tapping away, swallows already swooping over the stream in their eternal quest for gnats and midges. The air was full of mating and display calls, birds seeking their mates through melody and sheer noise. Ember felt herself relaxing; since swallowing the dew she seemed to be at home here, the woodland alive around her seeming to welcome her as it had not done the day before.

Even the spruce needles smelt better. Cleaner.

They mounted as the first shafts of sunlight began to stream through the branches, and set off in higher spirits than the day before. Ash kept his bow strung in case he could bring something down for the dogs, but although pink-footed geese flew high overhead, none came low enough for him to get a shot off.

THE LAST DOMAIN

Ash kept Thatch, his bay gelding, well back, letting Holly and her men take the lead. He wasn't even sure why he'd come. With such a well-armed, well-seasoned troop, Ember didn't need him or Cedar. Well, Cedar might be useful, if he could get control of his Sight. It came and went unpredictably these days, although their mam said it would settle down now he had his full growth and was man, not boy. Sight was always useful, even if it was sometimes hard to interpret.

But he himself was an extra wheel, that was sure. All he could offer was a good eye for the bow. And a shagging good bow. He slid his hand down the shaft, slung over his shoulder. A new type of bow, this one, designed in his master's workshop back in Hidden Valley. Barley had been unsure of the idea – not one piece of wood, but several, pieced together with horn and glue and sinew, and then covered with leather to protect the sinew from the rain.

He'd gotten the idea from a picture he'd seen of the bows they used in the Wind Cities, bows with twice the curve of the long shafted ones they used in the Domains. A longbow was accurate, and it could put some real punch behind the shaft, but it had a limited range in comparison to this little beauty – and what's more, his bow was easier to shoot from horseback, the extended recurve making it shorter. The Western Mountains' warlord had equipped his men with them already, with impressive results in their last battle against the Ice King's men.

He hoped he'd get a chance to show off its good points on this trip – Arvid had ordered fifty of them, but his men weren't so sure about changing from their tried-and-true methods. If Holly could be shown its merits, that would go a long way to convincing the others.

As they went past a field of blueberries, Ash saw a plover's feather caught in the top of one bush. Leaning precariously from Thatch, he snagged it and put it safely into his pouch. Plovers didn't have the greatest feathers for fletching, but they were strong enough and had a nice black and white section which looked smart. Some officers liked smart-looking arrows.

Today's journey was taking them into the Stinky Marsh. He'd had to suppress a smile when Holly had announced their route, but he wasn't the only one. Still, better a stinky marsh than the unknown. At least this way, by dipping southwards through the marsh and then coming up to the main track through the forest, they would avoid a whole day and night in the forest.

Which was fine with him.

Arvid's maps were detailed and specific, but Holly didn't seem to need them. She took them through the winding paths at the edge of the boggy ground without pause or hesitation.

It did stink, of something a bit like manure and a bit like rotten vegetables, and the midges bit every exposed piece of skin, but it was a pretty sight, nonetheless.

Reeds and sedges competed for the water space, but the small islands dotted between the marshes gleamed with the purple and gold of marsh thistles and dandelions, bog violets and meadowbrights. He could hear birds everywhere, even when he couldn't see them: bitterns booming, the honking of geese somewhere a long way off, warblers singing high and fast, sounding one moment like a lark and the next like a lapwing. Ash couldn't help but feel optimistic when he spotted a falcon circling; the smooth curve it made was a form of perfection, and he always considered seeing one a good omen.

The sky was high and wide, with small clouds racing fast and the sun shining bright in between, but it was surprisingly cold as they threaded their way through the waist-high sedges. The wind was northerly, which Ash thought was unusual for this time of year, and it brought the scent of snow with it.

Holly pointed to an island ahead of them, which was big enough to have sprouted a copse of willows.

'We'll spell the horses there,' she said.

The path to the island was narrow and they went in single file through the reeds. Ash felt the back of his neck creep; there were no birds singing here, no frogs. The only signs of life were swallows chasing midges, and Ash knew that swallows paid no attention to humans at all, unless they got too close to a nest. But while their own presence might bring silence to some birds, it should set others warning their mates. Where were the kik-kik-kik of woodpeckers' alarms? The sharp chirp of sandpipers? The trumpeting of whooper swans which should be nesting nearby?

Holdfast growled, her hackles rising as she stared at the swamp.

'Holly,' he called in warning.

Holly's mare had just set foot on the island. She half-turned in her saddle to hear him and at that moment shapes rose in the water on either side.

Water spirits was his first thought, but it couldn't be water spirits because these shapes came right up, out of the water, where spirits would melt into thin air, and they were solid and real and smelt disgusting and were carrying weapons. Spears, halberds, axes. Bandits' weapons.

His mind digested all of this slowly, it seemed to him, but his body was well ahead of his mind and he had brought his bow around, drawn an arrow, nocked it and shot before he had even finished the thought.

One of the shapes screamed and fell. Holly and the guards had their swords drawn and were attacking. Holdfast and Grip leaped and crashed into the one nearest, bringing him down into the mud.

Curlew and Tern were on either side of Ember, but the path was too narrow and Merry, her mare, didn't understand that she should splash into the water to get away. She baulked, putting Ember in danger. A bandit had reached the path and was grabbing for Ember's bridle. Ash reached out and poked an arrow-tip into Merry's rump. She sprang forward, knocking the man down, rushing up the path to the island. But who knew if she would be safe there?

Ash nocked another arrow and let fly as the man on the path struggled to his feet. He fell. Ash dug his heels in and Thatch, war-trained, kicked out at an attacker behind them that Ash hadn't even seen and then surged up the path after Merry. A body launched itself at him and tried to drag him from the saddle. He put an elbow into the man's eye and kicked him away as his grip loosened.

Ember had turned at the top of the trail and was hesitating.

'Stay where you are!' he yelled at her. He turned back to shoot at more figures emerging from the bog, shedding hats made of reeds as they did so. He turned Thatch and shot again, forcing their attackers to dive back into the bog, giving Holly and the others a chance to make it to the high ground.

He called the dogs off and took them up to the island to the others. They circled around until Ember was protected from all sides, weapons at the ready.

'Behind!' Curlew shouted, dragging his horse's head around to face the trees. A second group of bandits ran down, axes and halberds raised. Ash's arrow took one, a big man dressed only in trews, in the leg. The man roared and began to foam at the mouth. Oh, gods, protect them all. A berserker.

The man swung his battleaxe around his head and screamed. His companions hastily backed up, coming around wide, leaving him room. He was so *fast*. He'd swung and felled a horse before Ash had another arrow nocked. The head came half off, and the second blow of his axe took down the rider. Ash let fly. The arrow took him in the shoulder, but it didn't even slow him down. He brought his axe up from the guard's smashed head and sent it curving backhanded, spinning around with both hands to shatter the leg of another horse. It screamed, the shrill sound cutting through the shouts and clangs and thunder of fighting.

Ash was possessed by rage. He had been in battle before, but this was new to him, this fierce determination. Faster than he had ever done, Ash nocked and shot, nocked and shot. He sent arrow after arrow into the madman, who seemed to barely notice, dragging himself closer and closer to the centre of the guards, where Ember was. Was it just her bright hair which drew him, or was something else acting through him? Ash forced himself to breathe; to take a moment to aim. At the crucial moment, the wind died and he let off the perfect shot: straight into the berserker's eye. The man hesitated, swayed, and fell with a thud, back onto the rump of the horse he had killed.

Ash allowed himself a quick look around. Ember had her dagger out, ready. Good girl.

'Holdfast, Grip, *guard*,' he ordered, pointing at Ember, and the dogs set themselves ready, one on either side of her.

Cedar was safe; several of the others were down and still, although a brown-haired young man was struggling to crawl further up the island, leaving blood in his wake. He had grumbled about having no cha that morning. Ash gulped.

Holly and Tern were still horsed and unhurt; Curlew had fought off the berserker's companions, but the others whose horses had been killed were dead – one crushed under her mount, the other gutted by a pike.

'Adon's down!' one of the enemy yelled and then the bandits were running, and running hard. There were few left to run, and two of those were limping. Tern began to follow.

'Let them go!' Holly called. 'Don't separate to chase them.'

He hesitated, then spurred his horse just a little, leaned out and over and hit one of the fleeing men with the hilt of his sword. The man fell like a poleaxed steer. Tern leaped off his horse and dragged the man back to Holly.

Ash breathed. It was the first breath he could remember taking for some time. He became aware that he had a knife wound on his leg, a long but not deep slice. The man who had jumped on him must have done it as he fell.

Ember.

'Are you all right?' he demanded roughly. She was pale, but she smiled at him valiantly. He rubbed the dogs' ears, murmuring praise. Holdfast's muzzle was bloody.

'I'm fine, but you're hurt,' she said. She turned to Holly. 'Is it safe to tend the wounded?' It made his heart ache that she should be so well trained in the protocol of guarding and attack. Holly sent Curlew and Tern out to scout before she gave the all-clear for them to dismount and see to the wounded.

There were so few of them left.

Ember saw to Ash herself, pouring clean water over his wound and binding it with lint and linen, kept clean in a special bag on one of the horses. Her hands were gentle but it still hurt. Tern had a scratch on one hand, but that was all.

There were two other wounded; the brown-haired boy was badly injured in the thigh, and an older woman had a lighter shoulder cut.

Holly pointed to a body rolling in the shallow water at the foot of the island. One of her men; middle-aged, grey-haired. Ash didn't even know his name, and felt ashamed that he didn't.

Holly left Tern on guard with Curlew and took Ash down to fish him out.

'Vetch,' she said. 'A good man.'

They assembled the other corpses. Three more. Horn, Onion and Violet.

There were tears in Ember's eyes. 'The first deaths,' she whispered, as though she thought there were going to be others.

'Not the last,' he said, and pointed to the bandits lying still on the pathway or half submerged in the bog. Three of those bodies lay still with his arrows in them. It made him feel sick, and he wasn't sure if it was their deaths or the ease with which he had killed them that made him want to vomit. He might need those arrows. He had trained Holdfast to collect those that missed their mark, so together they went out, Holdfast finding the loose-lying arrows, and he reclaiming those that had found a target. It was bloody, horrible work, but the day had shown that their lives might depend on it, later. Ash tried not to think about what he was doing, and cleaned the arrowheads thoroughly afterwards.

The bandit Tern had knocked out was groaning. Holly walked over and kicked him in the guts to wake him fully.

'You killed my people,' she said.

'Not me, lady!' he protested. 'I stayed well back.'

'One and all the same,' Holly said. She was angry; the deep lines that ran from nose to chin were etched sharply on her face; her voice growled. 'You'll face my lord's justice for this.'

As though the knowledge of the certain death that awaited him gave him courage, the man stood up. He was around forty, Ash thought, and not all that bright, but he was as angry as Holly.

'Justice? There's no justice under the warlords, woman! Was it justice for my da to be run off his farm what we'd had for a hundred years, just so some black-haired bastard could ruin the best cropping land in the domain? Was it justice that Da got a piece of rubbish land, no good for anything but goats? He wore his heart out trying to make a crop come out of that ground, and for what? A shagging warlord?' He spat on the ground. 'Look for justice from a warlord and you're spitting in the wind.'

As a farmer, Ash felt sympathy. His own family owned their farm, but he knew plenty of families who worked the warlord's land, and had for generations. Arvid was the only warlord who believed in Valuing, the idea that each person had an equal value. The other warlords – including his own lord in the Western Mountains Domain – did what they liked with their people's lives. How would he feel in this man's place?

Holly listened impassively and then, when the bandit had finished, hit him full across the face with the back of her hand, a massive blow which rocked him on his feet.

'You killed my people,' she repeated. 'You can choose to die here, now, or be taken back to the warlord for punishment.'

'Kill me now,' the man said sullenly. 'Might as well.'

'Say any prayers you have, then,' Holly said.

He laughed. 'No god's ever listened to me before. Why would they now?'

'Are you ready?' Holly said implacably. Ash drew in a breath and looked across at Ember. Was she going to allow this? She looked uncertain. He shook his head at her and she nodded.

'Holly,' she said. 'I think it would be better if you sent him to my father.'

'His choice, my lady,' Holly said.

'No. No, I think it is my father's choice.' Ember's voice was quiet. Not pleading. Not ordering. But calm. Holly looked down, bringing the sword in her hand to rest position, with both hands on the hilt and the point on the earth.

'My father wants more information about these bandits,' Ember said, her voice sounding odd this time. Holly nodded and pointed to the two guards who had been hurt.

'You two, bind him, lash him on a pack horse and take him back to the fort. *After* he's buried our people.' She paused for a moment, looking down at the dead bodies of her guards. 'I am so tired of death,' she murmured. Ash knew she hadn't meant anyone to hear.

The burial service was brief but complete, and then they rode on, leaving the bandit and his guards to deal with the other bodies.

'They won't come back, but better to be safe,' Holly said. Her face had closed in completely; it would be a mistake to try to talk to her. But Ember was different.

On this side of the island, the path was wider and Ash could bring Thatch up next to Merry.

'Did your father really tell you he wanted more information?' he asked Ember.

She flushed a little. 'I'm sure he would have, if we'd talked about it.' A lie. She had lied to save a man's life. Was that wrong? It made him profoundly uncomfortable.

'Mm. Princess, this journey we're on – it's not a time for lies. Lies throw up dust that blinds the teller as well as the listener.'

She cast him a sideways glance, but she didn't roll her eyes, as his younger sister Saffron would have done. She sighed instead.

'I didn't know what else to do,' she said.

'Try the truth, next time,' he suggested. 'That might have worked too.'

'Or he might have had his throat cut,' she said, bristling a little. 'My way was safer.'

He paused, thinking hard. 'Safer for him, maybe,' he said eventually. 'But not for you.'

Thatch took his momentary inattention as an opportunity to slow down, so he had dropped behind Ember before he realised. He let her go ahead. He wasn't her big brother, who had the right to lecture her. He was surprised she hadn't lost her temper at him. Two of his three sisters would have. She was more complicated than he had thought.

He spent the rest of the day's ride saying prayers for the souls of the men he had killed. Perhaps it would help them on to rebirth.

THE LAST DOMAIN

Poppy's next stop was Acorn, a village of only five houses, perched on the side of a hill which overlooked the deep woods. The people here lived from hunting on the outskirts of the Forest and from woodwork – 'as fine as Acorn work' was a byword across the Domains for intricate and precise carving and marquetry.

At least their work wouldn't suffer from having no fire, Poppy thought.

But the carpenters were appalled, and so were the hunters.

'How can we make glue?' one complained.

'I do poker work,' a woman said blankly. 'Without fire, I can't burn the designs ...'

'I'm not shagging going into that wood without a fire,' a tough, nuggety little woman dressed in men's clothes said. 'Can't scare off a wolverine without fire.'

'Or bear,' a man added.

They looked a lot alike, these villagers, as remote towns-people often did: slight, light brown hair, flat cheekbones. Only one stood out – a woman with hair as red as Ember's and a small, pointed chin. She was nursing a young baby, so Poppy invited her to go to the fort. But the man beside her scowled.

'No wife of mine's going to go live with soldiers!' he said, and there was a murmur of agreement. The woman herself looked undecided, but it wasn't Poppy's job to persuade people, only to give them the invitation.

'Straw boxes,' the oldest woman there suddenly said, in a thick northern accent. 'If we c'n put t'food out in t'midday sun and get it mostly hot, we can put it into t'straw box and it'll keep cookin'.'

'Fire!' a man said dubiously. 'No woman here's ever seen Him.'

Poppy noticed a woman at the back, with darker hair than the others, look away as he spoke. A Traveller pretending to be one of Acton's people? she wondered. She'd heard of them, although it was rarer since the Resettlement. But one woman, of the old blood, might well feel safer still if others thought she was a blondie.

No business of hers, Poppy decided.

'I swear to you, it happened as I told you.'

'Can we, like, make sacrifices to Him?' a woman asked. 'The local gods like young lambs and fawns. Maybe He would, too. Does He have an altar?'

'Good idea, May,' someone said. They turned expectantly to Poppy, and she felt burdened by the knowledge that they would be disappointed.

'He has never asked for sacrifices,' she said.

'Still, can't hurt to try,' May mused. 'If'n we ask the local gods maybe they'll let us use their altar.'

'Fire might want more than an animal, if'n He's so tough,' a man said thoughtfully. 'The old gods, they liked human sacrifice, they say.'

Silence fell. The woman with the baby hugged it tighter, and stepped forward.

'I think I'll come with you,' she said. 'Go to the fort, like you said.' Her voice was high with nerves.

'No you won't!' her husband said belligerently. He wasn't very bright, Poppy thought. He didn't seem to realise why she was leaving. He took hold of the woman's arm roughly, and the baby started to cry.

Poppy looked at Larch. This was warlords' business.

Larch seemed to realise that at the same time. She stepped forward, her hand on her sword hilt.

'My Lord Arvid will welcome your wife and my Lady Martine will care for her, be assured,' she said politely, but there was strength in her voice. She was taller than the man. He tried to stare her down.

'I don't shagging believe any of this,' he said. 'Fire! Just some enchanter playing tricks, I reckon.'

There was a murmur of agreement from the others.

'Some *Traveller*,' one of the older men said, with venom in his voice. There was still a lot of ill feeling towards Travellers among the older people, Poppy knew. It was so in Hidden Valley. The younger ones didn't care, but the oldsters harboured grudges that went back decades. It had been a Traveller enchanter who had killed so many people before the Resettlement, and their relations and friends were slow to forget that. It might be so here, too.

Time to show the strong hand.

'Ash the Prowman has confirmed the existence of both Fire and Water,' she said. 'It is not an enchanter.'

That caused an uproar, and the husband let go of his wife's hand to stare at Poppy blankly.

'Ash is back?' he exclaimed. 'Gods help us, things must be bad!'

'I'm going to the fort,' the mother said firmly, and this time he didn't argue.

'Pack your things,' Larch told her. 'Not too much. Do you have a horse?'

She laughed bitterly, rubbing her arm. 'I used to, before I came here.' She glared at her husband and hoisted her baby higher in her arms, rocking him.

'You can use the pony,' he mumbled, looking at the ground, but her expression didn't soften.

'Good,' she said. She turned on her heel and went to one of the cottages, followed by two of the other women, including the tough little hunter, who hesitated, and then spoke directly to Larch.

'Don't you bother. I'll take her straight to the fort,' she said. 'Make sure my grandson is safe.' She glared at the man who must be her son. 'If you're lucky I might be able to convince her to come back!'

Best to ignore that.

'Our horses need a spell before we leave,' Larch said mildly, and a boy jumped forward to lead her to a stable. Poppy was left standing in front of the slightly smaller crowd, who inspected her with interest.

'Lady Martine's granddaughter, eh?' a woman said avidly. 'You'd be that white woman's daughter, then, the unchancy one.'

She was used to this. They all were, all six of Elva's children. Elva's white hair and pale eyes had marked her out from birth.

'Yes,' she said. 'My mother is the prophet.'

'What's she say about all this, then?' the husband demanded.

'She says that Ember must go to Fire Mountain,' Poppy said, matter of fact. 'She has given two of my brothers to help guard her on the way.'

They looked askance at her, but they let it be, walking away from her talking in twos and threes, leaving her standing there, feeling conspicuous and out of place. But she had done her job.

Palisade Fort, the Last Domain

Arvid and Martine stood together, looking at the innocent-seeming fire that had consumed Osfrid. It burned steadily, gently, without even crackling or snapping. Arvid felt a combination of anger and outrage – not just at Fire, but at Martine for keeping so many secrets from him for so long. He couldn't bear to gaze at the flames any longer. They just reminded him of the terrible, awe-filled moments when the Power had risen up and demanded his daughter.

He tilted his head back. Above the high wooden palisade which surrounded the fort, clouds were gathering. High, still, but grey.

'Build a shelter over this fire. Now,' he ordered Cat, his steward. Cat was a wiry older man who had once served his father. He was known to relish change and disruption as both a diversion and a way to prove his competence, but today his face matched his grey hair and there were deep lines scored between his mouth and chin.

Cat glanced up at the clouds and paled even further.

'Aye, my lord!' he said, and ran to the carpenter's workshop, calling, 'Moss, Moss, come quick!'

'That was well thought of,' Martine said. He scowled at her and marched inside. Not yet. He wasn't ready to pretend that he forgave her yet; nor ready to discuss the situation. There was, in any case, too much to do.

Arvid was a methodical man, and he kept methodical people around him. He had lists of every citizen in every village, including even the babies. His scribe, Reed, was ready with them in his workroom, and was totting up the number of women with children under one year old, as Arvid had instructed him to do.

'There are more than I estimated, my lord,' Reed said, his quill scratching as he tallied the lists. 'We will be hard pressed to house them all.'

Arvid nodded and turned on his heel, making his way back to the carpenter's workshop. Cat and Moss, the fort carpenter, were there, with Swan, the girl who was Moss's apprentice, gathering what Moss needed for the fire shelter.

'After you finish,' Arvid said, 'we will need more shelters. I am bringing the women with young babies here, and we cannot house them all. Make the shelters watertight. Get the thatchers to help. Send out boys to harvest the reeds. And Cat—'

Cat stood straighter, ready for the order. It was good to have someone so dependable on hand.

'Get privies dug. Outside the fort, past the sally gate. Well away from the stream.'

Cat made a face, but he nodded. 'We should maybe start bringing water in, too, my lord?'

'A good thought. Do so, but we need salt before we need water,' Arvid said. 'Send a caravan of carts to Salt. Poppy should be there by tomorrow and she has taken orders for them to supply as much as they can.'

Salt was the northern town which got its name from the salt

mine which supplied all the Last Domain with the precious stuff.

Moss was frowning. He was a big man, with soft brown eyes and tough hands. A craftsman, but not a thinker. It was as though he felt his way through his buildings rather than planned them.

'Salt, my lord?'

'We can cure meat, even if we can't cook it,' Arvid said, as gently as he could. 'Bacon, ham, salt beef – they're more appetising cooked, but they are safe to eat. We can't cook for everyone over one fire.'

'Aye,' Cat said. 'Eat raw meat and everyone here'll have worms, if they don't puke themselves to death.'

'The same with fish, and eggs,' Arvid added. 'We will need as much salt as we can get.'

The men nodded, but the girl was frowning. He hadn't survived as warlord in a domain full of Valuers by ignoring the small voices.

'What is it, Swan?' he asked.

'My da's a farmer,' she said.

'Yes?'

'Our muck heap at home gets plenty hot.'

Arvid blinked. Muck heaps. Compost heaps. Aye. He'd never worked with one himself, of course, but he'd seen them steaming as he rode by on cold mornings.

'Might be enough to coddle eggs for the babbies,' Swan said.

'That was well thought of,' Arvid said, the words bringing Martine to mind with unwelcome force. Swan flushed with pleasure, though, and Moss was regarding him with approval.

Oh, they all loved it when the warlord acted like a humble man. Arvid wished, sometimes, that he was naïve enough not to notice it, not to use it as a way of binding his people closer to him. He was genuine enough – gods knew, he was no one special, and if he'd been born a merchant it probably would have suited him better – but like a merchant he noticed things about people, and he would have been a fool if he hadn't sweetened the honey pot just a little from time to time.

'I depend on you all,' he said seriously, and saw them swell, just a little, with pride and responsibility. Even Cat. He was full of affection for them, suddenly. They were so staunch, his people. So brave and loyal.

He went back to his workroom and found Martine waiting for him, alone. Reed was gone, his lists still laid out neatly on the table, the tip of his quill resting on his inkstone, as he always left it. Arvid looked at the papers there – Reed hadn't finished his count.

She had ordered his scribe to leave. Interrupted his work. Countermanded his own orders.

Fury overtook him. She opened her mouth to speak but he cut her off.

'I gave Reed a task,' he said. 'You have not the authority to rescind that command.'

He'd never spoken to her in that way before. She swallowed, her pale skin reddening and her eyes, those green, green eyes, widening in shock. That was satisfying. He wanted to hurt her, to cause her heart to twist in the way his had when he had realised how she had betrayed him. And he could. He was the warlord, and he could do *whatever* he chose to a wife who had broken faith.

'I wanted to explain—' she began.

'There is no explanation which I would find acceptable,' he said. 'You have withheld information of immeasurable importance from your lord, and you have done so over a period of many years. You have placed this domain, and the people of this domain, in mortal danger. You have set in chain events which may result in the death of my heir, and the destruction of everything which has been built in this land. This, by any assessment, is treason.'

She gasped. Good. Let her understand the enormity of her crime. Her betrayal. At least she didn't try to speak again.

'You have placed loyalty to a dead culture over your sworn loyalty to your lord and ...' his voice faltered a little, 'to your husband.' He paused, and made himself breathe. He must appear calm. 'I will consider what punishment is appropriate. In the meantime, you will continue your duties among my people and do what you can to ameliorate the burden you have placed upon them. Now, recall my scribe and allow us to do the work you have made necessary.'

She bowed. Just bowed, silently, formally, with that lithe grace he loved so much, and then she left, closing the door quietly behind her. Arvid rested his knuckles on the edge of his worktable and let them take his weight, his head drooping. He felt as though his guts had been drawn out of him, as though the centre of him were being pulled away, gone with her. But he couldn't let himself feel like that, or run after her and pull her into his arms. He had work to do.

A knock on the door made him stand up and straighten his back.

'Come,' he said.

It was Ash, the Prowman, his dark hair a reminder of Martine. They were thick as thieves, those two, even though it had been fifteen years since Ash's last visit. He looked the same now as he had then. Exactly.

'How long is it since I last saw you, in your life?' Arvid asked abruptly. Ash stopped just inside the doorway. He hadn't been expecting that question, and Arvid could see he wasn't sure he liked it. Good.

'Three months,' he said. 'The Lake moved me in time. She thought I was more use here, now, than then and there.'

Arvid had heard stories about the power of the Lake. They all had, from the time they were children. But to see the proof standing in front of him just reminded him of how much he didn't know. The warlords lived their lives in the sunlight, their actions open to everyone. Always observed, always public. That was how power should be: clear and honest. But these – these *old bloods*, they consorted with power in secret and used enchantment to bend time and place and life itself. It was wrong. It could not be allowed to continue.

'Does She do that often?' he asked, seemingly just curious. If the Domains were to free themselves from these secret alliances, they would need information.

The Prowman shrugged. 'It was the first time for me. But She moved Baluch, the Prowman before me, from time into time for a thousand years. He said it was like being a stone skipped over water.'

Arvid shivered. A horrible fate. Horrible.

'There are things you don't know,' the Prowman continued.

Arvid motioned him to a seat, and sat himself.

'Then tell me,' he said.

Those keen dark eyes searched his face, and grew troubled, but he spoke willingly enough.

'When Acton came over the mountains to invade what is now the Domains, the people of the old blood here had a long and complex relationship with the five Powers. Women to Fire, men to Water – that's the way it had been for thousands of years. And the other Powers were part of life, too, She tells me, especially the Great Forest.'

Arvid nodded. Women to Fire indeed. That must end.

'Acton's people cut the Forest down,' the Prowman said

gently. 'Instead of working with it, in clearings and glades, as the old blood had done, they just chopped it down. They'd never seen a forest before, I think. They had no idea what they were doing.'

'So?'

'So the Powers withdrew from them, especially when the Five realised they were killing off the people of the old blood.'

'That is very old history, and here in the Last Domain no forest has been harmed.'

'Because the Forest learned its lesson, and knows how to protect itself. It's just too shagging dangerous to do harm to the Forest now. Isn't it?'

Arvid sat still. That was true. The Forest guarded itself. Pain twisted his face. Ember was riding into that Forest; he had been forced to risk the most precious thing in the world, because these dark-haired fools had held on to their secrets too long. He stood up abruptly, and gestured to the scribe's table.

'Write it all down,' he ordered. 'I will read it later.'

The Prowman rose slowly, and Arvid was suddenly aware that Ash was fifteen years younger and in much better shape. He had been a safeguarder, they said, and he had killed more than once. He had saved Martine's life, she had told him, by killing two trained assassins who had come after her with knives. Arvid tensed, his hand on his belt knife, aware of the anger in the dark eyes. He had killed a few times himself, defending against the Ice King. He wouldn't be easy prey.

'For a thousand years,' the Prowman said softly, 'Acton's people persecuted, murdered, raped and oppressed those of my blood. The only refuge we had was the Powers. The only loyalty anyone showed us was theirs. The only strength we had was the secret knowledge that we were valued by powers far greater than a petty warlord.' He paused. 'And the price we paid was secrecy. Absolute secrecy. The penalty was death. If Martine had told you what she knew, any Traveller woman would have been right to kill her. Because it was only secrecy which saved us from complete annihilation.'

Arvid felt anger bloom beautifully in him. Felt it fill him. How dare this pawn of the Powers lecture him on Martine? It was satisfying to shout, 'Sandpiper!' and have his guard run to the door immediately. It was enormously satisfying to say, 'Sandpiper, this man is going to write me a report. Make sure he doesn't leave until he is finished, and I have read it.'

'Aye, my lord,' Sandpiper said.

The Prowman looked at him with a mixture of anger and pity, which just made him angrier.

'She loves you,' he said. 'She forsook everything she believed in to marry you.'

'Not everything,' Arvid snarled. 'She kept her secrets.'

He strode out the door and slammed it behind him, with Sandpiper inside the workroom to ensure that his orders were carried out. Which was as it should be, because Valuer or not, sympathiser with the old bloods or not, he did not believe that the Prowman's secrets were worth even a single one of his people's lives.

A scurry of workers surrounded the bonfire. Moss had the uprights in already, the thatchers were bundling reeds, Swan was cutting cross-beams and Cat was directing a team from the kitchen in setting up a permanent tripod over the flame.

Good.

Arvid went to see the blacksmith. Lily was a huge man, of course, as blacksmiths were – so huge and so black-tempered that no one had ever been known to make a joke about his name. Arvid had never seen him sit still. But when he walked into the smithy, Lily was slumped on the tree trunk he balanced his knee on when he hammered hard, staring at the empty fire pit.

His tools were hung up neatly; the straight iron bars he used to make swords were leaning in a corner. There was the scent of dead smoke and ash. His two apprentices had made themselves scarce.

'Lily. I need your help.'

Lily slowly raised his head and stared at him blankly. His eyes were dead. He seemed to be having trouble focusing on Arvid's face.

'I need your help, Lily,' he repeated. Moving forward, he placed a hand on Lily's shoulder. The muscles were slack under his hand. 'I need you.'

Slowly, slowly, Lily sat up. He put his big hands on his knees and pushed himself up.

'I am useless,' he said. Without looking, he pointed back at the fire pit and the bellows.

'No,' Arvid said. 'You cannot ply your trade at present, but you are not useless. I need men I can trust – men who can stop panic, who can take command.'

'I'm not an officer,' Lily said slowly.

'My officers will be busy enough organising their own estates. I have sent messengers everywhere – I have very few guards left here in the fort. Who else can I trust to protect us but the one who has armed us all?'

Lily stood a little straighter. He was a fine swordsman, and if he'd been born an officer he'd have been a terror on the battle-field, if they could have found a horse big enough to hold him. But he was too good a smith to risk as a footsoldier.

'You know the men who can use weapons. Find them. Bring them from other villages if you must. Promise them hot food if they baulk. And garrison my fort.'

'Aye, my lord,' Lily said. He strode out of the smithy without even waiting for Arvid to leave, energy renewed.

Arvid stayed in the cool dark smithy for a moment longer, enjoying the brief respite from other people's eyes. He wondered where Martine was, and then pushed the thought away. He had other people to see. Salt. That was organised. Water.

The coopers weren't as dispirited as Lily had been. They worked more as a team, although the head cooper, Linnet, was the kind of woman who brooked no insolence. She had the other three, her journeyer and her two apprentices, soaking barrel staves in water. Nearby were bags which slumped oddly. He stared at them.

'Sandbags,' Linnet said briskly. 'We can't steam the staves, so we're going to curve them with weights alone.' She stood back so he could see a set of staves already balanced between two trestles, bags of sand on their middles so that they dipped down.

'Excellent,' Arvid said, his spirits lifting. One problem he didn't have to solve. 'We'll need as many as you can make. Draft help if you need it. Well done.'

The laundresses were cursing, as they often did, but they were resigned to their workload tripling without a copper of boiling water. He broke the news to them that there would be a troop of babies arriving soon, complete with dirty clouts, and fled as the curses rose to the treetops.

He couldn't see Martine anywhere.

If she had left him ...

He stood in the middle of the muster yard, breaking out in a cold sweat. She would not. She *could* not. He was the war-lord ... but Martine had never cared about that. And any other lord would give her sanctuary. The Last Domain wasn't impor-tant enough for them to be concerned about offending him, and Martine was not only the hero of the Compact Reweaving, she was the greatest stonecaster in the Domains. Arvid had used her skills too often to doubt that. The Ice King had almost stopped attacking them because they were always ready for each attack, since Martine's predictions were so accurate. Any warlord would welcome her for that ability alone.

That was the reason he went back to the hall, to his work-room, to her chamber, to search for her. He needed her skills to safeguard his domain, he told himself.

She wasn't there. In her chamber, he paused, and then, heart pounding, flung back the lids of the chests where she kept her clothes. They were there. His heart thudded harder than ever in relief. His hands were shaking. He dragged in breath after breath. His anger grew. Where *was* she?

He stormed out into the hall and into the kitchen. The cooks were busy cutting meat into wafer-thin slices. They looked up, saw his face, and immediately looked down and concentrated on their hands.

'Where is my lady?' he demanded.

'She is helping my Lady Sigurd to prepare for the road,' the head cook said in surprise. 'She has given us orders to prepare for the salt arriving.'

Arvid froze.

Merroc. Sigurd. Gods help him, in the rush to make his people safe, he had forgotten about them. He went back into the hall and climbed the stairs, dreading what he might find.

The guest chamber door stood open, and inside there were women moving about, folding clothes, stowing them into the travelling bales which southerners used, big square oiled canvas bags which lashed tight.

He couldn't see Martine, or Sigurd, or Merroc. The women were mostly Sigurd's servants, eager to go home, he guessed, from the brisk way they were packing.

Martine's parlour was the next door, and he approached it reluctantly. This was the only room in the fort which she had made her own – painted bright yellow as a southerner's room might be, with big lambskin rugs on the floor and a frieze of stars around the top of the walls, near the high ceiling.

'Stars are the Last Domain's treasure,' she had said, as though he should understand something by that, and when he'd looked puzzled she'd explained that the friezes were an ancient enchantment, meant to bring prosperity and peace. He'd wanted sheaves of corn and ripe apples instead, but she'd laughed and said no, each place had its proper treasure and it was bad luck to use any other.

Her parlour was where she cast the stones, and where she saw the few friends who would come to the fort – for most of her friends weren't officers' wives, and felt uncomfortable under his roof. A flash of irritation hit him. She had never really adjusted to being a warlord's wife. He knew that was unfair, that she had learned all the duties expected of her and carried them out with unflinching efficiency and calm. But it was still duty to her, and there was no joy in it. She despised what she was.

Which meant, surely, that she despised him.

There was a desolation in that thought that he couldn't face, so he pushed the door of the parlour open. Martine was sitting with Merroc at the small round table Arvid had made for her himself. Their hands were clasped.

Casting. He paused in the doorway, not wanting to interrupt this. If they could learn anything ...

Martine cast. The five stones twisted and fell, seeming to Arvid to take forever to reach the table. Then she put out a long finger and touched them, one by one, that listening look on her face. He had seen that look so many times, as she cast for him,

predicting attacks, droughts, blizzards, pestilence ... she had
saved his people twenty, thirty, *fifty* times over, because they had
had time to prepare. To be there when the Ice King attacked. To
stock the silos against the dry years and the woodpiles against
the long, long storms which sometimes swept down out of the
north.

Woodpiles. He reflected bitterly, in the moment before she
spoke, that the one thing he would not have to do was stock the
woodpiles.

'Death, Destiny, Chaos, face up,' Martine said clearly. Did she
know he was there? Probably not. When she was casting she
seemed to see and hear nothing but the stones. She turned the
other stones over. 'And hidden ... Joy, and Rebirth.' She looked
up at Merroc, compassion on her face. 'He has gone on to
rebirth already, Merroc.'

Merroc shook his hand free of hers.

'And that is supposed to comfort me?' he said harshly. 'That
I will not see him again, even in the darkness beyond death?'

Sigurd's voice came from a big wing chair by the window. It
usually sat by the fireplace, but someone had moved it so that
its back was to the hearth, and to the door.

'Perhaps Lady Death will be merciful to us, and take us soon,
so we may be reborn with him.'

Martine said nothing. She picked up the stones and placed
them back in her pouch, then looked up, straight at Arvid. She
had known he was there. Merroc followed her gaze and his face
darkened. He turned back to Martine.

'How may I take my revenge?' Merroc demanded. He spat in
his hand again and Martine took it. With reluctance, Arvid
thought.

She cast the stones.

'Chaos,' she said. 'Darkness. Danger. Death. Destiny. All face up.' A pause which seemed to lengthen beyond bearing. Merroc's breathing was loud in the silence, and Arvid found his hands were clenched into fists. 'I am sorry, my lord,' Martine said formally. 'This casting says that revenge is closed to you on pain of death. That *no* good will come to you or yours by attempting it.'

He loosened his hand slowly, staring at her.

'But you would say that, wouldn't you?'

'Ask any stonecaster, my lord,' she said. 'They will tell you the same.' A flicker of some strong emotion went across her face. 'I would not lie to you. If I did, the stones would never speak to me again.'

She hesitated, not looking at Arvid, but he knew that whatever she was going to say was for him too. Perhaps mainly for him.

'There is something you do not know. It was the relationship the old bloods had with the Powers which made the compact possible.'

A shudder went through Arvid. The compact. The spell which kept the wind wraiths, the water spirits, the fire wraiths, the delvers in the earth, from killing and eating and destroying humans. He followed that trail of thought and took an involuntary step forward.

'Do you mean,' he demanded, 'that the wraiths and spirits are creatures of the Powers?'

Martine stared at him in shock, as if she'd never thought that through. But she must have. She must have known.

'In a way,' she started, her tone placatory. 'But not in the way you mean. The Powers don't control them. They don't *use* them.'

'But these creatures come from the Powers? Are born from them, so to speak?'

She hesitated.

'Answer me,' he said coldly, in the tone he would use to a servant. It was a mistake. He saw her face close against him and her spine stiffen.

'I have no knowledge of that,' she said. 'You know as much as I, my lord.'

'But you suspect it!' Merroc snapped.

Her head moved sideways – not quite a denial, more a rejection. 'I suspect that the Powers are not the creators of this world, and it may be that whatever created them also created the wraiths and spirits. That there may be other beings we have never heard of, and mysteries we will never clarify. That life and death and rebirth is all we can be sure of.'

Merroc pushed himself back from the table with angry impatience.

'Come, Sigurd,' he said. He went to the wing chair and gently lifted his wife up, his hands at odds with the scowl on his face. 'Let us go home.'

'No,' Sigurd said. It was a flat no, an absolute denial.

Merroc blinked. 'I've ordered them to pack—' he began.

'Then they may unpack. I will not leave this place until my son has quickened, and I have said goodbye to him.'

'She says Osfrid has gone on to rebirth already, my dear,' he said. The pain and love in his voice were terrible to hear, and Arvid's throat tightened in sympathy.

'I believe nothing that Traveller bitch says,' Sigurd said clearly. Calmly. As though she spoke honey instead of vitriol. The flat voice was on the edge of madness. 'I will live in her house until I see my son, and then I will spit in her face and leave.'

Arvid flushed with anger and took a step forward, but Martine shook her head at him, her face full of pity. She stood up, and bowed to Merroc, who was staring at her with a combination of anger and uncertainty.

'Your lady is welcome in this house for as long as she chooses,' Martine said. 'But I must warn her, Osfrid will not quicken. He has chosen the path of rebirth already, and the gods rejoice in him.'

Sigurd thrust herself out of the chair so fast that it slid backwards and teetered. She spun on Martine, her face contorted.

'You will not use my son's name, whore!' she shouted.

Martine bowed, calmly, and turned and walked out past Arvid. He looked at Merroc.

'I understand the pain of your lady,' he said formally, 'but it will be better if she does not speak of my wife again in that fashion.'

'Better if they don't see each other again,' Merroc said. For a moment they were just men together, trying to deal with contrary women. Arvid nodded and went out.

Martine was in the guest chamber, telling Sigurd's women the unwelcome news. They protested, and she raised her voice.

'Will you tell your mistress that she cannot attend the quickening of her son?' Silence fell. 'I thought not,' Martine went on. 'Ready everything here as she would like it. She may have the use of my parlour also. If anything is needed, see me or my lord's steward.'

There was a chorus of 'Aye, my lady' and Martine came out, shutting the door behind her. She stopped when she saw Arvid, her back straight and her mouth firm. She had looked like that the first time he had seen her, near the Great Forest, sitting on a restive chestnut gelding. The gelding had died, long since. He noticed, as if for the first time, the grey in her hair.

She waited with perfect composure, a wall of serenity between them.

'How can you be so calm when she insults you like that?' It was all he could think of to say.

A flicker of amusement went over her face.

'I'm a Traveller,' she said. 'I've spent my life being insulted. If I had objected, my lord, I would have been lashed or garrotted or hung or killed in the pressing box. It's not so hard to swallow an insult when that is the alternative.'

She stared at him across a gulf he realised they would never cross.

'You are safe now,' he said.

'Am I?' she asked drily. 'It did not seem so, earlier.'

His anger came back. Why would she throw that up at him, when he was able for the first time to talk to her calmly? It was anger laced with that irritation all men felt at women, at times. She should not be *able* to be calm when his own emotions were churned so hard and so fast.

'Safe from *others*, I meant,' he said, knowing it was vicious but unable to control himself.

She flinched.

'I am at your mercy, my Lord Arvid,' she said formally, and bowed, then waited.

He turned on his heel and went downstairs, slamming the outside door as he left.

MOUNTAINSIDE,
THE ICE KING'S COUNTRY

The king's footsteps always boomed along the corridor as he returned. The boy who had been set to listen came running for the queen, so that when Ari, Hárugur King, pale as uncooked bread, stumbled out of the King's Passage, it was into her waiting arms. Nyr was there, too, ready to lend a strong shoulder to support his father over to the throne.

They said nothing. It was better not to talk to the king when he came back, until he had readjusted himself to the real world again. Halda put a mug of warm mead into Ari's hand, and guided it to his lips. He drank, shuddered, and drank again, the colour slowly coming back into his face. She could see Nyr wondering, not for the first time, whether he would have the necessary courage, when it was his time to confront the Ice King.

Finally, Ari stood up. It was time to call the others in. Nyr went to the door of the Council Cave and announced: 'Ari, Hárugur King, has returned!'

A cheer went up. It was never certain that a king would come back sane and whole, and Ari was a respected and valued ruler. The council crowded through the door first, as was their right, but Ari waved them back out again and went to stand by the central hearth of the big hall, where everyone could see him.

He basked in its warmth for a moment, then he said, 'The Ice King sends his greetings to his people.'

Halda and Nyr knelt on one knee, along with everyone else. It was always a moment of wonder, that the Power of Ice would deign to notice them. Ari went on, 'I asked our king if we should send a trading party to the east, and He had no objection.'

Another cheer went up, from the younger men who wanted to go with Nyr, and from their mothers and sweethearts, who would much rather they went trading than into battle. Except for some older women, who looked sour. They didn't like any change, Halda thought.

After the return feast and the dancing, Ari took Halda and Nyr aside privately in the Council Cave. 'He didn't care,' Ari said, frowning and puzzled. 'It was like something else was holding his attention. He just didn't care, one way or the other.'

'That's good, isn't it?' Nyr asked.

'I don't know,' Ari said. 'It may mean that the attempt at trading is doomed, and you will have to fight anyway. When you go, make sure you are fully armed.'

Halda felt her heart clench. She couldn't bear it if Nyr was taken from her, too.

'Yes,' she said. 'Be even more careful than on a raid. You may not mean to attack, but they don't know that.'

Someone sniffed loudly, with disapproval.

'Trading!' a voice said over Halda's shoulder. 'Like weaklings or southerners. It wasn't so in my day.'

It was Gytta, the oldest woman in Mountainside, standing just inside the entrance to the main tunnel, where the sun would not get in her eyes. Halda could only spare her a glance – her eyes were fixed on Nyr's golden head as he rode at the front of the trading party. He rode without a hat. The snow was only fetlock high on their horses, and the sun was clear on the eastern horizon. A fine spring day. She hoped it was a good omen.

'Our men should take what we need, like their fathers and grandfathers did,' Gytta went on.

Ari rode next to Nyr; he would leave them at the plateau's edge and return home, and he would be in no mood to hear criticism of his decision.

'The Ice King agreed,' Halda said firmly. But Gytta was past the age of being intimidated by anyone, even the queen.

'The king said he didn't care either way. It was that boy of yours that convinced the Hárugur King.' Her tone rang with disdain. 'You'd think he didn't want to fight.'

Even age didn't excuse that. Halda turned to look Gytta right in the eyes.

'Nyr, as you know, is a fine and courageous warrior,' she said, her voice as sharp as an icicle. 'As for trading – tell me, Gytta, how many sons and grandsons have you mourned when they did not return from a raid?'

Gytta met her eyes defiantly for a moment, but as memory overwhelmed her she turned away, looking at the granite doorstep beneath their feet.

'Aye, it was too many, too many, I'll grant you that.' She looked after the trading party wistfully. 'Your boy had better keep my youngest safe.'

Bren, Gytta's youngest, was older than the king. Ari had insisted that his trusted adviser accompany Nyr, and Halda was glad of it. Bren had a canny mind and a smooth tongue. It made her feel better, remembering he was there to shepherd Nyr through this unprecedented journey. Halda smiled and took Gytta's arm, leading her back in. She had too much to do to stand around wasting time. 'I'm sure he will,' she said.

But instead of organising the cleaning out of the caves, ready for their spring exodus, Halda went to the women's altar. It was a small cave. The women came in twos and threes, when they could slip away, unlike the men, who worshipped together at sunset, to welcome the night cold, the Child of the Ice.

It was just a simple space with benches around the walls and a small hot pool, gift of the king, to warm it. Like the other women, Halda loved this quiet nest. This was a space where she felt protected, cherished. Loved, even. It was as though the face the king showed the women was a different face altogether to the one he showed the men. But that was not spoken of; women's worship was private.

She sat and prayed for Nyr's safety and the success of the venture. The pool of hot rock flared suddenly, and she took it for a good omen from the king and was comforted. Then, for a blessed moment, she just sat, her thoughts wandering to her own first venture away from home, when she had come from her tribute tribe, the High Fjord People, to become Ari's wife.

It was a great honour, and it was what she had been born and bred for, but she had been frightened none the less, as all girls were who were sent off to marry strangers for the good of the tribe.

When she had seen Mountainside, its forbidding cliffs rearing up above the plateau, she had gasped with awe. For the first time she had believed the stories, that the Mountainside people, the Hárugur King's people, were specially chosen by the Ice King.

It wasn't until after her marriage to Ari, in the dark early days when she still hated him, that the older women had taken her to this place, to the altar, and explained *why* He had chosen them, and had sung the Song of the Sacrifice to her.

Ari's mother, Asi, had begun the story:

'Once, there was a brave warrior called Sebbi, from the peoples of the far south,' she began. 'And it was in his time that the Ice King woke, and being freshly woken was hungry, as hungry as a wolverine, and He came from the north, and ate everything, and left nothing behind.'

This was a version of the same story her own people told, about the coming of the king.

'But Sebbi was braver than all others, and he offered himself as a sacrifice to the king,' Asi said.

Then the women started to sing the Song of the Sacrifice.

I was there and I saw it
I was there and I smelt it
Sebbi's bright blood sprayed out on the ice

In her mind's eye, Halda could see it even now: the small valley being eaten by the king, Sebbi offering himself, the hunters chasing the prey with prayer and desperation, the women rending their garments and wailing afterwards as they scattered the flesh and bones before the king.

It had not bought their valley safety; the king had eaten it anyway. But He had communed with the first Hárugur King, and told him of a way through to the middle of the mountains, to safety, to Mountainside. He had granted them Mountainside as a sanctuary, when he had pushed all the other tribes far south. He had made the Hárugur King his mouthpiece to the tribes.

They were blessed. The hot pools, the eternal fire, the strong stalwart walls of the mountain – these were the gifts of the king, and they meant that the king's tribe was the only one not to fear the dread claws of winter.

So Sebbi had not died in vain.

Halda wondered how old he had been. Young, she thought. The young are always eager to trade death for glory.

She pushed down the thought that she would rather spend her winters shivering in the women's longhouse, as she had done all her childhood, than be caged under a mountain of rock for months on end. Without the warmth and brightness of the fire she would go mad, she thought, and sent a prayer of thanks to the king. The fire flared again as if in answer, and she smiled.

Time to get the caverns ready; although the end of winter was a ceaseless round of work, she welcomed it, both because it meant spring was coming, and because it would stop her worrying about Nyr. She said another prayer, for her son Andur's soul, feasting somewhere in the King's Hall. No doubt the fire there was warmer still.

THE GREAT FOREST

They camped again that night on a hilltop at the western edge of the marshes, in the best defensible position Holly could find, uneasily aware of how much smaller their group now was. None of them slept well, and they were up early, eager to be free of the marsh smell, which reminded them all, Ember thought, of death.

By mid-morning, they had come to a ridge which was the last high ground before the foothills. To their left, the road wound south to parallel the river that led to Starkling, the summer fort town of Northern Mountains Domain. Before them, a much narrower track led down into a vast bowl of land filled by the Great Forest.

All northern children were raised on tales of the Great Forest, in the same way the children of the south heard stories of the Weeping Caverns, the home of Lady Death. The Forest was vast, stretching over the two Domains, and once it had reached from cliff to cove in the south, too, right down to the desert which separated the Domains from the Wind Cities. But people had come and settled and farmed, and cut down the trees in great swathes, and slowly, over hundreds of years, it seemed that the Forest became aware of the depredations.

'Time in the Great Forest does not run as time runs for us,' her mother had told her, a note in her voice which meant that this was knowledge personally won, at high cost. 'But it has learned, at last, not to welcome humans.'

For that reason it was dangerous to go into the Forest alone. No one in her right mind would cut down a living tree here. No one would light a fire. No one would leave the path.

'Each one who ventures under Its trees finds a different Forest,' Martine had said, eyes distant, remembering. 'And there are places there where the wall between this world and the next is easily breached.'

The compact which forbade wind wraiths and water spirits to attack humans in settled areas did not run in the Forest, but at least the Power here kept wind wraiths and water spirits away as well.

The Forest was still full of morning fog, and they looked across the tops of high black spruces spearing through a milky cloud, and beyond that to the shimmering heights of the Eye Teeth Mountains. In the south of the range, they could just make out the perfect cone of Fire Mountain, wreathed with clouds – or smoke.

The day seemed to pause as they looked, although Ember could hear birdsong below them, in the Forest.

'A long way to go,' Holly said.

'We're at the border,' Ember replied. 'From here, we're in the Northern Mountains Domain.'

They looked at each other, Holly with compressed lips, Tern with eyes wide. Curlew shrugged.

'It's no different from the Last Domain,' he said. 'The rest is children's tales.'

'The power in the Great Forest is not a tale,' Cedar said softly. His hand went to his belt as though expecting to find something there, but came away empty.

Holly pointed north a little.

'The Power isn't always against us,' she said. 'I was born not far from here. The way my mam tells it, I was born under the shade of the Forest itself, when she got took short gathering berries. She reckons It welcomed her. We played a lot on the edges, when we were little. Saw some strange things, but nothing ever hurt us.'

There was a note of nostalgia in her voice, which surprised them all. Holly was usually so matter of fact.

'They say if you treat the Forest with respect,' Ash volunteered, 'you will be – well, not safe, perhaps, but not attacked.'

He smiled reassuringly at Ember as he spoke, and she bit her lip with chagrin. Did she look so frightened? Of course she was, but she didn't want to show it so clearly.

'The sooner we start, the sooner we're there,' she said, and kicked Merry into a quick walk down the rough track and into the mist, the dogs breaking away and joining her in exuberant chase.

'My lady! Wait!' Holly called, exasperated. Ember drew rein and twisted to look back, guiltily aware of having broken protocol – a protocol which existed for her safety. Grip and Holdfast shot past her and then circled back, tails waving happily.

The others were riding willy-nilly down the trail, through the waist-high saplings and low bushes which bordered the tall trees of the forest. Someone had cut the bordering trees down a few years back, it looked like, to leave a clear division between their land and the forest. But Forest was reclaiming Its territory, and the farmer, whoever it was, was nowhere to be seen. Ember shivered. There wasn't even any sign of grazing animals. She wondered what had happened, when Forest had realised the trees were gone.

As Ash and Holly cantered down towards her, there was a flicker of light, like sun through leaves, and behind them, around her, were no longer saplings, but huge and towering trees. Ember blinked, shook her head, feeling that if only she could shake it just the right way her addled mind would go back to normal and she'd stop seeing impossible things ...

Cedar and Tern and Curlew came into view, the sun flickered again, and it was a cloudy, dull day and the trees were gone, replaced by a kind of fern which grew higher than her head. The sounds were different, too – no birds calling, none ... The horses laid their ears back, neighing with fear and their eyes showed white.

'Dragon's fart!' Tern said. They were all looking around, frightened, alert for danger. 'Where have the others gone?'

Most of their rearguard group had simply vanished. Ember prayed that they'd not entered the Forest at all – that they had seen the first group disappear and held back.

'The dogs aren't here either,' Ash said, worry deep in his voice.

'Stay together,' Holly said.

Ember found some reassurance in the others' closeness, the horses' animal warmth. She bent to pat Merry on the neck, calming her. When she looked up, the forest had changed again. Trees, but softer and greener than any she had known. These were southern trees, surely, with luxuriant wide-leaved under-growth ... and the air was balmy, summer-warm and moist, although she could see the sun and it was still at spring height in the sky.

The horses began to calm down. Thatch even bent his head to crop at the grass.

'No!' Ember called. Ash had already pulled Thatch's head up.

They all knew the stories. If you ate in the other world, you had to stay there. All the old stories said so, and stories were all they had to guide them.

'We're adrift in Time,' Cedar said.

'But not in place,' Ash added. He pointed to a big rock outcrop halfway up the hill. 'That's shifted, but it was there in our – before, when we arrived.'

'Forest holds all of Time in Its palm,' Holly said. Her eyes were looking past Ember to the deep forest beyond. 'Death is nothing to It. Everything lives, and goes on living, within Its grasp.'

'But can we get back?' Ember asked. Someone had to be practical. She nudged Merry to take a few steps back up the trail, but the trail had disappeared. The hill was covered with rocks that would break a horse's leg with one misstep. Reluctantly, she turned her head to stare down – the trail was clear enough, here, though it was no more than a deer's track. At least the birdsong had come back.

Uncertain, Ember looked at Ash and Holly.

The world flickered again and the ancient huge trees were back, but not the same ones … a different species, some kind of conifer that Ember had never seen before. And this time, the rock outcrop was much, much smaller than it had been.

She began to shake. She couldn't think. It was like the moment when Fire had first appeared … when a Power displayed Its strength, humans were left adrift and confused.

'We are seeing the history of the world,' Cedar said in wonder. Annoyance flared in Ember. As if that was a good thing! With the anger, the shaking stopped and she could begin to consider what they should do.

'This is a message,' Holly said. 'Forest wants to remind us of Its power. And of our weakness. Humans may cut a few trees down, but It exists forever, and It will reclaim what has been taken, in time.'

'As it should,' Cedar said. Ash glanced at him, and Ember realised it had been an odd thing for a farmer's son to say. Cedar's dark eyes seemed larger when he looked at the Forest, as though they reflected a world rather than a scene. But she wasn't about to argue the limits of Forest's power here.

'We have to go on,' Ember said. The only way to get through the Forest was to *go* through the Forest.

Ash was nodding. Tern and Curlew looked appalled. Cedar stared off into the darkening trees with surmise.

It was up to Holly.

'Aye, my lady,' Holly said. Ember almost fell off Merry in astonishment. That was the first time Holly had ever taken any notice of her opinion. She realised belatedly that she herself was of highest rank in this party; not that Holly would pay attention to that if it were a matter of her safety.

Ember licked dry lips. She'd planned to do this when they reached the first of the big trees, but she'd clearly left it too late. Worth trying, still.

'By your leave, Great Forest, we seek permission to travel through your borders, doing no harm, seeking only safe passage.'

There was no response. Which could have been good.

Holly nodded at her, then went forward, taking point, and Ash, then Cedar, followed her. Ember went next, Tern and Curlew behind.

At least the horses didn't seem afraid. Holly clicked her tongue at her mare and they went forward at a walk.

The sky flickered.

Saplings were only waist high. The air was cooler, the rock outcrop the right size. The trees ahead ... they were black spruce and larch, as they should be. With a bound of her heart, Ember saw the dogs, waiting at the edge of the trees. They barked a welcome and dashed back to the horses, then away again, into the woods.

'Don't stop!' Cedar called, and Ember could hear Sight speaking through him, so she nudged Merry with her heels and kept on, into the Great Forest, into what she hoped was the Forest of her own time.

As the shade of the trees fell on her, she felt Merry twitch all over, but that was all. No terrifying shapes swooping from the branches above, no strange sounds. No malignant thorns reaching for her soft flesh. The sky stayed still, as it should. Just trees, and a deepening mist, thickening as they descended into the valley.

Unlike the pine forests nearer to her home, there was enough light filtering through the branches to allow mosses to grow beneath them. The curving light green of feathermoss, the bright tiny stars of sphagnum moss shoots, even some red fireweed lining the edge of the track, its flowerstalks reaching high but the bells not yet open. There were other trees occasionally, too – aspen, birch, balsam fir, each bringing its different green to the whispering patchwork of boughs. They emerged from the fog and slipped away again as Ember rode past, Merry's hoof-falls muted by the damp.

'We're being watched,' Ash said, bringing his bay up beside her. He was right. Ember could feel eyes on them from beyond the screen of mist. The horses were happy enough, though, their ears pricked forwards, their steps light but unhesitating. Holdfast and Grip padded before them, alert but not growling. Surely they would sense danger before the humans?

As they rode along the path, the horses' hooves splashing in the boggy ground, shifting sunlight began to pierce the cloud around them. But Ember could hear something, feel something, see something flicker at the corners of her vision which was never there when she turned her head.

It seemed that Forest was allowing them to pass, and allowing them to stay in their own time. Nothing barred their way except small, fast-running streams and the occasional sapling fallen across the path, which the horses stepped over easily. Spruce had shallow roots and were prone to being wind-blown, but most of the fallen trees were aspen, and she wondered if the black spruce guarded their territory. Anything seemed possible.

They spelled the horses every couple of hours, whenever they came to a clearing with enough sunlight in it to feel safe, although Ember was sure that feeling was an illusion. At least the clearings gave her something to do. She searched the ground for plants that the horses found edible and harvested as much as she could, stuffing it into a sack, knowing that in the mountains feed would be scarce. Tern helped her, while Ash and Cedar scouted for small game, and Holly and Curlew kept watch.

'Don't go far,' she said to her cousins, and Cedar grinned.

'Yes, Mam,' he said mockingly, but when he looked out into the shifting shadows of the trees, his face clouded and his hand again went to his belt, as if to find something that wasn't there.

Most of the plants Martine had taught her to recognise, and she knew which to avoid: baneberry, nightshade, dogbane. But there were many others, like the heart-shaped twayblade and cow wheat, horsetail fern and bracken and even some sedges by the streams that she could cut with her belt knife and stash away. She came back triumphant from one sortie with a handful of tiny strawberries, sweet as honey in the mouth. Only one berry for each of them, and one over which she gave to Tern, who blushed.

All the herbs were in blossom. She walked through them surrounded by butterflies and bees, busily harvesting too, finding the meagre drops of nectar in the heart of the tiny wildflowers.

She looked up from collecting some fresh tight-curled fronds of bracken to find Ash staring at her, a dog on either side, also staring. Her red hair crinkled so much, it was impossible to keep tightly bound, and she was abruptly aware of the strands across her face and neck, of the sweat under her arms. She must look as mucky as a cowgirl. She grinned and shrugged at him and the corners of his mouth lifted in a small smile. Then Grip bayed once and was away, across the clearing, chasing the black ear tips of a hare above the grass.

'Grip!' she called. 'Not in the Forest!'

Fast as thought, Ash grabbed his bow, nocked an arrow and let fly. The hare leaped once and lay still, the arrow quivering in its side. Grip happily collected it and brought it back to Ash, laying it at his feet and sitting back as he'd been trained.

Ember looked at Ash wonderingly. She'd known he had talent with the bow, but nothing like that.

'I couldn't let him go off into the Forest,' Ash said, almost apologetically. 'Besides, they need fresh meat.'

He gutted and jointed the hare swiftly and fed the dogs. The hare's fur was thick and full so close to winter, but it was in moult, changing from its white winter coat to its brown summer one, so it was less valuable.

'No way of tanning it, anyway,' Ash said, throwing it to Holdfast to play with. She and Grip had a joyful game of tug-o'-war with it before they all set off again.

Holly called camp when they came to a clearing with a running stream about an hour before sunset.

They saw to the horses in a watchful silence. Birds were settling down in their nests and the quiet whispering of the trees was easier to hear as the evening breeze began. The mosses and small shrubs rustled as the night creatures emerged.

Merry shivered under the curry as an owl called sleepily and was answered. Ember patted her.

'Settle down, you're all right,' she said, and the cheerful, familiar scolding tone worked. She stood placidly as Ember finished with the polishing rag and then combed her mane and tail free of the burrs and twigs they'd picked up. Not as many burrs as in mid-summer, thank the gods.

Holly had stopped grooming her mare Simple, and was standing, brush in hand, her head cocked to listen.

'Can you hear that?' she asked Curlew, but he shook his head.

'Birds,' he said. Holly frowned.

'No, something else,' she said. 'Something calling.'

'Calling what? Who?' Ember asked, but Holly shrugged.

'It's gone now. It sounded like ... I don't know. Like someone calling the cows home.'

As they sat in the growing dusk to their hard bread and cheese and dried fenberries, Ash sat next to Ember and said quietly, 'Don't think about fire tonight.'

'I'm not that stupid!' she flashed. The very idea of calling Fire within the Forest brought her out in a cold sweat. She had never realised how many ways there were to be afraid. At home there were, of course, lots of ways to die, most of them linked to the intensely cold winters: frostbite, the dry cough that turned to coughing blood, windbite, wolves, wolverines, snow blindness that led you over crevasses and into drifts, simply failing to make it home by nightfall. But they were known dangers, and there were methods to deal with all of them – mostly involving being home by nightfall.

But here there was no home, and no shelter, and the dangers were so many and so different that there was nothing which could protect them. And that was without the Powers of Forest and Fire stalking them.

Life was not easy in the Last Domain, so its people worked together, kept each other safe, stayed in groups. She had lived her life in a warlord's fort, surrounded by people whose job it was to keep her safe and well. To be out here, with so few other humans, was deeply unsettling. It was like walking out onto the lake ice the first time in early winter, when you weren't sure it would bear your weight. Every creak of the ice brought your heart to your mouth; every hint of danger here brought her out in a sweat.

Remembering the dead they had already left behind, her eyes filled. A tear dropped onto her fenberries, and she wiped her eyes surreptitiously, but Ash saw.

'I can't tell you it will be all right,' he said.

'I don't need you to tell me that!' she snapped, getting up and moving away. 'I'm not a child!' She was sorry a moment later, but when she turned back to look at him, his face was only a blur in the failing twilight and she couldn't tell if she had hurt his feelings. She sat down again, a little nearer to him, feeling his warmth strike across the air between them, making her heart beat more strongly. She was achingly aware of his bare forearms where he had rolled up his shirt. A crescent of moon edged over the trees, the moonlight showing Ash's muscles and tendons clearly, his big crafter's hands ... she shivered at the thought of those hands touching her and couldn't remember what she should be saying.

'I wish I were braver,' she said randomly. 'Like Mam.'

'Aye,' Holly said, 'your mam's brave all right. I saw her rebuild the compact and face down the wraiths. Saved us all, her and the other three.'

The compact. The spell which allowed humans to go about their business without attack from wind wraiths, or water spirits, fire sprites or delvers, the dark beings who lived underground.

Without that spell, existence would be terrifying and hand-to-mouth; every move out of doors fraught with danger, every hunting trip, every attempt to sow seed, an invitation to disaster. The compact had made the Domains possible. Sometimes it had seemed impossible to Ember that it was her mother, with three others, who had remade that spell when it began to fray twenty-one years ago. Her mother who had such trouble sewing or brewing or even ordering servants, though she did all those things because a warlord's lady must, in the northern domains. But there were times when her mother cast the stones to predict when the Ice King's men would attack. When she had sent men out to fight, and die. Then Ember had watched her with awe; her green eyes seemed like gateways to other places, other Powers, and Ember had been fervently glad that she had no Sight at all, that the gods had no interest in her, had given her no responsibility. Her mouth quirked, thinking of that unfounded relief.

The night was growing darker, despite the thin moon which showed through the very tops of the trees around them but cast the clearing into deeper shadow.

Holly lifted her head, on alert.

'Hear it?' she asked. Ember shook her head. Cedar got up and went to the edge of the clearing.

'There's something . . .' he said.

'Aye. A calling,' Holly said slowly.

'I can't hear anything,' Ash said.

'You've got about as much Sight as a rock,' Cedar said dismissively, although not unkindly. Ash nodded as though that were old news.

'It's gone now,' Holly said, almost regretfully.

Ember slept with difficulty, aware of Ash's warm bulk lying next to her, tormented by dreams where that warmth grew into an inferno of passion but never reached satisfaction.

THE LAST DOMAIN

Poppy and Larch spent the night in a village even smaller than Acorn, where the Voice turfed his family out so they would have somewhere to sleep. Poppy would have protested, but Larch shook her head. 'It's the warlord's dignity we uphold,' she whispered to Poppy. 'He wouldn't sleep in a barn, so we shouldn't.'

'I thought you were all Valuers around here?' Poppy whispered back. Valuers believed that all people were worth the same. The Last Domain was a stronghold for them, the place where the Valuers' Plantation had been set up as a refuge for those running from injustice or for those who simply wanted to work towards equality.

Larch laughed silently. 'Still working on it.'

Lord Arvid's mother had been a Valuer, and Poppy knew that he respected those beliefs, even if he felt he still had to be the warlord. Why, he had set up a Domain Council even before the Resettlement. Grammer Martine was Valuer through and through, of course, although she wouldn't say so. 'I'm no respecter of rank,' was how she put it, which was funny because she was a warlord's lady.

The mattress on the cupboard bed was thick linen over gorse branches, and it smelt wonderful, like honey and nuts and apricots, but the gorse prickles worked their way through the linen and woke her in the middle of the night. Poppy wriggled them flat and lay, listening to the dark.

The wind had risen and it was colder. She burrowed under the blankets and breathed the warm scented air, hoping the wind would drop before dawn.

But in the morning it was still cold, with a steady breeze blowing from the north. Her family never came to visit Grammer without bringing the felt coats her Aunty Drema had made them, and Poppy was glad of it as she pulled on the bright blue and black warmth and fastened the toggles.

'Nice,' Larch said as they mounted, and they talked clothes for a while as they rode further north, to Salt, a town in a low range of hills which owed its prosperity to a salt mine. They met the Salt Town Council in the Moot Hall, a big building for a town this size, with gilding on the doorframe that wouldn't have disgraced a lady's chamber.

The council, including its Voice, a woman of about sixty with jet-black hair who reminded Poppy strongly of her grandmother, were shocked and afraid at their news, although since they had spent a whole night without fire they were more prepared to believe it.

Then Poppy saw the Voice exchange a meaningful glance with another councillor, a younger man, and saw a small, acquisitive smile light his face. They would see this as an opportunity to make money, she realised. Salt would be the most sought-after commodity in the domain, the only sure way to cure raw meat and make it safe to eat.

Larch saw the smile, too, and stepped forward, holding out a letter.

'My lord Arvid knows that you will understand when he requests that you keep the price of salt to its normal level.'

The Voice looked sour, but she took the letter.

'Your trade will increase anyway,' Poppy ventured. It didn't make them any happier, but then the Voice looked up from the letter and said, 'He's going to let us off taxes this year if we hold the price steady.'

That was Granfer Arvid, all right, a trader to his bones. The council relaxed a little and variously grinned or smiled or sniffed in disparagement, but the atmosphere had shifted to acceptance.

Outside the Moot Hall, the weather was sharper than ever. The Voice looked north, towards the higher hills, and shook her head.

'Not seasonable, a north wind this time of spring,' she said. 'But there you are – might as well spit at the stars as complain about the weather.' She brooded a little. 'If this goes on, we'll all end up sleeping in the mines. Won't be the first time. Last blizzard the whole town was down there.'

Poppy's face must have displayed her puzzlement, because the Voice laughed, kindly. 'Always the same down there, lass. Winter or summer, always a little bit cool but nothing more than that.'

She stomped off, waving to a boy to go and get their horses.

The wind picked up Poppy's hair and flicked it painfully into her eyes. She blinked back tears, dug her coat's matching hat out of her pocket and put it on, but she was still cold.

Larch reached out to tuck a strand of hair back behind Poppy's ear, her fingers chilly. Poppy blinked in surprise and Larch snatched her hand back and stuck it in her pocket, looking down at the ground with a red face.

Oh, Poppy thought. *Oh*. Her body was swept with warmth. Looking at Larch's face, she felt a sense of horizons widening, like taking the last few steps out of a valley and standing on a ridge, with all the world laid out before you.

'Thanks,' she said softly. Larch shot her a look and then paused, both of them caught by the gaze, both slowly smiling. The boy came back with their horses and waited impatiently. It wasn't good to keep the horses standing in this cold wind.

'White Springs next, then Pine Hill, Shell Lake, and Timbertop,' Larch said, trying to sound businesslike.

'Aye,' Poppy said. 'Let's go.'

They rode off together as if they'd been doing it for years instead of days.

THE GREAT FOREST

The path narrowed between sharp black trunks like spears. Curlew went first, Holly last, with Ember safely in the middle position with Tern.

Under the thick shade they were walking into silence. Bird calls fell behind them and they no longer even heard the warning kik-kik-kik of the woodpeckers. Ember looked up. There was a strip of sky above them, palest blue. It floated, looking unreal. Outside that strip, what was happening? Clouds? Storm? Sunlight streaming golden and hazy with the scent from the trees below? She wondered if the two guards who had turned back had reached home safely, and sent a prayer after them.

'Halt!' Curlew called. Ember reined in Merry and stood in the stirrups for a better view, but Ash, ahead of her, was doing the same and she couldn't see past his broad shoulders.

Impatiently, she dismounted and tied Merry off to a nearby branch, then slid forwards past Thatch with a 'Good boy', a reassuring hand on his rump so he wouldn't kick. Ash followed her.

There was an elk on the path, taller than any Ember had ever seen. Its antlers were in full summer growth even this early in the season, and it was unquestionably a bull. It stood broadside across the path, turning its head to stare at them impassively.

Holly, Tern and Cedar arrived to stand behind them. The path was so crowded that even dismounted they could not all stand abreast.

Cedar smiled.

'So, do we just stand here until the world freezes again?'

'We can't go off the path,' Ash said.

Ember shivered at the thought. No, she wasn't going to leave the path.

'It has to move sometime,' Holly said.

Ash's hand, as though moving without his conscious thought, went to his bow, but Cedar grabbed his wrist.

'No, brother,' he said. 'I really wouldn't.'

'Maybe it's a messenger from the Forest,' Tern piped up.

'But what's the message?' Ash pondered.

Ember walked forward, shrugging off Curlew's cautionary hand. Her heart was beating uncomfortably fast, but if this was a messenger from the Forest, then she was the proper person to treat with it. She stopped a double arm's length from the animal, so close she could smell it: musky and a little rank.

'Greetings,' she said clearly, and gave her best formal bow, even allowing her head to tip flat as she bent, to indicate the respect given to those superior in office, although not in birth. 'We entreat you, let us pass.'

The elk turned its head and looked, not at her, but straight at Cedar. He stirred in surprise and came forward, and Ember ceded her place to him, easing past him and rejoining the others. Ash nodded approval at her, and she was thankful for the reassurance.

Cedar stood on the balls of his feet, prepared for battle and then, as if realising it, visibly forced his muscles to go lax until he was in his normal lounging posture.

'I greet you,' he said, and bowed, but differently. Lower, to indicate respect, but with his head raised. It was a Valuer's bow, and the elk snorted as though he found it funny, his brown eyes apparently amused.

Then the elk turned his back on Cedar, raised his tail, and deposited a hot stream of dung at his feet. The elk looked back at Cedar as if inviting protest, but Cedar was laughing, laughing hard.

'So that's what the Forest thinks of us!' he gasped.

It was infectious. Ember's fear twisted into surprise and laughter, and the others were chuckling, too.

'Thinks of *you*, my lad!' Ash said, smiling broadly.

As if approving their mirth, the elk moved, threading its way through the narrow tree trunks, disappearing into the shadows surprisingly fast, and they were left with only a pile of fresh dung to say it had been there at all.

The loose pat steamed. Cedar bowed mockingly to it.

'I salute you, message from the Forest,' he said.

Immediately, the dung shifted slightly. Curlew called, 'Get back, lass!' and Ash took Ember by the elbows and swung her around behind him, lifting her clean off her feet.

'*Ash!*' she protested, but he kept an arm out, preventing her from squirming back, so that she had to peer over the top of his elbow.

A plant was growing out of the dung. Fast, too fast, it sprouted one leaf, then two, then the stem grew and grew until it was waist high. Not a plant she recognised: green and mottled brown, it kept the look and scent of its origin. Cedar stared at it with a mixture of astonishment and elation.

'Wondrous!' he muttered.

On his word, it put forth a flower, black as pitch, black as the endless night sky, four-petalled like a briar rose, with deep purple stamens. It seemed to wait, poised at the moment of full display. Then a breeze lifted its head, stirred the pollen from its stamens, spreading it across the face of the flower. The petals withered and fell, velvet black turning to grey ash-like fragments, and the seed pod at the centre swelled.

Ember held her breath, and she could see that Cedar was doing the same. He stared at the plant with a ferocious intensity, as though all he had ever wanted was there before him, as a man hanging onto the side of a cliff might stare at the rope that will save him as it spirals down.

The pod opened silently.

Inside, it was bright orange, and in the middle lay a blackness, round as the full moon, about the size of a man's thumbnail. Slowly, Cedar put out his hand.

'Careful!' Holly called.

'It's singing!' Cedar said. 'Can't you hear it?'

He put his palm below the seed pod, hoping whatever this was would fall into it, but the blackness stayed resolutely where it was. Cedar swallowed and took a breath so big Ember could see it lift his shoulders.

'I thank you for this gift,' he said, and plucked the darkness from its bright home.

The plant withered in a heartbeat, and the dried dung blew away in a quick wind, leaving only the empty path, and Cedar standing there, holding—

'It's a casting stone,' he said wonderingly. 'The Evenness stone.'

They crowded forward to look as he turned and held it out to them. Black, round, perfect as the full moon.

'It sings to me!' he said, his face full of joy, more open than

Ember had ever seen him. And then he reverted to his normal manner and laughed. 'Typical, isn't it? Other people get given their stones in a pouch – mine comes from a pile of dung!'

'If Evenness comes out of dung,' Ash said, chuckling, 'gods help us when you get Chaos!'

'Ah,' said Cedar. 'Chaos was much easier.'

He pulled a kerchief from his pocket. It was tied up around what had to be a pile of stones. Cedar crouched and laid it on the ground, spreading it so they could see the collection – all casting stones.

'I've been finding them for months,' he said. 'This is the last one.' He hesitated. 'This is where I find out if I'm a stonemaker or a stonecaster. If they all sing for me, I'm a caster.'

Ember fished in her petticoat pocket for her coinpouch and emptied the coins into her hand. She handed the pale yellow pouch to Cedar.

'You'll need this, I think.'

Cedar smiled at her, acknowledging his own excitement and her generosity, but with that twist to his mouth that she was coming to understand. Not meanness, but a deep appreciation of how ridiculous life could be.

He put the stones from the kerchief inside the pouch and then slowly slid the Evenness stone in on top of them. Ember held her breath. Would they all hear the stones sing, or only him? She had never seen a caster receive his stone set before.

Cedar's head bowed towards the pouch. Oh, no, Ember thought, but then he raised his head and his eyes were alight, shining with unshed tears.

'They sing like a choir of water spirits,' he said unsteadily.

'So, you're a caster after all,' Ash said, beaming.

'You can earn a good living, casting,' Curlew said approvingly, and somehow the prosaic comment was what they all needed to return them from the realm of the extraordinary to ordinary life.

Cedar laughed and said, 'Aye, I hope so!' He drew the pouch strings tight, then tied it at his belt and rested his hand on it, in that spot Ember had seen him touch so many times.

Ember piled her coins onto Cedar's kerchief and tied it up. When she slipped it back into her pocket, it banged uncomfortably against her knee, so she handed it to Ash. 'Put that inside your jerkin,' she said. 'Or in your own pouch.'

'Mine's not big enough for this much coin!' he teased her.

They were all in good spirits. Perhaps the Forest had decided to welcome them, Ember thought happily, although a deep part of her wondered what would have happened if Cedar had not done everything exactly right, from greeting the dung to thanking the Forest for the gift. Without the right response ... the Forest, the old saying went, had no mercy and gave no second chances.

Which seemed to be true of all the Powers.

'Why is She helping us?' Cedar mused as they set up their sleeping pockets on the driest piece of ground they could find, a high bank beside the stream.

'She?' Why do you think the Forest is a She?' Ember asked. The Lake People had always referred to the Lake as 'She', but the Great Forest had never been spoken of in the same way. Cedar paused, his sleeping pocket hanging loosely from his hands.

'I don't know,' he said slowly. 'It feels female to me.'

'Feels male to me,' Holly said firmly. Ember let her mind reach out to the Forest in the way she imagined those with Sight did. She was Sight-blind, of course, but still ... in her imagination she coursed through the trees, whispering in the night breeze, new growth reaching for the stars and roots covered with rotting needles, flicked past the owls waking, the voles and shrews hiding in their burrows with their tiny blind young, the woodpeckers, the cuckoos, the nuthatches settling into their nests ... and other presences: bear, wolf, wolverine, elk and deer, weasel and hare. She had no sense of male or female, just of predator and prey. Life and death. Growth and decay.

'Both,' she said. 'The Forest is both.'

Ash had been watching her as she stood there, and now he came over to help her lay out her sleeping pocket.

'Both and everything,' he suggested quietly. 'Like some trees only need themselves to set fruit.'

Ember nodded.

'So why is *It* helping us?' Cedar demanded, taking his boots off. He slid into his pocket and propped himself on one elbow to stare at Ash and Ember.

'Maybe It's not,' Ash said.

'But—'

Ash smiled, his mouth twisting in the teasing grin he only gave his brothers and sisters. 'You said Evenness sang – maybe the singing was driving the Forest crazy and it just wanted to get rid of the bloody stone!'

Ember began to laugh, but then felt the Forest grow quiet around them. The breeze dropped. The owls fell silent. Even the stream seemed to pause in its song.

'I ask forgiveness if I misspoke,' Ash said. Ember could see the pulse beating at the side of his throat – fast and strong. He was wary, but not afraid. She wished she could be like him. Her own heart, as always, was leaping and jumping in fear.

With a sound like an avalanche so far off it was invisible, a giant sigh went through the trees and the noises of the Forest began again. They prepared for bed in silence, Holly, Curlew and Tern sleeping this time and Ash taking first watch, Holdfast at his side.

'I'll wake you at midnight,' Ash murmured to Ember. She nodded, pleased that he wasn't trying to exclude her from responsibility. But it took her a long time to sleep. Part of her was waiting. Waiting for the avalanche to hit.

Ember woke at midnight to find Ash gone. She scrambled into her boots and stood up, scanning the edges of the tiny clearing. The moon was up, a little larger, and the trees cast steel-sharp shadows across the ground, making it hard to see anything else. Then she spotted him, by one of the larches, standing with his bow where a long bough had broken off and made a cleft in the skirt of branches that swept the ground. His back was to the tree and he was staring across the open space, but not at her.

She turned slowly. A wolf. On the other side of the stream, a wolf silver in the moonlight, muzzle lifted as if howling, but silent, silent as a ghost. Cedar was standing on their side of the water, staring at it.

Ash had an arrow nocked, but his bow hung in his hands, ready to be raised if the wolf leaped the stream, but not threatening. Not hunting. The two dogs were with him, alert, ears pricked, on point, but not antagonistic. Interested.

Then Ember heard the wolf's howl. She was expecting the familiar ululation that she had heard all her life, when the winters were fierce and the wolves came down from the north to feed on the Last Domain flocks, on anything they could find or scavenge around human settlements – including children.

She knew that howl, that salute to the moon, as all northern children did. Wolf howls were loud, meant to carry across the silent night woods, across the hard-packed snow, claiming territory, gathering the pack, seeking a mate.

But this wolf howled almost silently; a thin thread of sound that raised the hairs on her neck crept like ice down her spine, curled her fingers into claws. A silver crooning, barely heard over the stream, spiralling up into the sky on a long, rising single note. It took her breath and her heart with it, and she looked up, too, following the wolf's gaze to the clear moon above them, to the milk-pale curve of moon breast, the silver tipping cradle, and the stars beyond it.

Cedar began singing in response, starting low and rising, climbing, as if the tone could take his heart and his soul higher and higher, as if they could together reach the sky.

The wolf's tone changed to meet his, as wolf howls do when a pack mate joins the salute. Ash took a step forward, the dogs following, and Cedar's attention turned to them for a second, and so did the wolf's. Their song faltered. Then their gazes locked and the wolf started the note again, its eyes fixed on Cedar's as if asking, 'Are you pack or not-pack?' Among wolves, such a look was a challenge to a subordinate. He began to sing again, at first deliberately matching its tone, then as it tilted its head back to again watch the sky, he looked up too.

Ember felt his song free itself from deliberation, felt it soar, matched and matching with the wolf's, yearning, longing, rising and falling, rising again, and from every part of the Forest she could hear the fragile, slender howl go up, from pack after pack, throat after throat ...

Time fell away. She did not feel cold, or frightened, or even excited. She was simply there, listening, and the moon above her was cold and silver and white and out of reach, all the things Fire was not, and she yearned towards the peace it promised, towards the idea of silence and peace beyond the confines of the world.

When the moon's lower tip touched the edge of the highest trees, the wolf fell silent, and a heartbeat later so did Cedar. Ember looked back down at it and bowed a little in respect. It met her eyes for a brief moment only and then looked away, as wolves do with their pack mates; then it was gone into the dense shadow. Cedar stood, swaying.

While he had sung, Ash had come forward and now stood beside her, his bow still strung but his arrow back in its quiver. The others were awake, sitting up with their furs around them; she was aware for the first time that Ash had draped her with his sleeping pocket to keep her warm.

Holly stared at Cedar consideringly.

'I think that was well done,' she said. 'But I don't pretend to understand why you did it.'

Cedar smiled at her, exalted but obviously tired.

'My turn to watch,' Holly said. 'After all that, I think you both need some sleep.'

Ember was tired. Yes. Exhausted. But she felt light, as though Cedar had sung out her weaknesses, as though he had twined a bridge across a chasm with that singing, and she could walk out over empty air without fear.

'Go to sleep, princess,' Ash said, but his voice was gentle. He turned to Cedar. 'Little wolf, go to sleep.'

She gave Ash back his pocket and slid down into her own, not even bothering to take off her boots. From down on the ground, only the very edge of the moon showed over the tree-tops, and as she watched it disappeared, leaving a halo of light around the highest branches.

Ember fell asleep, and did not dream.

In the morning, she was relieved to see paw prints in the bank on the other side of the stream. Not a vision, then, or a sending of the Forest, but a real wolf.

She supposed that was good.

PALISADE FORT, THE LAST DOMAIN

Arvid spent the next day organising. The first women with babies were arriving from the nearby villages, and Cat was billeting them within the fort where possible, and then in Two Springs, the village which surrounded the fort. By tomorrow, Moss would have the first of the shelters ready. Rough and no doubt draughty, but it was spring and they would cope well enough. He sent boys to the shallow lake a few miles away to harvest reeds and put another group to weeding and stamping down the ground where the shelters would go. They were losing some of the ground where the milk cows grazed, but they could be tethered in one of the open areas near the coppice.

They had taken the barrels and salt they already had and begun to pickle the meat on hand. The butchers had been told that a large slaughter would be needed as soon as the salt arrived. They had to give the meat time to cure, unfortunately. Brine was faster than dry curing, but it didn't happen overnight, although slicing the meat first would hasten things.

'A week,' the cook had said. 'A week to be really sure it's safe.'

At least they had plenty of workers. Cat had drafted all the people whose trades had been disrupted – and it was astonishing how many of them there were. The smiths, of course, black and gold and silver, the potters, candlemakers, even the fletchers had spread their hands at him and shrugged. 'Glue, my lord,' the fletcher had said. 'I can't make glue without fire. I can make shafts, but I can't fletch them.'

'Make the shafts,' he had ordered, a vague sense of anxiety sitting in his belly. They were weak, at the moment, and when a domain was weak it was likely to be attacked. If the Ice King chose this moment to assault their defences, things would go badly. They had to be prepared as far as they could be. Even an unfletched shaft would cause damage. It wouldn't be accurate, but if there was a wide enough target to shoot at ... he remembered an assault by the Ice King's men, thirty or forty of them, storming down a mountainside in the north of the domain. They hadn't needed accuracy that day, they had just shot and shot and shot until the attack reached them and then it had been sword and knife and pike and blood.

He needed a stonecaster.

For a moment he stood in the fletcher's doorway, irresolute. He could not humble himself to ask her ... but it was the safety of his domain at stake.

'Are there no glues which do not need fire?' he asked.

The fletcher shrugged, her shoulders rising almost to her ears. 'Egg, maybe. Mixed with blood ... It won't last longer than a single flight, my lord, if that.'

'Try it,' he said. 'If we need these arrows, the first shot will be the most important.'

She had blanched and nodded, then started snapping orders to her apprentices, her three sons, lanky and pimpled and completely cowed by their mother. They ran to obey while Arvid walked back through the increasingly full muster yard to the hall.

Martine was not there.

He found her in his workroom, reading the report the Prowman had written. But the man himself was nowhere to be seen. Arvid said to Sandpiper, 'I told you—'

The man was shaking. Already shaking, before Arvid had spoken to him. His people did not fear him to that degree. Surely.

'My lord, I couldn't stop him! Truly, truly, I didn't even know what he was going to do—'

'True, my lord,' Martine said. 'Sandpiper couldn't have stopped it.'

Arvid felt the calm of battle come over him, that sense of time slowing down to allow the time to do what must be done.

'Tell me,' he said.

'He finished the report and then he asked to see the lady, so I sent one of the girls for her and she came.'

Arvid looked at Martine, but there was nothing to see except that calm, impersonal front she had assumed earlier.

'He handed her the report and then he, he, he just disappeared!'

Sandpiper was shaking harder as he spoke. This was what he feared. The demonstration of a power far greater than a warlord's. Arvid ignored him. 'Where has he gone?' he demanded. Martine spread her hands, exactly as the fletcher had done.

'Wherever She has sent him,' she said. 'I doubt he knew himself.'

'How?'

'The Lake's secrets are Her own,' she said. 'I know he has moved in time. Whether She can move him across country as well, I don't know.'

'Did he say anything to you?'

'Not in words,' she said. And then, as if to pay him back for what he had said upstairs, she added, 'If you do not have the Sight you will not understand.'

'Tell me what he said,' Arvid replied, low and dangerous. He could hear the growl in his voice, and he didn't care that Sandpiper could hear it too. Let them gossip.

'He offered me refuge, if I needed it,' she said.

That was a punch in the guts. He needed a moment to recover from it, and in that moment she walked past him. He grabbed at her arm and she froze. Ignore the Prowman, his instinct said. Ignore everything except your duty.

'I need a stonecaster,' he said. 'Cast for me.' It wasn't a request, but it wasn't quite an order. She flicked a glance at Sandpiper and turned back, sitting not at Arvid's worktable but at Reed's desk. She took the linen square from her belt and spread it carefully, then put her pouch – red leather, he had given it to her when her old one split from long usage – on the edge of the linen.

'I am ready, my lord,' she said.

'You can go, Sandpiper.'

Arvid waited until the guard had shut the door behind him, and then brought a stool and sat across from her.

'Ask your question,' she said.

'Is the Ice King preparing an attack?'

She waited, sitting absolutely still. Reluctantly, he spat in his hand and stretched it to her. The first time they had touched since ... All the other times they had done this together ran through his mind. Winter, summer, night, day ... a ritual that was as much a part of their lives as lovemaking. He tore his thoughts from that and clasped her hand, the smooth fingers cool in his.

She dug in the pouch with her other hand and cast. He knew some of her stones by sight, but today he could not concentrate on anything except her long fingers, delicately touching one after the other.

'I don't ...' Her voice was puzzled. He looked up to find her frowning at the stones, a thing he had only seen once or twice before. 'Destiny,' she said, touching a stone. 'Danger. Ice.' Two of the stones were face down, and she turned them over. 'Evenness. And the blank stone.'

The blank stone was a bastard, and a source of hope. It meant the future was uncertain, that the actions they took would determine the outcome.

'How can you have Destiny and the blank stone in the same casting?' he asked.

'I've never seen it before,' she said. 'And never with the Evenness stone, which stands for balance restored and justice.'

'So what does it *mean*?'

Martine's green eyes were wide and unguarded, as they might have been the day before. 'The stone for a warlord isn't there. No stone for fighting, or death, or battle ...'

'So. No attack?'

'But there is Ice, and Danger,' she muttered.

She cocked her head, touching the stones again and bending to listen to them. He would never quite get used to that. The idea that the stones actually *talked* ...

'I think,' she said slowly, 'that there will be danger, but not in the form you expect.'

Arvid let out an exasperated sigh. Yesterday his life had been simple. He had been sad about losing Ember to the south, but they would visit, and he'd already agreed with Merroc that the first son would stay in the Far South Domain and the second would come here to be fostered and eventually be his heir.

Martine had argued about that, wanting Ember to inherit, and using the Lady Sorn, ruler of Central Domain, as her precedent. But although Ember was far smarter than she ever let on, she was not the slightest bit interested in ruling a domain. If ever there was a girl designed to be a ruler's wife, it was her. Even Martine had agreed with that, eventually, once Ember had finished begging to go south with Osfrid, away from the winters she loathed. A wedding, future grandchildren, a domain safe and secure, a loved and deeply trusted wife. All gone.

'Danger,' he repeated. 'Wonderful.'

THE GREAT FOREST

Black spruce and more black spruce. The Forest stretched on endlessly, with only the change in the direction of the shadows as the sun climbed and sank to make Ember believe time had passed at all.

She wasn't even sure how many days ago they had come under the shadow of the spruces.

Each clearing was like a gift; each small glade a fairing which shone bright. The horses were happy and the dogs loved it, although they complained about not being allowed to follow the tantalising scent trails which crossed their path.

Occasionally Holly cocked her head as if hearing something, and looked at Cedar inquiringly. Sometimes he nodded; sometimes he shrugged a 'no'. Ember wondered what she was hearing, and why it brought a strange kind of calm to her face, like the look of a crafter absorbed in making something, her whole mind and body attuned to the one thing.

They stopped for the night while it was still light, in a clearing with a stream on one side and a standing pool on the other. One side of the pool was taken up entirely by a massive holly tree, bright with white blossoms, which Holly regarded with amusement.

'May be a good sign,' she said. Ember found the holly tree disquieting, but then she always did. There was something about the dark glossy leaves and sharp points of a holly that made it unwelcoming.

Ash whistled the dogs back from the edge of the clearing where they had been investigating a shrew's hole. Grip came happily, loping over and butting Ash's side with his head, but Holdfast turned towards the holly tree, and showed her teeth in a silent growl. She was warning of something.

'What is it, girl?' Ash went over to her. 'What is it, then?'

He had picked up his bow as he went and now he strung it and nocked an arrow, holding it loosely, as Ember had seen her father's guards do at archery practice, waiting for the signal to shoot.

Holly went to stand beside him, her sword in her hand.

'Calling ...' she said again, and there was a yearning in her voice that worried Ember.

'Not calling me,' Cedar said. 'I hear it, but it sounds far away, and I can't make out the words.'

'What does it sound like?' Ember asked.

'The wind in the trees, the stream in its bed,' Cedar replied.

'No,' Holly said. 'It's a voice.'

'What does it say?'

'Come. Come home. Come home.'

Ember took a step towards the pool. None of them had drunk from that pool, preferring the running stream to the standing water.

'Stay back, my lady,' Holly said. Ember had been schooled in this type of obedience by her parents; it was her duty as war-lord's daughter to let her guards protect her. To not get in their way. So she stayed where she was, by the big log they had all sat on. Curlew and Tern flanked her, swords in hands.

The last of the twilight was almost gone now, and the moon was barely up, not showing yet above the encircling trees. Holly moved into shadow as she approached the pool, but something about the way her foot slid on the ground brought a memory back to Ember, a realisation of why the holly bush had seemed odd to her earlier. Berries. There had been holly berries all around the foot of the tree, and in the water. Berries fallen from the tree, and not eaten.

In the harsh northern winter, when every edible scrap was the difference between life and death, a carpet of holly berries uneaten by birds was impossible.

'Come back!' she called softly. 'Come away from the tree.'

'There's something in the pool,' Holly said, ignoring her, standing next to the holly tree and peering down. 'That's where it's coming from.'

'Holly, don't!' Cedar said.

'Don't touch it!' Ember cried.

Ash moved forward at the same moment they spoke, but it was too late. Holly bent and dipped a hand in the water, scooping some up and looking at it closely in the dim light. Ash paused, drawing his belt knife, but nothing happened.

'Don't drink it,' Cedar advised. Grip and Holdfast were both growling softly, now, a long undulating sound that sent chills down Ember's spine.

'It smells of – home,' Holly said. Her voice was odd. Younger, like a child's.

'Guard, to your duty!' Ember said in her best imitation of her father. Her heart was beating so fast she could feel it shaking her body. She began to move, to force herself to walk towards Holly. She had to be brave. She had to be. Holly would listen to her.

She took a step, two, but Curlew pulled her back and it took her a moment to break free of him, her resolution suddenly stronger, so Ash was there before her, reaching out, putting his hand on Holly's arm, forcing it down so that the water in her palm fell back into the pool. She shook off his touch irritably, and some drops of water flicked across her face, her cheeks, her lips. Her tongue came out reflexively and tasted them.

'I'm not an idiot!' she said, but she didn't move away. 'Can't you hear it?'

'Come away,' Ash said. 'Or I'll pick you up and carry you.'

Ember had reached her now, and took her hand, pulling her towards the centre of the clearing.

'Come away, Holly,' she pleaded. 'It's unchancy, this tree.'

Holly looked resigned and allowed her to pull, but before Holly had taken a step she looked down at her feet and frowned.

'I can't,' she said in surprise. The dogs had stopped growling and begun whining instead, as if they weren't sure whether they faced an enemy or not.

'Ember, move back,' Ash said.

'Get her away!' Cedar shouted. When Ember kept pulling Holly, Ash simply picked her up by her waist and dragged her backwards, ripping their hands apart, leaving Holly standing, puzzled, alone next to the tree. Curlew helped him pull Ember into the centre of the clearing.

'Put me down! Help her instead!' Ember shouted. Then Holly cried out. Around her feet, holly roots were writhing. It's trying to trap her! Ember thought. Tern and Curlew moved forwards, swinging their swords, cutting the roots as close to Holly's feet as they dared.

She screamed. The dogs were barking, teeth bared, the noise horrible.

'Stop! Stop it!'

'They're her,' Cedar said, sounding sickened. 'They're her.'

Straining through the dim light, Ember didn't understand what he meant at first. Then she saw.

'Dragon's breath,' Ash whispered.

The roots were not coming to Holly; they were coming out of her. And up her body, on her arms, her legs, her fingers, shoots were springing forth, like a dead winter tree coming to life in the spring, but fast, so fast.

Ember screamed, too. The holly twigs, so sharp and hard, punctured Holly's skin at a hundred points and immediately sprouted leaves. Holly's mouth was wide with astonishment and pain but then, suddenly, impossibly, she smiled. She looked straight at Cedar, as though he were the only one who could understand, and said, 'Called me home.'

Then her head tipped back, her eyes and mouth opened wide and holly shoots pierced her, emerging from mouth and eyes and ears and nostrils, growing frantically, writhing, reaching, and a moment later, a breath later, a heartbeat later, there was no human body standing there at all, only a second holly tree, smaller than the first.

They gathered together, staring, waiting, although Ember didn't know for what. Didn't understand why they weren't running screaming into the darkness, away from the horror. The dogs had gone – they were curled up together in a corner of the glade, whimpering.

Ash stood next to her and she reached out to grip his hand hard. Cedar took her other hand, and Curlew and Tern flanked them, swords still in hand, dripping a sap that was not white, like holly sap, but red. Tears ran down Curlew's face ceaselessly.

They stood, waiting, for what seemed like a long time, until the moon had risen enough to touch the tip of Holly's tree. As the first ray silvered the topmost leaf, flowers began appearing all over the tree; the white, pure blossoms like stars in the darkness.

Ember let go of her cousins' hands and walked forwards, and no one tried to stop her.

'You are very beautiful, Holly,' she said. 'Are you home?'

As if in answer, petals drifted from the tree and landed on her face and hair, surrounding her with scent. Ash leaped forwards in alarm, followed by Curlew and Tern, but she was safe, she knew. They all were.

The Forest had wanted only Holly.

THE GREAT FOREST

Sleepless, they waited for the light before dawn and saddled the horses. Holly's mare was gone. Her tracks led off into the deep wood and, although it tore Ember's heart in two, they all knew they couldn't search for her, especially since her hobbles lay beside the holly tree, cut clean through, although none of them had heard anything in the night, and the dogs had not woken. The Forest had its own way of taking what it wanted.

They left the two holly trees behind them with deep sadness.

Ember sought for the right words to say goodbye, but in the end all she could think of was, 'Gods bless and keep you,' which she felt the Forest might not like. 'We will miss you and pray for you,' she whispered to the living tree, instead, and watered its roots with her tears.

Curlew led the way out of the clearing, his face set against tears, but he looked back for as long as he could until Holly was out of sight.

They began to climb upwards soon after, the path curving in a long, gentle rise, so gradual that they didn't know how high they had climbed until at sunset they paused at the top of a small knoll and looked back. The tall larches and black spruce were still on either side, but if Ember looked straight back down the path she could see an expanse of forest below them, tree tips emerging from the evening mist, the shadows falling blue.

They were out of the huge bowl they had seen from the far ridge.

'We're in the foothills,' Curlew said, staring upwards to where the rounded hills were raised, rank on rank. They were too close to them to see the peaks beyond, but they could feel their eternally snow-covered presence in the chill of the evening breeze flowing down the slopes towards them.

Ember knew that they were safer out of the Forest than in, but she felt, as they climbed higher, that a familiar blanket was being slowly pulled away from her shoulders and leaving her exposed to the chill air. Cedar seemed to share her discomfort. He looked behind often, back at the bowl of Forest. When he caught her watching him, his mouth twisted wryly and he shrugged.

'It feels too easy,' he said.

'We paid our toll,' Curlew said harshly, his eyes red from weeping.

'Even so,' Cedar replied.

It was not a straight climb. The foothills were reached by ridge after ridge, each one appearing to be the last, and each time they came to the top to find what seemed like exactly the same view, as though they had been climbing the same ridge over and over. Even the trees looked the same.

Ash was riding in front, his horse flanked by the two dogs. Ember brought Merry up beside Thatch and said quietly, 'Are we just going over and over the same ground?'

Ash flicked a surprised look at her, and then his eyes narrowed.

'We'll see,' he said. He reined Thatch in and dismounted, then went to the side of the track and overturned a big lichen-covered rock. Underneath, insects scurried for shelter in the dark earth. Grip sniffed at them and sneezed, and they all laughed. As if embarrassed, he lifted his leg onto the rock and pissed.

Ash smiled up at Ember.

'We should be able to recognise that again,' she said.

They toiled up the ridge and down into the next valley, over the stream at the bottom and on. Halfway up the hill on the other side, there was the overturned rock, the earth below it beginning to pale as it dried out. Grip sniffed at his own mark and looked puzzled.

'Dragon's fart!' Curlew said. 'Have we been climbing the same hill all morning?'

Cedar cocked an eyebrow at Ember and she said, 'Yes, I know you said it was too easy. Now what?'

'It seems to me,' Ash said, 'that this hill is a gate.'

Following his thought, Ember nodded. 'So where is the gate-keeper?'

'Let's go to the top,' Curlew said to Ash. It was a suggestion, not an order. With Holly gone, Ember had expected Curlew to take control, but the other men looked to Ash as the leader. She never quite understood how they worked those things out. In every group of men there was a leader, she'd noticed, but it wasn't always the one a woman would have expected. None of them even considered her as a possible chief. She smiled ruefully. She'd have chosen Ash, too.

'Aye,' Ash replied to Curlew. 'Best get our bearings if we can.'

The view from the top of the ridge was the same as before. Ember had half-hoped that just noticing the spell would be enough to break it but, as Cedar had said, nothing was that easy.

The path was wide enough here for them to range across it abreast, each of them looking hard to see if there were any other way to go than straight down again.

'Cedar?' Ash said. 'Can you See anything?'

'No. Nothing that wasn't there before.'

Curlew's hand was at the pommel of his sword, but there was no enemy in sight.

Courtesy was a warlord's daughter's main training. Courtesy, rank, honour, hospitality, command. Perhaps this was one of those times when a soft word was more powerful than a sword.

Ember edged Merry forward just a little, until he was poised so that one more step would take him on the downhill track.

'Humbly we request passage through this land,' she said clearly, making her voice as sweet and pleasant as she could. 'To whomever guards this place, we make promise: we will respect the life we find here, we will journey through without malice or greed.'

The ring of scar on her wrist burned suddenly, and she bit back an exclamation. Was it Fire which barred their way?

The air shimmered like a heat haze and the expanse of trees, hills, ridges before them shifted and disappeared. Beyond was grassland dotted with trees and small streams; a plateau with knee-high grasses and wildflowers blooming sky blue and sun gold. Beyond, the Eye Teeth Mountains rose sheer and astonishing, much closer than they had looked only moments before.

A wisp of fog along the ridge thickened and became two figures. Ghosts.

Of course, Ember had seen ghosts before. In the Last Domain, the quickening ceremony, held three days after someone had died, was a well-attended affair; the kind of wake that other places had after the burial. But burial in the north was often difficult during the winter months, when any corpses were reverently stored in a special cabin at the fort until the ground had thawed enough to dig graves. Unlike the southern domains, there were no caves near most of the northern settlements to take the dead and the ground was too hard or too marshy lower down to dig anything but single graves.

So the quickening ceremony had come to take the place of the burial feast, and everyone came, hoping that the spirit of the dead person had gone on peacefully to rebirth. But sometimes, when the death had been an accident, or an assault (more common as the long winters dragged on), the person didn't realise they were dead, and three days later their spirit rose at the place they had died. Then, if someone had caused their death, that person admitted guilt and gave blood to the spirit in recompense. Ember had seen her first ghost when she was four years old – a cranky old woman she'd never liked who had been speared by an icicle dropping from the eaves of her house when she went out to get snow for cooking. She was used to seeing the pale, insubstantial form flow together. But normally ghosts were a shimmer in the air, a suggestion rather than a shape, although people with Sight saw them more clearly, she'd been told. And the Prowman could even make them speak.

She wished that the Prowman were with them now.

'Greetings,' she said to the ghosts. Squinting, she could just make out male shapes. Cedar said quietly, 'Men of the Northern Mountains Domain,' and she realised that he could see them clearly enough to make out the insignia on their uniforms.

'We greet you, men of the Northern Mountains Domain,' Ember said clearly, inclining her head graciously at the correct angle. 'We ask permission to pass through this land to the mountains beyond.'

The ghosts turned to stare behind them, at the cold shapes of the Eye Teeth jutting dark grey against the pale sky. There were clouds at the snowy peaks, twisting in a distant wind.

Then, moving together as though they were the same being, they raised their swords and crossed them. It was a clear signal: No passage. Then one freed a hand and pointed south.

Obediently, they looked: there was a path, now, just below the rim of the ridge. A deer trail, Ember thought, or an elk walk. The bushes on either side were cropped, a sign that elks had been that way.

'South,' Ash said. 'Towards Starkling.' He swivelled in his saddle to face Ember. 'Best not go there if we can help it.'

Starkling ... it and Elgir, the warlord of Northern Mountains Domain, had an eerie reputation. This use of ghosts as gatekeepers was typical. In a world which had almost been destroyed by ghosts, who else would use them as warriors? It was unthinkable.

Ember studied the ghosts. They were still standing with crossed swords, one with his finger pointing, in exactly the same position. She supposed that ghosts didn't get tired. Her mother would know. Her mother was the one to deal with strange events and unchancy threats, not her. But they had to do something. They couldn't sit on their horses until the ghosts went away to be reborn.

Tentatively, she said, 'By your leave, good men, our task is urgent and we cannot risk delay. Let us pass.'

They didn't move.

'Ride through them!' Curlew said. 'They're just ghosts.'

He kicked his horse and she leaped forward as though glad to get moving again.

'No!' Cedar cried. 'Curlew, don't!'

Ash reached for Curlew's bridle, but too late. He had cantered past them and straight through the ghosts.

The horse screamed, threw up its head and fell, twisting as it went as though its legs had been swept out from the side. They all reached towards Curlew, but it was futile; he was falling, too. Ember had time to see that his face was astonished, not afraid, and then he hit the ground.

And disappeared, horse and rider both. Ember cried out in alarm, and heard Cedar and Tern echo her. The ghosts hadn't moved, hadn't reacted at all: they still stood with crossed swords, hand pointed south.

Ash had readied his bow, but there was nothing to shoot. The grasslands stretched out before them. But Curlew was simply gone.

'Where is he?' Ash demanded. 'What have you done with him?'

The ghosts ignored him.

'Perhaps,' Cedar said slowly, 'they are not gatekeepers, but guardians. Saving us from whatever took him ...'

'No,' Ember said bitterly. 'This is Elgir's work. My father warned me to avoid him. He gathers power like a dragon hoarding gold. He wants us to go to Starkling.'

'Then we should not go,' Cedar said. 'But I suspect we will, anyway.' He looked at Ash quizzically.

'Curlew may not be dead,' Ash said. 'Elgir might be able to bring him back from wherever he was sent. We will go and ask him.'

Ember had never heard him so grim. Part of her agreed with him, but that part was Curlew's friend, not the daughter of his lord.

'No,' she said, her eyes filling hot and sharp, because the part that was Curlew's friend was large in her. 'We cannot risk a whole domain for the sake of one man.'

Ash looked at her in astonishment and dismay, but then his face hardened and he nodded.

'North, then,' he said. 'Try to go around them.'

'But Curlew!' Tern protested. 'What if he's hurt, somewhere? What if we could save him?'

Ember brought Merry across to him and held his gaze so he could see that she meant what she said. 'I wish we could forget everything else and find him,' she said. 'But what do you think Curlew would tell us to do?'

Tern looked mutinous. 'Just because he'd say it doesn't mean it's right!'

Cedar laughed shortly.

'Well said, boy. But she *is* right. Do you want to go back to the mothers of dead children and tell them we were too late because we tried to find a missing soldier, who knew the risk when he agreed to come?'

Tern's lip trembled, his eyes blurring with tears. His shoulders sagged and he looked away, saying nothing.

'North,' Ash said again. They turned the horses to the north, and dismounted. The slope would put too much strain on the horses if they rode – there was no path this way, although the trees and shrubs were not dense and they could easily weave through them.

As they left, the ghosts turned their heads to watch but did not otherwise move, and Ember wondered how long they would stand there, barring the way.

Barely half a league to the north, they rounded a bend and found themselves headed back towards the path they had left, with the ghosts still standing there, swords crossed.

Cedar swore. 'They're laughing at us!'

'No doubt we look funny,' Ash said. He tilted his head back to watch a bird circling, high overhead, and sighed. 'Heron,' he remarked absently. 'Or crane, maybe. South, princess?'

Although the name was teasing, his tone was weary and Ember wished they could all fly away.

'Let's see what the stones say,' she said, turning to Cedar. As a family, they were used to consulting the stones. Ember hoped Cedar would have at least some of that talent.

Cedar handed his reins to Tern and came to them with a mixture of alacrity and nervousness. His first casting, she realised. He took the yellow pouch from his waist, and then looked dismayed.

'I don't have a cloth!' he said. It was odd to see the normally saturnine Cedar so discomfited. Ember concealed a smile and pulled a kerchief from her pocket. It was a little grubby, but it would do. Cedar took it and sat on the ground, smoothing the green fabric as carefully as if it were silk from the Wind Cities.

'Ask,' he said, looking up at her. But something made her turn to Ash instead.

'You ask,' she said. 'Make sure Fire doesn't get involved in this.'

He grimaced, but he squatted opposite Cedar and spat into his palm. Cedar did the same and they clasped hands.

'Should we go to Starkling?' Ash asked. Tern edged nearer, holding the horses, so that their hot breath swept over Ember and raised the hair on her neck. She waited, heart beating hard, aware from the corner of her eye that the ghosts had turned to stare at them.

Cedar dug in his pouch and cast the stones on the kerchief. That moment, watching the stones fall, was always long, always exciting. No matter how many times Ember saw it, she was still astonished at the gods' generosity – to share the future with humans, how amazing!

Five stones. Some face up, some down. Cedar touched each delicately with one long finger, as Martine did.

'Chaos,' he said, a rough edge to his voice, as though this wasn't easy. 'Loss. Face up, both. And hidden ...' he turned the others over. 'Love. Destiny. Hope.'

'Hope,' Ash repeated.

'Chaos and loss,' Tern muttered.

Cedar gathered the stones together slowly.

'That's what they are,' Ember asked, 'but what do they say to you?' The others looked at her strangely, but her mother had often talked about the stones speaking to her.

'They laugh,' Cedar said blankly. 'I think they think we have no choice.'

He put the stones back in the bag and dropped Ash's hands. They stood up, staring at each other, wiping the spit off on their legs with identical movements. They had never looked more like brothers. Cedar made to give the kerchief back to Ember, but she waved it away. He would need it again.

'So, south, princess?' Ash asked her, his eyes steady.

'South,' she said, fear welling in her chest and making it hard to breathe. 'South to Starkling.'

They turned and headed south, leading the horses, and the trail appeared in front of them, clear as day, where they had walked through scrub and grass only moments before. Oddly, Merry and the other horses seemed completely unconcerned by the change, as though there had been no change.

What kind of power did Elgir have? Had he clouded their minds or physically moved them? Had he looped a part of the world back on itself? How was that *possible*?

They mounted again. Ash held Thatch back until he was level with Ember, and asked, 'What has your father told you about this warlord?'

'Rumours, mostly,' she said, feeling better for being with him. 'That he's an enchanter. That he never does a thing in the ordinary way if there's an unchancy way to do it. That he's besotted with the forms and uses of power. No one is allowed into Starkling without his leave, and his people ...' She dropped her voice. Her father had hesitated to even say this out loud. 'They say his people mate with the water spirits and the forest sprites, and carry their blood.'

Ash paled. 'Can that *happen*?' he asked.

'Who knows? I didn't think so, but then I didn't think the world could be turned in on itself as it is around here.'

He looked up at the sky again, and to their left, where the Forest loomed, dark and somehow more mysterious since they had passed through it. Ember shivered at the thought of riding back into that gloomy shade, and told herself that they'd be lucky to make it that far.

PALISADE FORT, THE LAST DOMAIN

A rvid had thought that Lady Sigurd was a tall woman; but as she came down the steps from the hall, leaning on Merroc's arm, she seemed much smaller. Older, weaker, fragile. He heard Martine, beside him, take in a breath that was full of pity.

'She told me, before the wedding,' Martine murmured, 'that she lost two babies before Osfrid, and could have no more after him. He was her heart and breath.'

Compassion took him, imagining how he would feel if Ember, born so late and so unexpectedly in his life, had been burned in that fire as well as Osfrid. Not for the first time, he wondered why he'd had no other children. He'd put off marrying because he wanted what his parents had had, love and respect, instead of just political goodwill; but he'd had love affairs, with more than a few women, over the years, and none of them had borne him a child. Most warlords had a score of bastards – half the sergeants in the Domains were by-blows of their lord. He had only Ember. His heart contracted, thinking of her in the Great Forest, where anything could happen.

They waited silently while Sigurd made her way slowly across the muster yard to the fire. Arvid bowed to her. She nodded back, but when Martine bowed she ignored it completely. Martine said nothing.

'My lady, I have arranged for musicians, if you please,' Arvid said.

Some people believed that music helped the soul to quicken, and then to release its hold on this world and move on, to the darkness beyond death which was the threshold of rebirth. Sigurd nodded.

The flute and drum began to play; the musicians had come for the wedding, ready with love songs and ballads and dance tunes. But every musician was used to playing for quickenings, and the music was gentle and soothing. Martine signalled to Cat, the steward, to bring the chairs they had ready forward, so that Merroc and Sigurd could sit. Merroc, Arvid could see, would have preferred to stand, but he sat to make sure that his wife would sit, also.

Sigurd looked withered; ashen with bloodshot eyes, a fine tremble in her hands as they lay in her lap clutching a kerchief. She stared at the fire with terrible intensity. They had moved the cooks away for the time being, so the fire burned unrestricted with no pots or pans nearby. It would make the day harder, but it was a mark of respect they could show.

Ghosts didn't quicken to the minute, so they had gathered a full two hours before the time of Osfrid's death. The sun was well up, and shining, but the chill was strong. Sigurd was shivering. Martine sent Fox back to the hall for a cloak and Arvid placed it carefully around Sigurd's shoulders. She didn't notice. Her eyes never wavered from the flames.

Martine was in her red coat. Normally he liked to see her in it, her hair tucked up under its matching hat, but today the colour reminded him of blood, and she seemed like an enchanter out of the old stories, not to be trusted, not to be – not to be loved.

Waiting fruitlessly for Osfrid's ghost to appear left him with too much time to think. Too much time to remember. He had, with his own eyes, seen her and three others remake the compact spell when an enchanter's spell had unravelled it.

She had kept everyone safe, Traveller and Acton's people alike. He had been so proud of her, and later, so *sure* of her love ... Memories poured through him. Martine pregnant, holding little Ember as she tried to walk, doggedly learning etiquette so that they could visit the southern warlords without her disgracing him, Martine in his bed, in his arms ... he shuddered and disguised it by rubbing his arms as though even colder than he actually was.

Could all that, could all the twenty-one years of laughing and loving and working together have been a lie?

He couldn't begin to imagine the mind of someone who could live that lie.

If only she would come to him, say she was sorry, ask for his forgiveness ... He realised that his hands were clenched into fists. He loosened them, and glanced at the sun.

'This was the time, my lady,' he said quietly.

Sigurd gave no sign of hearing him, but Merroc nodded shortly, his eagle gaze fixed on the fire.

But Osfrid did not come.

Arvid didn't expect him to. If twenty-one years of living with Martine had taught him anything, it was that her castings were true. If she said that Osfrid had gone on to rebirth, then he had, and that was that. He felt sorry for Sigurd, all the same.

Two hours after the time, he touched Merroc on the arm and drew him aside.

'I think my lady's casting was true,' he said. 'Your son was a noble soul and has gone on to rebirth already.'

Merroc's eyes shone with tears. His hand was unsteady as he wiped them away.

'So it may be. But my lady will wish to wait longer.'

'She is welcome to wait as long as she wishes. But in a few hours we will need to cook the evening meal for the children ...'

Merroc closed his eyes for a moment and drew in a breath.

'Have you ever noticed,' he asked, almost conversationally, but with a thread of deep pain underneath his words, 'that dying in battle is easy compared to living?'

Arvid couldn't stop himself glancing at Martine, who still stood, calm and polite, behind and to one side of Sigurd's chair, where the lady did not have to look at her. Calm and beautiful, like a soapstone carving.

'Aye,' he said. 'But when you are the lord, you must go on caring for your people, in battle or after.'

Merroc nodded, and seemed to have trouble stopping the movement of his heavy head.

'Give her another hour or so,' he said. Arvid could see the effort it took not to plead.

'Of course,' Arvid said. 'I will give as much time as I can.'

He bowed and returned to waiting, standing a careful pace away from Martine. Merroc, after a moment's hesitation, put his hand on Sigurd's shoulder and whispered something in her ear. She shook her head fiercely and he shrugged at Arvid and sat down next to his lady.

Martine ordered food brought, but Sigurd would have nothing but water. She never moved in her chair otherwise.

Arvid waited as long as he could, but the sun was lowering and he could hear babies crying, children demanding food, mothers being exasperated, in the shelters and barns. Women who had left the grieving mother respectfully alone all day now gathered in the doorways and waited, watched, impatience growing with their own little ones' needs.

Finally, he had to act. He drew in a breath and stepped forward, but before he could say anything Martine had walked past him and knelt by Sigurd's chair.

'My lady,' she said formally, respectfully, 'we must begin to use the fire again, so that the children may be fed.'

Sigurd seemed to pull her gaze back from the fire with a great effort, but she did not look at Martine. She raised her eyes to Arvid.

'My son will come,' she said. Her tone had the flat certainty of madness or prophecy, and who was he to say which it was?

'He will be welcome when he does,' Arvid said. 'Welcome and honoured.' She nodded, and settled back into the same pose she had taken all day. 'But, my lady—'

Her head whipped around and she almost spat at him, '*My son will come.*'

'When he does, will he be pleased to find starving children?' Martine's voice was sharp. Merroc got up hastily and stepped towards her, but Sigurd kept watching the fire.

'What do I care about other women's sons?' she said.

'Sig,' Merroc said, touching her head. He looked up at the residence, at the floor where their rooms were. 'You could watch from your chamber.'

She moved her eyes slowly to his face, as though she had to remember how. 'From *inside*?' she asked. 'But he will not see me there.'

'If – when he comes, he will wait for you, my dear,' Merroc said, his tone dreadfully kind. 'Come. You go up and I will wait here and watch for him. When you are safe at the window, I will join you.'

For a long moment, Sigurd considered this. Then she shook her head, slowly, and at the end of one shake her head simply kept turning until she was staring once more at the fire.

'I will wait here,' she said. Arvid looked away from Merroc's face.

'I'm sorry,' he said, 'we will need to cook, anyway.'

Merroc nodded and sat down again, taking Sigurd's hand into his own. She let him, but her pale fingers lay lifelessly in his grasp. Arvid's throat tightened and he turned abruptly to gesture to the waiting servers and cooks.

Immediately, they moved in to set up the tripod and cauldron and load it with food and water. They set a few smaller pots around the edge. Supper would be late tonight, but at least the babies would get their porridge.

Sigurd ignored the cooks and the pots, watching only the flames. They reflected more and more clearly in her pale blue eyes as the night came down.

Arvid stayed with Merroc, taking turns at sitting with Sigurd while the other walked up and down, staying warm. After the night deepened, Martine brought hot bricks for Sigurd's feet.

'Take them away!' Sigurd screamed. 'I will have nothing from that accursed fire! Do you seek to curse me, too, Traveller whore?'

Martine said nothing, merely removed the bricks and handed them to a woman with several children, who accepted them thankfully and chivvied her children off to bed.

Merroc sent Arvid an apologetic glance. Arvid knew he should support his own wife, should object to Sigurd's insults, but in the face of such naked grief he could not.

It was second watch before Sigurd finally slumped in her chair, asleep. Merroc gathered her up and carried her to their chamber.

The fort was so quiet as Arvid went up to his chamber that he fancied he was the only one left awake, except the cook watching tomorrow's breakfast soup. Each creak of the wooden stair was like a reminder of his own mortality, a whisper of death in the night.

Martine was waiting at the door to her room and his heart leapt. Perhaps now, when they could be alone, she would come to him and explain, apologise, weep for her betrayal ...

'I have cast the stones again,' she said, like a sergeant reporting to an officer, 'and I definitely see danger approaching from the north.'

'The Ice King's men?' he made himself ask, suppressing the sharp pain of disappointment with duty.

'No,' she said, frowning. 'Not them. Weather. Deep cold and storm.'

'In *summer*?'

She shrugged, face wiped clean of emotion again.

'I tell you what the stones tell me, my lord,' she said, and disappeared, closing the door behind her.

Just once, he would like to forget the duty he owed his people to appear sane and responsible, and kick the shagging door in.

The next day Arvid spent an hour going over the Prowman's report. It was too short. It contained little that Arvid hadn't already heard. Five known Powers, and the possibility of more unknown, which made his blood run cold. Would the moon itself turn out to be a Power? Or the worms which writhed in the soil?

Women, the report said, encountered Fire at the Spring Equinox when they were young, and the Autumn Equinox when old. Men were introduced to the Water Power at adolescence.

Earth was slow to act and rarely concerned with humans.

Air was distant from humans, but interacted at times. She was hard to predict, hard to contact, impossible to constrain, even by the other Powers.

And the Great Forest ... 'You know the forms that Power takes,' the Prowman had written, and so he did. In the Forest, anything could happen. He had been trying all day to keep his thoughts away from Ember, but reading that simple sentence brought back all his fears, swamping thought with simple terror of what might happen to her. He should have gone with her.

Sitting in his workroom, he was astonished that he *hadn't* gone with her. What had he been thinking? At the time, in the moment, it hadn't even occurred to him. Was that because his domain meant more to him than his own child? Was his duty so overwhelming that he could ignore the promptings of his fatherly heart? It didn't feel so, now. He wanted to be with her, and bedamned to the domain.

But ... when the boys had said, 'We'll go with her,' it had seemed so simple. Straightforward. As though it was right that the younger ones should take the danger and he and Martine should stay to protect their people.

Was he just getting old?

Or had something manipulated him in that moment? Fire. Twisting his mind? Twisting his heart askew?

His anger rose again at the thought, and at the realisation that it could have been *any* Power, from Fire to the local gods, even to Elva herself. Without Sight he was fumbling in the dark and as lost as a baby in the Forest. His only guide was Martine ...

No. He would not go cap in hand to her. If she wanted to help him, she would offer. If the daylight world was all he had, he would use it as best he could to protect the people who depended on him. And to the cold hells with everything else.

He kept reading. The report said absolutely nothing about the Lake. How was that possible?

Page in hand, he found Martine in the kitchen, discussing the flavouring of the salted meat.

'Juniper berries, wild garlic, pepper if we've got it, onions, sage,' Martine said, the cook nodding his head as he ticked them off his fingers. 'Anything else?'

'Brandy?' the cook said doubtfully.

'If we must. Tell the butchers not to kill the spring lambs. The meat's too fatty for brining. Let them grow some more first.'

How long would this last? Arvid wondered. Gods help them all, it had better be over by Snowfall.

Martine turned to find him in the doorway and her face became calm again. Part of him wanted to grab her and shake her or kiss her or anything to get that look off her face – to make her *see* him again. He gestured to her to go before him into the empty hall, and offered the Prowman's page.

'He does not mention the Lake.'

'Not specifically. The Lake is Water.'

As if that should mean something to him.

'So?' he was forced to ask.

She was surprised. The first emotion he'd evoked from her, and it was surprise at his stupidity.

'All water, lakes, streams, rivers, pools – any running water is Her. The Lake is merely a strong seat of Her power, because the Lake People have never ceased their worship of Her. But Her influence reaches wherever water flows.'

Just as Fire was in every hearth. And Air in every breath he took. And Earth, he supposed, beneath his every step. The scope of it was too terrifying to confront. At least one could avoid the Forest. But they had been surrounded by enemies, all unknowing, all their lives. Everywhere.

Arvid stared at Martine blankly.

'The local gods,' he said. 'Have they no power at all?'

'They have great power,' she replied gently. 'Power over life and death, and the responsibility to keep the door between the two closed. But they do not try to control the Greater Powers, and I doubt they could. It is as though ...' She searched for words ... 'It is as though their strengths are so different that there is no overlap. Like – like dry and wet, or day and night. The local gods care very little about individual humans, you know, but the Powers like to have more ... personal relationships with us.'

Her voice shook, at last, and he knew that she was thinking about Ember. Worried about her. A tear slid down her cheek and she dashed it away impatiently.

'In the story of the Bynum girls, and in the moment I witnessed, He waited for the woman to come to him,' she said. 'To embrace Him. She won't do that.'

'He killed Osfrid.'

'A man,' she said. 'And one of Acton's people.' As though that made it all right.

'*My daughter* is one of Acton's people.'

Quietly, very quietly, she said, '*My* daughter has the old blood in her.'

Although the sun was setting, he left immediately and inspected the fire where they were cooking dinner in a huge cauldron slung over the hot ashes in Moss's shelter, and the new huts for the women and babies, and all the work that had been done that day, before he returned to the now crowded hall for the evening meal and was told that Martine had taken her food to her chamber to leave more room for their guests. Merroc and Sigurd were eating in the parlour.

The hall was almost dark, and he was glad of the long northern twilight. Days were shorter without fire. He ate soup because he needed food and it was his duty to stay strong, and then he went to his own chamber. Martine had always insisted on a bed of her own because he snored. Now he wondered if there had been another reason. A desire to think her own thoughts, away from him, was the most innocuous of the reasons he could imagine, and that was bad enough.

He slept in brief naps, worry about Ember fighting with anger at Martine and the desire, stupid, stupid, to go to her chamber and beg forgiveness. *She* was the one who should be at his door begging. But he would not forgive treason. Not without better cause than she had given him so far.

In a small part of his mind he knew that he must never say the word 'treason' in front of others, or things would happen which he could not control.

But here, he dwelt on it. Treason. Betrayal. Deception. A whole life, lived on a series of lies.

If he had been a woman, he would have wept.

The Road to Foreverfroze

Elva felt a bit sorry for the guard Arvid had sent with her. Bass clearly didn't like travelling at night, particularly when the moon was just a sliver. He understood that her white skin and hair, her oddly pink eyes, meant that she couldn't travel in sunlight without pain. He just wished that Arvid had picked someone else to go with her. But the poor man hadn't dared refuse the 'honour' – not when she was both his lady's daughter and the mouthpiece of the gods.

It was Martine's idea that she be the one to take the news to Foreverfroze, the distant harbour town which provided most of the Last Domain's fish. She had no idea why, but it didn't worry her. The first time the gods had spoken to her, she had been little more than a baby, and she had grown up accepting their will as her own. She knew that her husband, Mabry, sometimes found her amused acceptance irritating. She wished Mabry was here, instead of at home with their youngest son, Gorse, busy with the spring sowing. Spring wasn't a time a farmer could leave his fields, even one who mostly ran goats. It had been a real sacrifice for him to let the other children come to Ember's wedding, and part of her wished that they hadn't.

Then maybe the gods wouldn't have sent Ash and Cedar to Fire Mountain. That had been the hardest thing the gods had ever asked of her, to risk her sons. But it was the boys' choice, not hers. Fire Mountain. The volcano in the middle of the Eye Teeth Mountains, its perfect cone contrasting with the sharp irregular peaks around it. Mam and she had seen it once, from a long way off.

Her horse stumbled over something in the road and she was jerked back to the present. Pretty, her mare, recovered and they went on, with Bass muttering under his breath about laming the horses beyond repair. She ignored him, as he clearly wanted her to do.

They were riding through the scrubby trees just south of the Great Forest, a place Elva had no desire to go. The trees were mostly alder and spruce, with patches of open ground between. Catchfly bushes grew close to the trail so they rode through a cloud of scent. The white flowers seemed to glow in the moonlight.

Sometimes she wished she could see the world with all its colour ablaze, but the night was beautiful in its own way.

The wind began to rise, blowing from the north, bringing chill and the scent of snow. Elva turned to Bass.

'Do you normally get a north wind this time of year?'

'No, my lady,' he said, looking worried. 'It's unseasonable all right.'

They stopped to put on their coats, hats and gloves.

'We might as well eat now, my lady,' Bass said.

'I'm not a lady, Bass,' she replied, laughing. 'My name's Elva. I'm a Valuer, you know.'

That seemed to relax him. Gave them common ground, perhaps.

'Me too,' he said. They sat on stones by the side of the track and ate the bread and cheese that Mam had given them. It was good cheese, even if it was from cows instead of goats.

'Wonder when we'll get bread again,' Bass said gloomily. That was a sobering thought.

'Will we get to the Valuers' Plantation by dawn?' Elva asked. He shook his head.

'Sorry, my lady, but it's much further. We'll get to Oakmere, though. There's an inn there my lord uses.'

'Longer than I thought. I've walked most of the domains in my time, but I've never been to Foreverfroze.'

'It's a strange place,' Bass said, but that was all.

They passed Oakmere's black rock altar before they got to the town, and Elva sent a polite hello to the local gods.

Honoured ones, I greet you, she thought and felt them stream from the altar to surround her, slide into her mind to taste it, riffle through her memories of the last few days and then out again.

The world is changing, they said in their silent multi-layered voices. *The balance is shifting.*

How are my sons? she asked. The only thing she wanted to know.

There was a pause as they considered the question.

Alive, they answered. *In the Forest.*

The gods dealt with life and death, and cared about little else. But they loved her and her husband, and she thought sometimes that they cared somewhat about her children. At least, about Ash and Cedar and Poppy. The others they scarcely seemed to notice. It was often so, she'd realised. The quiet ones, the ones whose eyes saw beauty even if they didn't create it, those were the minds that the gods liked. Saffron was carelessly beautiful and as flamboyant as Poppy was painstaking, but it was Poppy to whom the gods flowed when the girls went to the altar. And Gorse at fifteen was loud and strong and bull-like with a soft heart. He'd make a fine farmer and a wonderful Village Voice, she thought, when his time came, but the gods were less interested in him than in Ash, whose spirit was light as air even though he seemed so solid and dependable. Cedar, of course, was the most like her, gifted with Sight and learning to use it. His journey would stretch those gifts to their limit, she feared.

But she'd been on the Road herself from when she was two to twenty-two, and Travelling itself held few fears for her. Her boys would be all right as far as that went. It was Fire who could not be predicted. Not around men.

Oakmere had a Town Council so she went to the Moot Hall and dutifully reported all she knew to a Mayor and Council who hadn't even tried to go to bed, then found Arvid's inn as the dawn was breaking, cold as contempt.

She'd never liked towns much, but even the daybreak bustle of the markets below couldn't stop her sleeping. As she drifted off, she felt the gods in her mind, gently saying, *You must speak to Sealmother,* and that led her into a dream of a dark cave, and cold water, and laughing green eyes which reminded her of her mam.

They left Oakmere in a sunset haze of gold which should have felt warm but which chilled instead. That night was colder; every breath steamed and they couldn't let the horses rest for too long.

An hour before dawn they came to a small inn that Bass had had good reports of. The innkeeper and her husband woke readily enough but were profuse in apologies for the lack of fire.

They had thought it was a local problem. Hearing Elva's news made them thoughtful.

The innkeeper brought them a meal of sliced ham and early greens, with fresh milk as the only drink.

'I'd kill for a mug of cha,' Bass said with deep feeling, and Elva agreed.

'How long were you thinking of staying?' the woman asked. She had a southern accent, Carlion maybe or a bit further down.

'Just today,' Elva replied. 'We will sleep today and be on the road again at sunset.'

The woman eyed her pale skin and odd eyes but said nothing. Most of the Last Domain had heard stories about their lady's unchancy daughter.

'Fair dealing,' the innkeeper said. 'We'll be off, too.'

'You're leaving?'

'We'll take the childer down to my family in Carlion, till this is over, one way or another, and then we'll decide whether we come back.' She looked around the pleasant room, her eyes wistful. 'We've worked hard for this place ... but it's a fool that can't see when it's time to leave.'

That was a Traveller's saying. It had another part: 'and a fool is soon a dead man'. Elva wondered how many people would be left in the Last Domain by autumn, if Ember did not return.

That night's journey was colder yet, and Elva wondered if it was because they were now heading north, or if something else was happening.

The Valuers' Plantation was like a lord's large estate, except that here the workers owned the fields in common.

The Plantation had been started hundreds of years ago. Some said that it was the first settlement ever made in the Last Domain, as a refuge for those who fled the warlords. Whoever

picked the spot had known what they were doing, Elva thought.
It was flat water meadows and gentle woods, surrounded by a
long curve of the Two Scarf River, with the houses and hall set
on a rise which would have a good view of the countryside. A
defensible position, Elva thought. And the hall, the oldest building, was built like a lord's garrison, with arrow slits instead of
windows and archers' positions built into the roof line. Whoever
founded this place had been a warrior.

Now, it was a place for farmers and crafters and merchants,
its population the size of a town.

Lamb, the head of the Plantation Council, was already on
the way to Palisade, but Elva explained the situation to the rest
of the council after a hasty breakfast of soaked meal and
raisins.

She and Bass retired exhausted to guest rooms off the main
hall, which smelt sweetly of the apples that had been dried in the
rafters and had left their scent behind them.

Elva was woken just before dusk by a gawky blond youth
who reminded her a little of Gorse, although Gorse was much
sturdier and far less shy.

''m Thyme,' he mumbled, and handed her a tray of bread and
thin-sliced bacon and early strawberries, then ducked away
again. Elva looked after him, speechless. Not because of his
awkwardness – she'd mothered three boys through the awkward stage, after all. But because the gods had streamed around
his head with joy, and he didn't even seem aware of it. Some
weren't, she knew. The Lady Sorn, who was ruler of the Central
Domain, was the darling of the gods yet completely unable to
sense them. But this boy ... this boy carried Sight with him like
a heavy rock, a burden he was trying to ignore.

She'd have to do something about him, but later, on the way
home.

She wasn't looking forward to another night on the track. Her thighs were sore and her back ached. The Road was easier, in some ways, on foot. That was what the body was meant for, after all: walking and singing, the two unfailing comforts.

Bass was even more unwilling to take horse again. The night was already sharp, and the north wind had picked up. The council had drawn together briefly to wish them farewell, but they were as busy as flies on a dung heap, trying hard to plan and manage an estate without fire. As Elva rode through the gates onto the north road, the stars as bright as she had ever seen them, she hoped that wasn't an unlucky image.

Foreverfroze was a deceptively big town. Large circles of thatched reeds around waist height were arranged in groups. It took Elva a while to realise that they were roofs – the houses were half underground, each house part of a circular group with their entrances pointing towards each other. In winter, the inhabitants would have only a few paces to go between houses, and yet each house had space around it and gardens planted, barely green so early in the late northern spring.

They came up over a rise and saw the still harbour reflecting a dawn sky of rose and gold clouds, the long breakwater lying like a giant fishhook. Beyond it, the sea ice had broken up but parts still lay like white lace in the distance. Only one ship was in the harbour, and Elva could just make out that it had a broken mast – no doubt the reason it had not left for the fishing season which started at Icebreak.

An edge of sun showed on the horizon and the harbour abruptly became a blaze of sunlight off water. Elva's eyes smarted and watered, and she had to wrap her scarf around her face and let Bass lead her horse. She was sure it was beautiful, if only she could have seen it properly …

He helped her dismount quite gently and shepherded her down some steps into one of the houses. Inside there was one large room with sleeping platforms to one side and kitchen to the other. It could have seemed primitive to someone who was used to walls and separate rooms, but instead it was full of homeliness: bright rugs across the beds and patterned tapestries on the walls, three very young children playing on tufted carpets and everywhere a smell of sweetgrass. It was warm, too. Elva unwound the scarf completely with some thankfulness, and turned to greet her host.

There was a fire. Burning brightly, bright as if it were any other day. And Bass, standing beside it with a face of utter delight and relief.

She looked astonished into old wise eyes in a face she knew ... surely she knew it, although she had never seen it before? Dark hair gone almost white, merry green eyes – she felt as though she were falling, as though a memory was calling her from some deep place in her mind that she had never known about before.

'You have a look of your mother about you,' the old woman said kindly. 'I know she's not your full blood, but everyone in a village shares some blood, somewhere along the way.'

That was it. Her earliest memories, back in the village of Cliffhaven, before she and Mam went on the Road. The aunties and grammers had looked like this, just like this.

Elva sat down on a bed and stared. There were three of them, as alike as three peas, and they patted her on the shoulder and tutted over her and said things like, 'You've come a long way then, rest,' and 'It's a shock to see her own kind.'

'No,' she said, rousing herself. 'It's a shock to see the fire!'

One of them, she now saw, was younger than the others. That one came forward and sat beside her.

'I am Sealdaughter,' she said in a lovely mellow voice. 'This is Gull, and Sweetgrass. Why is the fire a shock?'

'Because there are no fires anywhere else in this domain!' Elva said.

'Ah.' Sealdaughter nodded at the other two and they nodded back. 'What, a few days ago, was it? Sealmother was upset about something then. I've never known Her so angry. She asked for our strength, and we gave it to her.'

'Whole village,' one of the other women said. 'Went up to the cave and sat for an hour, singing.'

'And then we came back here,' the last woman said, her voice like scratchy wool. 'What was it all about, then?'

Bass looked at her and said, 'What are they saying?' and only then did Elva realise that the conversation had been in another language, one like the tongue she had spoken as a child, but not quite, not quite, so she shouldn't have been able to understand it, let alone make a sentence in it. How could she have?

'How do I know your language?' she asked Sealdaughter, and saw Sealdaughter's eyes cloud over, unfocus. Oh, she knew that feeling – Sealdaughter spoke to Sealmother as she spoke to the gods, and with that thought came understanding.

'Yes,' Sealdaughter said, watching her face. 'The gods gave it to you so you could meet Sealmother and learn from her.'

'Then I had better do so,' Elva managed to say, through a whirl of confusion and delight.

'Tonight,' Sealdaughter said. 'When it is safe for you, Gull and Sweetgrass will bring you. Sleep now, and eat, and be warm. This is your house.'

The three of them harried the children out of the house and closed the woven door behind them. Bass was still waiting, so she told him what they had said.

'I think their Sealmother is like our local gods,' she concluded. 'Or else a Power in Herself.'

'Stronger than the local gods,' Bass observed. '*These* fires are still burning!'

He looked thoughtful, until he glanced across at the table. The women had left a tray of steaming hot porridge and fresh-brewed cha.

No meal had ever tasted so good.

Bass built the fire up and they basked in it.

'I didn't know how much I missed it,' Elva said.

'Mm,' Bass said, eyes closed, a smile on his face as he stretched out his toes to the warmth.

It was wonderful. But Elva slept poorly, wondering what she would learn from Sealmother. To meet any Power was a test; a trial of dignity and strength and will. And humility, but she had had plenty of practice at that.

The two old women, Gull and Sweetgrass, pointed along the harbour to where the northern ridge met the sea. A well-worn path led to a group of caves there, dark holes like staring eyes in the shining grey rock. They were curiously disturbing. Elva shivered a little. She was feeling young and vulnerable. *I am about to become a grandmother*, she reminded herself, *I have six grown children,* but with the two old women next to her, taking an arm each and shepherding her along the path, she felt a child again, being taken by her aunties to see the Village Voice because of some naughtiness.

The women stopped at the first cave mouth as though they, too, were nervous. Gull cleared her throat and a voice came from inside, saying 'Enter'. Gull pushed her into the cave and the women both moved back. Not afraid, but reverent.

She walked forward cautiously, comforted by the darkness

after the sunset light. The cave made a natural room. In the middle was a pool, dark as ink. It drew Elva's eyes despite her desire to look around. She felt as though it should sing like the black rock altar did. Sealdaughter came forward, holding an oil lamp, which she placed on a conveniently flat rock next to the pool. The light reflected steadily in the dark water. It was absolutely still and completely mesmeric. Elva felt dizzy. She wanted to sink into that pool, but she forced herself to look up at Sealdaughter.

'Little Eel,' she said, in a voice deeper than any woman's, much deeper than the mellow voice she had used before. 'You are welcome.'

She had indeed been named after the baby eels which had been splashing in a stream outside her mother's bedroom window and were the first living thing her natural mother had seen after she was born. Only Mam, Martine, knew that. Her real mam, Lark, had been Mam's best friend and she had been there for Elva's birth; the first to hold her, she'd often said, as though it was meant. Elva's eyes filled with tears. She had few memories of her early life, but it was as though these people, this place, called them all up in her, and with them a longing, a yearning, for the mother she had once known, the family who had been taken from her. She was alive herself only because Mam had taken her on the Road, because her father, Cob, had been unable to cope with the strangeness of a child who spoke with the voice of the local gods. So her gift, her curse, her talent, whatever you wanted to call it, had saved her life, and Mam's, because they were gone when the warlord's son had massacred everyone in the village. And he was dead, now, too; hanged for another murder, in Turvite, twenty years ago. He'd gone unrepentant to the gallows, and she was pretty sure it would be a long time before he'd be reborn.

The past was dead. Beyond recall. She'd made up her mind to that twenty years ago, during the Resettlement. All the Travellers had been offered land, in recompense for having been displaced from their homes and forced upon the Road when the warlords invaded. It had been a great, a momentous change, the Resettlement. She had been offered her old home back in Cliffhaven. She had said no, then, because she had a real home and family in Hidden Valley, and it had been the right decision. The past might call her, here, but it was the future which mattered.

'Sealdaughter,' she said. 'What should I do?'

The question came out without thought or preparation. She had been exasperated herself, many times, by villagers who asked questions like that. Always she had to make them be specific. The gods needed concrete questions, or they became annoyed. But Sealdaughter did not have her limitations.

'Enter the water,' Sealdaughter said in a much lighter voice, her own voice. 'Ask Sealmother.'

Knowing that, just like her, Sealdaughter spoke in a different voice when she spoke for others made her feel safer. She had never met anyone quite like herself before. If I had been born here, she thought, perhaps I would have become Sealdaughter, or at least we could have been friends. They were sisters, the two of them, united in service. Sealdaughter smiled as if she shared the thought and helped Elva take off her clothes. The cool air struck her skin and she shivered, aware that the water itself would be near freezing.

'Fear not the water,' Sealdaughter said gently, her accent making the words sound like a phrase from a song. 'You must learn if you are one of our people. All the Sealmother's children enter the water when they are newborn.' She smiled, a mischievous glint in her eyes. 'It is late for you. Perhaps you will not fit!' She laughed. It was the kind of mischievousness that Elva had often seen in very old women, women who had seen so much death and life and pain that any minor panic seemed funny.

Elva held too much anticipation to laugh, but she tried to smile. She stepped towards the water and hesitated on the edge of the pool. All she could see in the pool was her own reflection, clearer than in any mirror. She half-turned towards Sealdaughter.

'How do I—' she started to ask. Sealdaughter put a firm hand in the small of her back and pushed.

The water took her in a rush and black swirl, cutting out light, bitingly cold. She almost gasped with the shock, but in time remembered to keep her mouth closed. Her eyes opened without volition, and she heard, dimly, Sealdaughter clap her hands and say, 'Lo! She is one of our daughters, Sealmother!' She went down, further down and then, as she reached the bottom of her plunge, instead of surging up to the light, her body paused. Held in the water, flailing arms stilled, the water a pressure around her like the pressure of the gods in the mind. She was aware of something, Someone, paying attention to her. Listening. The presence had the same merriness in its heart as Sealdaughter, but it was sharper, also, like old women often are, impatient of foolishness.

What should I do? Elva thought, as a child asks her mother.

What you are called to do. The response was unmistakable, as clear as any message from the gods, but it came as though her own voice had been reflected back at her, just as all she had seen in the water was her own reflection.

Well, that's a lot of help! She couldn't prevent the thought and tensed in case Sealmother resented it, but She laughed.

The Powers are too strong for single humans, child, and Fire is not the worst you have to fear.

Tell me.

Ice comes. Humans alone cannot withstand Him. Humans together may have a slim chance. A better chance, humans together with your gods … if you can convince them to fight for you.

How do we fight Ice? The very thought of a Power of Ice was terrifying. The Ice King, she realised. That's who the Ice King is. For the past twenty-three years she had lived in the mountains, where cold was the enemy as much as the attackers from the other side of the mountains were. More, because they could be beaten, but cold could only ever be held at bay.

Yes, Sealmother said. *Hold him at bay.*

Her mind flooded with waves of images, sounds, prayers. No one she knew, not even Mam, would have understood. But she had had a lifetime of interpreting for those greater than herself, and she could take it all in and understand it later. Love, song, connection, loyalty … a wall of strength to keep out the cold.

There must be no gap in the defence, Sealmother whispered, no longer laughing, *or He will sweep in like a spear.*

Her mind and heart overflowing, Elva began to rise in the water, to float as she should to the top, towards the light and Sealdaughter's waiting hands.

She clambered out of the pool exhausted and sat on the edge, huddling her knees to her chest, water streaming from her hair. Sealdaughter produced a linen towel and began to dry her as though she were a child. She roused at that and dried and dressed herself slowly, squeezing the water out of her plait until it stopped dripping.

Sealdaughter smiled kindly at her.

'Sealmother liked you,' she said. 'You are one of her children. But you do not belong here.'

'No,' Elva agreed. 'Not now. But I might have, once, if I hadn't met Mabry.'

She was swept by a longing for Mabry, for the real home not the remembered one, for the real family, messy and loud and happy and sad and arguing and content, all the work and joy and simplicity and complication of six children and a husband and a farm to run. She wanted to go home.

But she couldn't. She had learned a lesson, and she would need to put it into practice, soon, for the sake of those same children, and of many others.

Bass was waiting for her outside the house, eager and hopeful.

'Do you know how to get the fires back now?' he asked.

'No,' she said. 'It's too late for that. But we have to get back fast. There are more problems on the way, and I may know how to stop them.'

He asked nothing more, just went for the horses while she thanked Gull and Sweetgrass. She was still shivering a little, and dazed from the encounter with Sealmother, but she remembered her manners like a good child and thought even Arvid would have approved of her diplomacy. She even thought to organise shipments of smoked fish and other foods to the fort, promising payment on delivery.

'Warm food before you go,' Gull said firmly, and when Bass came back with the horses she ordered a young boy to hold them. She led them down to another house where there was grilled rabbit and fried onions and a big mug of cha to wash it down. They sat at a round table by a roaring fire with children who had clearly been allowed to stay up late to see the strangers.

Loving children, Elva always gained energy from talking to them and making them smile, so by the time they had finished eating she was warm and ready to ride. Sweetgrass brought them parcels of food for the journey – smoked salmon and lovely fresh bread, pickles, snowberries. A feast, for later.

As they rode west, into the last light lingering on the horizon in slabs of lilac and pale green, she wondered what her children would be eating that night, and where they would be sleeping.

I'll have to get Arvid to call back Poppy and Saffron, she thought. Before Ice comes.

NORTHERN MOUNTAINS DOMAIN

An hour's riding and they were approaching trees again, but these were not the unbroken spruces and larches of the Forest. Some larches there were, but they poked their sharp heads out from kinder foliage: the spring green of elms and oaks, and the brownish-red of young leaves on horse chestnuts, the almost yellow of unfurling beech leaves.

Birds were calling, too, a medley of calls and songs: larks and thrushes, robins and nuthatches, crows and doves. As they approached the seedlings which surrounded the wood, Ember waited for the calls to stop, or change to the alarm calls. But even when they rode past a lapwing nest in the grass, the bird simply went on feeding her young. Ember reined in Merry and watched. The nest was well hidden, but it was clear enough; the mother bird flew in with a grub, and appeared again with complete unconcern.

Ash glanced back and saw what she was watching. They were so close Ember could see the green sheen on the bird's back.

'She should be pretending to have a broken wing,' Ember

said, worried. 'She should be leading us away from the nest. They *always* do that.'

Cedar was following her, and stopped his chestnut to smile.

'She's not afraid of us,' he said. 'Perhaps that's a good sign.'

'I don't think so,' Tern said. 'It's just unchancy. They say the Northern Mountains Domain makes animals mad.'

They rode on, but Ember wasn't sure if the lapwing should have made her more hopeful, or more afraid. She was both, caught in a mixture of feelings that also included sheer, pure curiosity.

Entering the shade of the trees she braced herself for the same feeling of panic she had felt going into the Forest, but there was nothing. Just dappled light, and birds calling, and a rabbit hopping away from them in unconcern, its white tail bobbing slowly.

A squirrel chattered above, but not at them – at another squirrel, cleaning out a hole above in an oak, scattering brown leaf fragments onto the one below.

It was as though they were not there.

Perhaps they weren't.

Ember shook her head. Perhaps this was the way Elgir unsettled his visitors – a subtle discomfort which made them question their own ears and eyes.

The wood grew deeper and thicker, with new kinds of trees appearing as they crossed streams and small standing pools: alder and willow, birch and rowan. No holly trees, and Ember thanked the gods for that. She never wanted to see a holly tree ever again.

Deer raised their heads from grazing to stare at them, but not to run. Ash brought his bow around to the front, but then hesitated, and slung it over his shoulder again.

'This is a test,' Ember said, jumping at how loud her voice

seemed. Ash and Cedar looked at her and she saw that Cedar had understood that already. His dark eyes were bright with interest.

'Aye,' he said. 'There's power everywhere here. Best treat as we're being treated.'

Ash's hand left his bow, but he frowned. 'A gentle test for a place with such a dark reputation.'

'Just the first one,' Tern almost shouted. He was nervous, and his horse had picked it up, dancing from side to side of the trail. Cedar held back and put a calming hand on the bridle. The red roan eyed him wildly, but settled.

'Arvid wouldn't have sent you if he hadn't known you could deal with anything we met,' Cedar said quietly. 'Will you prove him wrong?'

A flush climbed Tern's face, and he let a breath out, looking down, seeming smaller and even younger with the movement. But his horse calmed further, and Cedar let go.

'No shame in being spooked,' Ash commented. 'But if that's what he wants, let's not give it to him.'

Tern's mouth firmed, and he nodded. A breeze swept around Ash and flicked up Thatch's mane. Ash laughed, his sense of humour surging up and lighting his eyes. Ember felt her heart flame in sympathy, and smiled. He had never looked better to her, with his hair turned almost golden by the light through the beech leaves above him. She half-wished the desire that speared through her wasn't a spell.

'Come on!' Ash called, turning Thatch and cantering forward. 'Let's find out what's next!'

Ember laughed and followed him, and the others came up behind.

It was like the best rides of her childhood, the first spring rides when the ground was firm enough after the thaw. Sun and leaves and a constant breeze which played with them, deer and birds and squirrels and pine martens, shrews in the grass, grasshoppers buzzing, bees and dragonflies and midges dancing in the air.

No butterflies, she thought at one moment, but forgot a second later when the ground began to go down again, into a wide, wide valley. The trees were older, higher, their trunks wider and the bark cracked and gnarled. The branches started further up the trunk, forming arches above their heads. Birdsong slipped away behind them, and the wind died.

Shade became shadow, trees giants, making Ember feel like a doll, playing someone else's game. They could see further, between the trees, yet seemed to see less because of the gloom. But it was still clear which way was down, which way led in.

To one side, a deep brown shape moved. Huge. It was huge. Ember caught her breath, ready to call a warning, when she recognised the shape: spreading antlers, wide and flat; an elk. A big male, watching them from beside a stream.

He gazed steadily at them, water dripping from his muzzle. Those eyes stared in a way foreign to animals. Ash turned to make sure she had seen him and they exchanged a quick glance of concern and surmise.

The elk turned and began to pace them, keeping well to one side but staying with them. Ember had seen wolves do that, keeping the prey in sight, letting them know they were being stalked so they would panic. But elks didn't hunt. They were like *cows*, for the sake of crying!

Yet the elk turned his head, time and again, to assess them, his long awkward-looking legs easily matching the horses' pace, his eyes alight with something very like intelligence.

And humour. Ember was reminded of an older friend of her father's, prone to teasing him about all the times he'd gotten into trouble as a boy. The elk's eyes had the same mixture of amusement and mischief.

'It's not funny!' she called to him. Ash wheeled Thatch to come between her and the elk, as though he feared the animal would charge. But of course he didn't. He faced her instead, those dark eyes still laughing at her. 'You took my man from me,' she said, suddenly and coldly angry. 'Your warlord's power stole my guard. And we have come to get him back. Is that a cause for laughter?'

Tern was staring at her as though she had run mad, but Cedar looked appraisingly from her to the elk, and Ash stared at nothing but the animal, his brow concentrated, his bow ready, arrow nocked. Ember hadn't even seen him reach for it.

The elk tipped his head to one side, clearly considering her words. The expression in his eyes changed, but this time it was pure animal. No laughter, no intelligence. Dull, like a cow's. He dropped his head and began to graze on the sweet grass under a hanging birch.

'Someone was riding that animal,' Cedar said. 'I Saw him leave, I think.'

'Riding?' Tern said. 'You can't ride an elk!' His voice was full of indignation, as though the very idea was an insult.

'Riding its mind,' Ash explained. 'Using its eyes. There are old stories about that, but I always thought ...'

'Riding the bloody animal *and* laughing at us!' Ember said savagely. 'Elgir, who else? I dislike this lord already.'

'Early days,' Ash said. 'It's a good trick, for scouting.' *His* voice, she was annoyed to notice, was half admiring.

'He'd better have prepared a welcome for us,' Ember said. She refused to consider what kind of welcome it might be. Elgir was unchancy, but he *was* a warlord, and not a fool. He would treat her as his equal's daughter, with proper protocol, or the

Northern Mountains Domain would be shunned by all war-lords, all his trading partners. Elgir knew that. But even so, there was a cold hand around her heart. Would a lord who rode the mind of an animal care about trade the way he should?

A month ago she would never have thought to question it.

She went to the front, and Ash let her, as though respecting her anger. But as she passed, he said quietly, 'Princess—' in a warning tone, and looked at her hair.

'What?' she snapped.

'You're glowing a bit,' he said, almost apologetically. 'Like you did just before – just before *He* came, back at the fort.'

Anger drained out of her and was replaced by fear. Ash nodded. 'That's better,' he said approvingly. 'You can't let your-self get angry, sweetheart.'

The endearment brought a deep warmth. Ash reached out to pat her hand, and Merry shifted her rump, bumping his bay and moving on a step, so that his hand fell short. She was glad of it – any touch from him seemed to ignite the fire within her, and that could be doubly dangerous right now.

Ember rode on quietly, making herself watch and listen. In the mornings, in spring and autumn, she sometimes got up early and went with her mother or father to the black rock altar where they worshipped the local gods at dawn. Before the sun came up, before the birds' chorus started, there was a pause where the world seemed to wait, breathless.

This forest was poised permanently in that moment. Breathless. Waiting. And where were the people? They had seen only animals.

The land levelled beneath them, so they were riding flat instead of down, and Ember began to hear water running. Rushing, leaping, splashing … lots of water. The sound lifted her spirits and Merry's pace quickened.

The trees changed to huge willows and alders. She had never

seen alders this size, as big as oak trees. Their dense round leaves grew much lower to the ground than the beeches they had been riding through, so that the view ahead was blocked. But the sound of water grew louder.

'Princess!' Ash called. 'Best dismount.'

Good advice. She swung down from Merry and led her forward, Ash coming up beside her, Cedar and Tern close behind. Merry was stepping high, almost prancing, wanting a drink. Ash pulled back a thick alder bough to let her go through, but Merry baulked and Ember stopped, astonished, as cold spray hit her face and bright light her eyes.

The alder stood with its roots half in the stream. River, not stream, she thought, as she looked out and further out, across a broad race of water which crashed against rocks and sprang high in the air to fall and shoot away again. The land rose sharply to their right, a long climb to a ridge that was almost a mountain, and the river surged down it in a series of cascades, white and almost green where it poured smoothly, a coruscation of rainbows and spray and flashes of reflected sunlight.

The light was glaring after the gloom under the trees. Squinting, she peered across the river, aware of Ash looking over her shoulder, his body warm against hers. She wanted to lean back against him, but she took a half step forward instead. Fire would get no help from her in setting them both aflame. Across the river, the land was different. Copses instead of forest, open glades with long grasses buzzing with insects, alive with meadow flowers, poppies and cornflowers and amaranth and, everywhere, the blue of cranesbill.

There were animals to be seen – deer and elk grazing, a couple of wild cattle, their auburn coats still shaggy from winter, some ponies, small and sturdy, but looking as wild as the deer. And the birds! Swallows in a frenzy, swooping on the midges and flies, swifts darting over the water and back across the meadow, a mother pheasant strutting in the grass, followed by her tiny striped babies ... a plover stalked along the opposite bank, eyes on the mud at its feet; a family of ducks sheltered in a quiet pool formed by a fallen tree. If the forest had been waiting, this place was waiting for no one and nothing. It was alive and purposeful, brilliant with colour and movement. She looked up at Ash and smiled, seeing his eyes crinkle in that way he had that made her half-sad, it clutched so hard at her heart. Oh, gods, she thought, remembering Osfrid smiling at her once, and how she had felt fluttery right through to her backbone. This was nothing like that, which proved it wasn't love. It was just Fire, tormenting her.

She looked back across the river. The individual trees in the copses – were they *carved*?

'How do we get across?' Tern asked, his voice high with excitement.

The horses shouldered Ember aside to get to the water, and she moved back to let them drink. There didn't seem to be a ford or a bridge anywhere. Below them, to their left, the river curved around in a long arc. In the distance, it was hard to see which part of the forest was on their side of the river and which was on the other.

'I think there is a bridge,' Cedar said. His voice was odd; there was suppressed excitement there.

'What can you See?' Ember said, but he shook his head.

'More a feeling,' he replied, pointing downriver. 'There. See it? I think that crosses over.'

About a league downstream there was a bump on the river bank. It was one of those spots where Ember struggled to make out the separate banks. The trees were so large, and their branches reached out so far across the stream ...

'No!' she said in astonishment.

'He's *grown* himself a bridge?' Ash asked, voice alive with amusement again. 'Now that's a trick we could use back home. I'd like to meet this warlord!'

'So would I,' Cedar said, but he wasn't joking. 'Come on.'

He led the way back under the trees purposefully, and they followed him without question. The undergrowth cleared not far from the bank and they followed its broad curve along the bank, keeping the sound of the water as close as they could. It was tantalising, hearing that sound and knowing the bright, busy world lay just beyond, while they trudged through gloom and dead leaves. A baby in the womb must feel like this, Ember thought, hearing the voices of the greater world but unable to join them.

They came to a wider space where there was evidence of tracks – not humans, but all the animals they had seen earlier. And others.

'Wolf,' Tern said, down on one knee, examining the soft ground. 'Definitely wolf, here.'

'And bear,' Ash said.

Ember shivered. Bears were unpredictable things, and a bear's claw could disembowel a human as easily as the stroke of a sword.

They followed the tracks to a great willow tree, leaning down over the stream, its enormous roots stretching so far back into the forest that she lost sight of them. The closest was so thick it stood higher than her head. Tentatively, she put out a hand to touch the crinkled brown bark. It felt like every other willow tree she had known, and its catkins had already given way to the slender yellow-green leaves of spring. Its familiarity made her uneasy. No willow tree grew to this size naturally, no matter how old it was.

There were ways to climb up – broad pathways of roots, as

wide as the watchtower walk around her father's fort, where four men could stride abreast. The tracks led to these.

'Elk,' Ash said, pointing to where tracks climbed a rootway. 'Where elk can go, so can horses.'

Cedar wasn't waiting. He led Snail up onto the broadest root, where the elk had gone, and she went willingly. Cedar glanced back. 'Come on!' he said. His enthusiasm worried her – it was so unlike his normal cool head.

'Wait—' she said, but he had already moved on. Ash came to stand next to her, dusting his hands off on his trews. A leaf fragment, dry and brown, clung to his boot.

'We don't have to take the obvious route,' he said.

'Come *on*!' Cedar called, waiting for them at the top of the rootway, just before the tree arched out over the stream.

'Can you even *see* the other side from there?' Ember asked.

'There's another tree,' he said confidently. 'They intertwine. It'll be all right.'

That was all the reassurance Tern needed. He and his red roan scrambled up easily and went after Cedar.

'You first,' Ash said. 'I'll keep the rear.'

So she took Merry and Ash followed. Merry wasn't sure about climbing the tree. Her ears went back and her eyes showed white. Ember tried to reassure her, but maybe her own fears came through, because it didn't help. The other horses had gone willingly enough, but Merry didn't like the drop to the ground below, or the sound her hooves made on the living wood; she flinched with each hoof-fall and finally pulled up short, quivering.

'She's always had a problem with bridges,' Ember said, exasperated. Now she'd made the decision to cross, she just wanted to *do* it. Ash wrapped his jacket around Merry's head and began to lead her.

'You take Thatch,' he said. Without sight and with her

hearing muffled, Merry let herself be led up. Ember followed, astonished at how broad and strong the tree seemed to be.

There were several branches reaching out, as well as the main trunk, and further on they grew together as if a giant girl had plaited them untidily into a braid, the thicker central trunk bulging through.

Tern and Cedar were waiting for them there. Cedar grinned at them and led Snail out over the water.

A huge slab of sound hit them without any warning, the sound of a full thaw flood down a narrow gully; thundering, deafening. The river was rising up against them.

It reared back against its own flow, sending waves from both sides to crash against and over the bridge. Great gouts of water, thumps and slaps and blows of water that tried to sweep Cedar and Snail into the torrent. Tern pulled back just in time to the shelter of the overhanging boughs.

Snail's hooves scrabbled for purchase on the wet wood, the other horses milling, neighing and whickering in alarm. Merry's reins were torn from Ash's hands as the mare bolted down the rootway, crowding past Ember and sending her flying to the wood. She rolled and clung as waves pounded into her. Ash hunched over her, trying to protect her.

Another wave hit Cedar and he fell to his knees, Snail's reins looped around his wrist. He kept down and crawled, Snail sliding and slipping, then finding her feet and overtaking him, pushing him to the side, dragging him until his grip on the reins gave way and he began to slide back.

Ash lunged forward, grabbing his hands, both of them lying full length, with Cedar's feet dangling over the raging water. The waves continued, rising higher still, higher than their heads, higher than the tops of the trees, falling like avalanches, the water hitting like rocks.

Ash strained to bring Cedar higher, but he began to slide forward too, and Ember realised that the water was sucking at Cedar's legs. She grabbed Ash's ankles and they lay for a moment, panting. The wind rose as they lay there, whirling the waves from side to side, the air rushing through and against the water as it crashed. It gave them a moment's clear sight.

'Both of your hands on my wrist!' Ash shouted to Cedar above the crash and buffet of the waves. What was he doing? Ember wanted to yell at him, to tell him to pull harder. But Cedar moved his grip so that he was hanging from Ash's left wrist. The strain on their shoulders must be terrible.

Then Ash fumbled at his belt for his knife. What is he *doing*? Ember thought with frustration. He couldn't quite reach it, so she wriggled up beside him and got it out, lying as far over him as she could to give him ballast. Their wet clothes might as well not have been there – it was like they were naked, skin to skin. Ember flushed with shame and desire. Why was Fire tormenting her like this when her life could be at stake? She was filled with anger, and that helped push down the heat in her loins. Ash took the knife without looking at her but with a nod of acknowledgement.

'I am Ash, son of Elva,' he said, as though reciting a lesson learned by heart. 'Whose blood has calmed the waters.'

He took a breath and brought the knife across his palm in a long bloody gash. Ember gasped with horror, all thought of desire leaving her. Ash let the blood drip into the water.

Instantly the river settled into its bank, calm and serene.

The sudden quiet was like another blow.

Ash pulled Cedar up and he came to his hands and knees, and then they both stood up, Ash inspecting the wound on his hand. Tern was behind them, having run to catch the horses before they could dash off. That was good thinking.

Slowly, shaking, Ember clambered to her feet, edging back a

little, away from the river. What kind of spell had Ash performed? It was as smooth as a millpond.

Except for one last wave. Out of the corner of her eye, Ember saw it coming – down the cascade, down the stream, a running ridge approaching at a gallop.

'Ash, ware!' she called. The wave hit the roots of the willow and curved up, higher than their heads, cutting off the sun, and splashed down – not on Ash, but just beyond him. The spray blinded them. When Ember blinked it away, the Prowman was standing on the willow road, where the wave had landed.

He looked around quickly, getting his bearings. He was bone dry, even to his boots.

'Starkling? What brings you here?' he asked Ash.

'Elgir,' Ash said.

They locked gazes for a moment, then the Prowman nodded.

'My Lady Water has an arrangement with him, to guard his sanctuary,' he said, nodding at Ash's bloody hand. 'I am glad of it – it let me find you.'

Ash had some relationship with Water? No. No, that couldn't be right. She would have to ask him about that later. For now … Ember moved forward. 'Why did you need to?'

'To warn you,' he answered. 'There is more at stake than we realised. The fires have gone out in all the Domains.'

For a moment, Ember didn't understand. Then she felt the magnitude of what he had said.

'Why would Fire—?' she asked, bewildered.

'He just doesn't distinguish between the Domains,' the Prowman said. 'To Him, they are all one.'

Frowning, Ember stood by the Prowman, noting that he was still in the same clothes she had last seen him in, down to the cha stain on his shirt. As though it had only been a matter of hours instead of days.

'The south is in less danger,' she said.

'Not by much,' Cedar said thoughtfully.

'A month or so,' Ash said.

'How cold does it get in the south?' Ember asked. She wanted badly to get off this bridge, but the men seemed to feel quite safe, now, and she didn't want to act like a coward.

'Cold enough that to be without fire is dangerous,' the Prowman said, his singer's voice grim. 'Your people have nowhere to run to. You must not fail.'

'That's helpful,' Cedar said.

The Prowman grimaced, acknowledging his tone, but he addressed Ember. 'I will do what I can,' he said. 'But the solution lies in Fire Mountain.'

He looked out over the moving water. 'I think the time has come to remind the Powers that the blood has been mixing for a thousand years now. To hurt one people is to hurt both.'

Ember nodded. She'd thought much the same, standing between her mother and Sigurd, just before the – before Osfrid's death. These were new times, since the Resettlement, and it was time to let go of the old divisions. Whether Fire would agree was another matter.

To Ash, the Prowman added, 'No need for the others to give blood. She will let them pass.'

He nodded to the others and then simply stepped off the bridge into the river below. Ember rushed to the edge, but he was gone, as if he'd never been there.

'That did happen, yes?' Ash joked, a smile twisting his mouth.

She had to ask.

'You are one of Water's men?' she said, staring into his hazel eyes, willing him to say 'No', although she didn't understand why it mattered to her so much. The wind was rising again, lifting his hair, drying their damp clothes.

He shook his head. 'Not at all,' he said. 'But we have been …
introduced.'

A sharp satisfaction pierced her and she pushed back the
curls which clung to her face, welcoming the cool breeze as it
dried her. She reached for the kerchief in her pocket and
wrapped it around his hand. He was all right.

The fires were gone everywhere, across all the Domains.

'Let's go,' she said. 'We have to hurry.'

THE ROAD FROM FOREVERFROZE

There were altars along the way, notably at Oakmere, but Elva decided to wait until they were back at the fort before she approached the local gods about defending the domain against the Ice King.

She had Travelled for eighteen years with her mam before she had met Mabry, and she had talked with the gods the length and breadth of the nine southern domains in that time. She had learned a great deal which was hard to describe to anyone else – although perhaps Sealdaughter would understand – but one thing she did know was that the gods were truly local and, at the same time, connected to the next world and to each other.

The altars were at the heart of their power, and she suspected that they allowed the gods in different places to be connected; to know what each knew. But not to *care* about what each cared about. Although wherever she went the gods recognised her and welcomed her, it was not the same with other humans. The gods at the fort knew of Mabry, but did not yearn towards him as the ones in Hidden Valley did, eager for the images of beauty his mind created.

So she thought that it was better to ask at the fort altar, where the gods were personally connected to the people she would be trying to protect. More likely to help. She hoped.

Entering the Valuers' Plantation was reassuring, like coming home from a foreign country into familiar lands. Lamb, the Council leader, was back from Palisade and welcomed her kindly even though she'd been roused from her bed. She listened to Sealmother's plan gravely, then took Elva to a guest cottage and left her and Bass to rest while she spread the news.

At dawn, Elva made her way to the black rock altar. Dawn light was harsh but not so strong that it caused her too much pain, and although she didn't usually go to the dawn ritual, at the moment she felt the need for the familiar touch of the gods' minds.

The altar was surrounded with worried faces, but they were glad to see her. Elva prayed with them and the gods were there, right enough, so she reassured the Valuers about that, and it was like any dawn ritual, except that afterwards the gods didn't leave, but streamed towards the young man, Thyme, who had brought her food on her last visit. He stood shyly at the back, alone. Elva wasn't sure if he was aware of the gods, but they certainly loved him, and she smiled at him as she went back to the cottage, too tired to talk to him right now. He looked confused to be singled out, and she felt maternal towards him. Mabry always laughed at her for that: 'You'd mother the whole world if you could,' he teased, and it was true enough, she sometimes thought. This boy looked as if he could do with some mothering.

In the later morning, after a nap, it was cloudy enough for Elva to go outside, as long as she wore a hat to shield her eyes from glare. With not much surprise, she found Thyme sitting on a log down by the mill stream drawing with a stick of charcoal

on the back of a smooth board. The curve of water and the tur-
bulence where the millrace met the main stream were taking
shape under his hand. She had seen Mabry work like this, silent
and concentrated on the wood he carved, but this boy reminded
her more of Ash, the Prowman, as he had stood in front of them
one night, reciting poems with such power that she had seemed
to hear and feel and even smell everything he described.

'Thyme,' she said. He jumped and turned, an expression of
alarm vanishing when he saw who it was.

She sat down beside him on the cool wood and smiled reassuringly. He was only about the same age as her youngest,
Gorse, about fifteen, maybe, and still mightily shy of strangers.

'I have a question for you,' she said. 'Do the gods speak to
you?'

He flushed, and ducked his head.

'My da says prayin's women's work,' he muttered, in a thick
northern accent. 'He reckons gods don't do no one no good, it's
hard work gets results.'

Wonderful.

'And I suppose he doesn't approve of your drawing, either?'
Elva asked.

He shrugged, that one-shouldered shrug young ones use to
agree without committing themselves to words.

'Your da is right, in some ways,' she said. He hadn't expected
that; his head came up in astonishment. 'The gods won't help
those who don't work; and they don't really care all that much
about individual humans unless those humans are special, somehow.' She paused, let the silence deepen. 'As you are special.' He
blinked with shy pleasure. 'You speak to the gods, don't you,
Thyme?'

He nodded, his head going back down again, half-ashamed
and half-excited.

'Excellent,' she said briskly. 'We are going to need you.'

He sat up and brushed the unruly yellow hair from his eyes. 'Why?' This time his voice was high and unguarded, like the boy he was.

'It will get colder, and colder still, and at some point we will have to fight, to hold Ice at bay. I will be the centre of the fight, at the fort, but we will all have to work together. The gods here will tell you when the time comes, and what you have to do, but you must be ready to do it, no matter what your da says – or everyone here might die.'

His eyes were huge.

'But—'

'I've spoken to the council here; they know what to expect. You'll have support.'

That scared him almost as much as it reassured him. Elva smiled and patted his arm, put on her best mam's voice.

'Don't worry, lad, we'll be fine. Just don't go too far afield. Make sure you're where you can hear the gods.'

He nodded, struck dumb by the responsibility. Sometimes, Elva thought, your life changes in a few moments, who you are shifts completely, and that had just happened to him. 'The gods trust you,' she said softly, 'and so do I.'

As she left he stared blankly at his drawing, and then, as though compelled, began to sketch in the small curves of primroses on the bank. Emblems of spring. Of coming warmth. She hoped, for his sake, that the flowers would survive Ice.

STARKLING

The weight on Ember's shoulders seemed almost physical. The whole Eleven Domains. In the back of her mind she had kept the south as a way out – if she failed, at least her people could go there; they would lose everything they had built in the north, but they would not die. Now there was no refuge anywhere.

The river flowed calmly beneath them, occasionally flicking her face with spray, and the willow branches lifted from the great roots and trunk like a fan, creating a living screen which trembled gently with each breath of wind. She was in a tree. No doubt. But although her eyes knew that, to her feet it felt like solid ground.

Ash went first, and they followed him, the river sweet and gentle below.

Two-thirds of the way across there was an intricate entanglement of trunks – the other tree was an alder, and its paler, smoother bark swept in curls and knots around the crinkled willow.

Ember paused before she stepped across onto the alder. Here, in the middle of the stream, she could feel a faint swaying from the trees, and the river rushing below seemed a long way down. Yet her fear had left her, and even the horses went across calmly. Ember took the step onto the smooth grey bark, and felt a small shudder run through the alder.

The alder still had its catkins, busy with bees, but its leaves were growing, so that they walked down into a darker green than the willow, a rushing windy green where leaves tossed on side branches and Ember's hair was lifted into a plume that streamed downriver. The breeze was making Ash's clothes billow and puff, but he kept his jacket snug over Merry's eyes.

Ahead of them, Cedar had reached the other side and leaped down, his chestnut scrambling off eagerly and immediately beginning to crop the sweet grass by the base of the tree.

Tern was next, and then it was her turn. The alder roots were not as long as the willow's, so the angle was steeper here and Thatch chose to simply jump off, pulling Ember down with her. It was a wild leap. Her arms flailed at the air and she tumbled, letting go of the reins, but she fell onto grass and lay, winded, staring up at the intricate lattice of alder branches which shut out the sky.

Ash led Merry down more carefully, but he didn't come over to see how she was. He stood still, staring at something. His bow was in his hands, arrow at the ready.

'Princess,' he said, his tone making her scramble to her feet and whirl to follow his gaze.

A man watched them from the edge of the alder's shade. His face was in shadow and his hands were hidden. He was more a silhouette than a figure. Tall, very tall. Brown. Brown clothes, leather maybe, brown hair, long to his shoulders and shaggy, browned skin. Her eyes adjusted some more to the light and she began to make out his features.

A long, solemn face, not young but not old, deep-set eyes. Brown eyes. Eyes that lit with amusement as she brushed her clothes off and tried to regain her dignity. Oh, she knew those eyes.

'My lord Elgir,' she said, her voice as tart as Martine's ever had been, scolding a dairymaid. 'How nice to see you finally in your own body.' She paused for a beat, judging it carefully. 'That *is* your own, is it not?'

Amusement broke out across his whole face, transforming it from solemn to mischievous.

'Aye, this is me, for what it's worth.' His voice was as dark as his hair, but soft, like fur. A voice that gave nothing away. He came forward and Ash moved instinctively to stand beside her, but she put a reassuring hand on his forearm. There might be danger here, but Elgir wouldn't just attack her. 'I'm sorry if you resented my other form – most wouldn't have noticed.'

He clicked his fingers to the dogs and Grip immediately pranced up to sniff his hand and be scratched behind the ears. Holdfast held back, tail down as if she weren't sure of what she was smelling.

'We have been forced to notice more than that,' Ember said, unrelenting. 'Where is my man Curlew?'

'The one who tried to ride past my guards?' he asked, smiling with disarming candour. 'He's in the high trees, I think.' He gestured beyond the curtain of leaves and Ember looked out. The curve of the river had brought them around so far that the ridge which had been on their right now stretched up ahead of them. It was crowned with trees, enormous things which stood higher, surely, than any mortal tree could.

Elgir glanced at Cedar, who was staring at him intently, and smiled a small, secret smile. 'They're cedars,' he said. Cedar blinked and looked up at the far trees, drawing a breath as though there was some significance to their species.

'You are *not* going to turn into a tree,' Ember said firmly. She glared at Elgir. 'Don't even think about it!'

He was taken aback. 'Turn into a tree?' he said. 'Why would he do that?' He had been thrown off balance by the idea, and Ember was glad of that. Better off balance than laughing at them.

'It happens,' she said shortly. 'Take me to my man, if you please, my lord.'

'Well,' he said slowly, 'I'll take you to the high trees, but from there you must go alone. I'm no hand at climbing.'

'It's hard, when you're used to four feet, isn't it?' she asked sweetly, and he shot her a look that was a mixture of surprise and admiration. She'd seen that look before, in younger men who had thought to cozen the warlord's daughter and found it was harder than they'd anticipated. The memories bolstered her confidence. Strange it might be, but this was a warlord's stronghold and, in some way, she was back in known territory. A place for civilised conversation, which her mother always said was more vicious than any battle. She was gripped by urgency, the need to move and move quickly.

As they walked out of the alder's shade and along a clear path through the long grass, she became less certain that she was anywhere near civilisation. The meadowland near the river was broken up further back into a series of glades, bounded and linked by trees. She'd thought them coppices, earlier, the kind of managed wood all villages had nearby, but now she saw the trees in them were too old and huge to have ever been coppiced.

Yet, they had been managed. Like the bridge, the growth of these trees had been controlled, twisted into shapes more like houses than living plants. Some had branches growing straight and flat from the trunk, and these had platforms made of inter-twined boughs, so closely laced that it was like good wickerwork, but solid as a floor. A small child sat on one of these, her bottom resting amid living leaves, her hand stroking a small branch as another child might stroke a cat.

Ember paused, looking up at the child, who stared back down at her with interest. The first human apart from Elgir they'd seen – or was she? There was something about the tex-ture of her skin, a slight shimmer that reminded Ember of heat haze on a road, or moonlight on water.

'Hello,' Ember said. Elgir looked on, his face unreadable, but his stance relaxed.

The child opened her mouth and replied, but the sound was more like birdsong than language. Ash laughed, delighted, and the girl smiled at him.

'Hello,' she said to him. 'This is my tree.' There was an accent to her words and she said them carefully, as a stranger to the language might. But her pride in the tree was unmistakable.

'It's beautiful,' Ash said. She nodded and rose, climbing swiftly up, showing off as children did. Her face peered down at them from behind leaves, and she smiled again, then disap-peared, giggling.

'Your daughter?' Ember asked Elgir politely.

'I have no children,' he said.

He led the way forward, staying just a little ahead of Ember as they kept on, passing trees which had grown into rooms and towers, the long sinuous branches curling and twining so that there were no straight lines anywhere. Lime trees, beeches, elms, even oaks had been coaxed or enchanted into use. Not every tree, not every group of trees. The birches were too small, the aspens too weak, and willows were uncommon, it seemed, away from the river. But chestnuts and walnuts, and old, old alders. In one copse, several yews made an aerial village, their branches forming corridors as well as rooms, the boughs forming a lattice for a may hedge, dripping white with blossom. And on the outside of most of the clumps, fruit trees grew: cherry and apple and pear. She wondered what it would be like to wake up in a bed surrounded by cherry blossom.

In between, the glades were full of food plants. Berry canes, hazel bushes, apricots trained against the trunks of other trees for shelter, and vegetables, their distinctive tops scattered at random: onions and carrots, small wild leeks and dandelion greens, sallet and parsnips.

What looked like wilderness was a farm, but who was tending the crops? And how were the grazing animals, which were everywhere, kept from the human food? Deer were great destroyers of early crops, and Ember couldn't believe they wouldn't have tried to get to this feast. But Ember caught glimpses of them, happily grazing in the meadowlands, just a little way away from the glades.

That was an enchantment the farmers of Last Domain would like to learn.

They had seen no one but the little girl, but there were sounds all around them, birdsong and animal calls, wind and water. Ash came up beside her and said quietly, 'Those birds sound a lot like the little one.'

Ember listened more closely. Were people talking to each other, over their heads, watching from the network of rooms and walkways which seemed to stretch from one side of this valley to the other? It was a disquieting thought, and she shivered. It was also a breach of protocol.

'Where are your people, my lord?' she asked.

Elgir turned to her and waved a hand.

'Around,' he said. 'Watching you. We have few visitors.'

That was clear enough.

'Why did you bring us here?' she asked.

He stopped and the others behind them had to stop too, the horses huffing a little and shuffling, the dogs coming forward to nose Ember's hand. Holdfast still stayed a little away from Elgir, but Grip treated him like a long-known friend. Elgir looked up at the nearest tree, a giant beech which wound its branches into a tall tower with small openings. A tower walled with leaves, she thought. They must freeze in winter.

'I brought you here because you carry power with you,' Elgir said eventually, choosing his words. 'And power is dangerous left uncontrolled, but it is more dangerous when it is unknown. To protect my people, I had to discover more about you.'

That's a lie, Ember thought. Or rather, it's the truth but not the deeper truth.

'No other reason?' she prodded. He lifted his chin, as the elk at the stream had done, to stare down his nose at her.

'There is probably another reason,' he said, voice soft as moss, 'but I do not know it.'

And that was the truth. Out of the corner of her eye she saw Ash nod, once, and knew he'd heard truth, too. Cedar moved forward, as if pulled unwillingly.

'Is it your spells that have shaped this place?' he asked. Now *that* was dangerous, to ask an enchanter about his power, but Elgir's face cleared and he answered readily.

'Mine, my father's, his father's ... and other friends.'

'Human friends?' Ash cut in. Elgir laughed.

'Sometimes,' he said, and it wasn't clear if he meant that some of his friends were human, or that his friends became human sometimes.

Ember decided to leave it at that until they had Curlew back.

They moved through glade after glade, past treerooms and

towers and winding stairs made from branches. The air was full of the scent of sap and mayflower. She couldn't help asking, 'What happens when the leaves fall? How do your folk stay warm during the winter?'

He looked sideways at her, amused again. 'Some leave,' he said. 'Some find other shelter. We manage, as we always have.'

And somehow that put images into her mind of birds migrating and badgers burrowing and bears curling up for their winter sleep. Elks, she knew, continued to graze through the winter, eating birch bark and buried grass.

The ground began to slope upwards, and Tern, behind them, began to move faster, pushing them forwards. He was right, Ember thought. They should be hurrying.

'Where will we find our sergeant, my lord?' she asked. 'And in what case?'

'How he'll be depends on him,' Elgir said. 'That spell is a strong one, to safeguard my people.'

'It was not safeguarding anyone,' Cedar said. 'It was coercing.'

His voice was not disapproving; more like a teacher's, or a storyteller's, explaining something to a child.

Elgir dropped back to walk next to him, and Ember listened intently. They were alike, these two, in looks and walk and manner – saturnine and complex, hard to predict. Perhaps Cedar could understand this lord better than she.

'In your case, that is so,' Elgir acknowledged. 'But the spell was not made just for you.'

'What are you protecting, up there on the plateau?'

'Some of my people need that space,' Elgir said. 'You may see them yourself, some day.' His tone was final; no more discussion. But Cedar pressed him.

'You control the ghosts of former warriors,' he said. 'Like the enchanter Saker, who once almost destroyed our world.'

Elgir shrugged. 'You think they were real ghosts?' He smiled, narrowly, in challenge. Bull elk, Ember thought. 'Would I constrain my own people and deprive them of their chance at rebirth?'

'Well, would you?' Cedar retorted. Elgir laughed.

'Only if they wanted me to,' he said.

The slope steepened and Elgir said, 'Leave the horses here,' when they came to the next glade, a small grassed enclave fed by a stream which was half waterfall, sliding down over rocks into a pool. From a small glade to the right a horse wandered over, whickering happily. Blackie, Curlew's mare, looking just fine. The dogs greeted her, bounding at her heels, teasing her. Feeling more hopeful, Ember and the others unsaddled the horses. Merry rolled in the grass and then shook herself to her feet. Tern got out their nosebags, but the horses ignored him, crowding around Elgir instead. He was talking to them, softly, in a language she didn't know. They listened. Nuzzled his arm. Blew breath into his face, as if he were a friend. His voice ended on what was clearly a question, and all of the horses huffed or whickered or whinnied in answer, then turned to graze. The dogs lay down in the sun and stretched, quite content.

'No need to hobble them,' Elgir said. 'They will wait for us.'

None of them commented. He was an enchanter and he had just done enchantment in front of them. It was enough for him to be deposed by the Warlords' Council, because no warlord could be an enchanter, but Ember doubted he ever considered the council at all. This land might be called the Northern Mountains Domain, but it was no part of the country she had grown up in.

The high trees began at the very top of the ridge, which was not peaked but flat, as though someone had run a knife along the top to smooth it. The scent of evergreen was very strong as they climbed; not pine, not even the familiar odour of the cedarwood chests her mother kept blankets in; these were the living trees, and they smelled of life, heady and invigorating. The scent filled her lungs and made the climb easier, lifting her up.

These trees did not seem to have been enchanted. There were no entwined branches, no rooms with green lath floors. The trunks rose high and straight, and only far above their heads did the branches sweep out. They were close together: leaning back, Ember could see that far up the branches did intertwine with each other, but whether that made rooms or floors or walkways she couldn't tell.

'You will find him on the highest level, I believe,' Elgir said.

'How do we get up there?' Tern asked, voice squeaking.

'Most of my people fly,' Elgir replied.

How useful, Ember thought dryly.

'And the others?' she asked.

'They climb the saplings.'

At the edge of the ridge, before the tall trees cut off the sunlight, smaller trees were growing. These had branches all the way to the ground, but they were spindly, still, and didn't reach quite high enough for an easy transfer to the more solid trunks.

'You are not climbing up there,' Ash said flatly.

She glared at him. Didn't he have *any* idea of protocol? No. Of course not. Farmers and bowyers rarely did. She would have to excuse that.

'My cousin,' she said to Elgir, 'fears for my safety.' Family were allowed license which other courtiers were not. Even if Elgir held no real court, she had to maintain her father's dignity.

'You are not cousins,' Elgir said. It wasn't a question. His face showed only mild interest.

'An honorary title,' she said. 'Ash's mother was adopted by my mother as a baby. Technically, we are not blood kin, but we are certainly family.'

'Nephew,' Elgir said. 'Honorary.'

Ash laughed. 'She tried calling me that, once,' he said. 'But I'm a year older, so I didn't think it was right.'

Ember couldn't help smiling at the memory. 'You pushed me into the pig trough,' she said.

Nodding, Elgir looked from one to the other. 'Family,' he said. 'But not blood kin. And that may matter, one day.'

Cedar shivered at his words, but Ember couldn't tell if it was a warning. Sight, perhaps? There were too many unchancy things around here and she was beginning to feel dizzy, like a child who'd been spun around too many times in Seeking Blind.

'You're not climbing up there,' Ash repeated. He held her gaze until she nodded. 'You stay with her,' he ordered Cedar, then turned to Tern. 'Come on, lad.'

He tossed the jacket he'd been carrying to Cedar, but he gave his bow to Ember, and she took it with due ceremony. He opened his mouth to say something, but she cut him off.

'Yes, I will look after it,' she said. Laughter lit his eyes. She wanted to reach forward and kiss him, to lean her body against his full length and feel his muscles move against her, his arms come around her. Her hand began to move, without her willing it, to touch his face, but she pulled it back before he noticed. Her shoulders ached with the effort of not touching him.

'That's my princess,' he said. He stood with his hand on the trunk of the highest sapling, looking up, his face clearing of all emotion. She wondered what he was thinking. 'With your permission,' he said, but he was talking to the tree, not to her.

Elgir nodded in approval.

'She grants you passage,' he said. Ash swung up into the lowest branch and began to climb, Tern close behind.

STARKLING

Ash climbed as swiftly as he could, ignoring the sway of the sapling, pretending for Tern's sake that there was no danger. The cedar bark was rough but years of sanding wood had made his hands tough as oak. Brushing against the needles let the cedar scent loose – it reminded him of Winterfest, when his mother used to bring the evergreen boughs into the house and hang them from the window – that was how Cedar got his name, being born at Winterfest.

As they climbed, his footholds became smaller and more tricky, but he'd got into a rhythm by then and was beginning to enjoy it. He'd been sitting on a horse too long. The trees beside them were solid, but being on top of the ridge the sense of space around them expanded as they climbed, so that they were climbing into moving breezes and free air. He could feel his heart calm; this was his place, high and moving, wind and sky.

The sapling was growing sparse and beginning to sway with each step up, but the lowest bough of the near tree was still some way up. He grinned and climbed higher, then braced himself against a solid bough and reached a hand down to Tern.

'Come up, lad,' he said. 'I'll boost you.'

It was like the games he and Cedar had played as boys, standing on each other's shoulders to dive into the mountain pool below the ford. He bent a knee so Tern could walk up it, then hoisted him under the backside until he was standing precariously on one shoulder, steadying himself against the other trunk.

'Up you go,' he said. Tern could just reach the bough with his fingertips, but not enough to get a good hold. Ash flexed his feet and eased up an inch or so – it was enough. Tern struggled and scrambled and swore a few good soldier's oaths, but he dragged himself up onto the branch and sat, panting.

With his weight out of the tree Ash dared to go a little higher, and then grinned to himself. It was a long way down, but there was no way Tern had the strength to lift him.

'Move back, lad,' Ash said. Tern, puzzled, held the branch above his head and slid across to another branch.

Ash moved as high as he could, until the sapling shivered and began to bend. He flexed his knees, yelled, 'Hah!' and sprang as high as he could, arms reaching. He wasn't going to make it. He could feel himself pause in the air, ready to drop. But the wind roared up the trunk beneath him and seemed to push him just a little higher. Just enough. His hands found the branch, his feet scrabbled against the trunk and, impossibly, found a knot to give him purchase, and he was up and on the bough, sweating and astonished.

Perhaps Elgir had sent that blast of air to help him. He shrugged. No telling here and now.

'Let's climb,' he said to Tern, reaching a hand to haul the boy up.

The branches were further apart on the big trees, but they were rock solid. His shoulders would feel it tomorrow, he thought, taking a break to give Tern a breather. Ash looked out and felt his heart lift. From here they could see right across Elgir's valley: the wide curve of the encircling river, the dark forest beyond, the glades and trees and streams of what he must think of as the town. South, mountains reaching west and east. He edged around the tree to see if he could look out to the west, but the ridge was too thickly wooded to let him see the western mountains. Fire Mountain was at the junction of the two ranges. Perhaps when they were higher he would be able to see it.

The air up here was cool and invigorating. They climbed with more energy after the rest, not speaking much, helping each other where necessary. Ash felt returned to childhood, and wished that Cedar were here instead of Tern. Thoughts of Cedar led him to dwell on Ember, so far below, so fragile, so strong.

His little cousin was someone he hadn't really known. Never thought about. Warlord's daughter, red-head, Grammer's daughter. Spoiled, like all officers' children, but nice enough. Familiar and taken for granted. Until now.

He wasn't even sure what was happening, except that whenever danger threatened her, he felt suddenly and fiercely protective. As for desire ... well, she was pretty, of course, and it had been a long time since he'd lain with anyone. It was only natural that when he came near to her, smelled her scent, that he felt need. He spared a moment, as he paused to haul Tern up to the branch next to him, to remember Berry, who had wavered all last summer between him and his cousin Pike, and had finally settled on the one who *didn't* have a mother who spoke for the gods. She'd been open enough about why, and he'd felt mostly a guilty relief. He'd have married her if she'd wanted – after all, he had to get married sometime and she was the best of the local girls. He'd been proud that she'd even thought of him, and the afternoons they'd spent in the meadow grasses had been better than good. But he'd danced at her wedding with a clear heart.

Ember's wedding ... he'd been looking forward to that. Whatever he was feeling, it had come after that; it had started, he thought now, in that room where she had challenged Fire so bravely, so recklessly ... he put the thought aside and concentrated on the next branch, the next foothold. His shoulders were aching harshly, but there was still a long way to go.

Glancing up, he could see that above was a kind of floor circling the trunk. All the trees had them, at different heights. These weren't the interlaced, grown floors of the other trees they had seen. They were constructed: dead branches, twigs, an intricate latticework which seemed to have been tied together with reeds.

There were no openings to let them up. He looked around – the tree nearest to them had a floor lower than the one they were climbing on. So if they went higher, they should be able to jump across to the next tree.

A few branches more and he could see across to the next tree. Even so high, the cedars were enormous, their branches spreading out larger than the main room in his parents' house. The platform encircled the tree, but he could not see across it, because there were partitions, also woven of branches and reeds, half thatch, half wattle without the daub. The nearest partition left only a foot or so of room for him to land on, and the gap to it was wide.

He grinned. The road is long and the end is death, he thought, remembering all the times his mother had said that. If we're lucky.

Edging out as far as he could on the branch, he turned until he was facing directly to the opposite tree. There was a game

they'd all played as children, running along tree branches as far
as they could before they leaped into the river below. Cedar,
lighter and lither than he was, had always beaten him.

He took a breath and ran, balancing, wobbling, but picking up
speed. Behind him, Tern shouted something, but the rushing speed
was pushing him, lifting him as it had as a child, and he whooped
as the branch dipped beneath his feet. He leaped, curving through
the air. There was no blast from beneath this time to support him,
but he didn't need it – he was across, slamming into the partition
wall and bouncing back. He dug his heels in, spun and grabbed
whatever he could – the end of the partition – and then half-slid,
half-fell, to the floor at the very edge. He ended with his head over
the long, long drop, seeing the ground below, the branches
between, a kingfisher flying beneath him, blue wings flashing in
a patch of sun, everything clear and sharp and the only sound his
own gulping breaths. He realised he was laughing.

'You're mad!' Tern was shouting. 'You're insane!'

Ash dragged himself back onto the platform and rolled over
onto his back, still chuckling quietly. The branches above him
had varying sizes of platforms, and here, at last, were things connecting them, although they seemed to be mostly vines strung
across the gaps and between levels.

He rolled to his feet and stood back as far as he could.

'Come on, lad,' he said. 'You're lighter. You'll be able to get
closer than I did before you jump.'

But Tern was shaking his head.

'No.'

'It's not so bad,' Ash reassured him. 'If I could make it, you
will too.'

Tern clung to the trunk and looked down. He was shaking.

'You could have fallen,' he said. His voice squeaked and fell,
but he didn't notice. 'You could have *fallen*.'

Ash glanced down at the drop. He always felt an urge to jump when he was in a high place, but he'd learned to ignore that, the way he ignored his dreams about flying once he'd woken up.

'I'll catch you,' he said soothingly.

Tern just shook his head and kept shaking it, clutching the bark.

'I can't,' he whispered.

'Don't look down,' Ash said.

'Too late.' His face collapsed and he suddenly looked very young. 'I have to go back down!' he wailed. 'I have to!'

No chance. Ash had seen panic like that before, when his little sisters found themselves out of their depth in the river and screamed for him to save them. He couldn't save Tern.

'Slowly!' Ash warned. 'Go slowly, and only look at the trunk.'

Very slowly, still shaking, Tern edged his feet down to the next branch, and the next one. After the third, he clung, sobbing, to the trunk.

'I can't,' he said.

'Sit down and wait for me,' Ash said. 'I'll get Curlew as fast as I can and we'll bring you down together.'

The thought of Curlew seemed to strengthen Tern. He looked up and nodded, but he didn't sit. He couldn't seem to let go of the tree. Well, he was safe enough where he was if he didn't get dizzy.

Ash finally turned around, his curiosity sparking. What kind of people made these eyries? How did they live?

He edged around the partition and found more and less than he expected. There were no people, and no furniture – but the room was alive with colour. Feathers in every shade of blue were tucked into the woven walls, with no attempt at pattern. He took a step inside, eyes wide. He saw kingfisher blue, the pale grey-blue of heron, jay's tail feathers, others he didn't know. It was like being in a speckled blue bowl. Hidden in the feathers, hanging from twigs stuck into the wall were objects, some familiar, some strange. A cup of carved wood was easy enough to recognise, but what was the long wooden stick for, its tip carefully curved just a little? There was a shallow bowl, a mirror the size of his palm (which was worth a warlord's bounty), some beads on strings – blue, all of them.

'Curlew?' he called. Nothing but wind in reply.

He walked gingerly across the room, but the uneven floor seemed to bear his weight well enough, although it creaked unnervingly beneath him. On the opposite wall there was a gap, through which he could glimpse the far trees and the edge of another wall, curving around.

He put his head through the gap. Another room, open to the sky like the last, but this one had feathers of black and white: magpie, crow, plover. He had a plover's feather in his pouch. Hesitantly, he pulled it out and smoothed the crisp barbs down, then found a spot on the wall which seemed bare and tucked his feather in amongst the others.

It looked good.

'Curlew?' he called again, and stayed still, listening. He wondered how many platforms, how many rooms, he would have to search, and whether Tern would have the patience – or the strength – to wait until he was done.

'Your friend is some way from here,' a woman's voice said.

He whirled around.

In the gap he had come through, a young woman stood. As tall as he was, dark-headed, she was dressed in a long straight grey gown with a black border which swept the floor. Her hair was plaited and piled on the top of her head in intricate folds.

Her eyes were hard to see: pale and clear. They appraised him, lingering on his hand, which was still touching the plover feather.

He felt a little dizzy, but there was one thought sharp in his mind: there had been no way onto that platform except the one he had taken. So how had she got there?

'Greetings,' he said, and bowed. 'I am Ash, son of Mabry and Elva, from the Hidden Valley.'

The formality surprised her, but she seemed pleased, bowing back far more gracefully.

'Greetings,' she said. Her voice was not musical, but it had a timbre he had never heard before; a depth like a hunting horn. 'I am Grus.'

'My friend?' he prompted.

'He is several trees away,' she said. 'Will you fly?'

She asked it as simply as a woman at a farm might have asked, 'Will you ride?'

'No,' he said, regret in his voice.

'Then you must climb,' Grus said, not at all put out. 'Come.'

He followed her through another doorgap, to the far edge of the platform. She pointed to a tree on the very highest part of the ridge.

'He is there, your friend.'

'Can we call him? Can he meet us halfway?'

A ghost of a smile flickered on her lips. 'I think he is not able to come.'

'Is he all right?' Ash's tone was sharp.

'He is not hurt,' Grus said consideringly. 'But he is like your other friend – the air lets him fall.'

Tern? Was Curlew simply afraid of the height? Only one way to find out.

'How do I get there?' Ash asked.

'Follow me.' Grus led him to where two living vines grew across to another tree, one at floor level, one at shoulder height. What were they doing here? It was the sort of vine that grew in the moist valleys of the south. Part of Elgir's enchantments? They looked barely able to support the weight of their leaves, but Grus took hold of the upper vine and simply walked across on the other, moving her hands along the top vine for balance. The vine dipped under her, but it held. Ash had heard of rope-walkers performing in the cities of the coast, but he had never seen one. It looked far too easy to actually *be* easy.

He waited until Grus turned and looked at him, waiting, then he took firm hold of the upper vine, a liana as thick as his wrist, and put his foot on the lower one. It dipped immediately, far lower than it had for Grus, but he could balance, just. Just. He put another tentative foot in front of him and was standing wholly on the vine, feeling it swing a little in the free air.

'It is easier if you go fast,' Grus said, smiling slightly.

Easier. He swallowed fear and made sure he didn't look down. Faster. One foot, then another, then another, gradually he made himself go faster, until he felt as he'd felt running along the branch before he leaped – the air rushing to his head, the risk making his nerves tingle. He was supposed to be the staid big brother, he thought out of nowhere. When did he get to like taking risks?

Sometime, obviously. He laughed as he stepped lightly from the vine to the platform floor, and Grus smiled at him, her pale eyes lighting with approval.

'Come,' she said. She turned and ran across the platform, through rooms of yellow feathers, of teal green, of robin red. They burst onto his sight and vanished as he ran after Grus. At the edge of the red room there were more vines, and Grus did not slow, running out along the lower vine with barely a finger touching the upper one. Ash laughed and followed, gripping more firmly but moving as fast as he dared, as fast as he could. It was *like* flying, running a tower's height above the ground, and his heart soared, unafraid.

On the opposite platform he seemed to see shapes out of the corner of his eye, but he couldn't tell if they were human or something else. They disappeared behind the wall screen as he turned to look.

Two more platforms, room after room of colour, even one as orange as a sunset sky, and twice more they ran out over nothing with only a narrow vine as pathway, faster each time.

Then there was a room of grey feathers, pale and dark and calm, and against the wall, as far from the edge as he could get, Curlew sat, chin to knees, arms wrapped around his head, blocking all sight. Around him the latticework was patchy with damp, and his clothes showed damp stains as well.

Ash knelt in a dry space next to him and put a hand on his shoulder. The flesh shuddered under his touch and kept quivering, as waves of shivering went through him.

'Curlew?' he asked gently. 'It's Ash. I've come to get you.'

Curlew's body stilled, slowly.

'It's Ash, Curlew. The others are nearby. Ember and Cedar and Tern. All of us came to get you.'

The tightly clenched fists dropped a little and Curlew raised his head. His eyes were red and exhausted, as though he had been through weeks without sleep.

'Did you fly?' he whispered hoarsely. His eyes flicked quick glances at Grus but flicked away again immediately, frightened. Ash looked up at her. Her face was calm, slightly interested perhaps. Not threatening.

'They fly, here,' Curlew whispered. 'They made me fly. Did they make you?'

'No,' Ash said gently. 'I climbed up. Just like anyone else.'

'I flew,' Curlew said. He vomited suddenly, but only water came up.

'You won't have to fly again,' Ash said. 'We'll climb down.'

Curlew shook his head and kept shaking it. 'Can't. I tried. No way. No way but wings.' He clutched Ash's sleeve. 'Don't fly. Gods protect you, boy, *don't fly.*'

He buried his head in his arms again. Ash felt anger straining against his chest. He stood and confronted Grus.

'What did you do to him?'

She stayed calm, but she turned her head so she was looking at him from the side. 'He went through the gate. All who go through the gate without leave are brought here for the lord's punishment.'

'What punishment?'

'He has not yet received it,' she said, surprised. 'But he had too much Earth in him to fly easily. His soul rejected it.'

'How did he fly?' Ash needed to know. This was the answer, surely, to the yearning he'd felt all his life. If Curlew could fly, he could too, couldn't he? But Grus merely shrugged.

'The same way anyone does,' she said.

He put aside his frustration as Curlew moaned. Elgir would know – it was his spell. He went back to Curlew and helped him up, ignoring the man's groans.

'Come on, lad,' he said, talking as if to his own younger brother, Gorse. 'Come along and we'll have you safe.'

But looking around, he could see that there was no way off this platform except the thin vine bridge he and Grus had used. Curlew was not capable of walking over that height. Even with Ash's support, he couldn't bear to look at the edge of the platform.

'Forgive me: I am going to wreck your floor,' Ash said to

Grus. She kept that half-smile on her face, but her head tilted as if in curiosity, and she looked sideways at him, at the floor, at Curlew, then shrugged.

'If you can,' she said. 'It is strong.'

It was strong. But not stronger than he was, or his belt knife. The wattles and reed lashings that bound the longer branches in place gave way under his blade, and once they were gone he could use brute strength to wrench the branches up and away. It took time, but after the first few moments Curlew became involved, eager to destroy his prison. The first small hole brought a little crow of triumph from him, and his energy grew as the gap widened. But when it became large enough to see down, down the long drop to the ground, he turned pale and sat back on his heels, shaking.

'Can't fly,' he said.

'Don't have to, man,' Ash said heartily. He went to the edge of the platform and used all his weight and strength to pull the vine loose from its moorings opposite. Then he cut the near end through, although it almost blunted his knife.

He tied the vine around his own waist, then around Curlew's. Curlew stood bewildered, like a granfer mazed by age.

'I won't let you fall,' Ash said. 'We will climb together, you and I, like boys in a wood at home.'

'Home,' Curlew echoed.

'Remember being a boy and climbing trees?' Curlew nodded slightly. 'That's us, man. Come along.'

He led Curlew to the gap in the floor and only then looked at Grus. The sun was westering and it gave her black hair a cap of red, warmed her skin and showed the delicate outline of her figure through the long dress. She was beautiful, that was certain.

'Your lord will answer for this,' he said.

'I have no lord,' she said. 'I answer only to the same Lady as you.'

He frowned, completely puzzled.

'Ember?'

Now Grus looked puzzled. 'My Lady bears me up,' she said, 'as She does you.'

He didn't have time to work this out. Curlew was beginning to shake, staring down at the gap.

'Don't look there, man,' he said briskly. 'You watch my hands, that's what you look at.'

He had made the gap twice as wide as his own body so they could go down to the first branch together, and he was thankful for it. Curlew froze a dozen times, shaking and sweating, before he manoeuvred the two of them onto a firm foothold on the branch below. He tilted his head back – Grus was just visible, staring down at him with bright, clear eyes.

'Next time we meet,' she said, 'perhaps we will fly together.'

His heart contracted at the thought, pierced by a longing so sharp it was almost sweet. He almost climbed back up, but he didn't. He couldn't leave Curlew. Not now. He had to get Curlew to the ground and then go back up and bring Tern down. And there was Ember, waiting for him. But it was a near thing. It was a very near thing.

STARKLING

'Now,' Elgir said, 'let us discuss your marriage.'

'My marriage?' Ember said slowly. Her heart was jumping and the scar around her wrist flamed suddenly, searing her. Her other hand cupped it. Memory overwhelmed her. Osfrid's face, screaming silently. The ashes ... the face of Fire ...

Reluctantly, Ember came away from the sapling and sat near Elgir, Cedar beside her. She stayed still, shaking, trying to seem calm.

'Has your father planned your marriage?' Elgir asked. His tone was courteous, the polite chitchat tone of the warlord's court. He was asking the question one asked of a young woman, as though she could have no greater concern than her wedding. She almost slapped his face. And then she thought, shame-faced, that a month ago he would have been right.

'A marriage was planned,' she said carefully. 'I was betrothed to Osfrid, Merroc's son.' She paused, her mind turning over all the possibilities. What would her father recommend? Truth, evasion, misdirection? There had never been enmity between the

Last and Northern Mountains domains ... but they had never been allies, either.

'It was ... interrupted,' she said. Ash didn't like her to lie. He thought it was unlucky. She glanced at Cedar, belatedly remembering he was there. He shrugged a little. 'My – Osfrid was killed.'

Elgir stared at her. 'Killed?'

Some chances had to be taken, her father had told her. To find the truth of an ally, you had to risk trust.

'By Fire.'

The dark head bent over his hands, his hair swinging forward to hide his face. She could hear a whispering, but couldn't make out words. Then he straightened and faced her, and there was suppressed excitement in his eyes.

'That was the Power I saw in you,' he said. 'You carry Fire with you.'

'Not by choice,' she said. 'He has laid a task on me, and my people's lives depend on it.'

'What task?' He sat forward, half on his knees, keen for her answer.

'To go to Fire Mountain and steal some of His fire.'

'Like Mim,' he said. 'The great firestealer. His first worshipper.'

'I do not worship Him!' she snarled. 'He killed Osfrid. He – He has torn my life apart!'

'Power does that,' Elgir said. He seemed calmer now, and thoughtful. 'Why, I wonder?' he mused. 'Why now?'

'What?'

'The Great Powers have made no move in human affairs for many years, and they have never interfered in the lives of Acton's people.'

'My mother is of the old blood,' Ember said.

'As all the world knows,' Elgir answered courteously. 'But Osfrid was not.' He rose and walked around the glade. 'When a Power intervenes in the world, it is wise to look at anything unusual, in case they are acting again. There is something happening here I have never seen before, and now I wonder ... is one of the Great Ones involved? Come, I will show you.'

He pointed down the slope. She looked at Cedar and stood up, slowly. Ash would not want her to go. But it would be a great breach of protocol to refuse ...

'He means you no harm,' Cedar said. 'I have Seen it.' His head lifted to the huge branches above them. 'Tern needs me,' he said. 'Go with Lord Elgir, and I will aid him.'

Ember had never heard Cedar speak so formally. He reminded her of an older man, one versed in courts and etiquette. Perhaps that was Sight speaking for him. She had lived with it all her life, and she recognised it in his eyes now, so she got up and brushed off her skirts.

'Lead the way, my lord,' she said. 'Show me this anomaly.'

The tree houses which had been deserted were alive now. She could see shapes move in the tower rooms, people looking out at them. Oddly shaped, some of them – one man had a small pair of antlers, she was sure. A woman with hair as blue as a jay's peeked out from behind a branch that curved into a staircase. A child whose legs were surely too long for its body jumped lightly to the ground, and ran, laughing, across their path. Elgir regarded it with amusement. Court life taught how to ignore what one was not supposed to see, so she pretended to have noticed nothing unusual. Elgir glanced at her, his eyes unreadable.

Elgir led her down to a stream, and they followed a thin path along its bank. The water swirled deep and brown over stones, and mosses edged it. On the opposite bank, there were holes: water voles, she thought, or otters, but when a face peered out at her from one of them, it had human eyes and the mischievous grin of a child. She almost exclaimed, but was glad she hadn't when Elgir said sternly, 'Sar, leave those poor otter cubs alone!'

The face disappeared in alarm and Elgir turned to her apologetically. 'The burrows connect all over this area,' he said, 'and it's hard to keep the little ones out.'

The stream fell rapidly over small waterfalls, and Ember was glad of her sturdy boots in the wet mud.

They passed through a screen of poplars and came out into a meadow where the tumbling stream spread into a wide, shallow pool which fell silently over a lip on the other side to become a broad snaking creek.

All around the pool were juniper bushes. The sharp smell hit the back of Ember's throat and brought her alert. Because on the bushes, on every bush, on every twig and leaf, were butterflies.

Swallowtails, she thought. Black and white and yellow-gold, some dappled blue, some green, they lay with their wide wings and long tails drooping against the bushes, unmoving.

'Are they dead?' she whispered.

'No,' Elgir said. 'They came from the cocoon yesterday, and this morning they should have flown north. But they do not move. And the wind has not come.'

'The wind?'

'The south wind blows always at this time of year. It carries them up, and north to their breeding grounds. It is cold when it comes over the mountains, but it warms over my meadows and rises, and these little ones rise with it, and sail away.'

Contemplating the silent, vibrant host was sad. Ember loved butterflies. Well, who did not? But there was something else odd.

'There are no birds eating them,' she said.

'No. They are easy prey, but there are no birds. That is why I think the Powers are acting – birds are alert to power, they avoid it as quick as may be.'

Ember realised that there had not been a bird in sight when she walked from her father's fort to her marriage fire, when normally there were birds everywhere in spring.

She moved out among the bushes, looking carefully at the butterflies. Some of them moved just a little as she passed, their wings waving gently, their antennae quivering.

'They're waiting for something,' she said.

'For the wind. If they do not fly soon, they will die before they have bred.'

Abruptly, she was angry. Power. Powers. Interfering with humans was bad enough, but to condemn a whole generation of beauty to death – to sacrifice the generations of beauty unborn – that was wanton evil, and it should not be countenanced.

'Can't you *do* something?' she asked Elgir. 'Raise a wind?'

'I am Earth and Forest,' he said. 'I have no power over Air.'

Fuming, she moved further in, lifting a butterfly onto her fingertips and holding it up, willing it to fly. It hung there, limp, and that enraged her, too. They should *fight*, these little beauties, fight for their lives.

Anger swelled in her: anger at the Powers, at the butterflies, at the gods, at the world itself which let these things happen.

'It's not *fair*,' she muttered. Her hair was standing up on her neck, and she thought, fleetingly, of Ash's warning about temper, but it was too late. Much too late to stop the wave of heat that swept over her. No, she prayed. Don't come. Don't come here.

Wind. Perhaps if she could stir up a breeze, the butterflies would lift … she spread out her arms and began to spin, holding her skirts out to make a fan. Slowly. Faster. Faster still, until the world became a blur and she lost all sense of left or right, up or down. There was only the blue of the sky and the green of the grass and the black, white, gold rainbow in between.

Around her, the air grew warm and her hair began to lift gently as it rose. *Air*, she thought. We need *air*, not fire. Don't come here.

She spun, and the air grew warmer. The butterfly on the tip of her finger lifted away, drifting. She caught glimpses of it, snatches as she went around and then around. It was moving. Flying. Flapping its wings. She spun faster, laughing, and the air was like honey, thick and warm, and then like summer itself, almost burning her, almost blinding her.

More butterflies lifted, flapped, followed the current of warm air around her up, up and around into a swirling cloud of colour, a waterspout of wings rising like hope, a ribbon spreading into a scarf, a skirt, a cape of colour that filled the sky and streamed northwards. She flung up her hands as she spun and the anger became delight, triumph, equally hot, equally strong, and she laughed as she spun until she was breathless and had to sink, panting, to the green earth.

Her gaze followed the rainbow trail across the sky. Hah! she thought. I hate Them so much. Let Them taste failure.

Elgir wound through the bushes and reached a hand down to help her stand. She realised again how tall he was, how massive, and felt a small shiver of fear. But he was smiling at her.

'So you use Their power against Them?' he asked. 'You are brave, but perhaps not wise.'

'You think They will retaliate?' she asked, suddenly *very* afraid. The sweat on her skin turned clammy.

'All things must be paid for,' he said. Ember was irritated. That was the kind of thing people said when they didn't want you to have fun.

'Well, of *course* everything has to be paid for,' she said. 'But sometimes you have to take a chance. Some things are worth it.'

'Butterflies?' he asked, and he was teasing her now.

'Butterflies,' she said firmly.

'I agree,' he said, 'and I will do what I can to help, since you have helped me and mine.'

'Butterflies are yours, too?' she asked.

'All that lives is mine, here,' he said seriously. She nodded. It was no more than she had suspected.

'Including humans?'

'Those who are alive,' he said. 'The ghosts look after themselves, mostly.'

'Even your guards?'

He pursed his lips, but he didn't get time to answer. A shout came from the ridge. Ash's voice, calling her.

She turned and ran back the way they had come, not waiting for Elgir. It seemed steeper the second time, but she panted up the rise. Ash wasn't anywhere near where he had left them.

'Ember!'

She followed his voice, and found Ash at the base of one of the trees, some way from where he had climbed up. His arm was around Curlew, and they were both scratched and bleeding on hands and face.

'It was a hard climb down,' Ash said.

'There were butterflies,' Curlew said dazedly.

Ash made a face, as if the butterflies hadn't helped. 'There certainly were! We could hardly see!' Then his face softened. 'But they *were* pretty.'

Cedar and Tern arrived and went to help Ash with Curlew, and Ember took her sergeant's hand. He was shockingly pale and drawn – older than when she had last seen him. His eyes didn't seem to see her. They focused past her, onto the ground. Slowly, he sank down and placed his palms on the grass, and then lay down fully, pressing his face into the dirt. He began to cry, as a child cries when it comes back to its mother's arms after being lost.

Ember regarded him helplessly. Should she comfort him? Or scold him, as a mother did when the reckless child was found? She knelt next to him and put a hand on his back.

'You're safe now,' she said. 'It's all right.' She kept her voice low, and rubbed his back, and gradually his sobs died away and he hid his eyes against his forearm in a mixture of exhaustion and embarrassment.

Elgir had arrived. She glared at him, but Tern spoke first.

'What have you done to him?' he demanded.

Ash answered. 'The spell made him fly.' Curlew shuddered under her hands at the words and Ash grimaced, putting a finger to his lips. Ember nodded. No more talk of what had happened – at least, not in front of Curlew. Tern looked distraught. He patted Curlew tentatively on the shoulder.

'I hope you're satisfied,' she said bitterly to Elgir, whose face was creased with concern.

'That was my father's spell,' he said. 'Perhaps it is time to revisit it.'

The sun was almost gone, sending the long shadows of the trees down the ridge and across the glades.

'You will stay here tonight,' Elgir said. It wasn't a question, but although Ember looked at Ash to see if he objected, he didn't say anything. He was brooding about something, she thought. Curlew's condition, or something that had happened up in the trees.

She wanted to say, 'No, we'll go on,' but it was sheer stupidity to travel in unknown country in the dark, and the moon wouldn't rise for hours.

Tern and Ash helped Curlew up and Ember used her last kerchief to wipe his face. His eyes were still unfocused, but he could walk, as long as the others held his elbows and guided him.

They went down the slope and Elgir led them to a group of elms which had grown into rooms and towers and staircases, bowers and balconies. The horses and dogs, brought by some signal they hadn't heard, met them at the trunk of the largest tree.

'The privies are over there,' Elgir said, pointing at a clump of densely planted aspens.

Ember made for them with relief. She hadn't liked to ask – that was the problem with there being no lady here – she shouldn't have had to ask.

It was odd, she thought, as she made her way through the narrow gap between two trees, that the privy she found was *exactly* the same as the one at home. Except that they used comfrey leaves here instead of dock.

And the waterbutt with its dipper was not a cooper's cask, but a single tree trunk, hollowed out.

She was overtaken by homesickness as she washed her hands and face. The linen towel smelt of rosemary, and it brought back a vivid memory of helping her mother and the other women lay out the bed linen over the rosemary bushes in the kitchen garden, to air after winter in the gentle spring sun. It had been part of the preparation for the wedding, and the day had been full of laughter and happiness. The scent brought that back and she missed her mother fiercely. If only she had her mother's Sight! Then perhaps she would understand this odd warlord, these peculiar circumstances.

The others were using the nearby privies, and they met back

at the elms, all of them looking cleaner and more relaxed, even Curlew.

'I have had your gear brought here. Come,' Elgir said, starting up one of the staircases, but Curlew began to shake.

'Not up. Not flying,' he muttered, and stood dead still. Grip whined in his throat and Holdfast nosed Curlew's hand, as if trying to give comfort.

'Better for Curlew to stay on the ground,' Ash said clearly.

'I'll stay with him,' Tern offered.

Looking from Elgir to Ember, Ash hesitated. He didn't want to leave her alone – and she didn't want to be left. But Curlew's need was greater than hers.

'I will too,' Cedar said quietly.

Ash nodded thanks and began to climb the staircase behind Elgir, but Ember went to Curlew and took his hands.

'Will you be all right, down here, with Tern and Cedar and the dogs?' she asked gently. 'Do you want me to stay, too?'

He stared at her dumbly, his eyes still fixed on the ground.

'Curlew?' she prompted.

With an effort, he brought his gaze to her face.

'Down here,' he said. 'Not up.'

'I must go up,' she said. 'Unless you want me here.'

'Don't fly, my lady!' he cried. 'Don't fly!'

'Shh, shh,' she soothed him. 'I won't fly. I promise.'

Dully, he turned away and sat down, his back to a large stone.

Ash came back and took her arm.

'He will be all right,' he said. He looked at Tern and Cedar. 'Just keep him warm and get him something to eat.'

Elgir called from above. 'Food will be brought.'

Ash nodded and exchanged glances with Cedar, who nodded.

'I'll stay by him,' he said. 'Feet on the ground.'

'There was Loss in your casting,' Ash reminded him. Cedar made a face.

'And Destiny. And Chaos. When they are there, who knows what will be lost? Anything from life to love to –' he looked at Curlew '– to something less nameable.'

Grimacing, Ash turned to the tree.

'I'll bring your packs down,' he said. With a last pat on Curlew's arm, Ember followed him up, marvelling at the smooth, easy climb. The long limbs of some sapling – she thought it was a kind of myrtle, from the leaves – had been trained to form a handrail, smooth and pleasant to the touch.

Elgir led them to a room woven from the central branches and minor leaves of the elm – a green room full of breezes and the rustling of leaves. The slanting sun put lozenges of gold light on the floor, which shifted and danced as the leaves moved. Ember stepped onto the floor with caution. It dipped a little under her weight and she had a moment of panic before it settled into firmness. Their packs were lying to one side – how had Elgir organised that? She'd been with him all the time ...

Ash picked up Curlew, Tern and Cedar's packs and simply tossed them over the side of the 'wall' into Cedar's waiting hands.

'There is food above,' Elgir said, climbing a narrower stair to a higher level in a nearby tree. Ember followed him, and Ash came behind, a reassuring presence at her back. This stair was not so solid – it creaked as she walked, and swayed alarmingly. Ash didn't even seem to notice. He moved as though on solid ground.

In the next tree, a dining room of sorts was laid out. A slice from a huge tree trunk formed the table. Plates and cups of wood held food. Ember took a bet with herself that there would be no meat, and she was right: berries, bread, a salad of purple carrots and baby beets, and ...

'Cheese?' she said to Elgir in surprise. 'You keep cows?'

'This is mare's cheese, from the ponies,' he said. 'The cows don't like to be milked, but the mares don't mind. Try it.'

She was abruptly hungry. The cheese had a hard white rind but inside it was soft. There were no knives on the table so Ember used her belt knife to cut some and spread it on the bread. Oat bread, crumbly and fresh. The slightly sour cheese and the sweet oat bread were delicious together.

Ash sat next to her and Elgir went to the other side of the table. Ember spared a thought for the men below.

'My men, Lord Elgir?'

'They will be cared for,' he assured her.

'Your people are shy,' Ash commented, biting into cheese and bread himself. 'I've spoken to only one so far, apart from the little girl.'

Who had he seen? Ember came alert, only then realising that she had relaxed into a drowsy state as soon as she had sat down. It had been such a long day ... she stifled a yawn and listened.

'You met one of the high people?' Elgir seemed genuinely interested.

'Grus helped me find Curlew,' Ash said. His face was unreadable, but Ember watched his hands, which played with his knife on the surface of the table. Something had happened up there ...

'Grus is the most comfortable with speaking to strangers,' Elgir nodded, 'but does not normally do so. I wonder why help was offered?'

Ash shrugged.

'Perhaps they wanted to get rid of Curlew,' he said, his voice harsh.

Elgir put down the cup he had raised to his lips.

'I did not intend harm to your man,' he said quietly. 'We intend harm to none but predators, here.'

'What, no wolves in this domain?' Ash jeered. That was so unlike him that Ember stared. He was more upset about Curlew than he had shown.

'There are wolves,' Elgir said. His voice was dark again, and held a warning. 'They guard our borders from the Ice King's men, and are honoured warriors. I would not cross them, if I were you.'

'If they attack my lady, they will die,' Ash said flatly.

The two men stared at each other, stony faced. Elgir looked down first.

'No wolf of this domain will attack the lady who danced for the butterflies,' he said, a smile making his face almost charming.

'What?' Ash demanded, and so she had to tell him the story.

'Oh, princess,' he said, shaking his head but with his eyes full of warmth, 'you take too many chances.'

His mouth was so tempting. An image of running her thumb along his lower lip flashed through her mind, of him pulling her into an embrace, a kiss, more ... there was a confusion of feelings: the harsh heat of desire and something else, a softness, a need to surrender. Fire's weaponry, she thought, and steeled herself against it. Ash looked puzzled by her expression.

'Elgir knows about Fire,' she said. That would distract Ash from whatever had been showing on her face. Would he be upset with her? He drew in a long considering breath, but then he nodded, thank the gods, and looked seriously at Elgir.

'We need to reach Fire Mountain as soon as possible,' he said.

'I will guide you,' Elgir said. 'It is west of here, and the journey is difficult.'

'Naturally,' Ember said gloomily, and yawned again. 'Everything always is.' *Except butterflies*, a small voice whispered in her mind. She was still smiling at the memory when Ash pulled her to her feet and guided her down to the room with their packs, where their sleeping pockets had been spread out and lit candles had been placed in shallow wooden bowls. The light filled the leafy room with a green glow.

'In you go, princess,' Ash said.

She was so tired she didn't even say goodnight to Elgir, just climbed into her pocket and laid her head down. Ash would say what was right. But a last instinct of courtesy made her raise her head and say into the shifting green walls, 'Thank you, my lord.'

Elgir's voice drifted back from above, 'Good night, my lady.'

The last thing she heard was Ash saying, 'Sleep well, princess.' His voice carried her safely into warmth and darkness.

PALISADE FORT, THE LAST DOMAIN

Lamb, the leader of the Valuers' Plantation, was the first of the Domain Council members to arrive. She came riding through the gate in a flurry which was strange to see – Lamb was a calm woman, normally. A grandmother of seventeen, fifteen of whom were still alive, she was unflappable as a rule, used to dealing with the minor crises of childhood and the major ones of a large plantation. But she was flushed and uncertain as she dismounted and came to talk to Arvid, who waited courteously for her.

'Fire *showed* himself?' was the first thing she said. Abruptly, Arvid remembered that Lamb's grandmother had been a Travelling barber who had made her way to the Plantation from the far south.

'You knew of Fire?' he asked. He tried to make his voice calm, but she knew him well, and flicked him a glance of sudden concern.

'I—' She hesitated. 'All the women of my family go to the altar at Equinox,' she said finally. 'It's a women's tradition. I thought ... a woman's secret, nothing more.'

Women, Arvid thought bitterly. But he nodded as though he accepted that pitiful excuse, and Lamb relaxed. He called a maidservant and she escorted Lamb to the hall, while he waited for the other council members to arrive.

Some wouldn't be there until the next day, but that afternoon four more came; women and men trusted by their towns or regions, elected by their people to represent them. Some were officers, most were not. Domain Councils had no real power separate from the warlord – their advice was simply advice, not law, and the warlord could disregard it if he chose. But in the thirty years Arvid had worked with a council, they had never come to outright disagreement. Negotiation, mutual understanding, mutual respect, that was the key. Other warlords, he knew, routinely ignored their councils, but that was a way to breed discontent and rebellion. He had invested his council with some of his own power – in the regions they represented they could judge minor crimes, decide what matters of policy needed to come before their fellow council members, even settle the smaller tax disputes in their area.

In two, perhaps three generations, Arvid thought, warlords would have returned to their oldest function – the leaders in battle – and ruling, lawmaking, dispensing justice, all would have descended to the councils. He wished fervently that that had happened before he was born.

The council members straggled in over the next day; some would be unable to come for days, but they would have enough to make decisions. What decisions, he had no idea. He walked into the hall unsure of what he was going to say.

When the council met, there was no glass table set on a dais for officers and lower tables for everyone else. Just one large board, made of four tables moved together, and *everyone*, not just the officers, was served their wine in the precious glass goblets. Arvid sat, as he always did, in the middle of one long side. There were gaps where the councillors from farthest out usually sat, but he saw most of the faces he expected: Sage, Elver, Lamb, the three officers from Long River, Brown Hill and Waterfall, and the Voices from the larger towns.

'I welcome you to Palisade,' he said, the formal greeting. Then he paused, took a breath, and leaned back a little. Only honesty would do here. 'Well, this is a shagging mess, isn't it?'

Laughter circled the table, and they plunged straight into planning: how to keep their people safe and fed and prosperous, how to survive.

It was wonderful. For the first time since the Fire, Arvid put Martine and Ember right out of his mind and concentrated on something else entirely.

Dinner that night was outside, tables set up in the cold twilight so they could all at least see what they were eating without starting the meal early. Martine presided as she always had, and the councillors reacted to her as they always had, with respect and affection and a little awe.

The council separated the next morning, right after the dawn ritual, all of them eager to get back to their families. Lamb paused before she mounted the sway-backed gelding she unaccountably loved so much.

'Your Lady has our best interests at heart, my lord,' she said, and then left hurriedly, before he could reply.

He stood, glaring after her, fists clenched by his side. His groom took one look at his face and veered off to Lily's smithy. Just as well. How dare she. How dare *anyone* speak to him of his wife.

Behind him, the fire flared up, sending sparks high into the sky. He hoped it was his imagination that it was laughing at him.

'Ice?' Arvid echoed, frowning. 'That's why it's so cold?'

'Fire is gone,' Mam said. Her voice was distant, as though she were Seeing things, but her eyes were sharper even than usual, and Elva wondered what had been happening here while she had been gone.

'Fire is gone,' Elva confirmed. 'So we are open to attack from Ice.'

'Are you saying,' Arvid said slowly, 'that this – this *Fire* has been *protecting* us?'

Elva simply nodded.

'For how long?'

Mam Martine spoke, and this time her eyes were clouded with Sight.

'A thousand years,' she said. 'They have battled for a thousand years.'

Arvid sat down in his chair, the old workworn chair at his desk that he refused to have replaced. It had been his great-grandfather's, Elva knew, and was one of the oldest objects in the Last Domain, having been brought from the south when the land was first claimed.

A thousand years was beyond his understanding.

'Ember,' Arvid said. 'Ember is caught up in this – *battle*?'

Martine had her hand up under her breasts, as though trying to still her heart. Elva knew that feeling. Her boys were out there, too, as well as her little sister. Even though they hadn't grown up together, Ember was family, dear and beloved. So young, just like Ash and Cedar. Against Powers, what chance did they have?

The gods spoke to her gently, *Together, they may prevail. Ice has no defence against love.* She repeated the words as they came into her mind, the voices of the gods speaking through her, turning her own voice dark and deep, rasping. It was always a surprise to her, that sound. A stranger's voice.

Mam and Arvid looked up with hope blazing. With the gods in her head, Elva could see them so clearly; they were unhappy, driven, half-crazed with worry and something else that she didn't fully recognise.

Ice comes, the gods said through her. Arvid flinched, standing up as though to meet the threat head-on; but Mam sat down and clenched her hands in her lap, as though Seeing too much.

We must work together, you and I and the other humans, Elva said to the gods.

They hesitated. She shared with them everything that Sealmother had taught her, and felt them stream away from her to consider it. They would make their decision in their own time, as they always did, but she had to be ready – they all had to be ready – to work with them when they came back. If they came back. No use worrying about that.

'There is a lot we need to do,' Elva said briskly. 'If we're going to hold off this Ice.'

THE LAST DOMAIN

Poppy's head came up like a sheepdog's hearing its master's whistle.

That was what she felt like. She'd heard – something. Her mother's voice, it had seemed. She looked again at the black rock altar. The dawn ritual was almost over. Despite the clawing cold, almost all of the inhabitants of this little town had come out to greet the gods. When danger threatens, her mother had said many times, people start praying.

If she was going to hear her mother's voice anywhere, it would be here, Poppy thought.

It had sounded like her mother had said: 'There is a lot we need to do, if we're going to hold off this Ice.'

The ritual finished and the people began to drift away, many looking up at the clear sky with worried faces. Poppy went closer to the altar, reached out to touch it.

'Gods of field and stream, hear your daughter,' she said softly. Bringing out her belt knife, she cut off a lock of her hair and laid it down on the altar. 'Gods of fire and storm, of earth and stone, of sky and wind, hear your daughter. Give me my mother's wisdom; give me my mother's guidance.'

A breeze stirred, making her eyes water. When she blinked the tears away, the hair had gone. The gods had accepted her offering. She waited, and gradually found herself becoming afraid. Afraid of the cold. Shivering, shuddering with cold, although she could see from Larch's manner that it was not truly any colder than before. Then her mother spoke into her mind, clear and achingly familiar.

We must bind ourselves into one, she said. *Like this.*

A cascade of images flooded Poppy's mind; a song, a movement, a sense of many needs plaited, woven into one strong strand – no, a fence, a wall, a woven barrier as solid as steel. And her mother in the middle, the weaver.

'When?' she whispered, and the gods said to her: *We will tell you. Go, prepare the others. Ice comes.*

Salt was the nearest big town, and they had the mines – safety for everyone while the battle was being fought. She just had to convince everyone to go there.

Hah! No one would listen to her, a farmer's daughter. They wouldn't even listen to Larch. But Poppy had lived all her life with gods and prophets and seers, and she knew what she needed. Stonecasters.

STARKLING

Cedar had signalled to Ash that he would take the first shift. It was a breach of protocol, no doubt, to set guards within a warlord's residence, if you could describe a tree village that way, but Ash was taking no chances. He would take second shift, and let Curlew and Tern have an uninterrupted rest. Tern needed it, he thought. The young one had been quiet ever since he had come down out of the trees – ashamed of his fear, no doubt, and worried about Curlew to boot. He'd be better for a good night's sleep. He should find a time tomorrow to talk to Tern, reassure him that everyone met something they couldn't handle, sooner or later. There was no shame in reaching your limit.

At midnight, Ash slid out of his sleeping pocket, feeling his way to the stair. The moon had set and the starlight came only faintly through the leaves. Ember was a slightly darker shape, breathing evenly. Dancing with butterflies! he thought. I would have liked to have seen that.

Quiet voices drifted up as he negotiated the staircase. Cedar and someone else. Elgir?

They were sitting to one side of the tree, on an old log. Curlew and Tern were asleep, Curlew buttressed on either side by the dogs. Holdfast raised her head as he went by and he signalled her to stay where she was.

The two men looked up as he walked towards them and nodded with almost identical motions. Something worried him about that. Were they so alike, these two? He waved them to go on talking, and sat down at Cedar's feet, his back against the cool wood. He'd clearly come into the middle of a conversation.

'Are all your people shapechangers, my lord?' Cedar asked.

'Many,' Elgir said readily.

A dark shape moved in the shade of the trees and Ash sprang to his feet, but Elgir said, 'It's all right.' The shape came forward – the huge bull elk from the day before. Elgir rose and flung an arm over its shoulder. 'This is my brother, Durst,' he added, as if it were the most natural thing in the world. 'He's one of those who only change once, and then stay that way. He prefers it.'

The elk lowered its head until it could butt Elgir in the shoulder affectionately. Ash kept silent. These were matters beyond him. He wished his mother were there. She was the one who understood strangeness. She and Grammer Martine.

'Greetings, Durst,' Cedar said. 'What about you, my lord? Do you change?'

Elgir hesitated. 'I change rarely ... My duties do not permit me more.'

There was definite regret in his voice.

'But why are there so many here, when they are the stuff of legend in the rest of the Domains?' Cedar asked.

'That story goes back a long way. You may have noticed, there are no altars here.'

Ash had noticed. His father had brought them up to honour

the local gods. At home, the family went to the altar every dawn for the morning prayers. Except his mother, Elva. He had always thought it odd that the gods' own prophet would care so little about the forms of worship, but Elva just shrugged. 'If they want me to know something, they'll tell me,' she'd say. 'And this way breakfast is ready when you get back.'

He'd missed the morning ritual on this trip, and he'd looked for an altar as they came through Elgir's lands, but had seen none.

'Yes,' Cedar said, 'I'd wondered about that.'

'The black rocks fell from the sky a long time ago, long before Acton's people came over the mountains. The largest was at Obsidian Lake, in your domain.'

Obsidian Lake was in the Last Domain, not in the Western Mountains where they were from, but better to let Elgir believe that he and Cedar were Arvid's men. Less complicated that way.

'Other rocks fell south, but none here. I don't know why. Just chance, perhaps. The black rocks ...' Elgir hesitated. 'It is hard to say whether the rocks gave the local gods power, or whether they simply attracted the gods and, coming together, they found they had more power than when they acted separately. In any case, the rocks changed things. Humans turned away from the Powers, who were so vast, so far removed from them, to worship the local gods, who knew their lands.'

'Gods of field and stream ...' Cedar murmured. It was the beginning of the morning prayer.

'Exactly,' Elgir said.

A slight breeze lifted Ash's hair, but didn't seem to rustle the leaves around them. An owl hooted; small animals scurried in the undergrowth. A normal night, and Elgir was welcoming, yet he felt ill at ease here. He had liked it better on the high platforms of the cedars. At least there he could see the mountains.

He shifted so he could see beyond the treetops. The stars were bright and high, with no clouds to mar them. His own local gods seemed very far away.

'But what does that have to do with shapechangers?'

'The local gods are uncomfortable with beings which are two things at once. Maintaining the divide between life and death is their main task, and I think all divisions are – sacred is the wrong word. Reassuring to them, maybe? They suppress that kind of power around them. So wherever there is an altar, shapechangers do not change. They yearn. They dream. But they never discover their true kind.'

Elgir sat back down again and his brother began to graze.

'This is the only settled place in the Domains where the world is as it was before the black rocks fell, and shapechangers can transform. And so it is my task, the task of the warlords of this domain, to find them and bring them here. It is my main duty ... I scry for the young ones and talk to them in their dreams. Come north, I say. Come to where you will be happy. My predecessor four generations ago began it. He was a bear, they say.' He seemed to think it was all very normal. Ash felt as if he were in a dream – the night, the distant stars, the man with his brother elk ...

'It comes down in the blood,' Elgir continued. 'So most children born here now have some of the ability. Some are mostly human, others mostly not. All have a place.'

Cedar was fascinated, Ash could see in his face.

'Do your children have the – ability?' Cedar asked.

'I have none, yet. There was a prophecy that I should choose an heir, rather than beget one. I have looked a long time. I was beginning to think he would never come and I should have to go out into the world to find him.'

He looked straight at Cedar. The hairs on Ash's neck rose in alarm. Cedar? No, no, not Cedar!

'Me?' Cedar said. He was astonished – and flattered. Ash got up and stood in front of Elgir, planting his feet firmly.

'You're inviting my *brother* to be your heir?' he demanded.

'He has the power,' Elgir said. 'I could teach him the enchantments which keep this place safe.'

Cedar's eyes lit up at the thought of learning spells. 'I'm not a shapechanger,' he said slowly.

'Are you not?' Elgir asked, smiling. 'That power is in you, too, in all of your blood, I suspect.' He flicked a glance at Ash, then focused back on Cedar. 'Your mother gave you more than Sight, son.'

'He's no son of yours,' Ash stated.

Cedar ignored him. 'What would I be?' he asked. 'What animal?'

Elgir smiled. 'I cannot know that until you change. But you know in your heart which form calls to you.'

Cedar looked down at the ground, flushing. Oh gods! Ash was dismayed. Don't do it, brer. Deny him. But he didn't say it out loud. Cedar's choice.

Cedar looked at him and then up at the tree above, and his own expression changed, the excitement dying out, replaced by resignation.

'I must go with Ember,' he said. 'She needs me.'

Ash felt relief sweep through him, followed by a kind of sadness. That was a sacrifice Cedar was making.

'Yes, of course!' Elgir said. 'But afterwards ... your home is here, and your inheritance, if you wish to claim it.'

Cedar looked into his eyes. They *were* alike, Ash could see. Creatures of ideas and thought. Cedar could be the son of Elgir's heart and mind, if not of his body. A warlord's son.

'Why don't you have children?' Ash demanded suddenly. 'Is there a curse or something else Cedar should know?'

Elgir paused, still looking at Cedar. 'Yes. Yes, it is true. No lord of this domain has ever had children of his body. Each one must find his successor, and train him, knowing that there will be no children.'

'And when were you going to tell him that? When it was too late?'

Elgir looked at the ground. 'It won't matter to Cedar,' he said gently, as if he broke bad news. 'For people like us, it never matters. We are seduced by the enchantments so deeply that nothing else compares.'

Cedar was nodding, slowly. Ash took his arm. 'Be careful,' he said. 'He is asking you to give up everything you know, every-*one* you know, as well as the possibility of a family. Of – of love.' They were brothers, and never spoke much about feelings, but he had to make the case as persuasively as he could. 'Don't you want a family of your own? To live with people you care about?'

Cedar's eyes held tears, but they were calm.

'Not the way you do,' he said. 'Now I know I can learn – all this—' His arm made a wide gesture, taking in the tree towers, the water meadows with their grazing animals, the high ridge crowned with trees. 'How can I turn my back on it?'

Elgir nodded. 'You will come back, and I will welcome you,' he said simply. Cedar put out his hand and they clasped fore-arms, a gesture of equals.

'Dragon's fart!' Ash said. He turned away so he wouldn't hit Elgir and stared up at the treeroom where Ember slept. Would she be happy about this, or sad? Pleased that her cousin would have the same rank? That the two domains would be tied closer together? That was the way Ember thought, he'd come to realise. As rulers did, or should. He called her 'princess' half in affection and half teasingly, but it was true. Could Cedar become a – a *prince*? And what else would he become? Ash remembered the naked half-men of the Deep and his own distaste. He didn't feel like that about Durst. True shapechanging was ... purer, somehow. Not a rejection of humanity, but an expansion of who the person was. Or it could be, if they didn't choose to stay an animal, as Durst had.

'Whatever you turn into,' he said to Cedar, his voice rough with tears held back, 'promise me you'll become human again.'

Cedar put an arm around his shoulders and squeezed. 'I promise,' he said. The elk called Durst snorted and coughed, and Elgir laughed in response.

'Durst says don't worry, Cedar's like me, too stupid to understand that animal life is best.'

That was cold comfort to Ash, but it was comfort of a sort.

'Sleep,' he said to Cedar. 'It's my watch.'

His younger brother might be a warlord's heir, but he still obeyed orders. Cedar said goodnight to Elgir and slid into his sleeping pocket. Ash looked at Elgir, who was standing next to Durst.

'If you don't look after him ...' he said.

'I swear to you and your family,' Elgir said, formal and solemn, 'I will care for him as my own son. As my right arm.'

There didn't seem to be anything left to say. He had lost his brother.

THE FOOTHILLS OF
THE EYE TEETH MOUNTAINS

The morning was full of fog. Ember looked out of her tree tower into a shifting mass of white. Every leaf was outlined with beads of water, and each step she took sent a shower down below. Her hair crinkled up and was hard to plait, as it always was in the damp. She cursed it under her breath and looked up to find Ash laughing at her from the entrance to the stairway, his eyes bright and his brown hair tousled.

Something clenched under her heart. So might a young husband laugh at his new wife. Osfrid ... Osfrid would never laugh at her like that. A whisper in her mind said that Osfrid would never have laughed like that anyway; he had been a serious young man, far more serious than Ash. And although he loved her – *had* loved her – and had desired her, he had never looked at her with such simple affection.

Well, they had not known each other very well, after all. If they had had time together ...

'What's the matter, lass?' Ash said. He came up and began to roll his sleeping pocket ready for travel.

'Just thinking about Osfrid,' she said, tying a blue ribbon tightly onto the end of her plait. She put the brush away and began to roll her own pocket.

Ash was silent for a moment, and then asked, not looking at her, 'Was it a warlord's marriage, with him, or a real one?'

She paused. 'I wanted to marry him. I was so happy ...' She wanted to say that she had loved him, but it was as though Fire had seared that feeling out of her, leaving only pain and fear behind. The day when Osfrid had asked for her hand, eyes warm and hands gentle, seemed a long long time ago. 'My father let me choose,' she concluded.

'From the warlords' sons,' Ash said. She felt a flicker of irritation. What did he know of politics?

'I would have chosen Osfrid anyway,' she said, but even as she said it, she wondered if it were true. She had wanted everything that Osfrid was and had – the life as warlord's lady, the move to the south, the promise of children and comfort, as well as Osfrid himself, handsome and straight and intelligent. If Osfrid had been a farmer's son like Ash, would she have chosen him?

She was ashamed to realise that she didn't know.

Ash didn't comment further. They packed in silence then went up the stairs to the dining room. Sure enough, there was breakfast waiting for them: porridge with honey and berries, and some food to take with them, wrapped in neat packets of leaves. She could smell the dried apple and apricots through the leaves. There were enough packets for all of them.

Ash stowed them away after they had eaten, and they went down and used the privies, having to search for them through the mist, then looked for the others.

They were in the glade behind the elms, saddling up, the fog swirling around their feet and curling over the horses' hooves.

At least, Tern and Cedar were. Curlew was holding the horses' reins slackly, not noticing anything. Ember hugged him and he looked at her with a spark of recognition. Perhaps away from here he would be better.

'Have you seen Elgir this morning?' she asked Cedar.

'I am here,' the deep voice came, from above. She looked up. Elgir was leaning from a treeroom. He grinned and leaped down, landing lightly on all fours. He had never looked more like an animal. 'I will guide you out,' he said. 'There is a shorter way than the way you came.'

He looked at the horses. 'It would be better,' he said, 'if you did not ride until after you left our borders.'

'Why?' Tern demanded.

'My people do not like animals being kept as slaves,' Elgir said seriously. 'Best not to anger them.'

Ember shivered. There was something about that tone ...

They walked on in silence, with Elgir and Cedar striding together at the front, the dogs trotting one on each side.

'Elgir wants Cedar to be his heir,' Ash said.

It didn't come as a surprise to Ember somehow. No doubt that had been the reason Elgir had needed to bring them here, the reason he hadn't known at first. Well, it was good for Cedar, she supposed. And good for her own domain, to have the nearest warlord be kin. Not that Ash would see it like that.

'At least I won't have to tell my parents,' he said gloomily.

She laughed a little, softly. 'I know. It's the only advantage to having a mother with Sight – you don't have to break bad news! Of course, you can't keep a secret either.'

He sighed. 'I suppose inheriting a domain is a good thing,' he said.

'I don't think Cedar is thinking of that,' Ember said. 'He just wants to learn. And ... Elgir is a good man, I think.'

'He's not just a man, though, is he? What will Cedar become?' There was a real pain in his voice, real loss. She wondered what it would be like to have a sister, to lose that sister.

'That's his choice, lad,' she said gently, and took his hand. He squeezed hers and continued to hold it firmly, as though he found it comforting. She tried to ignore the warmth that his touch started in her. The fog seemed to mute it a little, but still it was disconcerting how a simple contact could make her breath fast, her nipples tight. She hated it; hated the sense of being controlled by someone else, of having her affection for Ash twisted into something else.

Through the fog she could hear people working, laughing, talking in that bird-like language. As swirls of mist lifted and moved, they caught glimpses – the woman with blue hair smiled at her as she knelt, weeding turnips.

Swathed in fog, Elgir's people were braver, perhaps. She wished they had time to stay and get to know them.

Elgir led them south and west, up the high ridge where the cedars swayed far above them. They climbed out of the fog halfway up, and turned to look back on the cream-filled bowl. Cedar sighed.

'You'll be back, lad,' Elgir said. They went through the trees to the other side of the ridge, and there were the mountains. The Eye Teeth, raising their sharp spires to a blue spring sky. Snow on their summits, harsh grey stone bases covered by a thin, precarious film of green. Beautiful. Dangerous.

'The border of my domain is two ridges over, where the plateau starts,' Elgir said. 'Beyond that, it is the Ice King's land, and you must beware.' He hesitated. 'There were spells laid on that area long ago, to protect us from the Ice King. Even I do not know them all. If you have trouble, send a message and I will come.'

Ash came forward and confronted him.

'What about the wolves?' he said.

'Last night I heard a story about a lad who sang the moon down with my pack,' Elgir replied. 'Do you think they will harm *him*?'

'That was your pack?' Ember demanded. 'Your wolves?'

'Some of them, on the edges of the Forest,' Elgir said, half-smiling, half-wistful. He seemed to wish he had sung the moon down himself. 'The one who sang to you was not mine. But mine will know you are pack, and protect you as they would each other.' He hesitated, looking at the dogs. Holdfast and Grip were standing on either side of him, their tails waving gently. 'These wish to stay,' he said, 'and they are welcome.'

'Holdfast is my dog,' Ash said. 'Grip can wait here for Cedar to come back if he wants, but Holdfast comes with me.' He squatted in front of the elkhound and rubbed her ears. 'Don't you, girl?'

She rubbed against him with affection, but then she moved back and stood next to Elgir. Ash's face hardened and he looked up at Cedar.

'They'll be happy here,' Cedar said, but his face was troubled.

'She wasn't happy with me?'

Elgir interrupted. 'She says you won't need her, any more.'

Exasperated, Ember exclaimed, 'So now the dog is a seer? How does *that* work?'

Elgir said nothing. Holdfast whined and gave a single bark, staring up at Ash as he rose to his feet.

Cedar put his hand out to Grip and the dog came to him and stood for a pat. Cedar's eyes were full of Sight. 'She is right, however she knows. Ash will have no more use for her.'

'That's reassuring!' Ash said. 'Because I'll be dead?'

Ember felt her gut clench at the thought, but Cedar shook his head.

'I don't *think* so …' he said slowly.

'Go well,' Elgir said formally, putting an end to a discussion, Ember thought, which could have gone on all day. Who knew what a dog could know, here in Starkling? Perhaps Holdfast was a dog seer – or perhaps she had just sensed that Ash, no matter what happened, was not the same as he had been, and would probably not return to the life he had left behind.

Elgir clasped forearms with Cedar and offered the same gesture to Ash, who hesitated. Elgir misunderstood – Ember knew that the movement was not natural to a bowyer. It was an officer's gesture.

'We will be family, lad,' Elgir said. 'As much family as Martine and Arvid are to you.'

Ember laughed. 'Martine changed his clouts when he was a baby,' she said. 'I doubt you'll ever be quite as close!'

'Better not be,' Ash growled, but he was smiling, and he took Elgir's forearm firmly.

Elgir bowed to her and she bowed in return.

'Travel well, my lady,' he said, as formal as any warlord.

'Stay well, my lord,' she said.

He turned and strode back down the ridge without another word, and only a nod to Curlew and Tern. Ember felt curiously vulnerable without him.

'Let's go, princess,' Ash said.

The dogs watched them go, waving their tails, and then trotted down the trail after Elgir. Ash's face was sombre; he would miss Holdfast a great deal, Ember thought, and felt savage towards Elgir. Even if he hadn't bespelled the dogs, it was his influence which had led to their decision. And she thought how insane it was, to accept that two hunting dogs could not only *make* a decision, but had the right to do so. Starkling was a place which turned your assumptions upside down.

The sun gradually warmed Ember as they left the shadow of the cedars. Ash turned and shaded his eyes to gaze back up to the high platforms, but he turned away almost immediately.

'Looking for your friend?' Cedar said wickedly. 'Blow her a kiss.'

Ember felt as if she had been punched in the stomach. Grus was a woman? You have no right to care, she told herself fiercely. You have no rights over him at all. But her guts were clenched and she had to stop herself staring at Ash.

He ignored Cedar and walked on, not looking back. She drew breath once and then again. She knew nothing about this Grus, who might be eighty and hare-lipped, for all she knew. She *would not* ask. The warlord's fort taught dignity and restraint. She knew how to control herself, and she would, even if her chest was tight with the desire to blurt out question after question. She would *not* let Fire degrade her and Ash, both, with ridiculous false jealousy. Not now. Not ever.

'It's pretty country,' she managed to say. 'But harsh.'

Ash nodded. 'It breeds a hard people, too.'

The Ice King's men ... raiders and looters and stealers of women. Her father was gone almost every summer to lead the defence against them. Further north than this, of course, where the Last Domain curved around the Northern Mountains Domain to reach the mountains. That was where Tern came from, one of the villages that had been attacked. He'd followed her father home to take service, wanting to learn better how to protect himself and his family. A big ambition for a young lad.

He was quiet today, taking care of Curlew like a son. She smiled back at him and he bobbed his head to her, not quite meeting her eyes. She would talk to him later and make sure he was coping with all this oddity.

Two ridges took most of the morning – the going was steep

and rough, and they wouldn't have been able to ride the horses, anyway. Four times they had to stop to get loose stones from their hooves, and Curlew's Blackie went lame for half the morning.

They toiled to the top of the second ridge just before noon, and found the ghost guards waiting for them, spears crossed.

'I greet you, men of Northern Mountains Domain,' Ember said to the ghost warriors, as she had said before. She was every inch a warlord's daughter, Ash thought, with a mixture of pride and gloom.

They turned and bowed to her, swinging the spears wide like an opening gate, but instead of vanishing, fog came roiling up out of them, as though the ghosts had grown vast and formless. The fog engulfed them, a white soup that blinded Ash instantly.

The horses shied wildly and for a few moments Ash had no attention to give to anything else.

'Don't blame them,' Cedar said breathlessly. 'It spooks me.'

Ash agreed. The fog was much worse than it had been this morning, as deep as a snow blizzard, chilling their faces and curling into their lungs, making breathing harder. He could only just see his own feet. Sound from the outside was dampened but their own breaths and the horses' seemed harsh and loud.

'What's happening, lady?' Tern asked. He was trying to sound brave, but his voice squeaked a little.

Ash moved around his bay and clasped Ember's hand, trying to comfort. He felt a twitch in his belly at the contact, but she wasn't even looking at him.

'Keep together,' he ordered. 'I've got some rope in my pack. We'll tie the horses together and keep hold of them as we move. Keep hold of someone at all times.'

Ash extricated the rope from his pack and moved from horse

to horse, tying it to the saddle ring which all Last Domain horses had, for linking together in a blizzard. Above the ring was a strap for the human to hold onto, and as their horses were tied each of them dutifully took hold of the strap and waited for the order to move off. The familiar ritual of being tied quietened the horses, allowed them to fall back into a routine.

Ash tied Ember's horse just behind his and took her hand again to guide it to the strap. It brought him very close to her, and he cursed the desire that struck through him. He looked down to the ground so she wouldn't notice anything, but looking up again he saw that her green eyes were huge with worry.

'Don't worry, little one,' he said gently, touching her cheek, playing the big brother. 'We'll get out of this.'

Startled, she looked up into his eyes. Her mouth trembled and he wanted to kiss her, to shelter her and make sure nothing would ever scare her again. He forced himself to look away.

'Should we send to Elgir?' she asked.

'Let's just see what's ahead first,' he answered, his eyes trying to pierce the fog.

'Because we'd look stupid asking him for help if it's just a narrow belt of mist?' she asked wryly. 'Of course we can't have that.'

He laughed, and tousled her hair, restored to normality.

'That's my girl,' he said.

He followed his own rope to Thatch and then went beyond, taking the poler's position. Although there were no snow drifts now, he still pulled the jointed pole out of his pack and screwed it together. Essential for winter travel, they had brought one each because the Eye Teeth kept their snows year round, and who knew if they would need to cross drifts?

With a poler out front, a train of horses could travel safely, the poler checking for deep drifts or sudden drops in the trail.

Ash did so now, using the long pole to search out the flattest, safest route he could.

Travelling in blizzards was ear-splitting. The wind always howled away any chance of hearing. Fog was eerily quiet. It gave the familiar process of walking, waiting for the poler and walking again, a dream-like quality. Ash let himself fall into the rhythm of pole, step, pole, step.

Gradually, he became aware of some other noise apart from the horses' hoof-falls and breathing. Something other than the tapping of the pole. He slowed his progress.

An odd sound. A combination of sounds, perhaps. Scratching, slapping, slithering ... above them, behind them, no, in front – a harsh shriek pierced him, and then another. High, sharp, it hurt his ears, and yet it was curiously exciting. One, and then another, sometimes with a second lower shriek following. Thatch reared, whinnying with pain as his more sensitive ears were attacked. Ash hung onto the strap, pulling him down, calming him, until he stood trembling. By the pull and slack of the ropes, the others were doing the same, but he couldn't hear them. The world was full of the shrieks. A hundred times louder, his ears were needled, his eyes were burning. Looking back, he saw that Ember had wrapped one hand around her head and buried her face in Merry's side, but at least she hadn't let go of the saddle strap.

Thatch was scenting the air, snuffing great gulps of it; and then, astonishingly, he calmed down, neighed a couple of times as though reassuring the other horses, and stood, still quivering a little, but not ready to bolt.

While his attention had been claimed by Thatch, Ash had been able to ignore the sounds, ignore his own heart leaping when they came. Now they hit him again, but Thatch's calmness was reassuring. He looked around, ahead.

The fog was thinning a little. As it did, the shrieks stopped.

There was only the slight, slight breeze and their own breathing. Ash counted two breaths, three, four, watching intently as the mist lightened.

Shapes beyond the mist. Shadows that changed as he watched: small and thin and then huge, stretching up and widening impossibly. The other sounds had returned, too, the scratching and dull tapping.

'We should go forward,' Ash said. He walked a pace forward, then another, and Ember and the rest were pulled willy-nilly after him. The shapes spun and bowed, stretched and shrank like poppy-juice visions.

Ash took another step towards the closest one and it shrieked: high, inhuman, piercing. He knew that shape.

'It's a bird!' he exclaimed.

Ember followed the rope to stand by Ash's side, and peered ahead.

Birds, he thought. Yes. Cranes, or something like them. Tall and thin, when they stretched out and spread their wings they were suddenly huge.

The one in front of them was still obscured by the mist so that it seemed like a grey, screaming ghost. It reared up and spread its wings, still shrieking, and the ones next to it did the same.

Grey-winged, black-necked, each had a red patch of feathers on their heads, a jewel shining in the cool light. They were so big! And their beaks were long and sharp, their wings powerful. The fog lightened a little more. Hundreds of them, reaching back as far as he could see. And each of them, every one of them, was staring with a red eye straight at him.

'Are you sure they're birds?' Ember asked. 'Not spirits in disguise?'

The one in front tilted her head to the side and gazed at him. After all that talk about shapechanging back in Starkling, it was easy to recognise her. Grus, her grey gown transformed to feathers, her hair to a topknot of red.

She cawed at him, and then turned towards the other cranes as they began to dance. Bobbing their heads, almost pecking the ground, they paced across the path, left to right, right to left, circling the group until they were surrounded. No longer shrieking, they gave out booming notes which made the horses shift uncomfortably. Thatch was unhappy, moving from hoof to hoof, ears back.

Ash felt wary, but not afraid. He had never heard of cranes attacking humans, but he had never heard of cranes surrounding them, either. They were in a strange land, and anything might happen. And yet ... he didn't believe Grus would hurt him.

'Friends, I think,' he said to Ember.

He put Thatch's leading rein and the pole into her hands and stepped forwards, his hands spread wide. Better to greet them all, not just Grus.

'I greet you, noble cranes,' he said.

The birds cocked their heads so they could see him, some turning their heads right around on the long long necks, but they kept pacing, kept dancing. Grus paced towards Ash, then backed away, like a partner in a step-dance, and he laughed.

'Hello, Grus,' he said. He couldn't help but laugh – what else could you do, when a bird asked you to dance?

Still chuckling, he bowed to Grus and began to dance, too, aware of Ember watching open-mouthed behind him.

Grus clucked and boomed to Ash and he laughed again and hit his chest to make a booming sound in response. They paced side by side, towards one another, back again, and other birds crossed and joined them, moving gradually into a great circle, which seemed to push the fog back with it as it widened.

He knew what to do. From some place, either inside him or

sent from Grus, the knowledge of the steps and their meaning came to him.

Grus's movements, towards him, away from him, back again. She was courting him.

Should he respond?

The bones of his ribs and arms felt light at the thought. Ember was at the corner of his vision, but she was a warlord's daughter, and not for him. This was shapechanging land, and here, perhaps, maybe, he could actually fly ...

Ash tucked his hands under his arms and then spread them out in unison with the cranes, picking his feet up in mimicry, feeling emptied out, full of air, as simple as thistledown.

They paced and stamped together, and he could feel humanity begin to drop away from him, as a light breeze lets dust it has collected fall. Grus encouraged him with small shrieks and calls, and he saw the red topknot make the dips and circles which it should in the first stage of a mating dance. How he knew that, he did not question. He was caught up in the rhythm, the noise booming through him, the tuneful shrieking and the step, slide, pace, step of the dance.

The cranes were breaking up the circle. One by one they flapped their great wings, ran a few steps and took off, soaring higher. They took the mist with them. It shredded against their great beating pinions and melted away into a clear sky as they climbed.

Watching their flight was filling him with yearning, desire, the need to soar, to be free, to shake off the bonds of the earth. He stretched out his arms, fingers splayed as their flight feathers were splayed into arcs of the palest grey and black. He could feel the change starting, the feathers beginning to break his skin. It hurt, each feather a separate pain, the hollowing-out of his bones hurting even more.

But just a few more minutes of pain and he would be able to fly. His neck was lengthening, he could turn it so far ...

He turned his head, testing it, and Ember was there, gazing at him with despair.

His eyes could see more than they used to: he saw the strange halo of fire that surrounded her, saw the leash the Power had put on her, binding her tight. It made him angry, as anything bound always made him angry.

Their gaze met. His sight was so good that he could make out his own eye reflected in hers: the eye of a bird, orange around black, hard and inhuman. She didn't have the right to call him back. She had no rights over him at all. If he wanted Grus and flight, he had the right to choose. He flexed his fingers, feeling the feathers slide further down.

Tears spilled over onto her cheeks. She reached out her hand to him, and then snatched it back, as though she knew she had no right. But her face, her face was full of pain.

Ash let his arms drop. Beside him, Grus, her tuft high, shrieked to him: *Come*, she said quite clearly. *Fly!*

'No,' he said to her, sorrowing, formal as at a funeral. 'No, I cannot come.'

You said you would give anything to fly! she cawed.

'Not quite anything,' he said. He bowed, his foot lifting as the cranes' did when they danced. Grus bowed back and, last of them all, lifted into the air, circling with the others above their heads as they climbed in a long leisurely spiral. Leaving him alone, heavy, full of earth, as dull and plodding as a toad.

Ash watched, standing quite still, until they were so high that there was nothing left to see but a scatter of dots against the sky. Then he turned to Ember and simply stood while she dropped the rope and pole and walked to him, put her arms around him and laid her head on his chest. His arms came around her slowly. She gave a long sobbing sigh and his arms tightened, his head coming to rest on hers.

He could still hear the beating of their wings across the sky, and his heart was speared by regret.

'I'll never get the chance again,' he whispered.

'But they chose you,' she said. She tilted her head back and stared at him seriously. 'They chose you.'

'Yes.' He was half-smiling, half-crying, sure at least that all his lifelong yearning had been for something real, not just a boy's silly dream. That was worth a great deal.

They turned to find Cedar staring at them – no, at him – with a mixture of awe and compassion, as he might gaze at a stranger. It was a hard look to bear from a brother. Ash straightened and moved away from Ember immediately, regaining his calm.

'Come on,' he said roughly. 'Whatever was guarding this passage is letting us pass. Let's go before it changes its mind.'

TIMBERTOP, THE LAST DOMAIN

There was only one stonecaster near Timbertop, and she was a reclusive older woman called Jelica, who lived in an isolated cabin and supported herself by trapping.

'She's an odd one,' the Village Voice had told them, but Poppy took no notice of that. Her family were described that way, too.

'Not enough people around here to live on stonecasting alone, I imagine,' she said to Larch as they rode along the trail to Jelica's house. The spring sun was bright but not warm, and it filtered through the big pine trees lining the path and slid over Starling's hide, showing the warm red of his coat and how badly he needed a proper grooming. Poppy had brought only a small curry comb and a hoof pick with her, thinking that she'd be able to borrow what she needed, but they weren't used to horses, out here on the edge of things. Horses needed too much care and feeding for too little return, where there was no ploughing done and a one-man sled could take a whole year's worth of trade goods.

The woods smelt of pine and water, of catchfly blossom and

violets. Larch's golden hair shone in the sunlight. Despite their
serious purpose, Poppy felt a small bloom of happiness.

As they rounded a curve of track and saw the small grey
cabin, an arrow thwanged into the tree trunk nearest to Larch.
Instantly, Larch grabbed her bridle, rounded the horses and
moved back along the trail, shouting, 'Warlord's messengers!
Hold!'

Larch kicked the horses into a canter and didn't stop until
they were well out of arrow range, then halted, cursing under
her breath.

'Pox-ridden backwood inbreds!' she said. Larch had never
sounded so much like a soldier. But she *was* a soldier. She dismounted, strung her bow and nocked an arrow, loosened her
sword in its scabbard, and her dagger in its boot sheath. Then
she looked sternly at Poppy. 'You stay here until I say it's safe.'

Her head picked up the sun and she looked like a shield
maiden in one of the old, old songs. Poppy felt both adoration
and panic rise in her, and pushed them down, hard. This was no
place for either. She obediently took the reins of both horses, her
hand shaking. Larch nodded, face softening for a brief moment
before she turned and slid back into the trees, making her way
to the cabin silently and with great skill.

Her heart was pounding, her breath shorter now she was still
than when they were fleeing. Because Larch was in danger? She
started to count silently, to regain calm, to keep from calling out
after Larch, and maybe putting her in more danger.

After two hundred and thirty-seven, Larch called her, sounding a little breathless, and she clicked her tongue to the horses,
moving back up the trail at a walk. She had to force herself to
breathe, her heart still pumping hard. When she reached the
curve where the arrow had come, she could see the cabin again,
and Larch, standing in front of it with an older woman, dressed

in the trews and leathers of a trapper. Larch's sword was at the woman's throat. Although she was flooded with relief, Poppy bit her lip. Surely that wasn't necessary?

But the woman – it must be Jelica – glared at her with real hatred as she rode up and dismounted. She had a knife of her own, but it was reversed, pointing at her own heart. Larch looked confused, as if she didn't know what to do with a prisoner who threatened to kill herself.

'Here's something new,' Jelica sneered. 'A warlord's whore sent as messenger.'

Some old and deep injustice there, which they had no time to investigate.

'The gods have sent me,' Poppy said simply.

Jelica slowly put down her knife and pushed a strand of her grey hair aside with the back of her wrist, ignoring Larch completely. Larch sheathed her sword with an air of relief.

'Tell me,' Jelica said.

The message from her mother, from the gods, was succinct, but the implications were large. Jelica thought them through.

'What d'ye need me for?'

Poppy smiled ruefully. 'Because half of them think the same as you, that I'm the warlord's whore, or his by-blow, or at best his wife's granddaughter, and they won't listen to a girl still wet behind the ears. But you – they'll listen to a stonecaster.'

Jelica stared at the ground and scratched her head. She seemed disgruntled, or uncertain, or simply put out.

'Haven't been to town these long years,' she said. 'Do all for m'self, out here. Traders come out to get my trappings.'

'We'll be with you,' Poppy said gently. Jelica's eyes flashed.

'Doan't need no striplings for comfort,' she said. 'Stay here. I'll cast and then we'll know.'

She went inside. Larch moved uncertainly to follow her, but

Poppy shook her head. Jelica's bow was on the ground – what other weapons could she turn against them?

'If she'd really wanted to kill us, I think we'd be dead,' she said, her mouth quirking. Larch grinned.

'Aye,' she said. 'She had a chance with me, a minute ago, but she didn't take it.'

Jelica flung open the cabin door and came out.

'Come in, then,' she said.

'You Saw it?' Larch asked, as if she couldn't help it.

Jelica stared her full in the eyes. 'I Saw Cold and Ice and Death Herself flying on frozen wings.' She turned to glance sideways at Poppy. 'And I saw Fire, too, and a red-headed girl.'

'Ember,' Poppy breathed. 'She's all right?'

'She's heading for trouble,' Jelica said. 'But aren't we all?' She paused, fiddling with the strings of her pouch. 'He wanted her?'

Poppy thought back to the terrible moment when Osfrid had died.

'He wanted *something*,' she said, 'but I'm not sure it was her.'

Jelica relaxed a little, and pushed the pouch back more firmly, standing up straight.

'What will you tell them, at Timbertop?' Poppy asked.

'To get moving!' Jelica replied grimly. 'Bolt for a hole like badgers, and dig ourselfs in, that's what I'll tell them.'

'The salt mines—' Poppy began.

'Aye,' Jelica nodded. 'I Saw Salt, too, and Dark, and ...' she paused, her eyes worried. 'And the blank stone.'

'We'll avoid the worst if we can get them to the mines,' Larch said firmly.

'Five towns,' Poppy said. 'We have five towns to rally and get moving.'

'Tomorrow,' Jelica answered, frowning, casting an eye at the sunset sky. 'First thing tomorrow, girl.'

'We could get halfway back to Timbertop by dark,' Larch protested.

'Aye, and freeze in the night,' Jelica retorted, stamping back to the cabin. ''Sides, there's a thing I've a mind to do tonight.'

She stared at Poppy, and then at Larch, as if considering what she could say, then shrugged.

'There's an altar here, just a bit of a one out back,' she said quietly. All her belligerence had fallen away, and her surety, too. She looked much younger, despite her grey hair. 'I'm going to call Him.'

'Him?' Larch asked.

'Fire,' Poppy breathed, her skin turning cold. 'He'll kill us.'

'He'll answer to me first,' Jelica said. 'Woman and girl, I've lit the wildfire for Him, and He owes me truth.'

'Larch has no Traveller blood,' Poppy whispered. To take one of Acton's people to Fire was to invite destruction.

'Um ...' Larch hesitated. 'My great-great-grammer was a Traveller, they say. Is that enough?'

Poppy and Jelica looked at each other, and it seemed to Poppy that neither of them were certain.

'Let's hope it is,' Jelica said eventually. 'It works best with three.'

THE ICE KING'S COUNTRY

They made their way along the narrow path along the valley floor. Ash kept one eye up on the cliffs and craggy boulders that littered the hillside; it was prime country for ambush, but also prime hunting country.

Part of him sincerely wished that Ember wasn't so reluctant to call a campfire in the evening. Now they were out of the forest he'd love a hot meal. But he couldn't blame her, he supposed. The memory of Fire towering over her at the wedding feast haunted his dreams, too. He'd never liked Osfrid much – a bit too satisfied with himself – but to be erased from the world like that, in a breath, turned to ash and scattered on the wind ... he wouldn't wish that on the Ice King himself.

High above, an eagle circled. He sorted through the various mountain sounds, as familiar as his own hand. Wind. The horses' hoof-falls. Scratching to the left, as a small animal hid. A mountain thrush poured out his mating call from a scraggy juniper tree halfway up the slope.

Rocks skittered down and he looked up in time to see a mountain goat bound away. He had the arrow nocked when he saw that she was pregnant, and he lowered the bow, but kept it ready nocked. Goats were flock animals. Where there was one, there would be more soon, although they spooked easily and would be impossible to track over this stony ground.

'Let's go quietly,' he suggested, taking Thatch to the lead. 'Watch for goats,' he added.

Cedar nodded understandingly and took his own bow from his saddle. It wasn't good for the bows to ride with them strung, but in unknown country it was safest.

Ahead, the path twisted around a large boulder and turned sharply into the next valley. With luck, the goats would be there. Ash clicked his tongue to Thatch and he picked up his pace, drawing ahead of the others. If he could get a couple of shots off before the others caught up with him, they might eat well in a few days, once the meat had dried. He wound his reins around one wrist and brought his bow up.

'Quietly, now,' he whispered to Thatch. An old hand at hunting, the bay slowed and edged around the turn as Ash scanned the hillsides.

Below, on the path, voices rang out suddenly with words he didn't know. A group of soldiers – bearded, long-haired, in furs and leathers, were shouting and pointing at him, drawing swords, raising their own bows. He whipped Thatch around and headed back, yelling, 'Back! Back!' as he charged towards the others. The horses milled, confused.

'Ice King's men!' he shouted. Cedar already had his bow at the ready, and he let an arrow fly as the first man rounded the boulder. Ash left him to guard the rear and made straight for Ember, passing Curlew who sat in the saddle, looking confused.

'Fight, man!' he yelled at Curlew, who hesitatingly took his sword out. Tern was fumbling for his quiver.

Ember had turned Merry but she was resisting being taken

away from the other horses. Ash swept up behind her, Thatch
having to scramble up the slope to make it past her, his hooves
sliding on the loose rocks. Ash grabbed Merry's reins and
pushed both horses to the fastest pace he dared on the narrow,
winding track.

Ember's face was set with a mixture of fear and determination, but she made no stupid protests at being protected. She
was the key to saving her people, and she knew it. She was
braver than she realised, he thought, and his heart wrenched at
the idea of her falling into the Ice King's grasp.

He urged the horses to go faster. The noise of fighting was
unmistakable. The Ice King's men were yelling their war cry,
'Hárugur, Hárugur Konung!' He'd heard it before, when he had
fought beside his father and brothers and friends to defend their
domain. Someone always died.

If they could make it out of the valley, it might not be Ember.

Horses were gaining on them. He could hear the steps
resounding from the sides of the defile. He let Ember's bridle go
and fell back, turning in his saddle, bow coming to his hand and
arrow finding the string without thought.

'Get clear!' he yelled to Ember, and shot, and shot again, back
into the melee behind him. Although it went to his heart, he
aimed at the horses. A better target, and all it would take was
bringing one down to unhorse the other riders.

But they saw as he brought the bow to bear and were ahead
of him, shooting at Thatch. He loosed one arrow before he felt
the shock go through Thatch, felt the stumble, heard the scream.

'Don't stop!' he shouted, kicking his feet free of the stirrups,
jumping as Thatch slewed and dropped, blood spurting from his
neck.

At least Thatch's body would block the track and give her a
chance to get away.

He landed on his shoulder and his head jerked back and hit the ground.

Thatch screamed and Ash fell behind her. She had to stop. She had to stop. She couldn't stop. One man wasn't important. A quick look behind her showed ponies jumping Thatch's body. Ash was lying on the ground, insensible. Further back, Curlew and Tern were using their swords. Cedar didn't have one – even in the Last Domain, only warlord's men had swords. But he had his knife out and was slashing wildly. One of the hairy men launched himself from the saddle and dragged Cedar down.

Curlew fell at the same moment, a sword stroke from his opponent cutting into his neck. Ember let her hands drop and Merry's pace faltered. Then she set her teeth and kicked Merry to go faster. But the ponies behind her were mountain bred, and they outpaced her on the shifting stones. Merry was tired, too, after the endless days of travel, and was labouring already. A few paces more and the ponies were on either side, their riders whooping and shouting at her. Hopeless. She would not be pulled down, she decided, reining Merry in.

They overshot and spun around, the ponies seeming to turn on the spot, then surrounded her with much jostling and joking amongst themselves. She knew something of the Ice King's language. Only a few words, and the ones they were using were, perhaps fortunately, unfamiliar. She could feel her cheeks reddening as they looked her over.

Their leader was a surprisingly young man, not much older than she was, so young his blond beard was still sparse on his cheeks. He looked at her with surprise.

'Husmothir?' he said. It was a polite term, she remembered from her father's lessons. The title of an adult female. The man thought again, and said, pronouncing the word with care, 'Mistress?'

She hesitated. In their language, her proper title would be 'konungsdottir'. Should she reveal herself? Political consequences tumbled through her mind. They'd keep her for ransom, they'd use her to put pressure on her father, they'd eviscerate her and send her body parts back to her father as a message of war.

In any other year, despite the lascivious looks they were giving her, she would have concealed who she was. But she couldn't take the risk. They wouldn't let some chance-caught woman go. All the world knew that women captured by the Ice King were used as slaves. Thralls, they called them.

She had to give them reason to respect her. And to help her men. 'Never show fear,' her father had advised her. 'Negotiations are just battle concealed.'

'Konungsdottir,' she said in a tone of correction, tilting her head up and looking the leader right in the eyes.

The young man blinked.

He tapped himself on the chest.

'Konungsen,' he said, and grinned.

The Ice King's own son! A wave of fear went through her, but she mustn't show it.

'Elgirsdottir?' he asked. She shook her head.

'Arvidsdottir,' she replied. His face lit at that and he said something rapidly to the men with him. One of them, an older man with a ginger beard and deep-set grey eyes, pointed back to where Ash was struggling to his feet, watched by two hairy men. Tern was nursing an arm, and Cedar had the marks of a blow across his face. But Curlew lay still.

The older man said something, wagging his hand in the air to show doubt. Reading their bodies and expressions as her father had taught her, it seemed to Ember that they regretted having killed one of her men. Which was ridiculous, unless ... unless they wanted something from her father.

She was thinking like a merchant, while her liege man lay dead.

Her eyes filled with tears and she turned Merry back towards his body. Watching her carefully, the leader motioned to his men to let her go. Merry didn't like the smell of blood, or the smell coming from the men – a mixture of smoke and old fat. Ember patted her soothingly, but kept her firmly under control, guiding her past Ash with only a look. Ash's eyes looked dazed, but he met her gaze with reassurance, not dismay, and she was filled with thankfulness for his strength.

As she swung down, Tern knelt next to Curlew, tears streaming down his cheeks. She wondered if the Ice King's men would disdain this show of emotion, but the three men standing nearby seemed to watch with approval. For the first time, she realised that there was a long string of pack ponies behind them. Had they already raided, and were on their way home? Or were they greedily heading back into the Domains to raid again? Her mind swirled with possibilities, but then her attention narrowed to Curlew.

She knelt beside Tern. Curlew's eyes were closed. She took his hands and placed them by his side. They wouldn't be allowed to bury him, but the farewells should be said. She looked around for what they needed.

Ash, stumbling a little, staggered up the slope to a scrubby pine and grabbed some twigs. There was no rosemary, but there was, right next to Curlew's head, the blue of speedwell gleaming in the dust. Forget-me-not, they called it in the south. She plucked it and Ash handed her the pine twigs.

'Go before us to rebirth,' she said, her voice choked with

tears, remembering years and years when Curlew had gone before her on the road, in the woods, making sure the path was safe for her. She placed the speedwell in his mouth. 'May you not linger on the road, may you not linger in the fields. Time is, and time is gone.'

'Time is, and time is gone,' Ash and Tern echoed her, Cedar's voice chiming in a moment later.

'May you find friends; may you find those you loved,' she said. 'Time is, and time is gone.'

'Time is, and time is gone,' they said

'Under your tongue is forget-me-not. Remember us.'

She placed the pine sprigs between Curlew's fingers. 'In your hands is evergreen: may our memories of you be evergreen. Time is, and time is gone.'

'Time is, and time is gone.'

To her astonishment, she heard the voice of the princeling joining in. *How dare he!* she thought, furious, and rose to blast him with a glare. But he was staring at the ground, hands joined on the hilt of his sword, and all of his men were in the same position. A sign of respect.

She paused, astonished. Nothing in the stories of combat against the Ice King had prepared her for this. They were vicious enemies, who took no prisoners but the thrall women, who killed their wounded opponents as they lay on the battlefield and left them for the crows.

The princeling said something quickly to his men and they began to collect rocks from the hillsides and pile them over Curlew. She noticed that off their ponies, they were still shorter than her men, although solidly built. Even Tern was taller.

Ash, Cedar and Tern also began collecting rocks, but the princeling stayed where he was, so Ember did the same. She had to match her rank to his, or he would not believe her, and no one knew better than a warlord's daughter how important servants were in establishing position.

Now that she was standing still, she began to shake. Ash came to hold her elbow, his hand strong and reassuring. She wanted to just lean back against him and let him hold her. At least Fire had the decency not to send a stab of lust at this forlorn moment.

'Are you hurt?' he asked.

'No,' she said firmly. 'Merely tired.' She flicked a glance to where the princeling was watching them, and Ash understood. He took a step back and bowed slightly, before returning to the burial party.

The princeling moved a little towards her and indicated Ash. 'Konungsen?'

She shook her head.

'Husband?' he asked with care. His eyes were sharp, she thought, and clever.

If only he were! Ember thought. None of this would have happened. But aloud she said, 'Cousin.'

The word was unfamiliar to him, and he frowned.

'Family,' she explained. 'Kin.'

He nodded, then tapped his chest again.

'Nyr,' he said. 'Son of Hárugur Konung.'

'Ember,' she said in return, pointing to herself, then to the others, one by one. 'Ash, Cedar, Tern.'

He repeated the words under his breath.

'Kin all?' he asked.

'Yes,' she said firmly. Tern could be an honorary cousin. Perhaps it would keep him safe. Cedar looked up calmly and opened his mouth, but she shook her head. Claiming kinship with Elgir, which he had been about to do, just made the situation more complicated, and perhaps gave them a weapon to use against Elgir.

Curlew was covered and the men came back, sweating slightly.

The princeling, Nyr, turned away to consult with the older man. They spoke quietly for a few minutes, then Nyr stood in front of her and bowed, an unaccustomed movement by the look of it.

'We will take you to your father,' he said, the western accent strong, so that it sounded like, 'Ve vill take ya to ya vader.'

'No!' Ember protested. Nyr and his adviser glanced at each other, faces alive with speculation. They probably thought she was running away, as girls sometimes did. She had to put that to rest straight away. 'My father,' she said slowly, 'has sent me here.'

'Why?' the older man interrupted, moving forwards to stand next to Nyr. His accent wasn't as thick.

How much should she tell them? They would be delighted by anything which killed off most of a domain – or would they? Who would they raid then? And the pack ponies. If it were anyone else, she would say they were a trading party.

'A task,' she said. 'He has set me a task.'

'Task,' Nyr repeated blankly.

'I must go to the Fire Mountain,' she said.

'Bren?' Nyr asked.

Bren said, 'Eldur Fjall.'

Every hairy man there, including the princeling, made a complicated sign with their left thumb and then kissed the thumb. A sign of protection, for good luck, against evil – it was obvious.

'Vondur,' one of them said, a big burly man who looked like he should be scared of nothing. But his eyes showed white.

'Evil,' Nyr said. 'Evil—' He turned in frustration to the adviser.

'An evil place,' Bren explained.

'Yes,' Ash said. 'Evil fire.'

The men were nodding, but Ember felt an odd flash of rebellion. Fire was hateful, yes, but *evil?* Her mother didn't think so.

'There's a difference,' she said, steel in her voice, 'between evil and uncontrollable.'

'Not go Eldur Fjall,' Nyr said with finality. 'Back to father.'

Ember let her mouth tremble. She was in their power, no doubt, but officers' women were always in men's power, one way or another. There were ways to get what you wanted, although her mother despised them.

'I *must* go,' she wailed, and let all her fear and helplessness and need out in her voice. Tears welled up, and instead of fighting them back, she let them fall. 'It's a woman's task!'

The men, Ash especially, stared at her with consternation. Except Cedar, who half-smiled, then turned away as if to hide it.

'A woman's task?' Nyr asked, his shrewd eyes momentarily confused.

Bren muttered something. They stared at each other for a moment, considering.

Ember wondered what she would say if they asked more questions. She couldn't reveal how vulnerable her people were; that would invite a mass attack. An invasion.

Nyr and Bren talked quietly, with Bren shrugging and glancing at her. She tried to look both piteous and determined. The two men were disagreeing, but finally Nyr firmed his mouth and pointed to the string of pack ponies.

'Trade,' he said. 'Father trade?'

'Help me,' Ember said immediately. 'Father trade then.'

'Oath,' Nyr said.

'I swear,' Ember said, and put her hand on her heart, to show truth. 'I swear that if you help me, my father will trade with you in peace.'

An easy promise to make. Even if they didn't help her, Arvid would welcome trade with the Ice King. He was always talking about how the only future in the north was through trade. Trade instead of fighting; trade instead of starving. 'It's the centre of civilisation,' he said. 'The thing that makes prosperity and peace.' Oh, yes, Arvid would trade.

But she was only a woman, after all. Nyr looked at her for a moment, then turned to Ash, as the senior man there. Tern stood at his shoulder, as if for protection or reassurance.

'Father trade?' Nyr asked.

'Only if you help her,' Ash said. 'Then, yes.' And that was true, too, because if they didn't help then there'd be no one there to trade with.

'Oath.'

'I swear,' Ash said, as serious as she'd ever heard him, 'that Arvid, warlord of the Last Domain, will trade with you if you help his daughter to reach Fire Mountain.'

Again they made that sign with their thumbs.

Tern pointed back to the mound of stones. 'And Curlew?' he asked. 'Do we just forget Curlew?'

His voice was bitter and accusing. Ember flushed, but Ash glared at him.

'We will never forget him,' Ash said.

'Unmeant,' Nyr said to Cedar. He nodded to where one of his own men showed a long cut on his face, from Curlew's sword.

'A misunderstanding,' Ember said. 'Terrible, but not intentional.' Her voice trembled as she looked at Curlew's grave. 'He will understand.'

'Will we wait for the quickening?' Tern asked.

'We can't—' Ash began, but Ember cut across him.

'He won't quicken here, Tern,' she said. 'We're not in the Domains any more. We are too far from any altar, beyond the territory of the local gods.'

'That's why they're called local, I suppose,' Cedar said, smiling sardonically. Ember could have hit him, but part of her was comforted by his familiar dark humour.

'He has gone straight on to rebirth,' she said comfortingly to Tern. 'As he deserves.'

Tern was unconvinced. 'He is a man of the Domains, and he will quicken,' he said, mouth stubborn. 'I'll stay here and wait for him.'

What if he were right? But they couldn't wait, and they couldn't leave Tern here alone.

'I'll be all right,' he said. 'Afterwards, I'll go back to Starkling and wait for you.'

His face was no longer the face of a boy. It had aged as he'd knelt at Curlew's grave.

'Very well,' Ember said. 'We will meet you there.'

Nyr had not followed most of this, but Bren had.

'Boy come with us,' he said flatly.

'He wants to wait until—'

'No ghosts here,' Bren said. 'No evil. Spirit gone to feast with Swith.'

That old story! They still believed it, then. She wondered if it were possible, if there was a different afterlife for the Ice King's men. But the stories said that Acton, the First Warlord, had waited in the darkness beyond death for a thousand years before he was called back as a ghost by the Prowman, and Acton had expected to feast in Swith's hall too.

There was no point in challenging these people's beliefs.

Nyr, after a quick word with Bren, was firm.

'Boy come,' he said. She was learning his tones, as her father recommended, and this one had no room for negotiation in it.

'Leave Curlew a note somewhere he will see it,' she said to Tern. 'They will not let you stay.'

Tern looked at Nyr and Bren with pure hatred and their hands went to their swords in response, without thought.

'Tern,' Ember said. 'We are travelling in peace and friendship.'

He ducked his head and went to their horses. Cedar was there before him, and handed him a stick of charcoal and a piece of vellum. Tern looked at it helplessly.

'I'll write it for you,' Cedar said gently. He wrote to Tern's dictation and together they fixed it to the scrubby pine. But all the way, Tern's shoulders were tense with resentment.

THE ICE KING'S COUNTRY

Nyr made them ride in the middle of the group, behind the warriors and in front of the pack ponies. But apart from that he treated them with respect. The ponies could travel only at a walk and the afternoon seemed endless as they worked their way back into the mountains. Ash, on Curlew's Blackie, gradually lost the dazed look, much to Ember's relief.

There was plenty of evidence that the ponies had come that way in the morning, and Ember found the piles of dung reassuring. They were on the right track.

They came to a valley hidden by several twisting turns between high valley walls. The hillsides opened out to show rough grass pasture, a stream falling in white mist from a cliff to the right and forming a wide pool before it meandered away across the valley floor. Quickening their pace, the ponies made for a campsite near the pool, where a big blackened circle of rocks showed where the campfire had been the night before. Ember wondered, with a quick squeeze of her breath, how the fire would react tonight. Would it come when the men struck flint? Or would she have to call it?

The sky above was darkening and Nyr's men dismounted thankfully and went about the prosaic tasks of making camp: looking after the horses, gathering the sparse wood from the hillsides, as well as old dung pats, getting out food and cooking pots.

Ember slid down from Merry to find Ash ready to take the reins.

'Allow me, princess,' he said. She met his eyes steadily. No sign of the teasing cousin; he must be her servant now, even if he was family. Somehow that was hard for her to take; losing her laughing, challenging Ash seemed like too high a price to pay. But she handed the reins over with a nod and went to sit on a large stone near the campfire, allowing the men to work around her.

They glanced at her occasionally, but didn't seem to resent her idleness, although Nyr was feeding and watering his own horse.

Then the youngest of them knelt by the kindling and tried to start the fire.

Tried and failed. Ember almost panicked, but Ash's hand came down on her shoulder and he whispered, 'Help him.' She took a breath, steadied, and as the young man struck his flint again she called the fire. Gently, gently, she imagined the sparks forming on the kindling; imagined the small flames licking at the twigs; imagined the fire growing bit by bit, stick by stick.

The young man sat back, satisfied, as the flames took hold, bathing him in yellow light. But Ember could see that the colours were the intense, deep hues of true Fire, and something in her belly curled up and shrivelled. Would she take the curse of dead fires to Nyr's people, too? Could she risk others so much?

Stricken, she looked up at Ash, and he patted her shoulder.

'They're with us,' he said. 'They had no trouble last night, and they won't again, once they let us go.'

She moved forward before the young man could reach to place more wood on the pile.

'I will tend the fire,' she said. He nodded, unsurprised, moving off to collect water from the pool.

She knelt on the soft grass and added stick after stick carefully, hoping past hope that Fire would not appear. When she placed the first dried horse pat on the edge of the flames, she tensed, but nothing happened.

'He wants you to come to him,' Ash said quietly, squatting next to her. 'He won't show himself to these men, because that might stop you.'

She hoped it would be that simple, but remembering the sulky, smouldering eyes of Fire, she wasn't sure. There had been a bitter note in Ash's voice she hadn't heard before, and she wondered, as he moved away, what had brought it out now. Curlew's death? The flames built as she looked at him, and she felt again the surge of pure desire she had experienced in the Forest. Fire-wrought; false, but still hard to bear, hard to resist. She forced herself to look away before her very bones melted.

Once the cooking pot was full of water and the food laid out, the men looked at her. Ah. Women's work. No doubt they'd be quite capable of cooking for themselves, but since she was here ... even Nyr seemed to expect it of her. With an inward grin, she remembered her mother insisting on teaching her to cook.

'I'll never need it!' she'd protested. 'I'll always have a cook!'

'Always is a long time,' Martine had said. 'And a good mistress can do everything she asks of a servant.'

Martine herself had, Ember knew, doggedly learned all the skills of the women in the fort: butter and cheese making, spinning, weaving, tending the kitchen garden, preserving, and, of course, brewing, the mistress's main responsibility. She had insisted that Ember learn them all, too, as well as the fine sewing and embroidery that were appropriate to her rank.

'Find me some herbs,' Ember said now to Tern. 'Rosemary, thyme, bay, whatever you can.'

She approached the pot confidently and inspected the food they'd laid out. It was barely recognisable; dried meat, by the look of it, and hard black bread. Onions, at least, she knew. Something purple that looked like a carrot. She sniffed it – yes, it smelt like carrot, too, only more bitter. Small dried some-things – peas? Berries? She couldn't tell.

'This will take a while,' she said grimly, pulling out her belt knife and beginning to chop the onions.

The Ice King's men were accustomed to waiting for their meal, it seemed, as they'd scattered again, looking after the horses and their tack. Several of them were gathered around Ash, looking at his bow from a polite distance, and at him, too.

'Their bows aren't as good,' Cedar said quietly to him. Ash had noticed that, of course. They were using single recurved bows, too long for horseback. Good for stalking and accuracy close up, but without the reach of his new bow.

He knew that if the Ice King took his bow, they could make their own, with a little trial and error. They might not be able to make the fish-skin glue he used, but there were other glues, not quite as good, that would serve. And the sinew backing which was the core of its strength was easy enough to come by in a land with deer and elk.

Nyr approached and sat on a stone next to him and Cedar, and pointed at the bow, his eyes bright with interest.

'Arvid trade?' he asked.

'I don't know,' Ash said. He was pretty sure the answer would be 'no', but Arvid was a strange one, not like a normal warlord. Who knew what he would decide?

'It may be,' Cedar said. 'Arvid Warlord likes trade.'

Nyr nodded with satisfaction.

'Good bow.'

'Thank you,' Ash said.

Nyr's eyes sharpened. 'You make?' he asked.

Ash cursed himself. If the bow was valuable to them, how much more the bowyer?

He shrugged.

'You teach,' Nyr said.

Ash shook his head, and saw Nyr's face harden.

Nyr glared at him and rose abruptly to go and talk to Bren. They spoke earnestly for a few moments, shooting glances at Ash and Cedar.

'I'm a fool,' Ash said.

'Yes,' Cedar said, but he put his hand on Ash's shoulder.

Bren and Nyr came back and stood in front of them, shoulder to shoulder. Ember noticed and came back from the fire circle to stand to one side, looking a question at Ash.

'You teach,' Bren said. 'Fire Mountain long way. You teach on way. Or not go.'

'Teach what?' Ember said.

'How to make bow.'

'He can't,' she said flatly.

'He is maker,' Bren said, scowling.

Ember laughed.

'Him? He is polisher.'

She mimed smoothing down the wood. Ash flushed. What was she doing?

'He is still learning to make the perfect bow,' she said. 'Aren't you?'

She wasn't lying. She was selecting her statements very carefully. Clever, but on a trip like this, he felt it was dangerous to twist the truth. He couldn't gainsay her, so he nodded, shamefaced, as though he'd claimed more skill than he had. And who was twisting the truth now? he thought.

'Too young,' Ember said dismissively. 'Could so young a man have made so good a bow?'

Nyr still looked suspicious, but that argument seemed to carry weight with Bren. He shrugged and tapped Nyr on the arm, to come back to the fire. Nyr left with a backward glance at Ash's bow; hungry for it. Ash doubted if they'd be allowed to leave with it, and thought he should probably break it right now, to make sure the Ice King didn't get hold of it. But he couldn't bring himself to do it yet. They might need it, he told himself.

Cedar had turned away, as if uninterested, but Ash knew that he just wanted to make sure they didn't ask him what the truth was. Stonecasters didn't lie. If they did, their castings went astray, doubled back to bite them. Cedar was only at the beginning of being a caster, and Ash knew he didn't want to do anything to endanger that.

But the space at his back felt cold and empty, nonetheless.

He looked across at Ember. She kept surprising him. That little piece of misdirection – how often had she done something like that before? It had been so polished. Practised. Warlords' daughters ... Always on show, always watched. No wonder she'd developed skills at deception. But it left him frustrated for her. She shouldn't have to lie. She should blaze as clear and pure as the red of her hair. Well. No business of his. Never could be. And that was, suddenly, a grief he hadn't expected. A farmer's son couldn't even have a place at her eventual husband's fort, except as the lord's bowyer, and then he'd be expected to dip his head and bow as she went past. He would miss their teasing conversations.

Cedar had returned and stood by his shoulder again, watching with him as Ember tended the fire and the cooking pots. Something was beginning to smell good.

'She cooks? Astonishing!' Cedar said, the ready laughter back in his voice. Ash smiled.

'She has more surprises than that in store, I'm thinking,' he said. Cedar looked at him with a question in his eyes, but it wasn't one Ash could answer. 'Grammer's taught her more than a warlord's daughter usually knows,' he explained, but it wasn't what he had meant, and Cedar knew it. Ash moved off to the horses, checking Merry's hooves again, although he'd checked them thoroughly already.

The food was all right, Ember decided. Not up to the standards of her mother's cook, Ailsa, but good enough for the trail. The men ate it fast enough, and grunted appreciation as they swallowed, which she supposed was all any cook could expect. Cedar caught her eye and mimed astonishment at the taste, and she grinned. For Cedar, at least, there was no flame raised in her, and she was thankful for it.

She banked the fire with horse pats and carefully did not speak to it, but nothing untoward happened. Ash set up their sleeping pockets with hers between him and Cedar, and she slid into it with a queer combination of fear and thankfulness. A horrible day was over, but here they were in the middle of their enemies, going into the vulnerable state of sleep. Oddly, the one thing that she should have been frightened of, as a girl alone among men, she was sure wasn't going to happen.

But what else would happen – not knowing that was the source of all her fear.

Ash smiled at her, as if reading her thoughts.

'Cedar and I will take turns at watch,' he said reassuringly. But they would be no protection against the fire. Her wrist, which had been cooled by the sweet water of the Forest, had begun to ache again, as if He were reclaiming her.

Her last thought was of Curlew, in his dark rock tomb.

The Ice King's men, it seemed, didn't believe in breakfast. They got up, packed and saddled the horses, grabbed some of the dried meat from their packs, and were off. Threading through the tortuous valleys, climbing higher with each turn, Ember felt as though she had moved into a world beyond this one. The high pale sun in a clear sky, the white-capped mountains which were revealed from time to time as they turned into a new valley, the taste of the air; all strange. Only the cold was familiar. How she hated the cold!

Then they turned a corner and came to the most spectacular place she had ever seen. A long, long valley, floored with welcome green by the sides of a flashing stream. On either side of the grass, rising to the sheer peaks, was a scree of loose rocks that had fallen or been ground from the mountainside by year after year of snow. Above those, a narrow belt of trees, small twisted pines whose branches curled like exploring fingers. And at the end of the valley, rising tor after tor, peak after peak, the sharp white edges of the Eye Teeth. Irregular, snowy, they lured her eye up and further up until she saw the straight grey sides and pure cone shape of a different kind of mountain. Alone of the peaks, it was not covered in snow, and was wreathed in cloud – but of course it was not cloud but smoke, white as the snow it reflected. His mountain. It had to be.

She hadn't expected it to be beautiful, to grasp her heart and twist it, to make her yearn towards it as – as the fish yearns towards the baited hook, she thought, giving herself a shake.

Nyr turned back and brought his pony up beside Merry.

'Fire Mountain,' he said, disapproval in his voice, as though she should now see how stupid it was to go there. 'See? No snow!'

Ember nodded. 'Fire melts snow,' she said.

He slapped his thigh, as though she'd proved his point. 'Evil.'

'Necessary. Without fire, we die,' she said.

That stopped him, and made him think. She could see that he was frustrated by his inability to say what he wanted to say; that he was intelligent and agile of mind, hampered by his poor command of her language. That was unfortunate. She had better begin to learn his, she thought, and distracted him by saying so. He considered, and she wanted to smile. It was the negotiator's face, and she could almost hear his thoughts. He was weighing up the advantages and disadvantages of her knowing his language. Eventually, he looked up at Bren, as though wondering what his opinion would be.

'I will teach you more of mine in exchange,' she said.

'Agreed,' he said immediately.

They began swapping words and phrases. Nyr was most interested in those related to trading, which confirmed her first view that he had been telling the truth about his trading trip and that Curlew's death had been a useless accident. It made her heart ache.

As they reached the valley floor she realised that the green patches were all in use: goats grazed there, and there were terraces cut into the side of the hills, invisible from a distance, but up close showing a tantalising glimpse of grass and low shrubs. The shrubs were orderly – too evenly spaced to be natural – but she saw no one tending them until Bren pulled a curved cow horn out and gave three blasts on it.

Children and young women came out from behind rocks and
slits in the cliff walls. Not many – perhaps ten on each side of
the valley, spread out over the terraces. They held farming tools
like hoes and sickles, but some also had spears, and the older
boys had bows, while the other children had slings tucked into
their belts.

Bren signalled to one of the older lads and he raised a hand
in reply, then turned and disappeared into one of the many
cracks along the cliff face. That made Ember uneasy, and Ash
brought his horse closer to hers as if sharing the thought.

'Ambush?' he murmured, fingering his own bow.

'Nothing we can do if it is,' she said, frowning. She was fairly
sure that Nyr had been honest with them, but Bren ... Bren
reminded her of the leader of the Valuers, the head of their council, a canny woman called Lamb, who put the safety of her
people above everything else, including honesty. Which her
father would say was her duty.

Bren came back to them and they reined in. He produced a
long scarf and handed it to Ash.

'Eyes,' he commanded, gesturing for Ash to tie it around his
head.

'Secret ways from here,' Nyr said.

Nodding, Ash took the scarf, although his face was troubled.
If there were an ambush, they'd be helpless. But they were helpless anyway, Ember told herself. She pulled her own scarf up and
wrapped it around her eyes. As she did, Cedar and Tern followed suit, Ash a heartbeat behind them. She didn't resist when
someone, Nyr, she thought, took Merry's reins from her fingers.

'Come,' Nyr said.

The bright day was just a vague outline of light above and
below her eyes. Ember felt fear curling in her belly. Helpless.
She strained to hear beyond the muffling scarf, but there was

nothing. No voices, and the sounds of the horses' hooves and the wind through the rocks was muted. Her hands felt distant to her as they clutched the front of her saddle. Only Merry's warmth was real.

She lost track of time, but she thought it was about an hour later when she heard hooves cantering along the rocky trail towards them. From ahead, from the Ice King's Country.

Men's voices shouted. Ember tried to hear, but only caught a few words: her father's name, Fire Mountain, death, or dead. Were they talking about Curlew, or about what to do with them? Frustration took her over and she pulled off the scarf, her whole body tightening with fear as she did so.

A party of around twenty men had joined them, all on the stocky, sure-footed ponies. They were a mixture of ages, but one stood out – his neck and arms were ringed with gold, and the others left a space around him as he and Nyr and Bren talked together. Ember recognised that deference. This was the king.

He was shorter and hairier than she'd thought he would be. The Ice King had been such a figure of terror in her childhood that she'd imagined him tall and ice blond, with sharp cheek-bones and deep-set, brooding eyes. Long clawlike hands.

This king was barrel-chested, with auburn hair and a ginger beard that covered his whole face, except for the startlingly blue eyes. His hands were hairy, too. He felt her gaze and whipped around, growling disapproval at her.

She raised her chin proudly. Here, she was Arvid's daughter, and had to be treated as such from the very start, or everything was lost.

'Well met, Konung,' she said in his own language. 'Ember Arvidsdottir greets you.'

That brought him up short and he snorted as if dismissing her greeting, but then he nodded brusquely. Something flickered in his eyes. Greed? Satisfaction?

'The Hárugur King greets Arvid King's dottir.'

Hárugur King. Hárugur meant – small? Small king? Not the Ice King? She was confused. Was he just a minor royalty then, who ruled over this part of the Ice King's Country? She would ask Nyr later.

Ash, hearing her voice, pulled off his own scarf and looked swiftly around. His hand went to his bow, but she shook her head at him and he took it away immediately. He looked up, as if involuntarily, and she followed his gaze for a brief moment. The valley had narrowed again, or they'd taken a couple of turnings away from it, and they were hemmed in on both sides by high grey cliffs. No terraces here, just rock. The pale sky shone clear above them and Ash seemed to take heart from it. He looked at her and grinned, shrugging helplessness.

Nyr and the king were arguing energetically. Cedar and Tern removed their own blindfolds and looked at Ash questioningly. Ember watched Bren. He was listening to the argument intently and when they at last paused for breath, he said one sentence. She didn't know what it was, but the word 'konung' was in there.

Both Nyr and the king paled. They looked at each other soberly, and Ember saw the resemblance in the tilt of their heads, the set of their mouths. They were agreed about this, whatever it was. As they turned together to look at her, she knew she wasn't going to like it.

Nyr glanced at his father for permission to speak. The king nodded.

'The Hárugur King does not wish you to go to the mountain. Danger. Evil.'

Ember listened quietly, but Nyr put up his hand as though she had protested. 'I tell him you must to obey father. Bren says, ask the Ice King. Hárugur King agrees.'

He sat back as though he had said something truly startling. When none of them reacted, he frowned.

'Hárugur King will ask the Ice King for you,' he chided. She knew that tone, even if she didn't understand what was really going on.

'Ember Arvidsdottir thanks the Hárugur King for his kindness,' she said dutifully. 'Arvid Konung will thank him greatly also.'

The Hárugur King nodded, as if that was no more than was due. Was asking the Ice King so large a favour? How far above the Hárugur King in rank was He? Had she been too friendly with Nyr, if he was only a minor princeling?

The Hárugur King gestured for them to put their blindfolds back on, and they complied silently, but Ember sneaked a glance at Ash as she did so. He was looking thoughtful, and he pursed his lips at her behind a screen of scarf before he wound it around his eyes. Behind him, Cedar raised an eyebrow. She noticed, as the light disappeared, that the Hárugur King was swallowing and wiping his hands on his trews. Nervous. She felt a small bone of ice lodge itself at the base of her spine. She knew men like the Hárugur King – they prided themselves on being afraid of nothing. So what made a man like that nervous? Who was the Ice King?

Palisade Fort, the Last Domain

'Has the word gone out to everyone? Every village?' Arvid demanded.

Elva shrugged. 'There are some small places which don't have an altar, or anyone who can hear the gods – but we've asked those who can hear to alert them. Whether they'll get to everyone ...'

Martine passed Elva a cup of hot cha. Luxury, in these circumstances, Arvid thought, but Elva deserved it. She was clearly exhausted after communing with the gods for hours. Martine didn't look at him. She hadn't looked at him directly for two days.

The cold was so intense now that frost had formed on the inside of the precious glasses which were used at his table. Everyone was in their winter gear – and the oddest thing, Arvid thought, was the length of the cold days. In the Last Domain, cold and dark were intertwined, the winter days brief and the nights long. But now the days were longer than the nights, and it was odd beyond belief to work through a long, cold watch and find yourself still waiting for sunset.

He was very worried about the outlying villages – they were all poor, all living on the edge, and if they didn't get the warning there would be deaths aplenty. Elva and Martine had done all they could – Martine had lent Elva strength in some way he didn't understand, to let her contact mind after mind. Saffron and Poppy had been easy, and the boy at the Plantation, but the others had needed convincing, and it had taken time and energy. Three days of dawns, three days of sunset rituals to reach them all.

Merroc had been listening, and now he asked, 'When will the crisis come?'

'It's already here, for some places,' Arvid said. 'But we are timing our defence for tomorrow's dawn.'

'The Summer Solstice?' Merroc said thoughtfully. 'Yes. That's sound.' He looked far older than when he had arrived with Sigurd and Osfrid, but his initial desire for revenge seemed to have dissipated in the face of the current threat. Elva's revelation that the Ice King was a Power had somehow calmed him. They had fought the Ice King for a thousand years, and the Domains had never completely lost. Some villages, some men, some women, but they had maintained their borders despite every attack.

We both think of this in the same way, Arvid realised. Another assault; and our only shield is this frail woman and her connection to the gods.

The Domains had been invaded once before, when Acton came over the mountains. It could happen again. He sat straighter in his chair. It will *not* happen, he promised himself. They would survive.

Martine looked straight at him as he sat up, half-smiling as though she had heard his thoughts and wanted to encourage him. Their gaze held and he felt his heart leap; his hand moved without his volition a scant inch towards her. Then he caught it back and she turned away, a faint flush on her pale cheeks. Arvid pushed himself to his feet and went out, inviting Merroc to join him by a nod towards the door. He had to get away from her. Every minute in her presence undermined him. Made him weak. It was because of her that his people were in danger of slow, cold death.

'Your wife,' he asked Merroc cautiously as they inspected the wedding fire, where the cooks brewed a constant supply of soup or porridge for the children and old people. 'How is she?'

Merroc sighed and thrust his hands into his jacket pockets. 'Convinced that Osfrid will quicken sometime. Soon. She watches the fire from her window constantly, hoping.'

His tone was leached of emotion, which meant a great deal. 'I am sorry,' Arvid said. 'If I had *known* ...'

'But you did not, although your wife did,' Merroc observed. His jaw was tight, and his eyes angry. 'Do you intend to take action in that respect?'

Arvid paused. There it was, the question which kept him awake night after night. What should he do about Martine's treachery?

'I will take action,' he promised Merroc. 'But I will not weaken the spirits of my people at this point.'

Merroc nodded abruptly. 'Understood. If you do not act later, however, I will.'

He walked off towards the gate, leaving Arvid to stare at the betraying, insouciant fire. His mind whirled with conflicting impulses: outrage that Merroc thought he could harm Martine; relief that someone else might take the action he could not; and overriding everything else, the desire to protect her.

'Fight the first fight first,' he told himself, as his granfer had always told him. Tomorrow was the solstice, and Martine might perish along with the rest of them if they did not succeed.

He went to the well, next, where he had set up a relay of boys to keep the surface ice free by drawing water constantly. If no one wanted it at the moment, it was poured back again. In winter they simply melted snow by the fire, but there was no snow – yet. Arvid had ordered Lily to set up the blizzard ropes, just in case. They stretched now from door to door across the muster yard, held firm on their customary posts, ready to guide when the snow blinded them all. They were a symbol of everything that was wrong: blizzard ropes at high summer.

The well was working fine and the boys, as boys will, had turned it into a competition, to see who could draw up a bucket fastest. He gave them the compliment of watching for a while and laughing, and then went on to the stream, to check how the animals were doing. In summer, the dairy goats were pastured outside the fort, but Lily had brought them back in again, in case they needed shelter. Arvid reflected that he hadn't valued Lily enough – the man was both imaginative and thorough, and should be given more permanent responsibility. If he could be lured from his blacksmithing, when the fires returned.

Ember. Arvid went through the day trying to concentrate on what had to be done, but every so often he would trip over the thought of her and his will to go on drained away, replaced by a desperate fear. She was so young ...

The goats were tethered well away from the stream, to keep it dung free, and they had plenty of feed. Perhaps too much. The dairymaid might have to ration that, if it got colder.

Arvid bent and scooped a handful of water to drink. Rising, he stumbled back in surprise. Ash – the Prowman – stood in the shallow water next to him, where there had been no one and nothing in sight a moment before.

'I am sorry to startle you,' the Prowman said with courtesy, his voice almost singing, 'but I have someone you must meet.'

In the distance, Merroc shouted out a warning. Reaching forward, the Prowman took hold of Arvid's arm above the wrist. Arvid moved, unthinking, to free himself, but it was too late.

*

There was water, rushing, streaming, jumping, and he was in the water, with the water, *was* the water. It was profoundly unpleasant, disquieting, like being turned into a fish.

Perhaps he was a fish.

On the horror of that thought, Arvid found himself standing again, in darkness, rock under his feet, up to his ankles in cold water, shaking. The Prowman's hand was still on his arm, but he let go, saying, 'A moment, while I make light.'

Arvid had wanted to break free of that hold, but with it gone he was adrift in darkness. He barely knew which way was up. Listening intently, he heard water trickling, dropping, plinking into pools, a constant murmur and susurration. And other, more homely sounds: a tinderbox being opened, a flint being struck. The tiny glow of lit tinder illuminated the Prowman's face and the relief the light brought made Arvid sweat. Blowing gently, the Prowman coaxed the small flame and lit a candle.

'Fire?' Arvid said.

'Fire's influence does not reach here.'

'Where are we?' He had to take control of this situation in any way he could, Arvid thought. Ask questions, demand answers.

The Prowman held the candle up high. They were in a cave, huge and grotesque, with pillars of stone and twisted shapes everywhere. Arvid was standing in a pool. He took a step up onto the bank and was astonished to find himself immediately dry, even to his boots.

'These are the Weeping Caverns,' the Prowman said conversationally. The Weeping Caverns! The home of Lady Death herself, it was said.

'Why have you brought me here?' He was proud that his voice didn't shake.

'To introduce you.' He put the candle down on a rock near him, and stood up straight, addressing Arvid in the tone a storyteller, a singer, might use to ensnare an audience. 'Imagine, Arvid Warlord, if you were twelve or thirteen years old. And your father or your uncle – a man you trusted – brought you to a place like this. Perhaps to a place even stranger.'

Arvid kept silent. He might learn, at last, what he needed to know. Ash went on.

'And he said to you: "This is the oath we ask of you: to be silent to death of what you see, of what you hear, of what you do." And you swore. Then he said: "Do you swear upon pain beyond death, the pain of never being reborn, to keep the secrets of this place with your honour, with your strength, with your life?" And you swore. Imagine that, Arvid Warlord, and then tell me: would you reveal those secrets later, to your wife?'

The silence in the cave was magnified by the constant dripping. The spaces in between the sounds were as deep as death. What could he say? If he *had* made that pledge, he would have kept it. But—

'Do the women so swear?'

The Prowman's voice took on a rueful tinge. 'I cannot say. What is done by women stays with women; what is done by men stays with men.' Arvid recognised a maxim when he heard one. 'But I would be surprised,' the Prowman went on, 'if they did not. The secrets have been kept a thousand years because the oaths are real. Any boy or man who talked was killed.'

'Yet Martine knew about – about the Lake, about your ...'

'Martine is a seer, and no one controls what the gods reveal to someone like her. But she knew, also, that it was a dangerous secret. I have another question for you, Arvid Warlord – if your fellow warlords were to find out that Traveller men were meeting in secret, what would they do?'

That was an easy question, but a hard answer. In honesty, he had to admit it.

'Kill them all.'

Arvid stared down at his hands. All this was very logical, but it did nothing to heal the scar of betrayal on his heart.

'You must understand, also, that we are not used to thinking of the Powers as enemies,' the Prowman said. 'They have been our refuge.'

His mind accepted it, but his belly was still tied in knots, and there was a stubborn part of his mind which simply repeated: *she should have told me*.

'I think you had better meet Her,' the Prowman said. 'Step back into the water.'

Reluctantly, Arvid put one foot into the shallow water. Reflections from the candle made it seem black and deep. The plash as his foot touched the surface echoed back a thousand times from the high walls, resounding.

Hello, lad, his mother's voice said, deep inside his mind.

He pulled his foot out in a startled jerk, stumbling back from the pool in horror.

'She says She is sorry to have distressed you.'

Arvid could barely make words. 'Why – why did it sound like my mother?'

The Prowman bit his lip. 'It often happens so. To me, She sounds quite different. Like music. But many men hear Her as the women they have loved. Or who have loved them.'

Slowly, not reassured, Arvid placed his foot back in the pool.

Arvid, She said.

This time, he was ready for the voice, but not for the affection it held. He made himself hold steady.

'I am here,' he said.

You are a good man, his mother's voice said, and that was

both a blessing and a blasphemy. *Fire has revealed us, and perhaps it was time for this to happen. It will be up to you to make sure the innocent do not suffer for His impatience.*

'Who is innocent?' he asked bitterly.

Those of the old blood who have Settled, believing the promises of the warlords, that they and their children will be safe, She chided. She was right. The Resettlement had been easy in the north, but in the south there were still simmering resentments and old griefs which had never been allayed. There were those who would take the news of the Powers as evidence that Travellers had betrayed them all, and act accordingly. Arvid had faced the ghosts of massacred Travellers twenty years ago, and sworn to himself and them that it would never happen again. He could not be foresworn.

'I will do my best,' he said stiffly. 'I will work with the other warlords to protect the innocent.'

Including Martine, his mother's voice insisted.

Every bit of the privilege he had lived with all his life reared up in him and spat at her. 'You will not dictate what I do in my own home!' he said. 'You will not give me orders!'

He was braced for anything – would She drown him, as Fire had burnt Osfrid? Astonishingly, She laughed.

Oh, you and your daughter are alike to the bone! She said. *Two fish from the same pool.*

Then She was gone. He didn't know how he knew that, but it was clear. He pulled his foot from the water and turned slowly to the Prowman, who was *not* laughing. He was considering Arvid, looking him up and down from head to toe.

'I am wondering,' he said conversationally, but with an edge to his tone, 'whether to kill you now. Martine would grieve, but at least she would stay safe.'

Arvid drew his sword, the steel ringing and the sharp note

echoing back. The Prowman merely smiled indulgently, his hand on a knife at his belt.

'You are a warrior, yes,' he said. 'But that would not help you.'

Arvid remembered Martine's stories about this man: trained as a safeguarder, she'd seen him take on two armed warlord's men without a single weapon, and defeat them both. He was a killer, and much younger. Time for negotiation.

'If I do not return and deal with Martine,' he said, 'Merroc has sworn revenge on her.'

The Prowman's nostrils flared with anger.

'And you let him?' he said with contempt. 'Martine is worth a dozen of you.'

'He has lost his *son*,' Arvid said, passion making his voice thick. 'If my daughter dies ...'

The Prowman paused.

'My namesake is travelling with her,' he said softly. 'He is the only stake in the future I am ever likely to have.' There was a kind of heartbreak in the quiet voice that Arvid recognised. Loss. Regret. Fear.

'I will deal with Martine as fairly as I can,' Arvid promised.

'If you treated her fairly you would go down on your knees and thank her for the life of service she has given to you and yours; thank her for giving up everything that she loved for you!'

'You love her!' Arvid accused him, jealousy striking up so hard it almost blinded him. The Prowman looked at him with pity.

'Have you never had a comrade-in-arms, warlord? Someone whom you trusted and valued beyond life itself? That is the love I bear for your wife.'

Without volition, Arvid thought of Holly. He had officers who took the place of second in command in battle, but Holly was always there at his shoulder, guarding his left side, reliable, brave, her fierce loyalty a shield in itself. That was why he had sent her with Ember, because she was the best he could offer.

'Yes,' he said. 'That I understand.'

He was suddenly weary. Thinking of Ember, of Holly, of Martine, of the huge enterprise of making the Domains accept news of the Powers without murder and massacre – it all seemed too much for one man. He stumbled a little, and his foot touched the water.

It seemed as though strength flowed up from the pool; warmth like hot cha filled him, energy came back.

I am glad that you were the first of the new blood to meet me, his mother's voice said gently, and then was gone, leaving him strong and revived.

'Come,' the Prowman said, a half-smile on his lips. 'I will take you home.'

Arvid found himself standing back at the stream, the Prowman three paces away from him, regarding him steadily.

'How long were we gone?' Arvid asked, and then cast an eye at the sun. It shone brightly, noon high, in a sky of warm summer blue. But even with his winter coat on, Arvid was shivering. The air wasn't even moving – it wasn't wind chill, just simple cold. Impossible cold. The edges of the stream were fringed with ice, each summer grass stalk outlined in filigree white. It made him feel physically sick.

'A few hours,' the Prowman said. He paused, searching Arvid's face. 'I can stay, if you want me to. I might be able to help.' He hesitated, seeming, surprisingly, shy. 'I have some power which is my own, which I can lend to Martine.'

'To Martine only?'

Yes, Prowman Ash was definitely embarrassed. 'To Elva, too, it may be … it seems to work best with women …' He paused again, and straightened, resumed the expression of someone who had nothing to hide. 'Or I can leave.' He indicated the water.

'I can't stop you,' Arvid said, thinking hard. Part of him, the part with twenty-year-old memories, liked Ash and trusted him. But he had trusted Martine, too. A surge of pain at the thought spiked through him, leaving him almost gasping. He would like to wipe from the earth everything which drew Martine away from him, which had encouraged her to deceive and betray him for so long. Like this black-haired man. This *young* man, who had not aged as they had aged, because he was in thrall to the Power of Water. He could not be trusted.

But Arvid was warlord, first, and husband second. He had to be, he told himself. Had to put his people's welfare first.

'Stay,' he said. 'We will need all the help we can find.'

The Prowman nodded, but his expression remained distant. 'And Martine?'

'We will need her strength even more,' Arvid said.

'Afterwards?'

'If she protects my people—' he paused, seeing a possible way out of Merroc's revenge. 'If she protects my people,' he said more slowly, 'I will protect her, even if she is no longer in a position of trust in this domain.'

It was as vague a promise as he could make, but it satisfied the Prowman. He nodded with relief and smiled gravely, the smile of someone who had seen too much danger. Arvid had seen that smile on the faces of old warriors before they went into battle. It felt wrong to see it on such a young man.

'If any of us survive, I'll hold you to that,' the Prowman said cheerfully, and walked off towards the hall with a lithe, swinging step.

Arvid felt more than his age as he followed, slowly.

THE ICE KING'S COUNTRY

For the rest of the day, they travelled blind, but Ember could tell they were gradually moving up, through narrow ways and over rocky passes that led to ever higher valleys.

The men talked very little, and she couldn't make out more than a word or two, most of which had to do with the ponies and the track. But as she listened, she began to realise how close their language was to her own. Over and over she heard words that were *almost* like her tongue, as though at one time the Ice King's people and hers had spoken the same.

It was a thousand years since Acton had led his men through Death Pass to invade the Domains. The Ice King's people had never been able to settle over the mountains. Legend said that Acton's son had brought down the rocks in Death Pass to bar their way, because they were enemies of Acton's folk.

Ember wondered if they still resented that. Resented being shut out of the fertile, kind lands of the southern domains. She would, if she were them.

The air was growing chillier, although she couldn't tell if that was because the day was lengthening or because they were higher up. She was grateful for her coat, and even grateful for the blindfold, which at least kept her ears and nose warm, but she regretted not putting on her hat.

She wished she knew exactly where Ash was.

The horses laboured up another steep slope, Merry breathing hard in the thin air. Ember tilted in the saddle to ease her back. Then they came out onto a flat space, and the horses stopped. Merry hung her head.

'My horse needs water,' she called out, trying to slide her words so they sounded like the Ice King's language. Maybe they would understand.

Another horse bumped her knee and a hand pulled the blindfold from her face, leaving her blinking. Nyr. He smiled at her.

'We're home,' he said. 'She be well cared now.'

The light brought tears to Ember's eyes, and she brushed them away impatiently. Ash, Cedar and Tern were safe behind her. They were on a plateau bounded a mile or so away on the west by a high cliff and on the east by a sharp drop – another cliff that led too far down for her to see the bottom.

The plateau itself stretched for as far as she could see. It was grassed, and there were goats grazing. A track led towards the cliff face. Between them and it, some houses stood – round homes made of stone, she thought, although at this distance it was hard to be sure, even with the clarity of the mountain air. Their roofs were brightly painted in some pattern she couldn't make out: blue and yellow, mostly.

'Come,' the Hárugur King said, and the word was the same as in her language, exactly. 'Come.'

They followed him through the grass.

Not only goats were grazing, she saw. Geese, too, and ponies. And – gracious, hares on long leashes, tied to a stake in the ground and watched over by a young girl. That was clever.

There was smoke coming out of one of the houses, more than you'd expect for a house fire. A smithy? She caught the unmistakable smell of tanning from a structure set far apart from the others – not a round house, this one, but more a long curved wall with a sheltering roof, the sides left open to show big stone vats like wide wells. Did these people use stone for everything? But the roofs, now she was closer, she could see were leather, great hides stitched together and then painted blue and yellow and red.

Nyr looked back and saw her observing. He held his pony back until she came alongside, and said, 'Strong, yes?'

'Stone is strong,' she agreed.

He nodded, satisfied by her appreciation.

'Wood, brick, not so strong,' he said, and she realised he wanted her admiration, to feel that his home was comparable to hers, was not contemptible. That was easy to give.

'It is very beautiful here,' she said, waving at the plateau and the mountains beyond. Nyr was surprised and looked around as though he'd never thought of that before.

'Good land,' he said. He reminded her of one of Arvid's officers, who assessed every acre of his property by its yield, and saw no other value in it or its people.

People came out of the houses to watch them pass and bow to their king as he went. Mostly women and older men, she noted. The men themselves – hunting? Raiding? Or off to trade, like Nyr?

They were closer to the windowless houses, now, and she could see that around their sides was all the normal clutter of living: tools, buckets, children's toys, the children themselves, getting underfoot and calling to the horsemen. They were sturdy but not tall; blond or red-headed, with rosy cheeks. Although they all looked healthy, bar one mewling infant in its mother's arms, they were thin.

Early spring, she thought. The hungry time. In the Last Domain, her father put grain aside for early spring, when the smoked meat was almost gone, the oat crocks almost empty, the jars of honey and salted fish dwindling. No one went hungry in the Last Domain except those too proud to ask for help. Arvid bought that grain from the south with furs and walrus tusks. She wondered if Nyr had planned to do the same thing with the goods on his pack ponies.

The women she saw were all dressed in red, in heavily embroidered shawls and long gowns that reached to the ground, unlike the calf-length dresses she was used to, worn over breeches and boots. The boots were there, right enough, under-neath – beautiful, beautiful boots with intricately decorated leather dyed red and blue. She'd *love* some of those boots!

Or the dyed leather thongs the women braided into their hair, which ended in beads and feathers and carved bone. Maybe they'd keep her unruly hair in trim.

The women eyed her as curiously as she did them, and she tried a smile or two, but no one smiled back. They didn't scowl, though, which was encouraging.

She smiled at some of the children, instead, and they grinned, calling in broken words that she couldn't make out.

Ash brought Blackie up next to her and nodded towards the cliff face. Long houses were built against it, their back walls the cliff itself. Although the cliff leaned away from them, she shiv-ered. What if the rock fell from above?

These houses had windows, and shutters too, made not of wood but of leather stretched over bone. She had seen no trees on the plateau, and in the valleys only small, stunted versions of the pines and larches which had towered over them in the Forest. Mountain ash grew a little taller on the sides of the val-leys, but not much.

The houses set against the cliff had slate roofs. Chimneys with thin threads of cream smoke that drifted up between the crannies of the cliff. Painted spells over doors and windows and on the shutters. Woven blankets in bright colours airing on the windowsills. Women came and went, carrying buckets, butter churns, baskets, crocks. Like the fort at home, Ember thought, where everyone has a task and knows how to do it.

There were few old women. Few old men. And no young ones.

Boys came running to take their horses and lead them away. Ember wanted to go with them, to see Merry's stable and make sure she was all right, but suspected that this would be seen as a slight, an insult to their hospitality.

So she followed the Hárugur King and Nyr, deliberately taking precedence over the others in the party, her own people and the Ice King's alike. The king's men fell back for her readily enough, but they closed in afterwards, and casting a look backwards she saw Ash scowling at her. She kept her face impassive. He had to learn diplomacy, and fast.

But a small warmth under her breastbone bloomed at the thought that he worried about her. She followed Nyr along the well-worn track to a double door set wide open.

At the door a woman stood, dressed not in red but in ice blue and the pale cream of undyed wool. Her golden braids were wound around her head and she carried herself erect, her long neck encircled by a golden torque. Her green eyes searched Nyr's face, and then came to Ember. That is a queen, Ember thought, and not used to bowing to anyone. She bowed herself, exactly as deep as she had bowed to Osfrid's mother the first time they met. The woman looked at her carefully, and then, surprisingly, smiled warmly and came to take Ember by the hand.

'Welcome to Mountainside,' she said. 'Come. These men of mine can explain later, when you are rested and clean.'

She had a strong accent, but she spoke in the language of home, and Ember's eyes swam with sudden homesickness. The queen saw, and squeezed her hand.

'I am Halda Geransdottir,' she said. 'And it seems my son has brought home more than he went trading for!'

Ember smiled.

'I am Ember Arvidsdottir. I think we were a surprise to him,' she said.

'No doubt.' Halda cast a critical eye over both son and husband.

'Show the king's men the baths and I will take care of his dottir,' she ordered them.

'Aye,' Nyr said hurriedly.

Ember followed Halda through room after room, far too many to fit in the long narrow house outside the cliff. She realised, with a little shiver of fear, that they were deep in the mountain itself.

Garn the Songkeeper, ever curious, had come to inspect the strangers, his eyes alight with interest.

Ari, Hárugur King, gave the three men into his care, and motioned Nyr to come aside and talk. Nyr watched as the three strangers disappeared into the men's passageway. Three very different men: a youngling, a seer – and the third, the large one who looked after his princess so carefully, what was he? A true bowyer, or a braggart apprentice? He didn't have the look of a braggart, Nyr thought, but then, who knew what braggarts looked like in the land beyond the mountains? Why had Arvid Warlord sent only these three, and no female companion for his daughter?

Ash, they said the big one's name was. An odd name, it made Nyr uneasy, as did the princess's. What kind of people named their children for the leavings of a fire?

The big man was carrying his bow and quiver, although they'd left most of their gear on the horses.

'We need that bow,' his father Ari said to him, following his glance.

'That is so,' Nyr said, resolutely formal.

'You will get it while I consult the king.'

'Let Garn get it. Take me with you.'

The Hárugur King hesitated, king fighting with father.

He'd been avoiding this ever since Andur, Nyr's older brother, had died. The heir should be presented to the king. It was custom – more, it was the king's order.

'Is it so terrible, to see his face?' Nyr asked softly.

'Yes.'

His father wiped his hands on his trews nervously, but he met Nyr's eyes, allowing him to see the true fear he felt. Nyr's stomach lurched. All the world knew that the Ice King was terrifying, but his father had faced him time after time since becoming Hárugur King eighteen years ago, and had come back each time none the worse.

'I must meet him, come wind or weather,' Nyr said. 'Better now than later, when he might be offended at the delay.'

Ari nodded, but only once, as though he resented having to agree. His face was pale under his ruddy beard.

'Come now, then,' he said, 'and prepare.'

Nyr followed his father through the men's passage to the main hall. The strangers were not there, but there were more people around the fire than he had ever seen on a fine day, and they were buzzing like lowland bees. The strangers had been here, for certain, on their way to the baths with Garn.

He spared a look up at Urno Ravenssen's great painting – the butterflies almost seemed to flutter in the wind. It lifted his spirits and he kept close behind his father as he entered the arch that led to his father's Council Cave. For the first time, he followed Ari behind his throne, to the narrow passageway in which only the king or his heir could set foot.

Next to the entrance was a basket filled with winter suits. Without speaking, Ari and Nyr climbed into the thick furs, closing the toggles firmly, overlapping the layers to prevent wind chill. Ari left his scarf hanging around his neck, so Nyr did the same.

Ari laid his gloved hand on Nyr's right shoulder.

'You are the heir,' he pronounced, speaking as though the whole clan were gathered to hear. 'You have the right to enter.'

Then he turned to face the passageway and squared his shoulders, taking a deep breath before moving forward. Nyr followed close behind.

'You can't get lost,' his father's voice reassured him. 'There is only one passageway, and it leads to only one place. Feel your way. But don't talk. You may not speak until you speak to the king, if he wishes.'

As Nyr took the first step between the rock walls, he shivered. It was cold, suddenly, as cold as winter. Although he could see the fire burning in the Council Cave if he looked over his shoulder, it sent no warmth into the passageway. They were already in the domain of the Ice King.

Then it was dark, the great formless darkness of the deeps.

It was forbidden to take fire to the Ice King. No light at all, that was the rule. Nyr felt his way along the rough wall, following his father as much by sound as by touch. It was like the game children played, Delver in the Deep Dark Cave, where they blew the lantern out and hid, and the child chosen as Delver had to feel their way to find the others.

He had hated that game as a child. Hated being Delver and hated being one of the Gemstones the Delver was seeking, waiting, muffled under some blanket that smelt of baby pee. He had never seen the point of it all. Why fumble in the dark when you could have light? But here he could not have light. As always in the great dark, his eyes made light for themselves – splashes and flecks of colour chased across his vision. As children, they were taught that these were the gift of the Ice King, to keep them company in the cold dark. They were unfailing, as the king himself was, and grew stronger the longer light was absent. Nyr welcomed them now, as he had welcomed them as a child, put to sleep in a winter cave with his brother, under the deep, sheltering rock.

The passage was long, and the cold grew sharper as they went further in. After a time, Nyr heard a familiar clink, rattle and slosh, repeated over and over. He smiled.

Like all winter suits, theirs had water flasks, complete with the small stones inside which broke up the ice when the flask was shaken, allowing the water to melt just a little, enough to drink. In a blizzard, you had to shake the flask all the time – apart from anything else, keeping close to the sound of the stones was a good way of staying with your companions.

His father was shaking his flask. Nyr fished his own out and settled into the rhythmic up and down motion that used up the least energy. He tried to match his own rhythm to his father's – that was a children's game, too. But he was taller than his father, with a different walking gait, so he had to concentrate. It helped still the growing fear in his belly.

He shouldn't be this afraid, not yet. They still had a long way to go. And he was no stranger to dark, or cold. But the cold was increasing, as though winter was advancing on them at a walking pace, as though they were walking out of season, going backwards or forwards into the coldest time of the year, when the sun fled and the stars failed and the wolves sang desperation to the shrouded moon.

A breeze touched his face with chill fingers, searching for a way inside his clothes, stroking him; it felt like real hands, real fingers, cold as hunger, but when he put his hand to his face there was only air.

His father reached back to pat him on the arm, but kept walking. Had he made some sound when the fingers touched him? He hoped not. Hoped his father didn't realise how scared he was. Then he remembered the fear in Ari's eyes, and knew that every heir, every Hárugur King, felt this terror as they walked the King's Passage.

Under his feet the floor was rising. He bent his knees and trudged on, one hand shaking his flask, the other feeling his way along the ragged wall. They had been walking for hours, now, he thought, and had only twice stopped to take a drink. He should be hungry, but he was not. He was getting tired. He could walk all day on the mountainside without feeling it, but this ...

The passage began to wind as it climbed, curving around in a wide circle. A spiral, Nyr thought, as they went further up. There was no sense of direction underground, but as they ascended he could feel the air change, becoming thinner and colder still. He wound his scarf over his face, breathing shallowly so the cold air did not burn his lungs.

He remembered sitting next to Andur, his brother, and his cousin Seid, in the Council Cave, listening open-mouthed to his father as he described the journey to the Ice King. All the heirs had to know the ritual, in case of disaster. It had happened before, more than once in the last thousand years, that the Hárugur King and his heir had both been killed by enemies or avalanche, and the younger heir had to take on the duties without warning.

'I do not know,' Ari had said slowly, his eyes on Andur, 'if the place we go to is in this world or another. But we must climb and climb far to get there. It will feel to you like we are at the very peak of the world. Maybe we are. But this is how the Hárugur King was first chosen – he was the one who was brave enough to stand on the peak of the world and look the Ice King in the face. You *must* look him in the face, or he will not speak to you, and you will be cast down as Hárugur King and your people will be left leaderless.'

It had not sounded too hard to Nyr at the time, despite Ari's solemn tones, but the night Andur had come back, weak and pale, from his first meeting with the king, Nyr had reconsidered. Andur was as strong as a bull elk, and yet he had staggered into the Council Cave and collapsed by the fire like a grandfather of eighty. He had stared into the fire, shaking, his face grey, and when his mother had come through the archway from the main hall he had turned his face into her skirt like a child.

Andur had been far braver than he was, Nyr thought. But he had wondered, in the seasons that followed, as Andur took risk after risk – including the late-season raid that got him killed – if he was trying to prove to himself that he still had courage, after that meeting.

Nyr was not a warrior born, like Andur. He was a thinker, a planner. A trader by inclination as well as need. He could fight, of course. Who couldn't? And he did well enough that the men followed him without complaint or snide remarks. He had more strategy than Andur, and since he had started leading the raids, last summer, they had lost only one man.

But he couldn't draw on the reserves of bravery that Andur had had. He would have to use stubbornness instead. His mother always said he was as stubborn as his father, and perhaps that was what was needed, on this long, long trek up the inside of a mountain.

The rhythm of his father's flask was slowing, faltering. He stopped shaking his own flask and came up close behind Ari, reaching forward to place his hand on his father's shoulder. Ari patted it reassuringly and moved forward again, but more slowly.

The flecks of light which still danced on his eyeballs were moving faster. Then his eyes started to water and he realised he could see a vague outline in front of him – his father's broad shoulders and head. Light.

Relief and fear washed over him. His body welcomed the light. His mind sheared away from it because it meant the end of the journey. Eyes smarting, he understood that his father was moving forward so slowly to let them get accustomed to the glare. Snow glare, he thought. Ice glare. The kind that can turn you blind.

The passage was widening. Nyr tucked the water flask into his belt and moved up next to his father, the two of them walking slowly, carefully, their feet oddly unbalanced now they could see where they were going.

The walls of the passage here were ice, not rock. Rough and smooth, blue and white, walls and roof and floor were all covered with it. But there was not one single icicle. This was not a place that ever grew warm enough for water to flow before it froze again. Their breath, coming through the scarfs, created a constellation of ice crystals which clung, sparkling, to the wool.

At the end of the passage his father waved him back again, turned hard left and then right, into a dazzle of blue and white. Ari went two more steps, and stopped. Nyr came up close behind him.

They were standing on a ledge, barely big enough for the two of them, above a cliff that curved back in beneath them, so they were suspended, with open air all around them. In front was – Nyr sucked his breath in, biting back an exclamation. He understood now why his father wondered if they were still in the real world. Below them, stretching as far into the distance as they could see, was ice. Not the snow-covered river of the glaciers which Nyr had often seen in the high reaches of the mountain. This was pure ice, swept clean by the constant whistling wind.

He leaned into the wind without thought, and his father put out an arm to push him back, shaking his head warningly. Nyr understood. Lean into the wind here and if it dropped ... so did you.

Beautiful. No one had ever told him the Ice King was beautiful. Deep blue and green in the shadows, blindingly white on the surface, it was curved and banked and carved by the wind into a great sculpture, a vast decoration over the face of the world. Clouds sped across the sun and light suddenly streamed down, striking sparks and fire from the ice. The light was unbearable, forcing him to look down, away, anywhere else.

His father knelt and covered his eyes with his hands, the mark of respect due to kings, a gesture he had never seen his father make. Nyr copied him.

It was profoundly unsettling, kneeling in the high air, cold shafting up through his knees and boots, his eyes shrouded by his hands but the terrible, searing light still blinding him.

Up through his knees and his boots a vibration began, a small steady shivering. He thought it was his own cold, but then the shiver turned to a thrum, a sound that was made using his own flesh, as though he were a drum in the hands of a musician.

It pulsed in him, harder and harder, louder and louder, shaking him, loosening his soul, he felt, from its bonds. Deep and high at the same time, a sound he finally recognised – it was the noise ice made as sections of it were scraped together in the bed of a glacier. A terrible, unliving noise. He wanted to piss with fear. He wanted to run away. Only his father kept him there. His father had faced this time after time.

Nyr bit the inside of his cheek to stop from crying out, to stop himself asking for mercy. This sound had no mercy in it, any more than the ice did as it froze a traveller to death; any more than the winter itself did.

The thrum and screech built and took shape, not in his ears, but in his mind.

'Speak.' The voice of the Ice King, dark and piercingly high, almost pushed him to the ground with its force. He would be deaf after this, he thought in a panic. But then it paused, the sudden silence ringing, and his father spoke. Nyr had never admired his father more. To be able to find your voice in the face of this power!

'Ari, Hárugur King, greets the Ice King with humility and devotion,' he said hoarsely. 'I present my heir, Nyr Arissen.'

In the moment that followed, Nyr felt the thrumming stream through him, a low pounding – the most dangerous of sounds, the telltale drumming of thin ice over a crevasse which might collapse at any moment. The sound of death.

It was an inspection, and he held still, hands clasping his face, and prayed hard that he would pass the test. But who he prayed to, he didn't know.

'You may uncover your face, Nyr Arissen,' the voice came at last.

Slowly, almost unwillingly, Nyr dropped his hands. He had expected a person, a great lord, a giant like the ones who would eat the sun in the last days. But there was nothing there except the ice sheet, duller now that the clouds had flowed back across the sun. He hadn't even noticed the light dimming, he had been so afraid.

Was still so afraid. Nothingness was worse, he thought. A giant you might bargain with, or plead with, but Ice ...

'Speak,' the voice said, reverberating in his own chest, shaking his bones. Nyr felt panic overwhelm him. Was he supposed to say something? What?

'A woman has come,' Ari said, rescuing him. 'The warlord's daughter from the Last Domain. She is tasked by her father to go to the Fire Mountain.'

A deep, deep vibration. Disapproving, uncertain – Nyr couldn't tell.

'Why?' the Ice King asked, the question spearing into Nyr's bowels.

'She will not say. But she promises trade concessions if we help her, and I think she is speaking the truth.'

'No. No one goes to the Mountain.'

And He was gone, just like that, letting go of Nyr's body as a boy drops an apple core after eating the sweet flesh.

His father collapsed onto the floor, but Nyr couldn't move, still. If he moved, he felt, he might break apart. He had to find some way to knit himself back together. He heard his breath, and listened. In and out, that was the sound of life, the only antidote to death. The only one.

Slowly, his father clambered to his feet and reached down to help him up. With human contact, he was finally able to move, to stand, to inch back from the edge and lean his back on the wall of the passageway.

He opened his mouth to say something – anything, to hear the sound of a human voice – but his father quickly put a hand over his mouth and shook his head. Nyr realised they had to make the whole long trek back through the dark in silence, as they had come.

Whatever was necessary. He would never, *never*, do anything which displeased the Ice King. Never.

MOUNTAINSIDE,
THE ICE KING'S COUNTRY

Ash, Cedar and Tern followed the older man, Garn, into a corridor cut through the rock. Ash was used to caves – the sides of Hidden Valley, where he had grown up, were full of them, and the children of the valley played in them all summer, once the bears had left. He'd always liked caves, but only when he could feel fresh air on his face. As they went downwards, he felt the air become stiller, and found himself drawing deeper breaths.

Cedar, he knew, did not like being underground at all, so he put a hand on his shoulder in encouragement. But Cedar, who avoided the caves which stank of bear even in mid-summer, met his eyes with delight and pointed up as they came out of the passageway into a natural cavern which had been shaped into a hall, huge and high-roofed. He looked where Cedar pointed, and gaped.

The long wall of the hall was covered with pictures. Paintings, row upon row of them, climbing the walls, becoming lighter and brighter as they went, as though the ones at the bottom were old. The hall was so far across that Ash couldn't make out the details, but he could see they were scenes of ordinary life. Green grass with animals, women spinning in the sunshine, a tree. Some of them were obscured by scaffolding, and looking up to its top he saw a burly man lying flat on the topmost platform, carefully daubing the wall with paint. His face was as blank as a stonecaster's as they let the stones fall. Behind him, stretching right across the long wall, was a flight of butterflies against a clear blue sky. Ash laughed. He couldn't help it – the painting was so full of light and joy in flight that it called deeply to him. It was very different from the careful, painstaking works below it.

Garn smiled at him, waiting patiently for him to stop gawking. Ash met Garn's eyes, and nodded. Garn reminded him of his father, Mabry, who was a woodcarver and had a keen appreciation of beauty. For a moment they stood side by side, looking up, united in pleasure.

'Urno is breaking many traditions,' he said, as if apologising, 'but he calls the Spring into our hearts, so we forgive him.'

He raised his voice at the end of the sentence, and the painter above popped his head over the side of the scaffolding and grinned at him. Ash heard Tern gasp. It did look high, he thought, but Tern's face was a mixture of shock and horror, which was strange.

He looked a question at him, but Tern had wiped the expression away and stared back at him blankly.

Garn sighed, noticing nothing of the exchange.

'Come,' he said. 'Or spring itself will have passed and winter will be nipping at our heels before we are done.'

There were very few people in the hall, and most of them were passing through on some errand, carrying pots or skeins of wool or tools or babies. Each person looked at them with frank

curiosity, especially the women, who eyed Cedar in particular
with real interest.

Garn chuckled. 'A new face as pretty as yours, lad, will have
them all talking!'

Cedar smiled at a young girl who giggled behind her hand
and ran away to join a couple of older women near the big central fire.

'Enough,' Ash growled at him, but he bowed anyway, with a
flourish.

The women hid smiles, but they kept looking, at Ash as well.
Tern they assessed and dismissed.

'A couple more years, lad, and they'll all be running after you,'
Garn reassured him, leading the way towards a curtained arch.

'I hope not!' Tern said with real horror, and they all chuckled.

It was too easy, Ash thought. They were in the heart of enemy
land, in the middle of the Ice King's Country, and they were
sharing a jest. It made him uneasy, when he suspected Garn was
trying to put him at ease. He would rather have met open hostility or suspicion.

They went downward again, on a path smoothed by centuries
of wear. Here the walls were decorated with hangings and objects
hung or displayed on shelves. With a shock Ash recognised a piece
of Domain pottery, a wine jug from the far south, with its unmistakable yellow and blue glaze. Thieves, he thought, glad of the
reminder. These were the killers of hundreds of Domain people.
Hidden Valley had been attacked three times in his own memory,
and many times before that. They had fought the invaders off, but
they had lost men – his own cousin, Aunty Gytha's oldest son, had
only one leg because of an Ice King attack. These people were not
their friends, no matter how friendly they seemed.

Alerted, he heard faint footfalls behind them. Garn might be
simply taking them to the baths, whatever they were, but the

Hárugur King was not a fool. There were other men watching them, ready for any trouble.

He tightened his grip on his bow. He could not let them have it, and there was only one way to make sure of that.

They passed turnings and archways hung with weavings; strange designs mostly in green and blue, as though these people were trying to bring the outside in. No, he realised, not the outside. The summer.

Pity struck him, then, but he shook it away. No matter how hard and long the winters were here in the mountains, it did not excuse generations of murder and pillage by the Ice King's men.

Garn turned into a smaller passageway, and then ducked under a low arch. This was a natural cleft in the rock, not one of the smooth doors made by human hands. Beyond, Ash was struck by a rush of damp, hot air smelling faintly of brimstone, and by light: lamps were set on a series of ledges around the empty cave.

In the middle was a pool – no, two, joined by a narrow channel. They were big enough to take a dozen men each, and steam wafted gently from their surface. Beyond the pools, far down in the corner of the long cave, was what looked like a small open fire pit. Ash took another step so he could see further, and found himself seared by the heat, his skin shrinking over his cheekbones. This was not a human fire. No fire that small could give out so much heat. It came from the mountain itself, and looked exactly like iron heated by a smith until it is white hot.

Cedar took his breath in and went still, his face in that blank stare that Ash knew meant Sight.

'There is power here,' he said, forcing the words out with difficulty.

Garn nodded.

'The power of the Ice King,' he said. 'He cares for his people.'

Cedar shook his head. 'No. No. Not the Ice King.'

Garn's face hardened. 'That is not a thing which you should say, stranger. You are talking of things you know nothing about.' His accent had worsened – this was something he felt very strongly about.

Cedar looked down at his hands, which were shaking.

'I thank you for the advice,' he said carefully, 'and will follow it.'

Nodding, Garn turned away. 'Strip and bathe,' he said, carefully casual. 'Enjoy the gift of the Ice King.'

He began to take off his boots, and Cedar and Tern followed suit. Ash could feel Cedar looking at him, waiting for him to take the lead. This was the time, Ash thought. The only time he could be sure of succeeding. He felt his heart twist. This bow had taken him so long, and was so beautiful. The arrows it loosed flew high and sure and certain, and they took his spirit with them as no other arrows ever had. He firmed his lips, took two steps towards the fire pit, until he couldn't bear the heat any longer, and threw the bow into the pit. It flashed into flame and burned in an instant, leaving only a squiggle of ash where the sinew had been. A breeze came from nowhere to lift the ash into the air, swirl it, and let it settle again. Then that was consumed, too, and there was only the glowing pit.

Tern exclaimed, 'Oh, no!'

When Ash turned back, Garn was frowning, and Cedar had a queer smile on his face, as though he had seen something he hadn't expected.

'You've made trouble for me, young man,' Garn said softly.

'Better for you than for my people,' Ash replied. Garn snorted as though agreeing, but he raised his voice and Ash realised that there were people listening outside the archway.

'You moved too fast for me, lad.'

Ash watched his steady eyes and nodded.

'I knew better than to give you warning,' he said loudly. 'You couldn't have stopped me.'

'I'll have to report this to the Hárugur King,' Garn said. 'Wait here.'

He went out the archway and they heard a quick conversation, then the sound of light running feet moving away from them. Garn came back.

'Well,' he said, and the look in his eyes reminded Ash again that they were among warriors. 'Get in the baths. You all stink to the roof.'

He went out again, leaving them alone.

Ash put a hand on Tern's shoulder.

'What was it, back there, lad, that had you so—' He didn't want to say 'upset'; the boy would take that as a criticism. 'So surprised?'

'That man, the painter,' Tern whispered urgently. 'He killed my uncle!' His face was hard with anger and grief. 'When I was ten. They raided. He killed him with an axe!'

Ash was vividly reminded of the first time he had seen the Ice King's men come towards Hidden Valley, their great battleaxes swinging, their battle screams filling the air. He had been seventeen, and had had nightmares for months afterwards.

Cedar put his hand on Tern's other shoulder. 'We are not here to take revenge,' he said seriously. 'We must convince them to let us go. That is all.'

Tern's eyes flashed with anger and tears. 'Aye. I know.'

He moved away from them brusquely, stripping off his clothes and easing himself into the first pool. Cedar looked grim, and Ash thought he probably looked the same. They could not forget that these people were the enemy.

*

Halda led Ember into a curtained cave with a sloping floor which led down to a pool of water. Hot water.

Too hot. She felt the heat begin in her cheeks, then just under her heart, then in her knees, feet, shoulders ... it spread and raged like a forest fire, and that thought made her realise that it wasn't the temperature. It was Him.

The pool below belonged to Him. He was in this cave, in the very air she breathed. She stepped back outside the doorway and bent over, struggling for breath, feeling her heart leap and race with terror. She just hadn't been *expecting* it! Not here. As if it were happening at that moment, she was plunged back into the memory of Osfrid's death, watching him shrivel and scream, feeling the whip of the burn around her wrist, the face of the Fire forming in the flames ... she sank to the floor, her hands over her face, shaking, rocking back and forth, trying to banish the images from her mind.

Halda followed her, concerned, and put a hand on her back.

'Child?' she said, her voice uncertain. 'Are you all right?'

Ember dragged air in, scrubbed the tears from her face and sat back, panting. Then she clambered to her feet like an old woman, swallowing tears in a dry throat. As she turned, she saw several men watching them from along the corridor, looking uncertain about whether they should move towards them – guards, she thought. Of course. They would watch her.

Politics and human threats calmed her down and let her smile with difficulty at Halda.

'I'm all right. I didn't expect ... there is power in there.' She gestured to the archway, but she didn't look at it.

'Few feel it,' Halda said slowly. 'None so strongly before ... you are a seer?'

Ember laughed shortly. 'Me? No, no. But I have, er, had some dealings with that Power.'

Halda blanched, making the gesture against evil which Nyr's men had made.

'The Ice King?' she gasped. 'You've had dealings with the Ice King?'

Her blue eyes were wide with a mixture of fear and awe and something buried underneath. Speculation.

Ember froze. What should she say? If these people believed Fire Mountain to be evil, how would Halda react to a claim that the heated pool came from Fire, not Ice? Then she realised what Halda was saying, what it meant – the Ice King was a power, one of the Great Powers, like Fire or Water. Oh gods, they'd all been fools. For a thousand years, they'd been idiots, all her people!

She'd been gaping for too long.

'The Ice King?' she said, trying to seem calm. 'No. No, I have never had dealings with the Ice King. With another Power. Perhaps I was mistaken. Power of that strength ... perhaps it all feels the same ...'

Not a lie. Not a lie. Ash was adamant that they shouldn't lie on this journey. 'Lies throw up dust that blind the teller,' he'd said.

Halda smoothed her long dress down over her thighs, considering. 'What Power?' she demanded. 'What Power have you had dealings with?'

Yes, that was the right question for the warlord's lady to ask. And she had promised Ash not to lie, but it was hard to say it. Dangerous.

'Fire,' she whispered.

Halda jerked back as though slapped and she made the sign against evil.

'That one is the bane of the world,' she said. 'The Enemy.'

'He killed my husband,' Ember said with real hate. 'On our wedding day.'

Suddenly she was crying, sobbing, and Halda's arms came around her in comfort.

'Evil,' Halda said flatly.

She led Ember away to a series of smaller chambers cut from the rock, furnished with narrow looms and spinning wheels, with felting tables and combing planks, and finally with beds and wall hangings. There were only a few women in the outer rooms, working by the light of closed lanterns. One was a young girl, younger than Ember, and Halda snapped some orders at her too fast for Ember to understand. The girl ran, her long red skirts flicking up around her ankles.

Halda led Ember to a wooden armchair beside one of the beds and settled her in it.

'Calm yourself,' she said kindly. 'No one will hurt you here.'

Ember sat and shook, feeling foolish, wishing she could be like her mother. Martine wouldn't be weak like this. She'd dealt with wicked enchanters, with evil ghosts, with the reweaving of the compact which kept all humanity safe from the wind wraiths and water spirits. *She* was a hero. She would never quiver and cry in front of a stranger.

The girl came back with a basin of steaming water and some cloths and put them carefully down on a small side table, staring at Ember with curiosity and a faint hostility.

'There you are,' she said.

'Thank you, Larra,' Halda said dismissively. Larra bobbed up and down, spreading out her skirts a little – something like a bow? Ember thought. Clearly a movement of respect to the lady. She would have to remember that.

'I'll leave you to wash,' Halda went on. 'Your clothes are there.'

Her pack was at the foot of the bed. Its familiarity in this strange, strange place made tears well up again, tightening her chest, but she managed not to cry.

'I thank you, Lady, for your hospitality,' she said.

Halda nodded and left, pulling a curtain which had been looped up over the archway down to cover the door.

Ember stood up and touched the rim of the bowl. The warm water had no trace of Fire in it. She relaxed a little. Undressing, washing and redressing in the one set of good clothes she had brought with her settled her more. She brushed her hair and wondered how she should arrange it. Should she wear it loose, as unmarried girls did, or bind it into plaits around her head, as married women did, or wear a cap, like a widow? She bit back a hysterical giggle. She was all three, gods help her. All three at once, so she might as well please herself.

She brushed her hair out and let it hang, bringing it flat next to her ears with combs to keep it out of her eyes. The strands crackled and spat sparks as she brushed, and she flinched each time. It was as though He was trying to reach her even here.

Finally she was ready. She tied her boots on securely and went to the archway, lifting back the curtain hesitantly.

'Halda?' she called.

The girl, Larra, was waiting.

'Queen Halda says to bring you to the hall,' she reported. As they walked together through the outer rooms, she glanced sideways at Ember's red hair. Her own was blonde as flax. 'Are you going to marry Nyr?' she asked.

The question was like a blow to the windbox. Ember gaped at her.

'Marry—' She smiled and shook her head. If it were only that simple! A diplomatic marriage, hah! 'No, I'm not here to marry anyone.'

Larra skipped a little, to go ahead, and Ember smiled at her back. So, Larra had plans for Nyr, did she?

'I'm a warrior's daughter,' Larra informed her, turning to

speak over her shoulder. Ember knew a claim for status when she heard it. The tone of voice was exactly the same as a girl in the Last Domain saying, 'I'm an officer's daughter.'

'A worthy wife for any man,' Ember acknowledged, and Larra nodded, as if they'd negotiated a settlement.

Winding through passage after passage, cave after cave, Ember began to realise that she was in a town. Mostly empty. All the people out with the goats, the hares, the crops, wherever they were planted; in winter all those people lived here, safe.

Winter was bad enough in the Last Domain, but at least there were doors and windows, even if they were often snowed over. At least there were glimpses of the sky, and days she could go out with her friends. To be cooped up underground for more than half the year ... She shuddered.

Then they emerged into the hall, and she stood astonished at the size, the colour, the height of the roof. The fire in the centre. She stood unmoving. If she went near it, would it die? Would she be revealed as an agent of the Enemy?

Ash and the others were standing in front of the fire, being confronted by Garn and Bren. Her men were weaponless. She couldn't remember the last time she had seen Ash without his bow. Bren had a hand on his belt knife, and two of the men who had ridden with Nyr were standing behind him, axes in hand. She went forward at a fast walk, but Halda was before her, coming swiftly from the other side of the fire.

'What happens here?' she asked with authority.

'He has destroyed the bow!' Bren spat.

Ember made herself laugh. As one, the hairy men spun to glare at her. Ash looked worried, as though she were walking into trouble. But she didn't spare him a glance. She looked straight at Bren instead.

'What did you expect him to do? Just hand it over to you so

your people could be better warriors? He knew his duty to his lord and he did it.'

Bren paused. 'Then he will teach us instead,' he said. 'And if he does not, he will regret it.'

The men with the axes moved towards Ash. Tern's hand went to his knife, but Ash shook his head, his eyes on Ember.

'Now is the moment,' Ember said gently to Bren, and to Halda, 'when you must decide if your people will gain more advantage from trade with my father than from a new bow.'

Halda was nodding, lips pursed, but Bren was unconvinced.

'We will let the Hárugur King decide!' he said.

'The Hárugur King,' Halda said, 'is consulting the Ice King, and no doubt has more to worry about than a single bow.'

Faces paled and hands made, not the sign against evil, but a different movement, a smoothing motion of one palm across the back of the other hand. Ember understood it – that was the smooth surface of ice.

'We are grateful beyond measure to the Hárugur King for his generosity in consulting the Ice King on our behalf,' Ember said. Her voice showed her sincerity. She was truly grateful – to deliberately go and face one of the Powers for a stranger was a great and generous act. As she said so, she cast a glance at Ash and Cedar, making sure they understood the implications.

Cedar certainly did. His eyes widened and he looked around as if reassessing everything he had seen. Tern just looked puzzled. Ash looked at the ground, then up again.

'Yes,' he said. 'We are grateful indeed.'

Bren wasn't mollified. He had wanted that bow badly. 'The Hárugur King knows his duty,' he snapped.

'And no doubt there will be benefits to us all in the future from his generosity,' Halda said, putting an end to the discussion. 'Come and eat.'

'No,' Bren said. 'He must be kept prisoner until the Hárugur King returns.'

People were trailing into the cave, watching them curiously. In the group around her, there was a silence that Ember knew was dangerous. These people did not respect their women much, any more than most warlords did. But Halda was the lady here, was she not? And in the lord's absence, she was the authority. Perhaps. Perhaps it worked differently here.

'After you have all eaten,' Halda said smoothly, with a lifetime's practice at defusing arguments, 'you shall take him to the inner cave. But you and your men have been travelling a long time and need food.'

This is a real lady, Ember thought with appreciation. I could learn a lot from her.

The younger men set up trestle tables on either side of the fire, and dinner began.

Men and women ate separately, but there was no distinction otherwise. No glass table for the king's family or for his closest officers. Everyone ate at the same long tables, mixed in.

Women served men first, then themselves, from a central trestle. Bacon and barley soup, bread, small strips of charred veal with onions. Almost familiar food, but the soup was spiced with something Ember didn't recognise, and the bread was flat. Children ate from their mothers' plates. The boys, not quite old enough to join the men, formed a group by themselves, imitating the way the men sat and joked with each other. Ember watched them with a smile. That was the same, at least.

Halda saw her looking at them, and smiled as well.

'Boys are the same everywhere, are they not?' she asked.

'You see a great deal, my lady,' Ember said.

'I know what it is like, to come to a strange place and search for something which is familiar.' Halda's voice was wistful.

'You are not from here?'

'I am the daughter of a tribute king, to the south,' Halda said. 'To be married to the Hárugur King's heir, as Ari was then, was a great honour. It bound our peoples close together.'

Ember made a face. 'My father let me choose my husband, but only from other warlords' sons. That's what daughters are for, after all – to forge alliances!'

A bitter smile crossed Halda's face, and she nodded. 'It is a great responsibility, none the less,' she said. She paused, and took a spoonful of soup, then put her spoon down and tilted her head. 'Has your father planned another marriage for you?'

Ember shook her head and shivered, her hand cupping the brand on her wrist.

'I must complete my task first,' she said.

'Nyr is not married, either,' Halda said, seemingly careless but with sharp eyes.

Oh, she knew that tone. Her heart beat slower as she thought through the implications. She had no doubt what her father would think. Her mother ... Martine had never reconciled herself to the need for Ember to make a political marriage. She had accepted Osfrid because Ember was so happy, but marrying the Ice King's son – or rather, the Hárugur King's son – that would be very different indeed. Ember didn't even like Nyr much. And to live in this cage of caves for most of the year – to be imprisoned by snow and ice for months and months and months ... oh, no, she couldn't do that. She just couldn't. Let them negotiate some other settlement.

Play for time, she thought. The essence of negotiation. Don't say yes, don't say no.

'I thought Larra had plans in that direction,' she said, trying to keep it light. Halda's hand brushed across the tabletop, sweeping Larra's ambitions away.

'I will find her a husband worthy of her,' she said. 'Someone in a neighbouring tribe, perhaps. She need not concern you.'

'My father believes in trade rather than warfare,' Ember said carefully. 'I suspect he would welcome anything which created a lasting bond between our peoples.'

There. That was both true and diplomatic. Halda nodded with satisfaction.

'It is not easy,' she said sympathetically, 'to be married off to a strange land. But peace is a great gift to bring to a people.'

Peace. There could be no peace if all her people were dead or gone south. Ember sighed, suddenly exhausted, and hoped that she could go to her bed soon.

But before that, Ash was taken away by Bren and his men. Ember forced herself to watch, seemingly unmoved. Ash smiled at her reassuringly and she smiled back, but Cedar was grave and Tern looked anguished.

'No doubt the Hárugur King will see fit to release him when he returns,' Halda said comfortingly. Perhaps she wasn't as good at seeming unmoved as she had thought.

'My father values Ash highly,' Ember replied. Time to raise the stakes and use what pressure she could to safeguard him. 'And of course, he is my mother's grandson.'

Halda frowned. 'Your mother's . . . '

'My mother adopted Ash's mother some years ago, before she met my father,' Ember explained. 'I was a late child. So Ash and I are of a generation, but he is my mother's grandson.' She laughed a little, trying to seem unconcerned. 'I suppose he might be called my nephew, but we have always called each other cousins.'

'But you are not cousins by blood,' Halda said thoughtfully. 'So you might marry.'

The thought of marrying Ash swept over her with all the

force Fire could generate, turning her knees weak and her guts liquid. Fire would accept him, because he had old blood, they could be together ... She took a breath, steadying herself. She would not submit to this interference with her emotions. She would not let a false desire, an *imposed* desire, control her. She would not insult Ash that way.

'My mother's first daughter married a farmer,' she said dismissively. 'Ash is not even an officer's son, let alone a warlord's.'

'Ah,' Halda said, satisfied. 'So he is in your service.'

'In my father's service,' Ember clarified. Something in her writhed as she said it. It was like a betrayal, but she knew that the less important Halda and Ari thought Ash was, the more likely he was to be set free. A loyal servant with some family ties to the warlord was not valuable enough to hold for ransom, or to kill as a message of defiance or strength. Ash must be her servant, even if she could not *ever* think of him that way.

'Your men will sleep with the others,' Halda said. 'Come.'

She led Ember to the chamber where she had left her pack. It was a mark of great condescension, for the lady to escort a guest to her chamber, and Ember thanked Halda for it.

'In the morning, one of the girls will fetch you,' Halda said. 'I must stay in the hall for when the Hárugur King returns.'

Ember stripped off her clothes and lay down in her shift, pulling the soft blankets up high under her chin. A bed, after so long sleeping on the ground! She was weary to her bones ... but after she blew out the single candle, she lay for a long time staring at the fathomless dark, wondering where Ash was and whether he could sleep safely.

THE LAST DOMAIN

None of them wanted to eat. Larch, being a good soldier, forced down cheese and old biscuits with a swig of cider, and bullied Poppy kindly until she did the same. Jelica shook her head.

'After,' she said.

They sat at the back of the cottage and waited for the sun to go down, then went inside and waited more, until the stars had wheeled almost halfway through their nightly course.

Jelica kept the shutters open so that the bright northern starlight could shine through. There was a moon, too. A beautiful night. Poppy sat and shook with cold and nerves, until Larch came over to her and crouched next to her chair.

'You're planning something,' she said, half-accusingly. Jelica looked at her, eyes picking up the light like a cat's.

'There might be a sure way to bring him,' Poppy said reluctantly. 'Dangerous, though.'

Jelica laughed shortly. 'Dangerous anyroad. What way?'

'My grammer once used the blank stone as the new flint.'

A sound came out of Jelica as though she'd been punched in the belly, a big 'whouf' of noise.

'She must have been mad!'

'They couldn't find a new flint for the third night,' Poppy apologised.

'What third night?' Larch asked.

She knew so little – were they right to take her to this calling? But the ritual demanded that there should always be three women, at least.

'Three nights, at Spring Equinox,' she explained to Larch, 'the women of the old blood go to the black rock altars and strike new fire, with an unused flint, and ... call Him.'

'And He *comes*?'

'Always,' Jelica confirmed, a note in her voice of remembered pleasure. 'Always. And never any harm.'

'But there must be a new flint each night, or He doesn't come, and that's ... bad luck.' How to explain it to one of Acton's blood, that deep, bone-deep bond; the three nights of mounting desire and yearning, the heated blood, the liquid touch ... She had a new image of love, now she'd met Larch, but even so she shook with the memory of His touch. To not finish, to not have the third night – there were stories about women who'd simply pined away if they'd been prevented from worshipping; or killed themselves, unable ever to satisfy their desire; or killed others.

'Bad luck,' Larch repeated. 'But we don't have three nights.'

'It's not Equinox,' Poppy said.

'Then why should He come?'

'Might not,' Jelica said. 'But it's worth trying.' There was a note in her voice that worried Poppy. Desperation.

The altar was so small that Poppy almost missed it in the dark; without the faint susurration of the gods' voices in her head, she would have stumbled past it. They fled away as Jelica approached and the stonecaster turned as if to watch them fly, her face, even in the moonlight, clearly troubled.

'They'll come back,' Poppy reassured her. Jelica shrugged and nodded, but Larch looked at her strangely, and she felt the point just below her breastbone grow suddenly heavy. She knew that look; it was the one that said, 'Strange. Freak.' Seeing it on Larch's face hurt a great deal.

Larch took a step towards her and stared into her eyes, her own guarded.

'What do you see?'

'I hear the gods,' Poppy whispered. 'Softly, like whispering. My mam can take them inside herself so they speak with her mouth, but I can't.'

The corner of Larch's mouth quirked up. 'Glad to know that.' Her shoulders lost their tension. 'Do we do the chanting now?'

Poppy smiled at her. Perhaps Larch would be one of those amazing ones, like her own father, who could just accept the gods without feeling tainted. 'Aye,' she said. 'Tinder and prayer and flint. One to prime, one to hold, one to strike, three to call.'

Obeying the instructions they had given her, Larch carefully put a nest of birch fungus tinder on the low surface of the altar. It was only a fragment of rock, barely larger than her foot. But it was a place of worship, none the less, and enough for their needs.

Poppy put her striking stone down by the tinder, and Jelica, last and oldest, placed the new flint next to it. The blank stone, which meant that anything could happen.

Poppy squeezed Larch's hand.

'We are daughters of Fire,' they said together, the three voices blending oddly: Jelica's strong and dark, Poppy high and certain, Larch's almost a whisper. 'Daughters of Mim the

Firestealer, Mim the Firelover, Mim the Fire's love. The fire must never die.'

They crouched next to the altar. Larch made a cup of her hands around the tinder, Poppy took up the striking stone, and Jelica raised the flint and brought it down smoothly in one motion. Sparks flew.

'Take our breath to speed your growth,' Poppy said quietly as Larch blew. She had watched as they'd tried this at the fort, over and over, striking sparks only to watch them die out. But no one, under Arvid's angry eye, had called Him properly.

'The fire will never die,' Jelica said, so clearly that Poppy jumped as if she'd shouted. 'Come on, my lord, you know me! Haven't I served you well?' Her voice dropped to a whisper, a plea, yearning so deep in it that Poppy felt her whole body ache in response. 'Kept myself just for you, didn't I?' Jelica whispered, her breath taking one of the sparks and fanning it. It glowed in the darkness. 'Don't let the fire die!' Jelica begged. Poppy wanted to look away. It wasn't right, to hear this from a stranger – from *anyone*. It was like spying on a marriage bed.

But the spark caught.

Quickly, they added more tinder, and then more, as the flames licked more strongly, more cleanly. They stood up.

And He came. The fire flared out impossible heat, far too much for the amount of fuel they had given it.

Every other time, on the higher altars, He had towered above her; now He was closer, barely taller than a man. It was curiously disturbing, as though He had come within her reach in a new way.

Larch took a step backward, and Poppy stood still, but Jelica moved close, her face turned up as though to the summer sun.

'Why did you abandon us?' she demanded.

There was His face, as it had been in the wedding fire which had consumed Osfrid. Terrible, wonderful; she felt herself melt through with a mixture of desire and fear, confusing and exhilarating. Larch clutched her hand, but she couldn't look away from Him.

Fire gazed down at Jelica as though she and Larch weren't there.

'Angelica,' He said, His voice as full of love as any bridegroom's. 'I had reason.'

'Ice is coming!'

'You are strong, here in the north,' He said, laughing. 'You will triumph, if your princess does. But I have business elsewhere!'

The flames began to die away. 'No!' Jelica howled, throwing out her hands as if to clasp Him.

He paused, and smiled, a long slow smile full of desire and – yes, surely it *was* affection. Surely. Poppy could hear Larch's breathing, ragged, beside her, and only that stopped her walking forward. 'Then come to me,' He said. He opened His arms.

'No, Jelica!' Poppy cried out.

But Jelica surged forwards and took His hands. He swept her into an embrace, into a column of flame, just like Osfrid, just like Osfrid. Larch screamed. Poppy felt the heat of desire consummated sweep through her, like on the third night of the Equinox; as Fire surged and climbed and then disappeared, all in an instant, she felt Jelica's joy.

There wasn't even ash left behind. It had happened so quickly, not even a smell remained. He had not hurt her, but He had taken her completely, as if she had never existed.

MOUNTAINSIDE,
THE ICE KING'S COUNTRY

It wasn't Larra but another girl, a bit younger, with hair almost white and skin like skimmed milk, who came with a mixture of diffidence and curiosity about the stranger. Ember was ready dressed and would have been hungry if her belly hadn't been roiling with worry about Ash.

She *was* a stranger here, and she needed to build connections with these people. 'What is your name?' she asked the girl in the best approximation of their language that she could manage. Amusement flashed across the girl's face, so probably her accent was terrible but, 'Iina,' she answered shyly, twisting the end of her plait around her fingers.

'I am pleased to meet you, Iina. I am Ember.'

'Ember Konungsdottir,' Iina said, making it half a question.

'Almost,' Ember said. 'Ember Arvidsdottir. Arvid is our konung.'

Iina curtseyed as though the information required deference.

'And your father?' Ember asked. Exchange of information meant equals.

'Bren,' she said proudly.

'Ah,' Ember said, careful to show how impressed she was. Iina dimpled.

'Will you come to the hall, konungsdottir?'

'Ember,' she said with a smile. 'Is the Hárugur King returned?'

'No.' Iina frowned with worry. She was choosing her words – to make it simple, or to hide something? 'It is often so.'

'It takes time?'

'Much time,' Iina confirmed.

The halls were fuller today, with more men, all of whom assessed her, not as a woman, but as a stranger. She was used to men being clean-shaven, or at most with a close-cropped, neat beard. None of these men seemed to have trimmed their beards since they first grew whiskers. It kept out the cold, she supposed, as fur did on animals. It made her feel she had stepped into an old story, one of the very old ballads about Acton and his men, the warriors who had originally come from this side of the mountain. And perhaps that was not too far from the truth. Perhaps these men thought as Acton would have thought, honouring only warriors and their skills. Enjoying battle, relishing danger. The thought dismayed her.

She was relieved to see Cedar and Tern sitting on stools by the central hearth, eating bowls of what smelled like porridge. They stood up as soon as they saw her, relief on their own faces, and came over to her. Cedar put his arm around her shoulders and she turned her face into his shoulder for just a moment of comfort.

'Where's Ash?' she asked. She could feel him tense.

'We don't know. No one understands us, and the lady just says to wait.' He hesitated. 'I think I would know if he was hurt.'

She nodded. Of course he would know. That was how Sight worked, in families. The number of times Mam had come running out of the fort to find her because she had fallen and skinned her knee, or bumped her head … She blinked tears away. It meant that Ash was fine. Ember drew a deep breath and let it out, then went to the fire to greet Halda.

She looked tired, and worried. Was it better to ignore that, or to be sympathetic? There was a point where simple compassion overrode diplomacy, Ember thought. She put her hand on Halda's arm.

'I'm sure they are all right,' she said.

Halda tried to smile, but there was a flicker of irritation in her eyes.

'Easy to say,' she said. 'Kings have been killed before when they displeased the Ice King.'

Ember beckoned Cedar over.

'Will you cast for the lady?' she asked. 'Discover how her family fares?'

'Of course,' he answered, and bowed formally, 'but where a Power is concerned, castings may be difficult.'

'Let's try anyway.'

Halda was puzzled.

'Cast?' she asked. 'What do you mean?'

Ember and Cedar both looked at her in astonishment.

'You don't have stonecasters?' Ember asked. 'People who can tell you the future, or what is happening elsewhere?'

She looked at them as though they were mad.

'That's impossible!'

Ember smiled. 'The past twenty years, how often have your people raided my father's domain and found it unprepared?'

As though a long mystery had been solved, Halda drew in a deep breath and let it out in a huff.

'That was my mother,' Ember said. 'She cast each week to discover your intentions.'

Halda glared at her.

'She has caused the death of many of us, then.'

'If you hadn't attacked, you wouldn't have been killed,' Ember said mildly.

'We need to raid. You can see how little we have,' Halda said, almost without thought, a fact so obvious, so ingrained, that she wasn't aware how it sounded. Cedar bristled, but Ember shook her head at him. No use challenging these people's deepest attitudes. Not yet. 'We wouldn't have been able to survive, the past twenty years, if the wraiths hadn't left,' Halda mused.

'The wind wraiths?' Cedar asked with interest.

'Wind, Water, Ice,' Halda confirmed. 'They had harried us for a thousand years. Growing crops was almost impossible, no child was safe outdoors ... and then they just left, one day, screaming and shrieking and flying high ... now they're only in the wild areas, in the high passes.'

'That was my mother, too,' Ember said with pride. 'She and her friends banished them from all settled lands. I don't think she realised that it would extend this far, but she would be happy that it did.'

Halda's face paled.

'What kind of witch *is* your mother?'

'Witch' was a word Ember had never heard, but the tone was plain. She raised her chin and stared Halda down. This was one of those moments which set the tone for a whole future, she thought.

'My mother is a stonecaster with some skill in enchantments,' she said. 'She is the warlord's lady of the Last Domain, and it is her duty to keep her people safe, which she does with all the skills she possesses. If you had been able to banish the wraiths, would you not have done it?'

Trouble clouded Halda's face, but eventually she nodded, reluctantly.

'Aye,' she said. 'I would have, if it cost me my soul.'

'But it would not,' Cedar said gently. 'There is nothing evil about what we do. It is the gift of our gods.'

This time, Halda's tone was dry. 'They are generous, then.'

Cedar took the pouch from his waist, but before he could speak there was a hubbub from the far wall, and a young boy came flying over to Halda.

'They're back, lady!'

'King be praised!' Halda exclaimed and hurried towards a curtained doorway. She stopped just outside as Bren lifted the curtain from inside and held it back for the Hárugur King and Nyr to come through.

They were staggering with fatigue, but no one tried to help them until they were through the doorway. Then Halda rushed forward to embrace and steady them both, but with her hands gentler on Nyr, her voice full of emotion as she exclaimed over his pallor. They were both pale, indeed, and their faces were drawn as though they had gone much longer than a day without food, as though they had traversed half the world to get here.

'Bring chairs!' Bren ordered. The men in the hall were already bringing them forwards. The first was the artist Ember had seen earlier, his shirt patched with paint, his long hair untidy but his hands beautifully clean and cared for. He met her gaze with a look of shock, and an involuntary glance up at his butterfly painting. Odd, she thought.

The Hárugur King slumped into a chair by the central fire and Nyr followed him. Women brought hot drinks and plates of

food and they ate gratefully, although their hands shook as they
lifted the food to their mouths. They had more of a look of each
other than she had seen before – the shape of the bones under
the concealing beards was the same, although Nyr had his
mother's eyes.

Ember hadn't been this close to the fire before, and she
realised, with a sinking heart, that although it burned cow pats
as fuel, or maybe horse dung, the base of it was much deeper,
and connected to the other fires in the bathing cave. This central
hearth was Fire's doing. His power was muted here, though, and
she wondered why.

Her stomach was flipping up and down with nerves, but she
knew better than to ask a king anything before he was ready to
speak. She waited, with all the rest, Cedar at her back and Tern
beside him, for the two men to be finished.

They didn't hurry. It was as though they wanted to settle into
the world again. She had seen Fire twice, and that was twice too
many. Humans weren't meant to encounter the Powers; it was
no wonder that the king and his son needed time to recover.

Nyr was finished first, but finally, Ari handed his plate to
someone and rubbed his eyes, then stood up with a sigh. Nyr
also stood.

'The Ice King greets his people,' Ari said formally. All
around, men and women both sank to one knee and bowed
their heads. Tern made a small movement to follow, but Ember
signalled him to stay upright. They were not worshippers of this
Power.

Ari noticed but seemed to accept their decision.

'This is the pronouncement of the Ice King: the man Nyr
Arissen is accepted as heir to the Hárugur King.'

Halda's face lit up with a mixture of pride and relief. Other
heads lifted with smiles of real joy and bodies shifted a little, as

though they wanted to jump up and cheer, but held themselves back.

'Nyr Arissen has looked the Ice King in the face and not trembled,' Ari went on, and this time the pride in his voice was clear. Nyr, oddly, was looking at the ground as though the praise made him uncomfortable. I'll bet he did tremble, even if only inside, Ember thought.

'The Ice King's pronouncement is this: the stranger Ember Arvidsdottir may not travel to the Fire Mountain, which is the site of evil, nor may her followers.'

Ember felt a hollow thump in her belly as the words hit home. Ari looked shrewdly at her, gauging her acceptance. Well, she knew how to seem complaisant. She bowed a little to indicate just that, keeping her face calm but allowing just a trace of disappointment to show through so that he would believe it.

Tern, on the other hand, tried to push forward, making an inarticulate exclamation. Cedar held him back, one hand on his arm, and Ember turned to frown at him.

'These were the pronouncements of the Ice King,' Ari concluded. People shifted, but didn't rise. Halda was looking at her. Something was expected from them.

'Will you translate?' she asked Halda quietly, and the lady nodded, rising to stand beside her.

'Ember Arvidsdottir thanks the Hárugur King and his son for their courtesy and their courage,' she said clearly, in her own language but very slowly, so that Halda could keep up. Halda translated easily, and Ember listened hard so that she'd know the words again. 'We will take counsel of them to decide what our next course should be.'

Ari nodded once, with satisfaction at both her courtesy and her humility. She stepped back, and at once the people around them rose and advanced on Nyr, his friends slapping him on the back and the girls exclaiming and fluttering their eyelashes, Larra well to the forefront. Ember exchanged an amused look with Halda, who shrugged and said softly, 'It's a great achievement, to be accepted as heir. Many have been rejected.' Her eyes were bright with pride and relief.

'Congratulations,' Ember said sincerely. 'I rejoice in your happiness.'

She moved back to let others get closer, and saw that Cedar was staring at the doorways to the inner caves. Ash was there, with three men guarding him. He looked all right, she thought, relief as strong as Halda's rushing through her, but he wasn't happy. He must have heard the Ice King's decision.

Ash was expecting her to go to him, but she couldn't. She had to maintain the illusion that he was just a servant; family, but not overly valued, not worth, for example, a ransom.

So she nodded and smiled with moderate warmth and gave him the hand signal he used with the dogs to say, 'stay'. His mouth twitched with amusement and he let his tongue hang out just a little, pretending to be a dog, but he didn't move and the men with him were too busy watching Nyr, broad smiles on their faces, to notice.

Cedar, on the other hand, could go to him with no harm done, and after a glance at her, he did so, with Tern close behind. Tern's expression as he looked at her was disapproving. He obviously thought she should rush to Ash's side.

Ari sent Larra to summon her, and Ember thought the girl quite enjoyed being singled out. She shepherded Ember most solicitously back to where Ari was sitting. Ember thanked her politely, and she made that little bob with a spread of her skirts, then went to stand behind Nyr's chair. Much good it would do her. Even if Ember wasn't prepared to marry Nyr, she didn't think Halda would countenance Larra as a daughter-in-law.

Iina, on the other hand, stood with her father, but her eyes were on Nyr just as much as Larra's were. She had a much better chance, Ember thought. Father close to the ruler, valued, important ... I'd put my money on her, if it were a two-horse chase. But no doubt there were other candidates.

She bowed to Ari.

'Bren tells me your man burned his bow,' he said roughly, his eyes bright, tiredness thrown off, peering at her from under his brows.

'As he should have, Hárugur King,' she answered calmly.

'Hmmph! So it was on your orders?'

She smiled, gently satiric. 'In so many words? No, I did not say "Burn the bow." I did say, "The bow must not fall into anyone else's hands." He found his own way of making sure of that, for which I commend him.' Turning, she bowed slightly to Ash, whose guards had brought him closer, although not within the inner circle.

'Mm,' Ari mused.

'What would you have done in my place, my lord?' Ember asked. 'Would you have handed over a new weapon to a traditional enemy?'

'We were helping you!' Ari barked.

She simply looked at him, a slight smile inviting him to share their common understanding of the situation. Nyr was smiling a little, but his father was far more experienced a negotiator.

'You have abused our hospitality,' he accused her.

'When I return to my father, I will tell him that you wish to trade for the new bows,' she said. 'But without his permission, how could I make that decision?'

Respect for a father and a ruler was an argument he could accept, although he harrumphed a few more times for good measure.

'He'll have to be punished, though,' he said finally.

'Believe me,' Ember said, sincerity blatant in her tone, 'burning that bow was punishment. He loved that thing.'

'So he *did* make it?' Nyr jumped in. She blinked.

'He sanded it down, I think,' she said, and turned to Ash as though to check her facts. 'Didn't you?' He nodded, face impassive. 'Yes. And I think maybe made the bow strings.'

'Who was your master?' Ari demanded of Ash.

'My master was Barley, in Western Mountains Domain,' he said.

'Yes,' Ari said grimly. 'We saw them used there last summer.'

'My father has ordered quite a few, so he may have some spare to trade.'

'Ah,' Ari said. 'Well, that can be discussed. But your man did something he knew I would disapprove of, and he must be punished.'

'How?' she made herself ask, as calmly as she could.

'Twenty blows with the stick,' he said, just as calmly. It was a challenge. She had no idea what a stick was, or how hard the blows would be.

'That seems excessive,' she said. 'Did you tell him you wanted the bow?'

He hesitated, and looked at Bren, who shook his head and sent her an appreciative smile.

'So he did not, in fact, disobey you,' Ember concluded. 'And he acted on the orders of his liege, to protect his people.'

'Ten, then,' Ari said, dismissing the problem and getting up. 'I am going to bed, and do not wish to be disturbed until evening. Bren, you see to the punishment.'

'Aye, Hárugur King,' Bren said.

Ari and Nyr left, still walking heavily, and Halda followed them. The three guards brought Ash forwards, and motioned him to take off his jacket. Urno, the painter, brought forward the stick. Tern glared at him.

It was long, almost as tall as a man, and thicker than her thumb. Some hard dark wood. She felt sick. Helpless. There was nothing she could do. They were surrounded, in the midst of their enemies. To protest, to question the will of the Hárugur King, might condemn them all.

Ash, damn him to the cold hells, smiled at her as though it were all just a joke. Bren took the stick.

'Hold onto something, lad,' he said. 'Brace yourself.'

Ash took his advice and braced against one of the tables, his back to them. They were encircled by the men, but there were no women to be seen. Bren stared at her, waiting for her to leave.

'He is my man,' she said. 'Acting under my orders. The least I can do is stay.'

A younger man growled something in disapproval, but Bren waved a hand at him and he fell silent.

Her father had rarely used physical punishments. He preferred to take the criminal's time, assigning them to work at the fort or for the person they had injured or stolen from. The kind of work no one else wanted, like digging privies or cleaning pigsties. Worst of all, cleaning out the tanner's vats. Thank the gods, there was never any need to torture to discover whether someone was guilty, as she'd heard they did in the Wind Cities. The stones could tell them, if the evidence did not.

Serious crimes were punishable by death: rapists, murderers, child-stealers, slavers were dispatched quickly, by a knife to the heart. Arvid had never let anyone but the victim or their family attend executions, and he did not use the pressing box or the garrotte, like the southern warlords. But all rulers had to punish wrongdoers, and Ember had been thankful that it would be Osfrid who would make those decisions for her.

The first stroke made a thud as it landed on Ash's back, and Ember felt the impact like a fist in her stomach. Tears came to her eyes. Ash didn't make a sound, just braced again.

'One,' the men yelled as it landed.

Ash was strong; like the oak tree she'd compared him to in her thoughts. But he was flesh and blood, and merely human. He had no Power to call on, no special skills. He was like her, vulnerable to pain and injury and death. She felt her heart shudder as each blow landed; as his flesh seemed to ripple under the force of each stroke.

The men counted the rest as Bren laid them on. On the fourth blow, blood appeared on his shirt. On the fifth, he rocked on his feet but grabbed at the table and saved himself.

Bren gave him a moment to set himself again and Ember caught a glimpse of Ash's face, sweat-streaked and determined. He planted his feet and nodded at Bren.

'Six!' the men shouted. Blood was flowing now, from a wide slash on his right shoulder.

'Seven!' His head was still up, but it bowed just a little as the blow landed.

Ember's knees were shaking and she wanted to run, to hide her head, to throw her skirt over her eyes as old grammers did when they mourned. But he was her man, following her orders, and in this place she was the only authority, the only protection, he had.

'Eight!' His fingers, gripping the table, were white, and his arms had begun to shake. Cedar stood at her shoulder, fists clenched.

'Why doesn't he go faster?' he muttered. Urno, the artist, stood beside them.

'To go quickly would be to treat him like a child,' he said. 'That would dishonour him.'

'You're all barbarians,' Tern said, glaring red-eyed. Urno frowned as if encountering a new thought, but he turned away without answering. Ember knew she should reprove Tern, but she agreed with him too much to force the words past her clenched throat. Every blow seemed to hit her own body; pain speared down into her as it did him. Only the long, long training as the warlord's daughter kept her on her feet and not screaming.

'Nine!' Ash's back was covered in blood; his shirt was in tatters, but his feet were still planted, although he swayed.

'Ten!' the men yelled, and then cheered and laughed, the groups breaking up.

Bren handed the stick back to Urno and went to Ash, but Ash dragged a breath in and stood up by himself. He turned, that challenging smile still on his lips, despite being as white as death. He even grinned at Bren while his blood was dripping onto the floor.

'A good arm on you, there,' he said. Bren smiled back and Ember thought that she would never understand men. Idiots! She took Ash's arm and Cedar went to his other side, but he shook them off.

'I'm not an old man, to need a shoulder to lean on,' he said, almost crossly, and Bren nodded approval. A few of the other men laughed at her and made comments which contained, she was sure, the word for 'hen' and 'chick'. Ash laughed too, although he could have understood nothing but the tone. Fine, if he wanted to play the man and show off, she would let him.

She let go and moved back, but his head came around to follow her movement and he smiled, properly this time, and said, 'Thank you for your eloquence.' She could feel tears fill her eyes, hot and stinging.

'Let Cedar look after you,' was all she could say.

'Aye,' Cedar confirmed. 'It's a brother's job.'

The men around accepted this with nods and Cedar led Ash off towards a corridor, Tern holding his other elbow.

Bren saw her tears and sighed. 'Punishments are not fit for women to see,' he said.

She ignored him.

'Now what happens to us?' she asked.

'Tomorrow, when your man has recovered, you come with us on the journey to your father.' He looked pleased by this, as well he might. She was guarantee they would not be attacked before they reached Arvid. Especially if they went the long way, around the Forest.

She nodded, as if she had expected nothing else.

They would have to leave tonight.

'I need to check my horses, then,' she said. 'Make sure their tack is ready.'

Bren pursed his lips, unsure.

'And to tell you the truth,' Ember added, 'I'd like to get out into the fresh air for a while.'

That brought a half-smile; it was a feeling everyone here had in spring, she suspected. Bren motioned one of the young boys over, a slight lad with corn-coloured hair and eyes so pale they were disconcerting.

'Take our guest to the stables and then show her the gardens,' Bren ordered. To Ember, with some pride, he added, 'This is Siggi.'

'Aye, Da,' Siggi said, staring at her with interest. He went ahead to one of the many passageways that led out of the hall. Ember noted which one – it was beneath a painting of a double-headed battleaxe dripping with blood. She hoped that wasn't an omen.

The horses were not far, and the passage led straight to their pasture. Merry was pleased to see her, and that simple affection lightened Ember's heart. She collected their dirty bridles in a basket and checked on the saddles, safe in a stone shed built against the cliff.

Siggi took her back to the hall with an air of having successfully performed a difficult task. He swaggered a little as he ushered her through the doorway and saw some of his friends watching.

'I need to see my men,' she said slowly, trying to get her accent right. She shook the basket a little, as if to say that she wasn't going to do their work.

He grinned, showing a gap in his teeth.

'Aye,' he nodded, and ran off to the passageway she had seen the men go through.

There were few people in the hall today, but there were some older women preparing food near the central hearth, who stared at her curiously. Her trousers, showing under the calf-length skirt, made them cluck their tongues with disapproval. They sounded like hens in a barnyard, and she had to fight not to smile. Instead, she mimicked Larra's little spread of the skirts with a bob, and discomfited them. They all bobbed their heads and then turned into a tight circle, pretending not to be looking at her.

Siggi ran out of the passageway and was followed, just as fast, by Cedar, who came hurrying over to her, looking alarmed.

'What is it?' she asked.

'Are you all right? This little one came running, calling "Arvidsdottir, Arvidsdottirsmen!"'

Siggi grinned cheekily at her and she mimed flicking his head with her hand. He grinned wider and ran off to some friends on the other side of the hall, no doubt to boast about being her guide.

'I'm fine,' she said to Cedar. 'How is Ash?'

'Resting,' Cedar said, 'and cross with anyone who tries to help. He's always been that way – it's best to just leave him alone. He'll recover.'

She must have looked surprised at his equanimity, because his mouth twisted awry a little. 'He's had worse than that falling out of trees or from cliffsides,' he added. 'He was always climbing, even as a little lad, Mam says. Always trying to get as high as he could, but he never seemed to hurt himself badly. He heals fast.'

It was reassuring, in a way, because they had very little time, and Ash had to travel tonight, come what may.

'Bren has told me,' Ember said, conscious that not far away a pair of women were picking over beans for supper, and alert for every word. No telling how much they could understand. 'We will be leaving for home tomorrow, with the trading party.'

He met her eyes and she held his steadily, warning him not to react.

'The Ice King's word is law here, and He says we must go,' she said. Out of the corner of her eye she saw one of the women nod, and knew they had been set as spies. Ember handed over the basket of tack to Cedar. He looked at it blankly, then his gaze sharpened as he recognised their own gear.

'I've been to see the horses,' she went on. 'They're ready to ride after such a good rest. Clean this and get it ready, too.' It was an order, lady to servitor. He nodded slowly.

'Aye, my lady,' he said. 'Should I check the saddles, too?'

'No, they're fine. I've looked at them.'

'Do you know what time we'll be leaving?' he asked.

'At dawn, I suppose, or soon after.' With one hand, concealed by her skirt from the women, Ember showed Cedar two fingers. The second watch. He nodded understanding. 'It will be a long day's travel,' she went on. 'I hope Ash can manage it, because we can't slow Prince Nyr down.' Again the woman nodded to herself. She wasn't a very good spy – maybe it was just natural curiosity which had set her to listening. But certainly what they had said would be reported to Bren.

'Let's hope your father won't be too angry with you for not completing your task,' Cedar said. Good, keeping up the act. He was learning, Cedar, how to choose his words, which was just as well if he was going to be a warlord.

'Well,' Ember replied comfortably, 'you know how he loves trade. If we bring a trading party back I think he will forgive me.'

The woman smirked. That's right, Ember thought. I'm just a lazy daughter who is taking the easy way out. I don't care one way or the other if I complete my task, whatever that is, do I? You go and tell Bren that.

Sure enough, as Cedar took the basket of tack back to the men's passageway, the two women picked up their own basket and headed for a small doorway on the other side of the hall.

Ember felt suddenly weary, although it couldn't have been later than noon. She sat down on a bench at a table and wondered what was happening at home.

TIMBERTOP, THE LAST DOMAIN

'The stonecaster saw what I told you, and you can make up your own mind about why she's not here to tell you herself,' Poppy said, loud and certain, to the people of Timbertop.

'Jelica doesn't leave that cabin,' an old woman said. 'You want her, you go to her.'

There were mumblings of discontent and uncertainty.

Poppy stilled her face with an effort. No use telling these people what had happened to Jelica. It had been her own choice, but would they believe that? Her job was simply to get them and others like them to the mine in Salt.

At least she didn't feel too young for the job. Watching Jelica surrender to Him had aged her in a moment.

'You can stay here and die, or you can come to Salt and live. That's the choice, and it's the only one you've got,' she said. They are afraid, she thought. I must remember that they are as afraid as I am. Larch stood at her shoulder, silent but strong. 'The gods speak to my mother, you all know that.' They nodded, muttered a few words to each other, looked back at her. She took a deep breath. Time to claim her inheritance. She'd never said the words aloud before, not even to her mam. The whisperings in her head had been so slight, so soft, that she had even wondered if they were real.

'They speak to me, too.'

The villagers exclaimed at that. Half of them cheered up, and the other half looked sour. But they listened.

'We must go to Salt.'

'We?' the Village Voice asked. 'You're going, too?'

'I need to collect the people from the other villages. But then, yes, I will be there.'

For some reason, this decided them and the group broke up to pack. Larch smiled at her puzzled face.

'Why should they trust someone unless that person is risking the same thing they are?' she asked.

'We're all at risk, no matter where we are,' Poppy said.

'But they will have a darling of the gods to protect them.'

That was more terrifying than anything else she could have said.

Palisade Fort, the Last Domain

In the evening before the Summer Solstice they began to gather: the women and children, the people of Two Springs, the fort guard and all the other workers who kept the fort running, complete with kin. Everyone from the dairymaid to the gardener to the boy who watched the geese. They filled the hall by an hour before sunset and then each room of the residence, one by one. Except the guest chamber and Martine's parlour, where Sigurd kept her vigil, undeterred by darkness or weariness.

Very few of them had washed much in the last two weeks, and the smell began to mount as people crowded in together. At least it was warmer that way.

At sunset, they said the evening prayers, led by the Voice of Two Springs, and Elva was there at the glass table, white head bowed as she sent their wishes and hopes and fears to the gods. They spoke back, to Arvid's relief, in that odd, deep voice so different to Elva's normal light tones.

'Be strong, be bound together in trust and love, and Ice will quail before you,' they said.

It was what they all needed to hear, but Arvid hoped that it wasn't one of those tricksy messages the gods sent, where there was a darker meaning underneath. If they were not bound together, what would happen?

After the prayers, concealing his fears, Arvid stood on the dais he used to pronounce judgement and spoke to his people, conscious of each trusting or fearful or cynical eye on him. He'd planned a long and reassuring speech, but he realised it wouldn't work. They deserved his honesty, not manipulation.

'The gods and Sealmother have given us a way to defend ourselves,' he said. 'You all know what must be done at dawn.' They nodded, looked briefly at each other, looked back at him. 'We are one people. Man, woman, Traveller, blondie –' there were some grins and some shocked looks at his using that word, '– guard or blacksmith or farmer or maid – or warlord – we are all Last Domainers first and forever!'

They cheered at that and he grinned at them, feeling for the first time that they might succeed. It was like this in battle, when you had your men behind you, trusting you, following you. He had forgotten, with all the enchantment and tricks, that this was a battle; and battle was a thing he understood. He said so.

'It doesn't matter if it's the Ice King's men or the Ice King himself!' he declared. 'We know how to fight the bastard, and we'll win, the way we always win!'

They were on their feet, now, shouting his name, calling out the battle cry of the Last Domain: 'North! North! North!'

He saluted them and they cheered more, then he leaped down from the dais and went around the room, as he went around a camp the night before a battle, talking to each of them, putting a hand on a shoulder here, giving a clap on the back there. As always, it uplifted him and sobered him at the same time. They were his strength, but also his weakness; he would feel their injuries as his own.

He was conscious that Martine and Elva watched him from the glass table. The Prowman was standing propped against the wall by his workroom, arms folded. His face was unreadable. Arvid would have given a great deal to know what he was thinking. He made his way over to the wall, chatting and laughing and encouraging as he went.

Ash nodded at him and they moved into a small space in the corner.

'Your defences, my lord, are incomplete,' the Prowman said soberly. That reined him in with a jolt.

'Where is the weakness?' Arvid demanded. The Prowman put out one long finger and touched Arvid's forehead.

'Here,' he said. He moved the finger down to Arvid's chest. 'And here.'

Anger spiked through Arvid, but he kept it in check.

'Explain.'

'Did you not hear the gods? We must be bound together in trust and love. *All* of us.'

Involuntarily, Arvid glanced over at Martine, and saw that she was staring out across the hall but not seeing; her eyes were abstracted with Sight. As though she felt his gaze – perhaps she did – she turned her head to stare him right in the eyes. His stomach lurched. It was the first time she had looked at him properly in days. There was pain in her eyes, and something he had never seen before, except when she was worrying about Ember. Martine was afraid.

Twenty years of married life allowed him to read her face, now that she was not shutting him out. She was afraid that he would not listen to the Prowman. They had been talking about him to each other. A hand squeezed his heart, but his mind over-rode the surge of jealousy and pain and said, *She is afraid*. Martine, who feared nothing.

'Bring her to the fire,' he said, and turned away from that look on her face with relief.

He left the protection of the hall in his full winter gear, and he needed it. The storm was rising, wind in gusts of chill that slit through his coats like needles, snow whirling around in circles of intense cold, a high keening piercing his ears. And yet the stars shone brightly above – the snow wasn't really snow, but flakes of ice blown off walls and ground. He followed one of the blizzard ropes (already frozen stiff) to the fire, which he could barely see in the distance. Closer, it seemed pitifully small to withstand the blown snow and ice, but it burned valiantly. There was a team feeding it, led by Lily.

'Good thing you ordered the woodstack filled, my lord!' he shouted cheerily against the howl of the wind. Arvid grinned and nodded. This had been a mistake. He and Martine couldn't talk here – but he should have thought to come out and encourage these men anyway, so it wasn't wasted effort. He spoke to each of the four, and by that time Martine had joined him with a pot of cha they could warm at the fire. They thanked her profusely, especially when she handed over a small flask of apple brandy.

'Ah, we're lucky to have you, my lady,' Lily said, taking a swig.

She smiled with genuine amusement, the first real smile Arvid had seen from her since Osfrid's death.

'Save it for the cha,' she advised. 'It'll last longer and do more good that way.'

'Aye, my lady,' Lily said, saluting her.

'Come to the barn,' Arvid said, and waited until she had found the right rope, then followed her across the yard to the solid bulk of the barn. They were in the lee, here, and it was a relief. The big doors were barred, but Arvid lifted the latch on the small door and held it open for her to slip inside, then went in too. Closing it behind him was a mistake – he had forgotten, again, that there was no light to be had after sunset.

Even the meagre starlight of the yard would have helped, but they were standing in velvet darkness, the wind distant, unable to know anything but each other's breathing. The animals had all been housed in the smaller barns; with all the people in the hall, this one was empty, although it smelled faintly of goats and more strongly of hay. They were alone for the first time in days. It was intimate; her breath in the darkness reminded him of so many nights, winter and summer, when the darkness had been a prelude to desire, to joy, to laughter ...

'Ash says,' he started, but she said at the same time, 'This is my fault.'

At last! he thought. At last.

'We would not be in this situation if I had done what I should,' Martine continued. Her voice shook a little. It was as though he heard that voice for the first time. It was like mead, dark and golden and mellow, but with a strength at the centre you didn't get from honey water. He was shaken with something more complex than desire; need, he thought. I need her. Her strength, the tenderness that she only shows to me and Ember, her desire for me, her competence and her vigour and her laughter, her understanding of people which somehow never made her too cynical, her compassion ... her wisdom.

'I was wrong,' she said, slowly. 'And this is hard to say ...' Her voice faltered, and he took a step towards the sound, his hand reaching out. She never gave up her pride, ever; admitting her mistake *would* be hard. 'I should not have married you.'

Arvid stopped dead. He could feel blood draining from his face, cramping in his guts, leaving him cold and astonished. Not even angry. Simply frozen. *This is what He wants*, he thought, *to freeze us all like this forever.*

'I loved you,' she said. 'Oh, gods, I loved you *so much*.' She paused. 'I still do; you know that, yes?'

He didn't answer. What could he say? The Ice King's cold hand was around his heart. How could she love him and say that she shouldn't have married him?

'So. As soon as I knew I was pregnant I should have left you. Gone to Hidden Valley with Elva, raised Ember there ... but I loved you too much, and you needed an heir ...' her voice was troubled by a mixture of shame and longing. He could read that voice so well, but had he ever understood her? 'I let my child be taken and used as a warlord's catspaw.'

'No!' he burst out. 'Never!'

'Oh, you can't even see what you did to her!' Martine said. 'It was all so *normal* for you. But I knew better. I should have raised her as a farmer's girl and let her choose her own life and her own love. And if I had, this wouldn't have happened.'

'I never made her a catspaw,' he insisted. 'I love her.'

'If she had come home, as you did, with a penniless Traveller, and said, "Da, this is the man I want to marry", what would you have done?'

He was silent for a long moment. It had never even occurred to him that such a thing might happen. He wanted to claim that he would have been happy, but that would be a lie.

'I don't know,' he said eventually. He rallied. 'I let her choose her own husband!'

'From a carefully picked bunch!' she retorted. He heard a rustle, as though she had raised her hands to her face. 'Oh, it doesn't matter! But I sacrificed her because I loved you so much, and that's the truth.'

It was the truth. He could hear it.

'Then why did you lie to me?'

Her voice was cold. 'I have *never* lied to you. I do not lie.'

Stonecasters were renowned for telling the truth. The stones, they said, wouldn't stay with a liar, and Martine was so accurate a caster that it was a joke around the fort that she must be Truth's own daughter.

He struggled with the memory of clasping her hand, time after time, as she cast for him, telling him truths plumbed from the gods and from time itself. The Prowman's words in the cavern came back to him, 'Would you have told your wife?'

'You left me in ignorance,' he said quietly, and it was the first time since Osfrid's death that he had spoken to her in a normal tone, without accusation, without defence.

'Yes,' she agreed, her voice quieter, warmer, too. 'I left you in ignorance. Partly because I had sworn to do so. Partly because I thought you were safer without that knowledge. Partly—' She stumbled over the word, and then recovered. 'Partly because I still don't know enough about how a warlord thinks, and I didn't know if you would feel honour-bound to share the knowledge with the other warlords. I knew the consequences of that would be bad.'

'So you didn't trust me,' he said, with difficulty.

'I knew you would act with integrity,' she said slowly. In the darkness, each word dropped clear and heavy. 'But I did not know what form that integrity would take. And I trust the other warlords not at all.'

She was right not to trust them – Sigurd's reaction to her was evidence enough of how southerners still thought of Travellers, deep down. If warlords had known that Travellers were meeting in secret ... would he have told them? The truth was, he didn't know. Couldn't know, now, how that younger Arvid would have reacted.

'I cast a couple of times,' she said, surprisingly, 'to see what I should do. But someone who casts for herself has a fool for a client.' It was an old saying, and it meant that stonecasters never Saw clear about their own worries.

Somehow, the fact that she had turned to the stones for guidance – that she had, at least, *considered* telling him – mattered. It meant that she hadn't reduced him to the status of a child, not fit for grown-up secrets.

'I never went to the Fire from the time I met you,' she said, in a much smaller voice. 'Never worshipped Him, or came from Him to you.'

And that mattered, too.

He took another step towards that strong, intoxicating voice, hand reaching out blindly to find her. It touched her shoulder, and he felt the deep shiver that went through her at his touch.

'I loved you too much,' she whispered again. There were tears in her voice; Martine never cried, never ...

'No,' he said quietly, standing next to her, breathing her in, the musky jasmine of her hair, the clear female scent that jolted his whole body into abrupt need. He forced himself to breathe slowly, but his breath was ragged. They were much the same height, he and his wife. He leaned forward until his cheek brushed her hair, so he could whisper into her ear. She swayed towards him. 'You cannot love me too much. Nor I you.'

Her head turned, her wet cheek sliding across his until their mouths found each other, clung desperately, kissed and clung again, bodies turning and pressing, trying to get closer, to cleave together, muscle and bone and sinew all with the same desire; to reunite.

There was clean straw under them, but he didn't think about that until much, much later, when she stirred in his arms and said, 'It's almost dawn. Elva will need us.'

The word 'us' brought a flood of happiness as great as the passion that had gone before.

MOUNTAINSIDE,
THE ICE KING'S COUNTRY

Ash was grateful that they could pack openly, pretending to be getting ready for the next day. It didn't take long, once Cedar brought the news back from Ember.

Being beaten by Bren had made the other men more friendly towards him, as though they'd all been through the same thing – as they probably had. One of the younger ones had even brought him some soup at lunchtime; then they had all disappeared outside, leaving the three of them to clean tack, with only one of Ari's men, Pib, sitting by the small fire, whittling a cup out of a sheep's horn. Pib spoke their language – his mother had been a thrall, taken, he said, from further south than Hidden Valley. She'd died a few years ago. Ash suspected that he'd been set to watch them, but that was fair. He'd do the same to strangers in his home.

The cuts on his back were shallow, but it had taken a while to stem the bleeding, and he was feeling groggy. Worse was the deep bruising, which would make him stiff as a granfer if he didn't move around soon. The pain wasn't as bad as being cooped up in the men's cave. Ash was oppressed by the stone roof, the unbroken walls, the eternal candlelight. Although the air was fresh, he longed for breeze on his face. He might do better with a hood on, like a falcon in a mews, he thought.

He lay on his stomach with his face in the crook of his arm, planning. Cedar had insisted on cleaning the tack with Tern's help, and Ash had seen the sense of that. He had to rest, or he wouldn't be able to ride tonight, and he could not, *must* not, hinder Ember's escape.

Second watch. Yes, by then they should all be asleep, except for the guards. He had no bow, but he and Cedar each had his belt knife and Tern had his dagger. The arrows might be useful, too.

Ash was uncomfortably aware that he might have to kill someone to get out. One of the men who'd joked with him; one of the guards who'd ridden with them. It was hard to think of them as enemies, as the ruthless horde who attacked without mercy.

He had never killed face to face. Never with a blade. Never someone he knew.

Seeing these people in their homes had made him realise why they raided. The pasture outside was the richest thing they owned, and it only lasted a few months a year. The valley earth was thin, producing spindly plants and lean grazing. They were poor, these people, living on a knife's edge of cold and wind. He hadn't even seen a chubby baby here – all the children were scrawny. A few men were solid enough, but Ash was taller by far and even Tern looked muscular compared to the others.

If they had nothing worth trading, how could they survive without raiding? If his children's future were at stake, would he attack strangers to ensure it? He thought he would, especially if a Power like the Ice King encouraged it.

He sat up, trying not to wince as the bruises caught, and slid around to sit on the side of the bed, stretching to stop himself stiffening up. Cedar scowled disapprovingly at him, but he just grinned and stood up, going over to the water barrel and dipping up a drink.

'What does Nyr have to trade?' he asked Pib in a tone of idle curiosity. Pib rested his whittling on his knee as if glad of the break.

'Furs, mostly,' he said. 'We've been able to trap a lot more now the wind wraiths are gone. It took a while to outfit everyone with winter gear, but now we've got enough for ourselves *and* some extra. And there's this—' He brandished the horn. 'We've made carvings, some silverwork, soapstone jewellery, a bit of weaving.'

'What do you want in return?' Cedar joined in.

Pib gave a bark of laughter. 'What *don't* we want? You southerners have more than you need. The women want pots and wooden things, platters and such, and herbs for healing. Ari Hárugur King wants steel, seeds, tools ... ' He shrugged.

'Dried fish would be useful, here, too,' Tern piped up. He was in a corner, rubbing tack industriously, but now he looked up. 'I'm from the north, where it gets as cold as here, and salt fish makes a good standby in winter for stews.'

Pib looked doubtful.

'Never had fish,' he said. 'What's it taste like?'

They looked at each other, trying to work out how to describe it. Cedar smiled. 'Salty,' he said.

'Salt's good,' Pib acknowledged. 'At least we've got salt.'

'Really? You can trade that, as well,' Cedar said. 'Especially down south.'

'I'll let Bren know that,' Pib said, and then, suspiciously, 'Why you bein' so helpful?'

Laughing, Ash sat back down on the bed. 'We've spent every summer of our lives defending our valley against you lot. I'd much rather sell you arrows than put arrows into you!'

That was a joke Pib could understand, and he laughed full-throatedly, throwing his head back.

I could slit his throat now, Ash thought, but that would be stupid. Which was a relief.

Cedar said Ember was fine, but Ash couldn't help worrying about her. He'd been surprised by how well she'd handled the king, but that was the courtier in her coming out – the part he liked the least. In the Forest they'd just been family and friends together; here she was the princess and they were servants, and that was increasingly hard to bear.

The trouble with being cooped up was that he had too much time to think. He lay down again and buried his face in his arms. Ember. No. Don't think about her. What about that girl, Iina? She was pretty, and much more the kind of girl he'd always fancied; slight, blonde, shy. He tried to summon up her face in his mind, but it wouldn't come; only Ember's green eyes, the freckles on her uptilted nose, the blazing hair which always escaped from its ties ... people talked about their hearts being sore, but it wasn't his heart but just under it that hurt. A hard knot that tightened every time he thought about her. He was her *cousin*, for Swith's sake! Or even worse, her nephew. *Not by blood*, his treacherous mind whispered.

He was a bowyer and she was a warlord's daughter and blood or not, she was forbidden to him.

Grammer would support you, he thought, but he banished it. Grammer Martine didn't rule the Last Domain, and he was as sure as he could be that Arvid would forbid any marriage between him and Ember.

He couldn't believe that he had even thought the word

'marriage'. His stomach clenched; she was beautiful, of course, but she drove him to distraction sometimes, with her tears and her spoilt assumptions about who would do the work for her. Yet, to be fair, on this journey she had pulled her weight, and if she'd cried, she'd had cause. And brave – she was as brave as Grammer, and that was saying something. She had stood up to Elgir as he wouldn't have dared; an enchanter, a warlord – that was a bad combination! But she was fierce in defence of her people.

That brought him to thoughts of Curlew and the cairn of rocks which covered him; and of Thatch, left behind for the wolves and crows. He mourned them both, in different ways, but the one he missed most was Holdfast, who had been his companion for five years, as Grip had been Cedar's. Holdfast's warm weight on his feet would have helped him sleep.

'I wonder how the dogs are?' he said to Cedar, and saw his eyes go out of focus as he thought about them. Sight.

'They're fine,' Cedar said, half-smiling. 'Playing like pups.'

Tern stared at him, wide-eyed, and Pib stared, too. Although he didn't quite understand what had just happened, he realised something had. Ash laughed. All of their family were so used to Sight and the gods talking that they forgot, sometimes, how odd it seemed to others.

'It doesn't always work like that, to order,' he said to Tern.

'That's the truth!' Cedar confirmed. 'When you most want to know something, that's when the Sight won't come.'

Pib came forward slowly. He pointed at the yellow pouch hanging from Cedar's belt.

'Are those stones?' he asked, with some awe. 'My mam told me about them. Can you really tell the future?'

Cedar nodded, taking the pouch and weighing it in his hand.

'Aye. Most of the time.'

'Can you tell *my* future?'

'You have to ask a question,' Cedar said gently. 'The more precise the question, the more precise the answer. I will cast for you, if you wish.'

He was talking more like an officer's son every day, Ash thought. They'd always been encouraged to speak properly; no Traveller slang, no slurring like most of the Hidden Valley people. But Cedar's speech had shifted, and it was a reflection of how he himself had moved away from his past, away from being a simple farmer's son to being a stonecaster, a seer – a warlord's heir. It was a strange thing, seeing a younger brother grow in stature like that.

Pib nodded.

'What do I do?'

Cedar spread out the kerchief Ember had given him on the bed, and motioned for Pib to sit down opposite him.

'You have to spit in your hand and then take mine,' he explained. 'Then ask your question. But remember, I *will* see the truth, so if there is anything you wish to hide from us, don't ask that question.'

Pib considered that carefully, then he spat in his hand and looked doubtfully at it before he clasped the hand Cedar held out.

'I'm going with you tomorrow, on the trading trip,' he said. 'How will the trading turn out?'

Cedar's brows rose. He dug in the pouch and cast the five stones. All face up.

'Success,' he said with relief. 'Prosperity, Rebirth, Certainty, Homecoming.'

Pib beamed. 'Well, that's good!' He hesitated. 'Lad, I wouldn't go around talking about this. *I* understand, because of my mother. But most around here would think you were consorting with demons, or that the evil one had sent you here to confuse us.'

'The evil one?'

'From the evil place – Fire Mountain,' Pib whispered. 'The Destroyer.'

Ash grimaced, and nodded. Wonderful. He couldn't argue with that description of Fire. Not after seeing Osfrid burn. But it wasn't reassuring, to hear their destination described as 'the evil place'. Not reassuring at all.

Their escape wouldn't doom Nyr's trading trip. That was good.

Ash slept for a while, and then was wakened towards evening by one of the young boys running in and shouting, 'Food's ready! A feast, a feast to celebrate Nyr our king's heir!' and running out again.

At least the men here didn't dress up, Ash thought, but when they got to the hall he found he was wrong. The men were all arrayed in blue or red tunics edged with bright embroidery, the women in long gowns with short sleeveless red jackets decorated similarly and edged with fur.

There were candles on every surface and the long trestle tables had been set up at the edge of the big space, leaving the area around the hearth clear.

Ember, he was relieved to see, was sitting safely next to Halda, in the position of honour. As trusted servants, they were placed with Ari's guard – a nice solution to the threat they posed. It meant that Ash was next to the man who had killed Curlew, with Tern on his other side, glowering at his plate and refusing to look up in case he met the man's gaze.

Oddly, Ash felt no anger towards the man, whose name turned out to be Sami. Curlew's death had been a genuine accident – a misunderstanding which happened, sometimes, when men with weapons encountered each other. Tern would understand in time. If he'd been Sami, Ash thought, he'd have struck out, too.

The feast made Ash even sorrier for these people, especially the women. While they had killed a couple of young kids and their hunting falcons had brought down a swan, that meat was shared out mainly among the men – the women got the scraps, and the children ate from their mother's plate. There were greens, and small turnips, flat bread with a sour cream and fennel dipping sauce and the big event was a sweet slice made with oats and honey, which had the children begging from table to table for crumbs. Ash thought of Ember's wedding feast. No one had had the stomach to eat much, but the tables had been overflowing: meats and breads and cakes and fruits, doves stuffed with raisins, spatchcocks and quail, as well as ordinary chicken and egg dishes, flummeries and fools, biscuits and salads and wine. At least here there was mead, and good mead it was. It eased the pain in his back, but he was careful not to drink too much.

After the food some of the men got up and fetched instruments. Drums were the same everywhere, but there were no flutes or harps. Instead, there were horns – short ones, made from cow or sheep horns, and long ones constructed of a combination of horn and wood and bands of metal. They made a low sonorous noise which set Ash's skull vibrating and then, as the drums came in, his feet tapping.

As soon as the first note sounded, everyone got up to dance. Ash was glad his beating excused him, but the other men dragged Cedar and Tern up, too, Tern blushing red. He was young for dancing, Ash thought; young enough to be embarrassed to approach a girl.

But none of the men went towards the women. They formed a big ring around the hearth and began stamping to the beat. The women formed a larger ring around them, clapping in time. Ari and Halda, standing opposite each other, threw their arms up into the air and everyone began to move. The two rings circled in different directions, both making intricate steps and stamps in time to the ever-faster beat. Ash clapped along, watching Ember's efforts to stay up with the other women. She was laughing, her face flushed, her feet nimble. In the circle of women she seemed to stand out like a beacon, a kingfisher among sparrows. As the ring passed him she looked up and smiled. Their gaze held for a moment, and then she blushed red and looked away.

He cursed himself. What had she seen in his face?

As the dancing grew faster and more energetic, Ash noticed that the central fire burned brighter. Did they see it, too? They couldn't possibly realise what it meant, not with the whole lot of them thinking the Fire was evil itself. He wondered why Fire let them go on thinking it. Why He didn't show Himself.

He got a clue when the musicians paused for a break. Everyone threw themselves down and drank and a singer, old Garn, came forward to chant a long ballad in a beautiful practised voice. Pib translated for them. It was the story of Sebbi, an ancient hero who had sacrificed himself willingly to the Ice King. That extraordinary act had gained the King's attention and had led to the first alliance between the Ice King and the Hárugur King of the day. The Ice King had told the Hárugur King about Mountainside, the complex of caves in which his people could survive the long winters.

'We are alive,' Pib said, tears standing in his eyes, 'because Sebbi bought us His approval with his own blood.' He paused, thinking something through. '*He* was a stranger, too,' he said.

When Garn finished, there was no clapping, but everyone drummed their feet on the floor of the cave in applause.

After that, the dancing went on for hours, until Ash's back was pained simply from sitting up. He said so to Pib on one of the musicians' breaks when everyone came back to the tables for a drink.

'Go to bed, then,' Pib suggested, his words a little slurred. 'After one of Bren's beatings, no one would blame you.'

Perversely, it made him want to stay up, but he couldn't risk slowing the others down later, so he dragged himself up and made sure he walked a little more weakly than he needed to. Ember looked at him with concern and came over to him.

'I'm all right,' he said, pretending to pretend, but his eyes were steady on her and she nodded in understanding.

'Oh, you men, always trying to seem brave!' she scolded, lending him her arm which he took with exaggerated reluctance, aware that many eyes were on them. 'Second watch is too early, with this going on,' she whispered. 'An hour later.'

'Aye,' he said, and stumbled a little to hide the fact that he was pulling the strip of leather from the end of her braid. She flinched but said nothing, and he slid the strip into his pocket. They would need it later.

He left her at the entrance to the men's caves, glad that the moment of awkwardness seemed to have been left behind. But the place where she had taken his arm burned beneath his shirt, and despite the quiet of the cave, sleep was a long time coming. He lay and listened to the distant bass beat of the dancing, praying to whatever local gods guarded this place that they would make it away safely.

The others trickled in later, waking him from a doze. Cedar and Tern were tired, which was bad, and Pib simply saluted him from the doorway and winked.

'Got myself a girl to see,' he said, letting the curtain fall. Could they be lucky enough not to have a guard tonight?

No. A moment later Sami appeared, dragging his bedroll, and lay down across the entrance to the passageway with an excusing shrug. Ash nodded at him. He'd have to make sure Tern didn't kill Sami. A knock on the head would be enough, surely, if they bound and gagged him?

Killing as few as possible was an investment in the future Nyr and Arvid were trying to build, he thought.

Sami had drunk deeply and started snoring almost immediately. Ash and Cedar cautiously rolled their sleeping pockets and stowed them, while Tern checked that they had not left anything behind.

Ash looked around to find Tern standing over Sami, his throat working, his hand clutching a long knife. He must have stolen that, Ash thought in alarm. That's not one of ours. Tern, of course, was trained as a soldier, used to carrying weapons. Moving as quietly as he could, Ash put a hand on Tern's arm. The boy's face was stone, his eyes dark with misery and the desire to kill. Ash shook his head.

Tern tightened his grip on the knife as if to disobey, but Cedar stepped forward next to Ash and put his hand out to mime 'Stop'. Tern's lip jutted mutinously, but he spun on his heel and went to the other side of the cave, leaning his head against the stone wall.

How hard should you hit a man to knock him out? Tern would probably know, but it would be a mistake to bring him back into it. They listened at the curtain – no noise beyond, but it wasn't that long since everyone had gone to bed.

Ash would have waited longer, but it was almost an hour past the second watch. He didn't understand how he knew – in the Forest he had noted the stars or the moon's position, but here, so deep underground, he just felt the passage of time as though it were a breeze that flowed through him at a constant rate.

Ember was expecting them at an hour past second watch. She could be out there now.

He pulled a kerchief and the strip of leather from his pocket and made sure Cedar had the cords they used to roll the sleeping pockets ready. He squatted behind Sami and gently pinched his nostrils closed. The man snorted and his mouth opened wide to drag in breath. Ash stuffed the kerchief in and used the leather strip to bind it in place, gagging him. His eyes opened wide and he fought for air through his nose, coming awake as if from a nightmare, arms flailing. Tern was back, ready, and he and Cedar grabbed an arm each and flipped Sami over onto his back, dragged his wrists together and bound them quickly. Ash pushed down on his shoulders as Sami bucked and writhed and grunted, but with three of them on top he had no chance.

They bound his ankles as well and hoisted him across to Ash's bed, leaving him face down and tying him to the bed frame for good measure. He was still jerking and pulling at his bonds, giving muffled shouts.

Ash bent and said quietly, 'We don't want to kill you.'

Sami stilled suddenly. Good. Not a martyr.

'No one will hear you. You made more noise snoring than you can now.'

Sami turned his head and glared.

'Yes, yes, I know, you think we've betrayed you. But believe me, it was necessary.'

Ash straightened up, aware of his bruises and the deep cut across his back.

'Let's go,' he said.

The passageway outside was empty, lit by a single candle at

the next turning. They had been through it often enough now to know it; there were four openings before the great hall, where the gods alone knew who they would meet. Surely there would be a guard somewhere.

Hoisting their packs, they walked as quietly as though they were stalking deer; or rather, Ash thought, grinning, as quietly as deer trying to avoid a tracker.

They passed the curtained doorways without a problem; at the second, they could hear a man's panting breaths and a woman's moans. Tern flushed red and Ash sent the couple a wish for good luck and a healthy baby.

It cheered him and he walked faster; but at the entrance to the hall he was cautious, peering out carefully. Nothing. Nothing but the central fire burning low, the tabletops leaning against the walls, the eerie shapes of the paintings climbing the walls, seeming to move slightly in the firelight.

No Ember. Should they emerge and wait for her, or wait here? He smiled to himself – she could be standing at the entrance to the women's rooms, asking herself the same thing. He moved out into the hall as though he belonged there, the image of an arrow leaving the bow carrying him forwards.

She *was* there, just inside a passage on the other side, under the paintings, and she came out to signal them as soon as she saw them, then slipped back into the darkness to wait.

Ash had his knife in his hand, although he couldn't remember drawing it. The walk across the hall seemed endless. Behind him, Tern and Cedar moved quietly. They had passed the central hearth and left its brief warmth behind when a man moved out of the shadows by the far wall. Bren.

He had a battleaxe, and merely by holding it he became their enemy – the traditional enemy, the Ice King's man, raider, marauder, the stuff of nightmares. Without the bow, without

Tern's sword, they had no hope against an axe. Ash slowed but Bren moved sideways, across the entrance to the passageway where Ember waited. Ash's hand tightened on his knife. Had Bren seen her? He didn't even glance into the passageway – it may be they'd been lucky. Whatever happened would happen to them and Ember could get away unscathed. He hoped she was moving already, heading for the horses. She was all that counted.

'You can't go,' Bren said simply. 'The Ice King must be obeyed.'

He said it as another man might have said, 'The sun must shine.'

Time to take a desperate chance.

'The Ice King doesn't keep you alive here,' Ash said. 'The fire, the bathing caves, they are all gifts from Fire Mountain.'

The axeblade flashed as Bren twitched in reaction.

'Blasphemy!' he hissed. 'I give you one chance – turn around and go back. I will say nothing to the Hárugur King. I would rather not kill you; Nyr is right, trade is our future. But I will kill you rather than disobey the king.'

He raised the axe across his chest, blade facing them – the classic attack stance. Tern and Cedar spread out so he could not come at them all at once. Ash raised his knife, hoping he could duck fast enough – knowing his injuries made that unlikely. Bren shuffled backwards into the beginning of the passage, wanting the protection of the walls on his flanks.

'One chance,' he said. Ash shrugged as if agreeing, half turned away, and then came back fast, ducking down and knife coming up, hoping to get under Bren's guard.

But as he turned back and felt Tern and Cedar move in from either side, Bren gasped and slumped to the floor, his axe hitting his boot and slicing off the toe.

Behind him, Ember stood, bloody knife in hand, tears flooding down her cheeks. She looked down at Bren, hiccuping a little.

Ash stood frozen for a long moment.

'He has a daughter, Iina, and a son, Siggi,' she whispered. That pierced his astonishment. He moved, grabbing her by the elbows, bending to pick up her pack, hustling her down the passageway as quietly as he could, while she walked as if in a dream, quietly enough, but with the tears still streaming down her face. The trip down the dim corridor was eerily easy.

There was fresh air on their faces. Ash hefted the knife in his hand. There would be a guard, surely, at the entrance?

He held Ember back and she stopped obediently. Cedar came forward, and motioned that he would go ahead. Ember pulled his head towards her.

'No more killing,' she breathed.

He shrugged. If he could, he meant. But he reversed his knife in his hand. That was a trick their father had taught them, to hit an opponent's temple with the pommel of the dagger, but Ash had never quite mastered it.

Cedar crept along the wall and the three of them tried to breathe like ghosts, to sink into the dark. His silhouette showed briefly against the slightly paler sky outside, and then there was a grunt, a shuffle, a groan. Ash pushed Ember back and went out, finding Cedar kneeling over a man, unknown in the darkness.

'Gag him,' Ash said quietly, but Cedar said, 'No need, I'm afraid.' His voice was flat, the voice he used when he was trying not to cry. For a moment, he envied Ember, who could kill and then cry without shame.

Another death.

Then they came out into the starlit night. Free.

Not quite. Merely out from under the suffocation of earth. Ember crouched by the guard and came up with an expressionless face.

She put a sympathetic hand on Cedar's arm, and Ash was ashamed that he envied Cedar that comfort. He craved any touch from her, even a sisterly pat.

The horses were hobbled nearby and they found them easily enough, not even having to whistle them up, their own horses towering over the sturdy little ponies and whickering to them eagerly.

They bridled and unhobbled their own horses and then, after some hesitation, unhobbled the others. Not stealing, but letting loose to make pursuit more difficult. Ember led them to a stone stable where they lit a candle, found their saddles and saddle-bags, and got the horses ready, filling the feed bags from the bins.

Ember asked him for her kerchief of coins and put a gold coin on the bin. Far more than this feed was worth in their country, but who knew how valuable grain was here?

She eyed him a little shamefacedly, but he nodded approval as he tucked the kerchief away again. No need to do more harm than they had to.

With the candle doused, the night seemed doubly dark as they led the horses through the narrow opening to the wider plateau. They weren't out of danger yet. There were stone houses and workshops all over this area. Their safest bet was to head straight for the edge of the plateau, where there were fewer buildings.

And hope they would realise the edge was there before they went over it.

He boosted Ember into the saddle and mounted Blackie, feeling his bruises twinge and the cuts hurt sharply for a moment until he settled into the saddle. At least Bren's blows hadn't reached his buttocks. He could sit comfortably enough. Holding the reins might prove a problem, later.

He took the lead, going slowly. They came out from the shadow of the cliff into the moonlight. The moon was going down, but they'd have a couple of hours' light before it grew too dark to ride. They had to make the best speed they could. Ash left the ponies behind, not wanting to risk them out on the plateau.

Passing the tanner's workshop gave him a sense of where they were. The path down was to their right, about a league. Should they take that path, which surely Nyr would expect them to head for, or should they just keep going south, towards the mountain? Arvid's maps hadn't reached this far. He had no guide but common sense.

These people had no dogs, thank the gods, or they would have been discovered by now. Why did they have no dogs? He didn't want to think about that, about dogs being eaten, maybe, in a hard winter. Just as well Grip and Holdfast had stayed with Elgir.

The air swirled around his head, intoxicatingly sweet and cool. This breeze was in their favour, carrying the horses' hoof-beats north, away from the houses. None showed a candle, but the moon lit their painted roofs brightly, and it was easy to imagine someone looking out of a window and, seeing them, raising the alarm. Except these houses had no windows, only solid doors. He kept coming up against differences in the small-est things, and every difference emphasised how narrow a life Ari's people lived.

He had grown up in a small mountain valley himself, but he had known what these people would think of as luxury: food aplenty, pottery ware to eat from, bread and honey every day, dogs, comfortable beds, long soft summer days. Apples, he thought. I haven't seen a single apple. Not even dried. Wine. Silk – it was rare enough, but a warlord's lady had it in plenty.

Even Grammer Martine wore it for feasts. The Lady Halda had worn wool last night, just like everyone else. Ari the king had worn a golden armband, but otherwise he had been dressed as the other men were.

Gabra, Acton's son, had closed Death Pass, the only way known through the mountains, a generation after the invasion. Had decided, guided by his mentor Asgarn, that there were enough people in the Domains. They had deliberately triggered a rockfall which choked the Pass, trapping the people on the other side, in the cold.

Over the centuries, the Ice King's men had found other ways over. Although none allowed a full-scale invasion such as Acton had undertaken, they were enough for raiding parties to sneak through. There were too many small valleys snaking between the peaks to guard them all, which was why stonecasters were valued so highly in the Western Mountains and the Last Domain. And someone like Grammer Martine, who was so accurate, was worth any price for the lives she saved.

Since the Resettlement, every warlord had a stonecaster permanently in their household, and the Ice King's attacks had been repulsed all along the border. Which was why, no doubt, Nyr had been able to convince his father to try trade. Ash wished him well.

The grass grew close along the path and goats moved nearby, their wooden neck plates clacking like frogs in a marsh. A shape rose up from the darkness and Ash drew his knife – not tall, a boy, he couldn't kill a boy—

'Kalla!' the shape said, interested but not alarmed. He asked a question too quickly for Ash to follow even the sounds.

'Kalla!' Ember replied before Ash could speak or move. Then she giggled. Actually giggled.

The boy laughed.

'Finn nott!' he said cheerfully, with a hint of teasing.

'Finn nott!' Ember agreed, sounding tipsy. 'Vertu.'

'Vertu!' the boy said.

She rode on in apparent unconcern and Ash followed her, heart pumping hard, wondering what in the cold hells she had said. He was aware, again, of every part of him that hurt, as though the shock of the boy's appearance had opened each cut afresh. But he could ignore that. It wasn't too bad.

They rode for a while and then she reined Merry in so he could come up beside her and said, 'He thought we were going home after the feast.'

She was so quick witted! Admiration warmed him but he made himself simply nod and ride ahead. Pay attention to the track, he thought. Or we all die.

The moon was sliding down behind the cliff, cutting their visibility moment by moment. Ash strained to see ahead, trying to find the edge before the light disappeared, but it was too dark, a wall of darkness.

He slowed Blackie even further, but it was a balancing act – they would be found gone by dawn, and then the pursuit would be fast. They couldn't afford to go too slowly.

Wind buffeted him and a swirl of flying shapes streamed up into the air, curving and swerving on the breeze. Blackie shied and propped, throwing her head up, and behind him he could hear the other horses neighing and shuffling.

Bats. Bats coming up from the cliff. They were right at the edge and the bats had saved them. He dismounted and quieted Blackie, then led her a few paces back. The others did the same with their horses, and they stood in a small circle.

'Do we try to find the path down?' Ash asked.

His eyes had adjusted to the starlight, but he could see very little.

'No,' Ember said. 'Not in the dark, do you think?'

'Too dangerous,' Cedar agreed. 'They'll look for us there.'

'So, south,' Ash concluded.

'Aye,' Tern agreed, his voice lighter and nervous, as though he wasn't sure he had a vote, but he wanted to be heard anyway. Cedar patted him on the shoulder.

'Aye,' he confirmed, and Ember simply mounted Merry and waited impatiently.

'We have to move,' she said. 'We've wasted enough time here. Who knows what's happening at home by now?'

They moved back from the edge and began to ride, perforce keeping to a walk but pushing the horses as fast as possible. Dawn wasn't far away, and light would help them, but it would help their pursuers as well. Ash was sure Ari would come after them. Blasphemy, Bren had called it, and Bren's death alone would push Ari to find and punish them. His shoulders twitched in memory of Bren's stick. It wouldn't be a stick this time, it would be a blade or a noose or some other barbarian way of execution. Beheading, perhaps, the way they often killed in battle.

At least that would be quick. But he would not, *not ever,* let that happen to Ember. He'd call up Fire himself and let Him consume this entire people before he would allow that.

PALISADE FORT, THE LAST DOMAIN

About twenty minutes after her mother had gone out to meet the warlord, Elva felt the gods relax, and knew that Martine and Arvid had resolved their coldness.

She didn't want to think about *how* they'd resolved it; Martine was her mother, after all, and imagining her and Arvid together was just plain wrong. She smiled at herself. She was always annoyed when her own children complained about her kissing their father in front of them, but here she was, feeling just the same about Martine.

We are all alike, under the surface, she thought, and that similarity may be what saves us now.

Ash joined her at the glass table, looking no older than one of her own sons. She sent a prayer for Ash and Cedar's safety out into the darkness, and the gods hushed her fears, but without giving her any solid news. Nothing beyond, *They are alive and travelling.*

'All's well, then,' Ash said, as if the gods kept him informed too. She raised her eyebrows at him and he touched the stonecaster's pouch at his side to show the source of his knowledge.

Stones. People thought she herself was extraordinary because the gods spoke through her, but that was straightforward compared to the stones. Everyone believed that the gods gave knowledge through the stones, but she had lived with the gods for her whole life and not once had they ever mentioned casting. And surely, if they were giving knowledge away like that, she should be able to cast? But stones were just stones to her; they told her nothing.

She wished Mabry were here. He'd stand at her back and lend her all the strength she would soon need. The eyes and hands of an artist, and the heart and hands of a farmer, that was her husband. Kind, gentle, strong ... she sighed. Also stubborn, shy, and sometimes aggravating. But she missed him with a physical pain under her heart.

Outside, the wind increased. The windows had been shuttered as though it were mid-winter, but through a couple of narrow cracks she could see that the moon had risen. It was almost full, and looked enormous, golden and full of promise. But she looked at it through a fern-pattern of frost on the horn windowpane, which distorted and smeared its light.

Not for long.

Elva had had a good life. Oh, yes, her parents and family had been massacred by warlord's men, but she had been so young that she didn't even remember them. Mam was the only family she'd known, and together they'd Travelled and laughed all the way from cliff to cove and back again. And then she'd taken the Road on her own and met Mabry, fallen in love, married, borne six children, and each and every one of them had lived to adulthood, which she thought was the greatest gift the gods had given her. Prophecy, which came to her as easy as breathing, had never seemed as important as her children's laughter and tears.

She knew, though, that she'd had that life because Martine, among others, had risked life and soul for the Domains.

Now it was her turn, so that her children could have a safe life, as she had done. And if she died in the doing, as she might well, that would be all right; but she wished she could kiss Mabry goodbye.

The others: women, children, men, old and young and in between, were mostly sleeping, curled up in family groups to keep warm. The cold was growing worse, even here with the human fug deepening each minute. Outside, she could hear the flick-flick of ice hitting the walls.

'Time to wake them,' Ash said.

'Aye,' she answered reluctantly. She didn't think she was a coward, but she knew all the power they raised this morning would funnel through her, like water through a millrace, and she had no idea what the consequences would be. She might end up a drooling idiot, like Widow Cowslip's daughter in the Valley. She might drop dead.

'I hate getting up early,' she sighed, and Ash laughed. It reminded her of the morning her own Ash had been born, and this boy had peeked through her window holding a potted cedar tree, because Mabry wanted to make sure the baby would be named something 'decent' – not Slug or Snail or, worse yet, Violet! So he'd tried to control what the first living thing she saw outside the birthing room would be; and like all attempts to control destiny, he had failed, because the first thing she had seen was Ash, not the cedar tree, and the baby was named after him. He had laughed then, too. It was a good name, she'd thought at the time, and she knew it had made the older Ash very happy. He'd gone red and quiet that morning and had smiled for months every time anyone said the baby's name. Then he had gone, and apart from a couple of flying visits when the childer were little, she had barely seen him again. But the winter he and Mam had stayed with them, after little Ash was born, had turned him into the brother she'd never had, and that bond was strong yet.

He put down a hand and pulled her to her feet. Her back creaked audibly and Ash bit back a comment.

'Easy for you to laugh,' Elva said sourly. 'You're escaping old age, seems to me.'

He sobered and shook his head. 'Not escaping. I'll get old – and when I do, I'll be among strangers, somewhere far in the future. I'd rather age here with the people I care about.'

That was sad. She patted his hand as though he'd been Gorse, her youngest. 'You can find people to love everywhere, if you try,' she said in her best mother's voice. He recognised it, and smiled.

'Aye, Mam,' he said. She cuffed him lightly on the ear and they laughed gently, but underneath was the tension of knowing what they had to do next.

'It's time to wake up,' Ash said, pitching his singer's voice to the back wall.

People started to rouse, childer chirping questions, wailing, trying to climb on tables and being pulled back, fathers wiping noses and mothers trying to get their childer to the room set aside for chamber pots before they wet themselves, grammers and granfers querulous or soothing, some unsure of where they were or why they were here. People. Just ordinary people. All they had to set against one of the Great Powers.

Stupid as new-hatched chicks, the lot of us! she thought, but she was cheered by the bustle of normality, none the less.

'There's something I haven't told you, yet,' Ash said to her quietly. 'The fires have gone out across all the other Domains.'

'You think the gods don't know that?' she said. 'No need to spread panic, though.'

He nodded, relaxing a little.

'Let's get them organised,' he said, and clapped his hands for attention.

Slowly, with much shushing, the people in the hall and on the stairs sat and looked at him. When there was enough quiet and everyone was watching, Ash became the Prowman. Elva saw him do it – saw him straighten up, deepen his voice, act like a stronger, wiser, braver version of himself. Or maybe this was the truth, and the other a jacket he put on to hide what he was.

His voice went out to the furthest corner of the rooms, up the stairs, through the open doorways, clear and compelling.

'My friends, you are welcome here. Together, we are going to defeat more than cold, tonight. We will defeat the Ice King himself, and send him reeling!'

There was no cheering, only listening so intent it almost hissed in Elva's ears.

'And this is what each one of you must do,' he said. 'Listen carefully.'

The ice was knocking sharper against the wooden walls by the time her mam and Arvid came back, looking tired and relaxed and happy. By then Ash had organised everyone into groups, sitting comfortably.

'Make sure you've been to the privy and are well set where you are, because once we start we can't stop, not for anything,' he had warned them.

After the scurry to the chamberpot room that caused, they had sat and set and begun to hum in unison, as the Sealmother had directed her. She had reached out through the gods and found the minds of the other leaders, spread throughout the Last Domain: her own two girls, Poppy and Saffron, whose minds were so much richer than she could have imagined, the boy at the Valuers' Plantation, and others, old and young, in big towns and tiny villages, at altars and in mines, huddled in animal barns, in shops, in houses.

Humming.

The Sealmother, no doubt, could pull all her people's minds together and hold them as She held a seal pup in the arms of a gentle spring swell. It was much, much harder for a human.

This was not the five-note safety spell which every Traveller girl learned. It was an undulation, like that gentle spring swell, which spoke of moderation and calmness and kindness and smooth, rolling motion. Movement, the enemy of Ice, who wanted to fix and freeze things in place, who desired permanence, eternity, instead of the slow drip of spring thaw, the yearly theft of His power, the inevitable cycle back to summer heat. That was what drove Him, Elva knew, although the gods had not told her so. Ice desired perfection which never changed, the purity of stillness, the calm grandeur of eternal stability. Death to a human.

So they countered it with motion. Opening her eyes, Elva saw that many in the crowd were swaying to the tune as it lifted and fell. She shut them again and reached out for the others, gathering them like strands for lacemaking, or weaving, neither of which she'd ever been good at. Another image, then: braiding her girls' hair in the morning, ready for a party. Intricate braids made with love, under and over and under again, coming together with patience and delight into a beautiful design.

THE ICE KING'S COUNTRY

Dawn crept up quietly; the cliff became a visible edge in the distance against a pale grey sky; then the edge to their left became clear, to Ash's relief, and when he looked back the others showed silhouettes instead of a moving shadow. Birds were nesting in the grass all around. As the sky lightened they could be heard, calling, singing, chirping to each other, to their nestlings. Then, as the eastern horizon flooded clouds with rose, gold, carnelian, crimson, the thrushes began to welcome the sun, the lapwings rose on the morning breeze, a pair of swallows flicked themselves up over the edge and arced through the sky.

High above, very high, geese were flying north in formation, heading for some far lake to breed. There was an eagle below them, circling the grassland, waiting for hare to leave its couch, or rockdove to launch from its nest on the cliffs. There were no signs of humans at all.

For a long moment Ash simply enjoyed the peace. Then, with a sigh, he turned to the others.

'We spell the horses at the next stream, and then ride as hard as they can take us,' he said. Ember nodded.

'They're not fully rested,' she said. 'They're better than they were, but that grazing wasn't enough for them. We should feed them too.'

'Aye.'

There were streams enough, snaking across the grass and emptying down into the valley below. At the next scurrying rill they loosened the girths and gave the horses time to drink and eat, and ate a little of what they had scavenged from the feast the night before. Tern had brought back the most. He shrugged.

'Everyone expects a lad my age to eat a lot.'

Ember hugged him with one arm and he flushed, but he didn't duck his head as he would have done at the beginning of this journey. He'd grown taller, too, it seemed, and his voice didn't waver as much.

'How far do we have to go?' Tern asked.

The Fire Mountain wasn't visible from here; it was hidden behind the long line of cliffs. But Ash could see the plateau curving to an end, the land sloping down to a narrow valley which wriggled its way south.

'A day, two days?' he shrugged. 'We have to get over that range.' He pointed to the cliffs. 'The valley might take us through.'

'Might need a few castings to find our way,' Tern said, looking at Cedar.

'As many as we need,' he confirmed cheerfully.

There was something uncomfortable about all this, and it was Ember. Apart from that hug for Tern, she had been distant since they left.

Since she had knifed Bren.

Ash moved across to where she was petting Merry, her back to them.

'Are you all right?' he asked. She didn't look at him, her head bent.

'Of course,' she said, her voice thin.

'You saved us,' Ash said. 'But you could have left it to us to kill him.'

She turned at that, eyes full of tears but angry, too. 'My father says a warlord has to be prepared to defend his people, even to death. I'm not a lord, but you are my people. I can't expect you to kill for my sake if I can't do the same.'

'You ask too much of yourself,' he said, exasperation and admiration mixing. 'You haven't been trained the way your father has, to fight and kill. Not like Holly.'

'But my duty is the same, whether I've been trained to it or not.'

'Duty! You and your bloody duty! If you hadn't been following your duty instead of your heart none of this would have happened!' He'd raised his voice and the others were watching, but he didn't care.

'I wanted to marry Osfrid,' she protested, but there was a waver in her voice.

'He was the best of them,' Ash said, low and fierce, 'but he wasn't your heart's desire, was he?'

She looked up at him in astonishment and he saw his own longing reflected in her eyes. His heart began to thud in hard, desperate beats. Admit it, he thought. Please. Admit it. Tell me the truth, let it be the truth I need to hear.

'No,' she said finally, red mounting in her cheeks and her breath coming faster. 'No. He wasn't.'

All he wanted was to hold her, snake his hand into her hair and pull her head back, feel her body soften and curve against his, taste her ... if she just made a small movement towards him, he would do it, he would drag her into his arms and bedamned to her father and her rank and her inheritance ... She straightened and raised her head proudly.

'But I would have had a good life with him, and I would have strengthened the ties between our domains, and—' she faltered, 'I would never have realised what I did not have.'

It was a challenge and an admission.

'But now you do,' he stated.

'Yes,' she said. 'Now I realise what I will never have.'

He closed his eyes so she wouldn't see his pain. Never. So. That was that.

Ash turned away and began to tighten Merry's girth. Never. There was no room for him in a warlord's daughter's life. Never. Merry, sensing his emotion, shifted uneasily, but he finished and went to Blackie. Cedar and Tern followed his lead. Ember was still standing where he had left her, looking away again.

He hoped she felt as bad as he did, but he doubted it.

The horses were not too tired, so they moved into a canter, hoping to avoid burrows and hidden holes, not daring to go slower. The plateau wound down gradually at this end and Ash hoped they would be able to simply ride into the valley, but the long slope finished in a small cliff and it took them more than an hour to find a narrow goat path down. They led the horses. Blackie didn't like heights, Ash found, so he went last.

'You first,' he said to Ember, not meeting her eyes. She slid past him without a word and led Merry down carefully. Tern followed her, and then Cedar, who gazed at him questioningly, but he ignored the look. No need to spill his heart out, not even to Cedar. Ash realised that he had started to think of Cedar as someone who was leaving, pulling away, instead of the constant companion he had always been. Perhaps that had begun even when the Prowman had taken him to the Deep, but not Cedar, because 'it wasn't the right time of year' for Cedar. He had to go when the stonecasters gathered, Ash thought, and wondered for the first time what Cedar would do when the Prowman offered to show him his true nature. If he ever went. If he ever came back from Starkling.

To calm Blackie, Ash needed to walk on the outside, which put him uncomfortably close to the sheer drop. Lower than the high edge near Ari's caves, but high enough to break his neck if he fell.

They sidled along carefully, each slow movement making him more impatient. They had to get out of sight into the valley before Ari's people found them. Surely that couldn't be long ...

As Ember reached the valley floor – a long winding strip of gravel on either side of a rocky stream – shouts came from above. Ari and his men, shaking spears and axes.

Ari's people were coming down the goat path behind them, Ember was certain. Their own horses were faster, she thought as they scrambled down the remaining path and made it to the valley floor, but they were tired from their long trek through the forest. Elgir had helped them bu—

Her thoughts were cut off by a shower of rocks – slingshots from above, aimed at the horses' heads.

Were they trying to kill Merry or spook her? It misfired for them – Merry bounded away as soon as her feet were on solid ground, racing with ears flat back in terror. The others followed, just as fast.

Her father bred his messenger horses from chasers, and they all had the racing instinct – when one ran, all ran. Ember risked a look behind, the wind whipping her hair across her eyes. Cedar's cheek was bleeding, Tern was nursing an arm, but Ash, thank the gods, was unscathed, and the horses all seemed fine.

Blackie was overtaking her. She'd always been the fastest. How Curlew had loved her! She shook all thought from her mind apart from speed. They had to get as big a head start as they could.

Merry's hooves pounded and breath whistled. Ember's teeth were rattling in her head; how could anyone *enjoy* doing this? She would never understand the chase-riders, but she would respect them more from now on.

Was Ash all right? She checked again and found him almost at her side, his face set with purpose. If she were killed, would Fire let him take the flame back to the Last Domain? It was her duty to sacrifice him if she needed to, but she couldn't. Better for them both to die, and then maybe Fire would forgo His revenge.

Ash called, 'Faster, princess!' and the familiar name lifted her spirits and gave her energy to urge Merry on.

The valley floor turned like a snake, heading west, which was good. They had to get over the next ridge before they would be able to see the Fire Mountain. Perhaps they could lose Ari – an arrow slid past her, almost silent, and flicked down to be cracked under Merry's hoof, the sharp sound making her lose her rhythm.

'Come on, Merry!' Ember cried. The mare took breath and went on, but she was labouring now in the thin air, slowing, and the others were slowing with her. One more turn, then they would be out of sight, out of aim.

They turned with the winding ground into a wall of cold. The horses shied and reared. Tern fell off.

There was no valley. No valley at all. It was filled with ice. Huge, blue-green, a wall of ice, a river of ice, cracked and melting at the edges, feeding the little stream that ran back down the valley ...

'This is the Ice King's work,' she said aloud.

Backing up a little, she looked west and there it was – Fire Mountain, perfect, even, wreathed with clouds. Surrounded by ice.

By Ice.

They would have to cross the ice to get to Him. Damn Him to the cold hells where His fire would go out forever! Ember thought.

Was there a path up? Behind them, they could hear the hoof-beats of Ari and his men. She exchanged a single, simple look with Ash, and then they both went forwards, looking for a way up. There was no path fit for horses; they would have to climb.

Without speaking, working as one, she and Ash pulled their winter gear out of their packs, found the ice poles, found the ropes to link them, the hatchets and spikes for ice work, dressed and roped up with the speed of desperation, Cedar moving as swiftly as they were.

Tern wasn't. Ember went to him to help, but he put up a hand, looking all of a sudden much older.

'You'll need someone to guard your backs,' he said. 'I'll stay here.'

He was collecting stones as he spoke, and pulled a slingshot out of his pocket. 'This was in the stable. I learned to use it as a boy, keeping the birds off my family's plot. Give them a bit of their own in return.'

She had to accept this gift. That was the hard part of being a ruler, she thought. You had to accept it when your people sac-rificed themselves for you. If only Valuers had settled all the Domains, so that she would be worth nothing more than anyone else. Or would she? Did Fire want her because she was a warlord's daughter, or because she was a seer's?

She kissed Tern on the cheek.

'Thank you,' she said, then went back to rope herself to Ash. He looked at her queerly.

'You're sure, lad?' he said to Tern.

'I don't much like the cold,' Tern joked. "'S'why I left home in the first place.'

Ash nodded and tossed him his own quiver of arrows.

'May not help, but it might,' he said.

The hooves were nearer.

'Come on,' Ash said to her. He was in front, Cedar roped behind. They took their little hatchets in one gloved hand and a spike in the other, and approached the cold wall.

She put her foot on the small ridge where Ash had stepped, pulled herself up by the spike he had set, and began to climb the ice.

PALISADE FORT, THE LAST DOMAIN

The gods had helped Elva communicate with her daughters and the others, but they had not committed themselves to lending their strength in the fight ahead. Elva still wasn't sure what they would do when the sticking point was reached. But she didn't say that to Arvid. Time enough to worry if it happened.

She began. Poppy first, in the mine at Salt. She was standing, as she should be, in front of the people of the Town, humming the long undulating note the Sealmother had taught them. As with the gods, Elva could feel what she felt, hear what she heard. Poppy's hand was tight gripped by that big girl guard, Larch, and Elva felt the strength that Poppy drew from the clasp. Strength and joy. Tears pricked Elva's eyes. So often, it happened so often, that love grew out of danger. She was happy that her daughter had found someone she could lean on; Poppy needed that.

She gathered her daughter's mind in, and with it Larch's strength and the growing power of the people of Salt.

Saffron next. A very different mind, quick and flickering and simple. But oh, so determined. Saffron was in a town hall, and her musical ear was being tortured by the townsfolk's inability to hold a tune. A whole family was off key.

Tell them to hum quieter, Elva instructed Saffron, and mind to mind she felt Saffie's quick amusement, translated instantly into action.

The boy at the Valuers' Plantation, Thyme, was next, and he and the Valuers were ready and powerful.

One by one she gathered them in. It was tiring, but she drew no strength from her mother, not yet. She would need it all later.

As she took them in and wove them, braid by braid, she understood what they knew, saw what they had seen.

When she reached the northernmost person with Sight, Atos, an old, old man in the little village of Purple Lights, she cried out at what she Saw. Wraiths attacking the flimsy cottage, wraiths made of ice and malice, claw and sleet.

Atos stood by a small window whose shutters hung askew, torn off their hinges by the ice wraiths. He swung an axe at the long clawed hand that reached through the gap, and as the metal blade touched the blue flesh it shattered, made brittle by the cold. A woman came from behind Atos with a broom and poked it right into the wraith's face. It screamed and backed away, leaving Atos panting and his protector in tears, which froze to her cheeks before they could roll down.

'He comes!' Elva cried. 'He is here! Gather in and sing! Together!'

Elva sent all the strength she could to Atos, in Purple Lights, but the old man was physically weak and not practised at the kind of concentration she was asking of him.

And he was frightened. Behind him, in the cottage, his whole village cowered away from the windows and doors where ice wraiths were shrieking and scratching. Only his wife, as old as he was, had enough courage to face them.

Sing! Elva cried to Atos, and he began to sing, turning to the others to encourage them, to lead them, to bring them into one voice, as they needed to be to repel the wraiths. But turning away left a gap and one wraith slid through the window, clicking its claws, bits of ice breaking off with sharp cracks as it forced its way through. Atos turned, but too late – the claws were outstretched, reaching for him.

His wife threw herself between them, crying, 'No!' and the wraith's claws went through her chest, right to the heart, her blood freezing in an instant, her face turning blue.

Elva felt Atos's heart stop for a long moment as he watched her fall, and then thud again, harder than ever, as anger took him. He screamed revenge and snatched a chair from under a woman nearby. She fell on the floor, scrabbling backwards, away from the wraith who had come wholly within the room. Atos swung the chair over his head with impossible strength and smashed it down on the wraith. The wraith fell to the floor. Another man, emboldened, grabbed a hoe from a corner and attacked another wraith at the window. Then the woman on the floor picked up a bowl and broke it, using a long shard to stab into the wraith on the floor.

It writhed and screamed – a dark, low sound that made Elva sick to her stomach. Then it melted. Its fellow at the window cried out and slid away, and Atos closed his eyes and sank to the floor, his hands gentling his wife's body, gathering her up to hold the cold, cold flesh close to his own heart.

Sing, Elva urged him. *Sing, or they will be back.* Slowly, painfully, Atos relayed her message, and the villagers began to hum. The woman who had stabbed the wraith led them, her shard shining in the streaks of light that came through the shutters. Shining clean, as though it had been new-washed.

ON THE ICE

She was a Last Domain girl – cold and snow and ice were as familiar to her as her heartbeat. She knew how to wind her scarf around her face to keep the air from freezing her lungs; she knew how to test the ice in front of her for cracks, for the drumming which was the most terrifying sound of all, because it meant a hollow drop under a thin cover; she knew how to pace herself, how to slide her feet forward rather than lift and drop them, how to work her arms so that her thighs weren't doing all the pushing. She knew how to survive.

But that was in the Last Domain, where ice had an end – where the end of the trek was home, and safety, and warmth.

Well, there would be warmth enough, if they reached Fire.

The hoofbeats behind them thudded and stopped just as they reached the top of the ice cliff. She stuck her pole in for balance and turned to watch. They were high – higher than a spear could reach, but perhaps not out of arrowshot.

Tern had taken cover behind one of the huge boulders which the glacier had pushed out in front of it, and he was waiting to see what their enemy would do. They didn't see him.

It was Ari, with Nyr close behind. Other men, too – she saw Urno on the edges, his eyes red. He and Bren had laughed together as they danced, she remembered, and felt guilt strike her in the heart.

Ari looked up at them with consternation as well as anger.

'Come down!' he shouted. 'Come down! No one is allowed on the ice!'

So he could speak their language, too, although he had pretended not to.

There was silence. Ash was going to let her deal with this, which was as it should be, but it still made her feel lonely.

'I have a task,' she said loudly. 'I must go to Fire Mountain. And there is something you should know, Ari Hárugur King. The fire in your hearth, the warmth of the bathing pools, these are not gifts from the Ice King. They come from Fire Mountain.'

'Blasphemy!' a man shouted, brandishing his spear.

Ari looked at her strangely, and there was no other sound but the slow creaking of the ice.

'It doesn't matter,' he said. 'We are bound to serve the Ice King. That was the ancient bargain, and it stands. We survive.'

'Just,' she said.

'Enough to make your people fear us!' he retorted.

'How many people have died to ensure that? How many of *your* people?'

Something crossed his face – a spasm of grief, of memory?

'We are bound to serve Him,' Ari repeated heavily. 'If you had met Him, you would know why.'

'I have met Fire,' Ember replied. 'And I will *never* serve Him!'

He blinked.

'Then why—?'

It was time for truth, as Ash kept telling her.

'He has taken back all the fires in my domain,' she said, her words dropping down like slow leaves into water. 'My people will freeze this winter unless I bring back fire from the mountain. He has said it.'

Ari's head came up, and she knew he was calculating how this changed the balance between the two domains.

'They will still be ready to repel your attacks,' she said quickly. 'My mother will still predict where you will come, and when.'

He nodded. 'And you are the witch's daughter,' he said slowly.

Tern had been edging around the boulder he hid behind. From the corner of her eye, Ember saw him ready a stone in the slingshot and stand, arm back. He was aiming at Urno.

'No, Tern!' she called. Ari whipped around, spear in hand, and sent that spear straight into Tern's chest.

It pierced him. He dropped the sling and his arms went wide. He fell back, slowly it seemed, spreadeagled on the harsh rocks.

Ember screamed as he fell, but no sound came. Ash and Cedar cried out. She was on her knees, hands clenched, imploring whatever gods that could hear to make it not be true, to make Tern get up, and live.

Ari looked up at her, a mixture of satisfaction and grief on his face. One of his men handed him another spear and he took it without looking, as if they had done this a thousand times before. As though a thousand men of the Domains had fallen to his spear. And perhaps they had.

'You took Bren from me,' Ari said heavily. 'My oldest friend, my councillor, my most valuable man. This boy's death is light repayment for that but I say, the debt is paid.'

Ember felt again how the knife had gone into Bren's side, how it had baulked at his shirt and then gone through, how it had slid easily into flesh and up under bone to find his heart. She remembered how he had fallen, as Tern had fallen, and she saw that Ari's face wore the same silent scream of grief as hers. Worse, perhaps.

This was another lesson her father had given her. Sometimes, he had said, there is nothing to be done because what has happened cannot be undone. Then you must find the best way forward.

She couldn't speak agreement; she couldn't say out loud that Tern's death had been justified. But she bowed her head in acknowledgement to Ari.

Astonishingly, he dropped the hand with his spear and let it rest by his side. 'The Ice King will deal with you,' he said, almost sadly, 'and then your people will die, and we will take your land.'

Fear gripped her so hard she could barely breathe. It sounded so *likely*, so inevitable. But Ash was there, shaking his head, helping her up.

'You forget, there is Fire to contend with. Do you think He would bring her all this way just so His enemy can kill her?'

That was true. That was true. Her heart began to beat again, swift and light.

Ari's mouth twisted awry.

'Then, it is between the two of them,' he said. 'So be it. If you return ...'

She stood as proudly as she could. Remember Sigurd, she thought, and raised her chin, stilled her shaking hands.

'When I return,' Ember said, putting every ounce of rank and privilege into her tone, 'we will discuss the future of our two lands.'

He nodded, glancing at Nyr, and she realised that he understood her. Halda must have spoken to him. Her father had done his best to prepare her for this, for the moment when she ceased to be a person and became a bargaining chip, but it was hard, none the less. She didn't even like Nyr all that much. But the futures of two peoples were more important than her personal preferences. Stepping onto the ice, raising her head above the edge of that cliff and seeing the endless expanse, the deathly eternal white, had shown her, finally, where her duty lay. Gods of field and stream, she prayed, help your daughter.

'Good luck,' Ari said, oddly enough, and raised a hand in farewell. He said something to his men who, apart from Nyr, hadn't understood their conversation. It sounded like, 'The King will deal with her.' They looked dissatisfied, but Nyr said something sharply and they shrugged. The man who had accused her of blasphemy – odd that it was the same word in both languages – glared at her and spat on the ground.

Then they simply rode away and there was only the ice.

There was less wind here than Ember had expected, just a light breeze which tossed Ash's hair, but the cold was fierce and the morning sun, reflecting from the ice, brought tears to her eyes. She wrapped one layer of her scarf over her eyes – there was still plenty of light coming through.

At least they could see their destination.

For the first time she realised the pressure which had pushed Acton to invading the Domains. The Ice King had taken everything – not as winter did, for a time, but for always. Ari's people lived on the edges as guillemots fought for nesting space on a seacliff, jostling for a toehold. They had nowhere to go, no way of expanding, of feeding their people, of doing more than survive.

It was not right.

Acton, she felt sure, would never have brought that rockfall down, sealing them on the other side. Acton would have let them all come through, bit by bit, settling throughout the Domains. The Last Domain hadn't been settled until a few generations ago – there was plenty of room without unhousing the original inhabitants. But there she came up against the truth of history, which was that the original inhabitants – her mother's people – had been massacred and dispossessed and forced into servitude and fear. It just would have happened faster if the Ice King's people had been allowed through.

'History is over,' her father had said to her more than once. 'Our job is to acknowledge its truth and then build for the future.'

So.

They had left thirteen days ago, if she had counted right. There was still time to get home before Snowfall – if they could return as quickly, if the horses were still there when they came back, if the Forest didn't stop them, if Ash didn't fly away with that shagging blue crane, if Ari didn't change his mind ... too many things to worry about. She put one foot in front of another, following in Ash's footsteps, hearing Cedar coming behind, concentrating everything on simply getting to Fire Mountain and doing what she had to do.

Ash took the lead. He was their eyes and ears, finding safe passage among the great clefts and crevasses, the sudden chasms and hidden traps of the ice kingdom.

Calling them into a huddle, he expressed surprise at how many tunnels and crevasses there were.

'As though it's been carved,' he said in puzzlement. Ember wondered whether there was a pattern to it – whether the Ice King had written a message in ice so large that only he could read it. Or perhaps Fire, from the mountain, could see it all.

'Follow *exactly* where I step,' Ash said. The leader. Ash was from the mountains, accustomed to ice and snow ... If Holly had been with them, would she still have led?

The Forest seemed like a lifetime ago, a different world. She had hated the everlasting shade of the trees, but now she would welcome the respite from glare. A headache was building behind her eyes, sharp and aching at the same time.

There were a thousand traps here, and many of them came from inside – lights dancing on her eyeballs where there were none; tears freezing her lids together; hands fumbling at the pole as they lost feeling. Her own desire to see a safe path would have made her reckless, but she curtailed her natural inclination to go first, to go fast, to *hurry*, and submitted to Ash's authority, stepping only where he had stepped.

They stopped regularly for rests, and to drink the little water that was still liquid in their flasks. On one halt, Ember looked back to see how pitifully short the distance they had come. Not worth thinking about. She looked forward, instead, to where the mountain seemed as far away as ever. But there was something different. More clouds, perhaps, around the summit? No. The clouds were darker.

'Smoke,' Ash said in her ear, making her jump. 'He is building His fire.'

'To welcome us, I hope,' she said, aware of his warm breath against her skin, his hand on her arm. She waited, but the flame didn't sweep through her as it had every other time he had come close. There was no sudden liquidity in her bones, no shortness of breath. She almost whooped with relief. Out here, on the ice, Fire had no power. He could not inflame her with false desire, not speed her heart, even a little. She was free of it; free of the sickness of fake need, of induced lust, washed clean by cold. Ash was simply Ash again, friend and cousin and stalwart support.

Happy, she turned to him, their heads close, and smiled into his eyes. There was a moment, a heartbeat, when the breath mingled between them, warm as homecoming, and then his eyes darkened and he caught his breath. Her heart turned over in her chest; a hand clenched her lungs so she could not breathe. Desire surged through her that was different, completely different to the manufactured lust Fire had plagued her with. Clear, aching, it filled her to her fingertips, to her toes, like warm mead, sweet honey, golden and molten and painful because of its tenderness.

Tears filled her eyes and Ash raised one gentle hand to brush them from her cheeks before they could freeze. Gods, she was undone. She had been fighting lust all this time when it was love she should have been wary of.

She raised her own hand to his cheek and his face changed, seeming almost like a stranger's, need and yearning in his eyes. She moved closer, just a little, just so she could feel his warmth against her, and as she did he said something under his breath, an oath, something, and pulled her to him, his hand against her back, the other sliding up and underneath her hat. The touch of his fingers against her neck made her weak, made her feel like crying. Him, too? Love? For *her*?

Ember turned her face up to him. His mouth was cold; her lips were chapped too and on the first kiss their skin snagged; but then it softened, their lips warmed, clung: eager, desperate, sweet.

Vaguely, she heard Cedar say, 'Oh, not now you two!' and felt Ash smile against her mouth before he kissed her again, his breathing faster than before, his hands a little unsteady.

She would stay with him forever, she thought in a daze, tasting him. They could live on one of her father's estates, one she would inherit in any case. They would raise a family, love, be merry, be happy, away from the fort and everyone who disapproved. Her father had married whom he chose, and so could she.

'Let's go,' Cedar ordered.

Reluctantly, they pulled apart, staring at each other. Ash's hazel eyes were dark with desire and wonderment. She smiled at him, just a little because that was all she could manage; she wanted to cry with happiness. His mouth moved in response, but it wasn't quite a smile.

She gulped a breath as Ash turned away, clearing his throat.

'Yes. Let's go,' he said. But he kept hold of her hand for the first few steps, until it became clear that she needed him to break the trail for her.

Only the habit of the last hour saved her; she trod in his footsteps because her feet had learned that path; she kept her head down because she needed to block out the glare; she kept going because otherwise, otherwise she was lost in a fluttering confusion, an insane world where Ash and she, she and Ash …

She wished she really believed it was possible.

PALISADE FORT, THE LAST DOMAIN

'How can wraiths attack?' Arvid demanded furiously. 'What about the compact?'

Martine shook her head. 'The compact is against air, water, fire and earth beings. We've never needed one against ice …'

Her voice faltered. 'Poppy. Saffron. They're both north of here.'

Elva listened and waved reassurance, and then signalled for them both to start singing. They would need everyone. Everyone.

The braid in her mind was growing thicker and more intricate as she brought in the new strands, from Salt and Oakmere and Purple Lights and Tinderbox and the Plantation and Brown Hill and Marsh River.

Each a different texture and colour, in her mind they were brown and blond and red and black, Traveller and Acton's people, townsfolk and farmer, woodster and crafter, officer and soldier.

This is the first time, she thought. *The first time ever we have been bound together, with no distinction made.* It made her vaguely proud, but a small part of her wondered what changes that would bring, if any. She could imagine her sister-in-law,

Drema, advising dryly, 'Don't get your hopes up, lass. People don't like changing the way things work.'

But now, but now ... now she wove them all in, every colour, every kind, and they were together, singing together, swaying together, a whole domain of unity. This was the time. She focused on Purple Lights, where Atos was still trying to sing while he nailed a board across the window, sobs interrupting his song.

As he did so, the door burst open to a flurry of sleet and the ice wraiths surged through.

SING! she shouted at him but he was too frightened, too slow. She was losing her ability to sense him. *Help me*, she begged the gods, but they didn't answer her. Then she felt her mother's hand on her shoulder, and her mother's calm strength enter her mind. She reached out to Atos. *Sing*, she begged him. The wraiths were playing as a cat plays with prey, making little feints to goad him further. Atos swallowed against a dry throat and hummed one note. Just one, but it was the note that every-one, everyone in the domain, was humming at that instant, and Elva gathered up the strength from Poppy and Saffron and Thyme and all the others and sent it down that note into the shabby hut at Purple Lights, sent it through the frailest vessel they had, an old, old man, and he put his hands out as though to ward off the wraiths.

Begone! Elva commanded them.

It was as though a wind had picked them up and sent them reeling back outside the door. He slammed it shut behind them and dragged the table over to hold it closed.

They'll be back, Atos sent to her.

Aye, Elva said. *It's time to attack.*

The braid had to become a wall which moved farther and far-ther north. That was the plan. Sealmother had showed her some of it, but She had protected a much smaller area. On the other hand, She had had fewer people powering her spell, if spell it was.

It was enchantment, sure enough, but spell was a small word for what they were making between them.

Elva opened her mind to her mother as she had opened it to the gods, time and again, sharing the image of the many-coloured braid. Martine caught her breath.

Beautiful, she thought. *Strong.*

Now we make it a wall.

Together, they began to take the strands from each place and strengthen them further, the image changing in Elva's mind from a braid – essentially decorative – to a woven wall. Martine helped. Arvid's father had owned a shield made in the Wind Cities; a shield of woven steel laid over a withy base. It was a beautiful thing, and had saved his father's life more than once in battles with the Ice King. That would be their model, now. Still singing, Martine went to Arvid's workroom and took the shield down from the wall, bringing it back to the glass table and holding it high.

The assembled people understood immediately. The soldiers punched the air, the women nodded, the children clapped. Martine placed it on the table in front of Elva and she stood, putting her hands flat on its surface.

Arvid stood up, too, and said clearly, 'Now we will make a shield so strong that nothing will penetrate it!' The singing grew louder in response, and Arvid was loudest of all.

Elva and Martine, because it was easiest, felt for Poppy and Saffron first, and shared the image with them. The four together began the reshaping of the braid into a shield, gradually bringing Thyme in, and Atos, and all the others, one by one. Elva was concentrating so hard that she wasn't aware of anything else except that image in her mind, the shield growing, lengthening, curving up and over the fort and moving north, getting bigger as it went.

'It's getting warmer!' a woman exclaimed. A few people broke off singing to happily agree, and Elva felt the shield weaken. She punched Arvid on the shoulder and he shouted out, 'It won't get warmer unless you sing!'

Those who had broken off resumed singing, shamed. Elva could feel the shame through the braided shield, but she also felt the joy the warmth was bringing, and she fed that in, too, because it had a warmth of its own which would work against ice.

As the shield moved further north, though, she began to feel *something*. Someone, it may be. Heavy, inimical, a brooding presence envious of and hating everything the braid contained: life, love, warmth, fellowship. Difference. She had never known one of the Great Powers, but this was unmistakable, and she understood what it was He wanted, could feel His desire for the unchanged, unchangeable permanence of Ice. For ice which never melted, for form which stayed, immutable. For an eternity of sameness, safe and solid and forever.

She knew that feeling. Every mother knew the feeling of wanting time to stop, wanting the child to stay a baby, wanting the youth to stay a child, wanting the moment when the little arms came around your neck to last forever. Every human knew that feeling, of wanting tomorrow to be the same as today, so that you could just go on being who you were, without the pains that age brought.

But as a mother, as a human, she knew the stupidity of that. Knew that the child could give more joy than the baby, as well as more grief; knew that age had its compensations; knew that growth always hurt.

Well, this shield was going to grow and it was going to hurt.

Just before she began to push it north in earnest, she wondered where Ash was, and why he hadn't joined in the singing. *We could use a voice like his*, she thought vaguely, then slid in a strand as strong as steel from a tiny village called Acorn, where a nut-brown aged woman stood over the corpse of an ice wraith as it melted on the floor, a flint knife in her hand.

'No one kills me or mine,' the woman said, and Elva fed her exultation and determination into the shield.

Then the Ice King struck back.

He struck from the north, where if you dug a foot down, the earth itself was ice all year round. From there he sent the ice down every channel of water he could find. Lakes and rivers froze every year, and there was no one hurt by that – but now, in an instant the groundwater froze and swelled, sending the earth above it into rolling hills and breaking chasms, undoing the foundations of house after house, hall after hall.

Panic broke out as the freeze hit each village. In Oakmere the singing faltered as the great columns which held up the Moot Hall roof tilted and began to sink on one side. The slate floor buckled and parents snatched their children up and began to run before the roof fell in. Elva heard the screams as the walls themselves shifted.

As the humming failed, He grew stronger, and Elva despaired. Ice would sweep down, the houses would be destroyed, forcing everyone out into the unforgiving cold. They would all die and lie, forever frozen, unrotting, in the eternal ice.

But then she felt a hand on her shoulder and felt a warm strength flow into her. It was unlike anything she had ever felt before, a mixture of male and female, fuelled by both love and anger.

'He is using water to destroy us,' the Prowman said, 'and that is not allowed. She can fight Him, now, as She always does, each spring. Give Her your trust.'

Beyond the warm humanness, the extraordinary strength of Ash's mind, underneath the music of flute and drum which sounded a war beat in his thoughts, there She was: cool but not cold, a Power but so intricately bound with humans that Elva slid easily into communion with Her. She was angry.

I will take my streams back, She said. *Be you ready to remount your shield.*

'Aye, my lady,' Elva said aloud. Ash's hand tightened on her shoulder in encouragement, and strength slid into her from that contact as easily as from her mother's mind. She felt her mother smile, and sent reassurance to everyone still in contact. *All is well*, she said. *Water fights with us.*

Elva felt the wave of power that went out from Her: the order to every drop of water in the domain to *flow, flow, be free.*

South and north the groundwater was melting, flowing, seeping back and flowing further.

Houses were still tilted, but they settled, uneasily, creaking. Ice fought it, but She was strong, unbelievably strong. And then, far north, She reached the limit of Her power, where the ground was frozen all year, where Ice held permanent sway. And from there, He was gathering His strength to attack again.

Elva called the gods in.

Now, she said, *if you are going to help us, it must be now.*

They came reluctantly, but they came. *It is not for us to defy the Powers*, they said, much as a commoner might have said, *It is not for me to defy the warlord.* But Elva had an answer for that, now. *Not the Powers, only Ice. Water fights with us.*

She sensed that it was only that which had brought them this far.

Very well, they said. *Use the altars to anchor your shield, and we will hold it fast.*

It was what they had needed. The shield was fragmented, fraying, failing. Painstakingly, as quickly as they could, Elva and Martine and Poppy and Saffron and Thyme and Atos rewove it, each village mind sending its strand first to their altar and then on to Elva, the lacemaker with her pillow laid out before her, each altar a pin to secure a single thread of power. This shield was far stronger, far, far stronger than the first. With triumph, Elva began to push it back, from the fort to the nearby villages, from those villages to towns, north and south and east and west, bringing all the domain under its protection. She could feel the hall warming around them as it worked, as Ice was pushed farther back.

The people were still singing, still feeding her power, and so were Martine and Ash and everyone else in the lace.

She heard, vaguely, a voice shrieking nearby, but she didn't pay any attention to it.

'You are making spells!' the voice screamed, its pitch interrupting the smooth humming of her people. 'This is the spell which stops my son returning to me! Stop! I command you to stop!'

And she turned sideways to see Sigurd, wild-eyed, being held back by Merroc, while the Prowman moved towards her to help him. *Back,* she thought to the shield, bringing Salt under its protection with a sigh of relief that Poppy was safe. And then Sigurd launched herself forwards, dragging out of Merroc's grip, ducking under Ash's elbow. He grabbed her from behind, but she snatched up the big pottery pitcher from the table and threw it straight at Elva. Her mind in Salt, her attention on the humming, Water, Ice, she reacted far too slowly.

The pitcher hit her head and all thought stopped.

PALISADE FORT, THE LAST DOMAIN

Arvid sprang forward as Elva fell onto the tabletop. Martine cried out and shoved Sigurd aside to get to her. She was unconscious, bleeding from one temple, pale and waxy.

Martine grabbed a napkin and tried to staunch the bleeding, but head wounds always bled like stuck pigs and it soon turned red. He offered his own kerchiefs and Martine took them without a word. A couple of other women came forward to help and he saw Martine take a deep, deep breath and move back to let them come to Elva. He didn't understand why she would do that – and then, as she closed her eyes and began to hum, he felt the cold hit.

One of the women dropped the soaked napkin onto the table. Elva's blood froze as it fell and the napkin stood like a tent on the tabletop, in stark folds.

'He's coming!' Martine said, and sang again.

'Sing!' Ash called, and lent his own voice to the choir – not his singing voice, that lovely smooth tenor, but the voice of power that Arvid had only heard him use once before, a voice like the screech of the rock being rolled across the burial cavemouth.

The people sang, but it was not enough. Martine was struggling, pale and trembling. He went to support her, but he couldn't give her the kind of strength she needed. The Prowman joined hands with her and she took a breath of relief, but Arvid could tell she was having far more difficulty than Elva had. Martine, he remembered, had never been able to hear the gods directly. Only through the stones.

He could feel his fingers turning blue and stuck his hands under his armpits; the skin on his face was tightening, drying out with cold; his lips where he had licked them a few moments before were ice; his eyelids were beginning to stick together.

The cold was so intense that he could not feel anything, anything at all.

He held onto Martine but could not feel the touch. He leaned his head against her sleek black hair, but there was nothing except a sense of pressure.

They were all going to die, unless the Prowman could save them.

'Water?' he croaked, hoping She could do something, *anything*.

But every drop of water in the room had been frozen. The Prowman's eyes were unfocused, staring at something, someone, far distant. He couldn't hear. Didn't speak. Martine leaned heavily against him, humming still, but even he could tell there wasn't as much power as Elva had summoned. Not summoned – organised.

From every wall, from every shutter, a clicking, flicking noise started. Scratching, scraping ... a small part of his brain thought of summer beetles, but then the shrieking began, and the hungry screaming, and he knew the ice wraiths had reached them. They were scrabbling at the doors and windows, trying to get in. To kill them. To eat them, as wind wraiths did? He didn't even know. Perhaps merely to pierce them to the heart with their cold talons.

He should defend the hall, but he was so tired. Arvid had heard it was like this, being frozen to death. That you got tired, so tired, and then just fell asleep and never woke up. It had sounded peaceful, but it wasn't. It was simply terrifying.

His eyelids were closing, but he couldn't lie down, no, he couldn't, *mustn't* lie down, because Martine needed him, everyone needed him. He drew his sword and staggered towards the windows, struggling to stay awake. All around, the others were sliding down into sleep, even Sigurd. The singing slowed, became softer as voice after voice dropped out. He *must not* sleep, or there would be no one to protect Martine when the wraiths broke in.

Martine swayed and he staggered as her weight came on him, but he managed to stay upright. The Prowman was talking, 'No, I can't leave them,' and he agreed with that, Ash shouldn't leave, but it was more important that he not fall asleep.

He was *so* tired. Perhaps it really was time to at least have a little nap. Just a few minutes ...

And then, it paused. He could *feel* the advance pause. Outside, the scraping and shrieking was suspended, the silence terrifying. What was He planning to do next?

With a sense of something being sucked away, the cold withdrew all at once, the wraiths' screaming began again but faded quickly into the far distance. The cold remained, but it was a natural cold, emanating from the ice, which still decorated every surface, every face.

It was deathly quiet. Most people were still asleep. Then he heard a small, small sound: a drop of water hitting the floor. Arvid looked up. The edging of ice which ran along each roof beam was melting, dripping. All around the room, ice was turning to water, and the drops hit and splashed faces, hands, backs, waking them all one by one.

They roused, and sat and looked up, and a woman started to cry with thankfulness. Arvid opened the doors and felt summer heat flood in, and distantly heard his people begin to cheer. The cold retreated sullenly, but it slid back and back, and out the door. The blood-soaked napkin melted.

Martine was still tending to Elva – it was as though she hadn't noticed anything; but then Arvid saw that tears were streaming down her cheeks. The Prowman gathered Elva up and carried her upstairs, Martine following.

Outside, the sun came up, dazzling the world with brilliant reflected rainbows. Every surface was a mirror, fracturing and repeating the light, so that the ice which had almost killed them was for a moment, just a moment, a celebration of beauty instead of evil.

Ember, he thought. Somehow he was sure this was her doing, that the Ice King had turned away from them because of her. He wished he didn't have the image of a snake, turning to better prey.

ON THE ICE

They moved along, through, over the ice in laborious stops and starts. Cedar spelled Ash as leader, testing the footing. The glacier curved around, following the valley, and they found themselves climbing higher, towards a broader river of ice which flowed straight towards Fire Mountain.

There was a ledge between the two streams of ice. Cedar went up first, using spikes and pole to make a path the other two could follow. Ember followed, breathing hard, wishing she'd done more walking, at least, in the lead-up to the wedding. She had concentrated all winter on sewing and packing, and had let her daily walks slide away. Now this was harder than it should be.

Cedar put a hand down to pull her up over the edge. Below, Ash waited until she was safe before he started the climb. She moved back from the edge, staring at the mountain, glad of the breather. She couldn't look down at him; there was a raw edge in her heart where she was aware of her love for him as one is aware of a wound. Heart's desire, she thought. Now I really know what I'll never have.

He pulled himself up with Cedar's help. Even not looking at him, Ember was aware of him glancing at her. It was as though his gaze was a touch, lighting her like tinder.

As Ash set foot on the higher level, the ice creaked. They hardly dared breathe, standing motionless. Nothing.

'Move away from the edge,' Cedar said.

Ash took a step towards the mountain. Ember followed him. The ice groaned.

'That's wrong,' Cedar said, worried. He unwound his scarf from his face and examined the ground. 'This ice is as deep as a house. It shouldn't be –'

'Get away from the edge,' Ash said to her urgently, taking hold of her arm and pulling her.

They moved fast, leaving their spikes still in the ice, and felt a shudder underneath their feet. A shriek buffeted them, the ice bucked and they fell full length. Behind them, the whole edge where they had climbed had fallen away, dragged downwards into a crevasse that had not existed a moment before.

Cedar was waxy pale, eyes clouded by Sight.

'They know we are here,' he said. 'Run! Run to the centre!'

Ember scrambled up and ran, heading straight for the mountain, straight for the middle of the ice, aware of Cedar on her left and Ash on her right.

In front of them, the light snow which lay across the ice rose like a dust devil, spinning in cones that grew, spread, became shapes.

Wraiths.

Ember jolted to a stop, aware that the ice was groaning again below her, the wraiths – *ice wraiths*? She had never even heard of ice wraiths, but they were unmistakable – the long claws like wind wraiths, a body made of flying ice and snow, of splinters and daggers of ice, with eyes that burned blue, teeth sharp as arrowheads, cold, cold, drifting towards them slower than she expected, but still too fast, their long clawed hands stretched out in anticipation.

Slivers of ice flicked from the claws, hitting like needles, piercing, cutting. Each needle brought not only pain, but cold, spearing deep inside. Blood sprang out along Ember's cheek; pain blossomed as the blood froze on her skin. Ash swore and tried to move in front of her, to protect her. The onslaught increased but she couldn't bear to turn her back, to let them come up behind her unseen. She wrapped her arms around her head but the ice spears cut through her jacket.

Cedar gulped down a curse and began to breathe hard, trying to make a noise, trying to – to *whistle*?

'There's a spell,' he shouted, through the sound of ice. 'To control wind wraiths. It might work.'

He tried to whistle again. Five notes. But Cedar, gods help them all, had the worst of whistles and almost never hit a true note. Still, she recognised it. Of course, he was right.

'You don't have to whistle,' she gasped. Mam had taught her this, at least, even if she'd kept silent about Fire. The spell for protection. Words, what words should she use? She fought for breath and sang. 'Safe, safe, warm and safe.' The five notes had to be equal in length and power, but the words could be changed to meet the need.

The wraiths were slowing, although the arrows of ice kept coming. Ash and Cedar picked up the song, their deeper voices twining through hers. 'Safe, safe, warm and safe,' they sang, memories of family celebrations where they had all sung rounds and ballads sliding through her mind, giving her strength and a sense of deep belonging.

The ice wraiths hovered, claws extended but no more needles flying towards them. The fragments of ice which swirled around them caught the sun so that they were enshrined in rainbows, beautiful, every colour dancing across their white faces and arms. They flung back their heads and howled.

Terrible, terrible – beings so ethereal should have voices high and piercing, but this sound was deep, thunder, rocks ground beneath ice, echoes resounding in the deepest cave.

Cedar stopped singing, but she and Ash kept on desperately.

'He sees us,' Cedar said again. The wraiths' howling was doing something – the ice beneath them shuddered again and again. Ash was looking around, still singing – he grabbed Ember's shoulder and spun her, pointing to where, bright in the sunlight, cracks were snaking towards them from the edge of the ice sheet. Lightning bolts of emptiness into which they would fall and die.

'I'll hold them,' Cedar said. 'You go.'

Ember kept singing, but she shook her head, and Ash took Cedar by the arms and did the same.

'Elgir taught me something,' Cedar said. 'I'll survive.'

The cracks were breaking wider, each movement bringing a whip of sound against their ears. Ash put both hands on Cedar's shoulders and nodded, once. Cedar nodded back and began to sing again, his voice stronger than before.

Still singing, Ash and Ember backed away, watching both the wraiths and Cedar. The wraiths were undecided: whom should they follow? They turned between the two, back and forth, until Cedar cried out something in a language Ember had never heard. Then they whipped back to him, like snakes following prey.

He sang, but this time he sang, 'Watch, watch, watch and hunt.'

Ember's breath caught in her throat. That was too dangerous, too dangerous! The cracks were heading for Cedar, straight for him, straight to him, and the wraiths also, drawn by power as thirst to water.

They advanced, slowly, hands coming up, claws reaching out. He still sang, but softer, and Ash pulled Ember away, as fast as she could go, both of them looking over their shoulders as the cracks and the wraiths converged towards him.

He looked up and grinned at them, across a distance which seemed much wider than it should have; how long had he been singing? How long ago had they left him there?

The largest of the ice chasms had almost reached him. He spread his arms, and shouted, 'Hunt!' on the last note of the song, and ice flew up around him in a flurry of white and dazzling rainbows.

As it fell, a grey wolf jumped forwards, leaping over the chasm as if it were a narrow stream. Tongue lolling, it sat on the other side and mocked the ice wraiths, who shrieked in high desperate voices and leaped after it.

Cedar ran, the wraiths following, moving out of sight towards the edge of the ice, jumping chasms and abysses, it seemed, for sheer fun.

'Gods help him,' Ash said, his voice trembling. 'We must run also.'

There was no more time to test the ice, to move slowly and carefully from firm footing to firm footing. Now they raced, guessing where the best surface was, their eyes attuned to the shading of the ground so that they anticipated the dips and chasms in time.

Behind them, the ice wraiths' shrieks still sounded from time to time; still desperate; still unsatisfied; and that was all the comfort they had.

ON THE ICE

The Mountain was closer. On its bare shoulders Ash could see hot springs steaming, leaking down the slopes to battle with the encircling ice. Smoke was gathering around the summit, darker and thicker than before. He hoped that was a good sign, but 'caught between fire and ice' was an old saying of his mother's, and he wondered if this battle had been fought with other footsoldiers, in other times.

He wondered, more than anything, why Fire had forced Ember to come here. It was clear, now, that everything He had done – killing Osfrid, taking the flame from the Domains, sending Ash and Cedar with her – had been done to bring her across the Ice. Even the detour to Starkling – had Fire organised that with the warlord so that Cedar would learn the spells he would need?

What did He want with her?

The old story of Sebbi, sacrificed to the Ice King a thousand years ago, haunted him. If anyone had to be sacrificed, it would be him, not her, but he would fight to his last gasp first.

Which would mean nothing against one of the Powers.

The closer they came to the Mountain, the colder it was. So cold that it was hard to breathe; so cold that it pressed down on him like a heavy weight, dragging at his hands and feet. Even though he was in his winter gear, the cold bit through the thick furs as though they were a linen shift. He began to imagine his toes turning black with frostbite, his penis shrivelling and dying.

Ember was in no better case. Although she was walking in his footsteps, she was struggling. He wondered if he should take her on his back, but wasn't sure he'd be able to walk at all if he did.

They paused for a moment to rest at the top of a carved ice slope and Ember came close to him, put her mouth to his ear.

'This is unnatural,' she said. He looked down into her blood-shot eyes; still startlingly green, but so tired. So afraid.

'Yes,' he said. What else was there to say? This cold, in summer, was deeply unnatural. They were being attacked, and the closer they went to the Mountain, the worse it would get.

He yearned to sink down onto the ice and simply sleep. That was death, but was death such a bad thing? Going on to rebirth, starting again ... He might have done it if Ember hadn't been there. But she was so vulnerable; and stronger than he was, because she pushed him in the small of the back to say, 'Get going!' He smiled at her and tucked his head down to bury as much of his face in his collar as he could, and got going.

It became colder still. So cold that with each step his foot froze to the ground and he had to break it free. He used an icicle, because oddly that froze his hand less than his knife did, and stepped and chipped, chipped and stepped, Ember doing the same behind him.

He wondered if they would just collapse from exhaustion, unable to go farther.

Then they were on the upward slope, at the bottom of the Mountain, and the cold seemed to lessen, just slightly. Ash

looked up. They were within bowshot of the first gravel slope.
A long bowshot, a long way to go, but at least his feet weren't
freezing to the ground now. He grinned back at Ember and her
eyes smiled at him over her scarf.

They paused and looked back over the ice field. From this
small height Ash could see the carvings the wind had made,
those crevasses and ledges which they had struggled over all day.
Beautiful, he thought. *So beautiful and so deadly.*

The Ice King came.

Invisible, silent, the sense of His presence sweeping in from
the north was so great that it forced Ash to his knees.

Not on your life, he thought, and struggled up again. Ember
had never fallen. She stood straighter than ever, facing the
oncoming Power with disdain.

No one must go to the Mountain!

It was more a scream of ice grinding together than a voice,
but it was thunderous, impossible, ripping mind and body apart,
and the mind behind it was colder than ice, full of long purpose
and deep desire. Ash stumbled and almost fell again, but he
recovered in time to steady Ember as she reeled back.

The two of them held each other up like two old grammers
helping each other to the privy.

'Call us no one, then,' Ember called back to the empty sky,
'because we must go there.'

She was so brave and so reckless. The weight of the Ice King's
mind fell on them, draining all warmth, all hope, all sense of life.
They were nothing, midges, ephemeral. Who were they to challenge the great purpose, the eternal creation of beauty, the
unchanging perfection of the Ice? Every time in his life that he
had ever felt unworthy swelled in his heart and told him that it
was true; that humans were nothing, the Ice was forever. His
own appreciation of its beauty fought against him; he was ugly,

pustulent, disgusting, while it was pure, clean, perfect. It was right that it should survive and he perish.

Ember's hand found his. Ash straightened his back and stood next to her. He knew how to talk to the gods; his mother had explained it when he was still a young boy. He formed the words in his mind and sent them out into the blank ice field, where he could see nothing but winter, lying under the high sun of summer. Which was wrong.

You have no right to bring cold in high summer, he said with certainty. All the other things were matters of Power versus Power, but this he knew, deep in his soul. Even the Powers should not subvert the cycle of the year. *You are doing wrong.*

You dare to judge me? The roar was the roar of an avalanche, and it drove them both to their knees and set the ice field groaning. They clambered up again and faced him, having to keep their eyes almost closed because of the glaring light which grew even more intense as they stood there.

'Ice is not eternal,' Ember said. 'And you must fade, each spring, as it is ordained for you.'

Humans, He said, the scorn so deep that it was like acid, *you will die now.*

The wraiths had found them, speeding up behind silently, grabbing Ember and tossing her to the ground, pushing him down, face in the ice.

He rolled and sprang up to find them clustered over her, greed in their burning eyes. They smiled at him, as if in challenge, and extended long, long claws to her back. She turned over, dazed, and he barrelled into them, standing over her, legs astride, bellowing defiance.

If he had been a crane, if he had known how to change, as Cedar had known, he could have flown her to safety, even if it destroyed him to lift her weight; or he could attack with beak and talons as they did. A knife in each hand, he lifted his arms as he had in the crane dance, willing the air to give him purchase, begging it to help him grow the feathers he needed, the ones he had almost had once. All he had were weak human fingers, soft human hands, heavy feet.

'Let me change!' he sang in five wobbly notes to whoever controlled these things. There was no change. But there was a pause, as the wraiths heard him sing and realised that he had no power – not like Cedar, not even like Ember; he had no Power behind him, no warmth or Sight or ability. They smiled, and gathered together, ready to attack again, claws out. The ice needles flicked out from them, spearing into his cheeks and chest. And all he had was himself, the centre of himself, which was, after all, just a single arrow in flight.

As though the thought had called it up, wind arose. It curved around both sides of the mountain, giant hands flipping the wraiths away from them, sending them sprawling across the ice, lifting into the sky, flapping futile hands, screeching, imploring, complaining to the relentless buffets and gusts which slid impossibly around him and Ember and barely lifted the hair on his head, but which hit the wraiths like a tornado. A warm tornado.

The Ice King howled with anguish, but it was as though He, too, were swept away in the wind, because the sense of heaviness, of being tied to the earth with lead chains, lifted and Ash could move freely again.

In his mind, a voice spoke, which was the sound of an arrow in flight, *Hurry*.

He dragged Ember up and pulled her, not caring where they stepped, further up, and further up, and step after step, stumbling together, gasping for breath, higher, steeper, until his foot came down on gravel and rock, not on ice, and they climbed on hands and knees as the slope grew steeper and they could look back, finally, at the brilliant ice below them, where there were no wraiths to be seen.

They leaned against each other, panting, and heard the triumphant howl of a wolf cut across the sky.

Ember had heard stories about the molten rock which could stream from places like this, but although the ground was warm under their feet, she wasn't sure if that was simply because they weren't on ice any more. There were no ribbons of glowing rock, no flames dancing over a deceptive crust, not even any smoke, except high above them, on the summit. There was no fire on Fire Mountain.

'So we climb,' Ash said. He looked tired.

'Rest first,' Ember said, but he shook his head.

'I don't think we have time,' he said. 'Something – whatever brought the wind – said, "Hurry" to me.'

'Are you tired of all this – this *enchantment*?' she asked, exasperated. That irrepressible smile broke across his face, his teeth white against the red sunglare burn of his cheeks.

'Part tired of it, but –' he shot a glance of pure mischief at her, 'but part fascinated, too. Who knew my little brother would turn grey so early?'

Laughing, they began to climb. They had lost their poles somewhere in the frantic scramble to the mountainside, so they had nothing but their hands and feet to help them up. The surface was loose with gravel and dirt, and under that the rock was harsh, sometimes cutting their gloves right through.

Wind still circled the base of the mountain, lifting currents of snow and dirt into drifts in the air and letting them drop. Ember felt the cold radiating from the ice, but the sun was summer hot and she shed her big winter furs and wore only her felt coat and hat. Ash did the same. They left the furs puddled against a boulder shaped like a hat, in the hope of finding them again. In the hope of making it home.

The slope was steady, at least, but it was hard work climbing the slippery scree. She fell often despite Ash's steadying hand. They were both covered with dirt and dust and sharp, powdery particles of stone which got into her nose and eyes and made Ash cough.

She laughed at him, once, as they rested on a ledge halfway up. He was grey with dust.

'You look like your name!' she teased.

'*I*,' he said, with mock hauteur, 'was named after my Uncle Ash, who was named after a tree. I am happy to look like the noble ash tree.'

Out here, in the bright light and wide blue sky, any barriers between them had vanished like the wraiths. Every time she looked at him she felt her heart swell. Love, she thought. It tingled to the tips of her fingers, climbed into her throat and blocked it, made her dissolve, every part of her aware of his breath, his movements, each strand of his hair.

Now they were off the ice she could feel the fake desire from Fire licking at her skin, but she shrugged it off like the counterfeit it was.

'Hurry,' Ash said, pulling her up. 'I think we have to get to the top.'

They started struggling upwards again. But two-thirds of the way up the slope there was a much broader ledge, and it led easily to a fissure in the mountainside, a cleft unpleasantly reminiscent of a gaping mouth. From inside came the unmistakable smell of fire, the burnt air shimmering up outside the cleft, floating Ember's hair as it had floated before the butterflies flew, creating a breeze which blew the dust from Ash's hair and made it shine brown again.

'Here,' she said with certainty. 'He will be waiting in here.'

Now they were so close to the end, fear hit her and her hands started to shake. Ash stripped off his gloves and hers, exposing the scratches and cuts from the sharp rocks, and took her right hand gently in his left. She gripped it, ignoring the pain, and he returned the pressure.

'Together,' he said.

The passageway through the rock was dark, with ragged peaks reaching down in unexpected places. They felt their way, but kept hands joined. Ember was afraid that if she let Ash go, they would lose each other completely in the dark.

Zigzagging, rough underfoot – this was not made for or by humans, Ember thought. This is the natural rock. It grew hotter as they moved in, and smelled more of brimstone.

Around another corner, and there was light – the red, flickering light of the bathing caves back at Mountainside. Ash stopped and she stood close to him, just behind his shoulder, and then forced herself to move forward, next to him, unprotected. This was her task.

She tried to free her hand from his and go on alone, but he held on tightly and walked with her.

FIRE MOUNTAIN

A round cave lay beyond the passageway. On its far side was a pool of the hot red rock mud, just like the bathing caves, glowing with heat, small flames dancing over it. That was all. Rock floor, walls, fire.

'I have to steal some of that fire,' Ember said. All through this trek she had kept secure the bone which was the only object that could withstand the fire rock. It was safe in her petticoat pocket. She took it out and held it tightly in her left hand, ready.

But she had nothing to fish the fire fragment out with. This, gods help her, was when they needed the poles. Even if they burned up in a moment, it might have been long enough to get the – the ember.

Her knife would have to do. And for that she would need her right hand back. Reluctantly, she freed her fingers from Ash's grasp, and this time he let her.

'My knife is longer,' he said, handing it to her.

She took it carefully and moved towards the pool, feeling that it *couldn't* be this easy, not after all the death and despair and anger and pain to get here. Surely He wouldn't just let her take it and go home again?

The heat from the pool was searing. She wrapped her scarf around her face as if protecting from cold, but it didn't help much. Kneeling just within arm's reach, Ember turned her face away, imagining her skin crisping in the dry air. Out of the corner of her eye she managed to locate a small chunk of hot rock floating on the surface of the mud, and stretched forwards, sliding Ash's knife delicately to it, the tip moving underneath, coming up …

The blade of the dagger melted; heat struck up the tang and hit her hand like a spear. She recoiled, dropping the knife in the pool where it spread like silver gauze across the surface as it melted and then disappeared. Her hand throbbed with pain.

She scrambled backwards as Ash came towards her and pulled her further, towards the passageway. But she wouldn't sprawl on the floor in front of Him. She struggled to her feet, nursing her hand.

'Damn you to the cold hells!' she shouted at the pool, at the walls, at Him. 'You never meant us to succeed! You're a shagging baby throwing a tantrum, taking revenge on a whole people because one of them displeased you!'

Fire sprang out of the pool in a surge of flame, a towering blaze that roared up. And the bastard was laughing.

'You have succeeded!' He said. He looked from her to Ash with great satisfaction. 'You are both here.'

The roar quietened – now the sound was no more than the safe crackle of a hearth fire, a kitchen fire. Tame.

'Both?' Ash said, moving in front of her.

'Both,' He confirmed, still laughing. Ember's anger mounted. Not Ash, too. He'd made puppets of all of them, and now Ash? No.

'What do you want him for?' she said, feeling dangerous. It was ridiculous, to feel as though she could do Him damage, but when it came to Ash she *was* dangerous; she would do whatever it took to protect him.

'*She* wants him,' Fire said, with an air of complacency, the beautiful sulky face looking for the first time satisfied. 'Air.'

It astonished both of them. They stood like dumb cattle, staring at Him. Finally, Ash said, 'Air? Air, like you're Fire?'

He laughed, the roar returning, and threw up his hands so that the whole cave was bright with golden light. Happy light.

'The first man in a thousand years to reject Water in favour of Air,' He said. 'My first ally.'

'What?' Ember asked, but Ash stood very still for a moment, and then turned to her, his eyes troubled.

'The Prowman offered me allegiance to Water,' he said slowly, 'but the shape of my soul is not in Her care.'

Fire nodded. 'You are a creature of Air, and had the sense to know it. And *you*,' He added to Ember, 'are a creature of Fire. Together ...'

'What?' Ember snapped, not sure she liked the idea of Ash owing allegiance to anyone but her. 'Together, what?'

'Together, you may lure Her back from the Ice King.' This time, His mutable voice was solemn, serious, and the light He gave off was red as blood. 'A thousand years She has played with Him. He tempted Her with a land's worth of ice to carve, and She accepted. A thousand years She has kept the Ice flowing south, so that She may make beauty out of it.'

He seemed to stare outwards, past the rock walls, to the ice beyond. 'Did you not see? She has made great beauty ... but She forgot me; and there has been no worshipper to draw her back for a thousand years ... until now.' He looked directly at Ash. 'She loves you, boy. She has saved you over and over again – and finally you forced her to act against His agents. Now She must choose.'

From a dry throat, Ember asked, 'But why me? What do you want from me?'

'In the cold, she has forgotten Love,' Fire said. His voice was like the low horns of Ari's people, soft and troubling, throbbing with pain. 'Together, you may remind Her of the glory which comes when Fire joins with Air.'

'Joins?' Ash said. His voice was furious and Ember looked at him, astonished at the anger on his face. Ash never got angry, not like this.

'You want to pimp her!' he shouted. 'You brought her all this way to turn her into a whore!'

Fire smiled strangely.

'I tried. But she would not be turned,' He said. 'She rejected every lick of desire for you I sent Her way.'

A stillness came over Ash and Ember saw his face harden. It was wrong. Wrong for Fire to taunt him so. Wrong for her to let him. She couldn't let Ash's face lose its sweetness, to turn hard, like Ari's and Nyr's. Even if it meant baring her soul before this bastard of a god.

She put her hand on his arm, and felt, deep within his muscles, a fine trembling.

'He sent desire that was false,' she said softly. As though against his will, Ash looked down at her, fear in his eyes at what she might say. 'I rejected it, because it came from outside me. True desire comes from within—' Oh, this was so hard to say! A warlord's daughter did not talk to a man of her own desire. Never. In this cave, though, she must be Martine's daughter, not Arvid's. '... as mine for you does. And – and my love.'

She gulped air. So hard to say. Ash's eyes were alight again, and warm as they had never been, even when they had kissed.

His hand covered hers on his arm and she felt his heartbeat running, fast and light. The feeling was too strong to allow her to smile at him, but she could feel joy coursing through them both.

'Love!' Fire said. 'Better even than I could have hoped. Love will lure Her back for certain. And then We will destroy the ice, and my mountain will be free again.'

That caught her attention.

'You *planned* this?' she demanded.

He laughed again, the column of fire shooting up to the roof and coming down again.

'Not the love, child. Love breaks all fates. I planned desire.' He smiled at her but it was a baring of teeth, and she shivered. 'You resisted me. The women of your family resist me too often.'

'Is that why You chose me? To punish my mother?'

'She deserved punishment,' He said. 'But that was not why.' He looked at Ash and smiled with the commiserating smile men give to each other over women. 'He wanted you. He wouldn't let himself know it, but he wanted you. And he wanted you because you are fire to your core – all anger and passion and heat. The butterflies proved that.'

'And now You need us,' she said. Ash made a movement with one hand, as if to warn her, stop her – but then he pulled the hand back and stood at her shoulder, where the lord's second-in-command stood in a place that was dangerous. She felt herself grow larger; Ash trusted her to handle this, to let her negotiate for them both, for all of them. For all the world. That wasn't just love, it was a respect she'd never expected to get. She felt as though she could do anything, with Ash at her back.

'You,' she said to the ancient Power, 'will give fire back to my people right now, or we will not even have this discussion.'

Fire shrank down until He could look her right in the eyes. If fire could be cold, those eyes were freezing.

'I could burn you where you stand until not even a flake of either of you remained,' He said softly.

'And wait another thousand years?' she asked sweetly. Oh, this was heady stuff! Negotiating with Ari had taught her a great deal, but she had learned more at her father's knee, and the one thing he had taught her above all was that the one who was most in need was the weak one in the bargaining. She waited a beat, until she saw the colour of His eyes change from white hot to red. 'Give them back their fire, my lord,' she said. 'You only took it from them to bring us here, and here we are. Why should they suffer further?' And the second lesson was: give them a way of saving face, so they can look like they have capitulated to reason, not superior strength.

'That's true,' He said magnanimously. 'And they have fought the Ice King well in your absence, much more strongly than the cave people ever did. They deserve reward.' He waved a hand. 'There. It is done. The fires blaze again.'

There was no way to prove or disprove it, but she suspected that He would not deign to lie. They had succeeded. No matter what happened, she doubted He would repeat Himself and steal the flames again, so her people were safe. Relief made her knees shake, but she stood firm. Now it was time to play for larger stakes.

Ember took a breath and reached back to squeeze Ash's hand in warning. He gripped her hand warmly and she welcomed even the sharpness as the scrapes and cuts on her palms stung. That was human; prone to hurts, but able to recover, given the chance.

'I thank you, my lord,' she said. Thanks cost nothing. 'Now. We must discuss the terms of our next agreement.' Her chin came up and she stared him in the eyes. Of course, she and Ash wanted to get rid of Ice, too, if for no other reason than that it would stop Ari's attacks on the Domains. But it was Fire who *needed* to break free.

'Agreement?' He hissed, like water drops landing on flame. 'You should be thanking me. Where else but here could you two come together?'

The truth of that hit her and she could see it register with Ash, too. He was right. Outside this cave, the barriers between them were huge. She could defy her father, and would, if all that was at stake was her own happiness. For just a moment she indulged herself in that dream again: she and Ash, living on one of her father's estates, raising a family, happy together. In the flash of a moment she imagined it all, and it was a good, good life.

Every decision she had ever made, she thought, had been selfish. To choose to marry Osfrid, which would have taken her so far south her parents – and her people – would rarely have seen her, just because he was handsome and she hated the cold. That had been selfish. She had fancied herself in love as a girl dressed in her mother's jewellery imagines herself to be grown up. She had barely known Osfrid; it had been a wisp of cloud compared to the thunderstorm of her love for Ash.

To defy Fire, back at the fort – that had been selfish, concerned only with her own dignity, not with the safety of her people.

It was time she let go of selfishness and did what was necessary instead, even if it broke her heart.

'Untrue,' she said to Fire. She felt Ash look at her in surprise. 'If we wished, we could defy the world. My father did.' She couldn't let Ash think she meant to do it, though. That would be cruel. 'But that is not what will happen.' He took that like a kick in the stomach. She felt the shock go through him; his hand tightened on hers painfully. 'When I leave here, my lord, I intend to marry Nyr, heir to the Hárugur King, and unite our peoples in peace.'

That was a shock to both of them. Ash jerked back, but she kept tight hold of his hand, keeping her eyes on the hard, flaring eyes of the Power.

'And I do *not* intend to watch my second husband die in the wedding fire.'

'You are mine,' He said.

'No.'

It wasn't smart. She knew it might break the negotiations – but this one thing she couldn't flatter or mislead about. She would *not* say that anyone owned her. This was the centre of her soul, and that was that. But she could challenge.

'I belong to myself,' she said. 'And if you kill me to disprove that, then you do no more than any thug or rapist.'

It stopped Him. It stopped Ash, who was turning to caution her. And around them, a breeze sprang up, twisting dust into the air, fanning the flames around His feet. The twisting, changing face lit up.

'She is here!' He said, as excited as a young boy. Press the advantage, Ember thought.

'And She agrees with me.'

He glared at her, but He wasn't prepared to argue the point.

'What do you want?' He asked and she felt her heart leap. Now. Now was the time to change the world.

'My father is of Acton's people. Ash's father is of Acton's people,' she stated. Ash nodded, next to her, understanding where she was heading.

'Yes,' he said. 'If you accept us, you must accept them.'

The air stilled around them and Fire seemed to freeze in place, even the small flames around His feet not moving.

'The Prowman says the time has come,' Ash added.

'Water agrees?'

Ember looked up to see Ash smile strangely. 'She will.'

'You've already shown yourself to Acton's people, my lord,' Ember said, trying to seem calm although her heart was suffocating her, it was so big in her chest. 'Unless you accept them, the old blood will suffer further in revenge.'

He hadn't thought *that* through, of course. That was Fire – oh, she knew Him because He was right, she was fire through and through, and she wanted what she wanted at the very minute, *now*, and would take it, if she could, and damn the consequences. She'd fought herself all her life because a warlord's daughter could not, must not, act on impulse. Ember had learned to watch what she said, and control what she did, and deny herself what she wanted, as this Fire never had.

'We have equality under the law now,' Ash said, his deep voice serious, his hand holding hers less tightly now they were talking about impersonal matters. 'But unless we have equality before the Powers we will never be one people.'

'Why should you be?' He said, the sulky boy back in full.

'Because there are more like us, half and half, every day, and it is our future, our country.'

'Watering down the old blood until it disappears!' He flashed.

'Enriching it,' Ash said. 'Bringing more to acknowledge their deepest allegiance, whether that is to Fire, or Water – or Air.'

In response, the breeze became a positive wind, swirling around them, around Ash, caressing him. Ember didn't like that at all, but she ignored it.

'She agrees,' Ember said, straight to Fire.

'The old blood must have control over who meets us,' He said, but it was the last hurdle, a feeble attempt to pretend control over the negotiation.

'Agreed,' Ember said.

The world was changed.

'Your part of the bargain must be kept,' He said. Almost pleaded.

'Not with you here!' Ash exclaimed.

He laughed, the flames shooting up, heat expanding to fill the cave. He held out His hand, but not to them.

'No. We dance above. Come, Beloved, and remember the glory of Fire and Air together.'

The fire reached to the roof, a column too bright to look at. They turned away, huddling together against the far wall, and then darkness fell.

PALISADE FORT, THE LAST DOMAIN

Elva was conscious, now, and seemed unharmed, so they left her to rest in her own room and went to Martine's parlour.

Sigurd sat in her chair by the window, rocking back and forth, staring avidly at the wedding fire. Her hands were clenched tight, her mouth turned down and in, her eyes too bright. Arvid doubted that she would ever be sane again. Merroc sat in a chair by the empty hearth, watching her, looking like a man beset by too many troubles, who sees no way out; a worse grief than death, Arvid thought.

Martine stood next to him as he hesitated, trying to find the right words to say to Merroc. Perhaps it would be better if he sat down.

The hearth flared up in roaring flames.

Arvid sat down in surprise, and Martine went with him, ending up in his lap. Ridiculously, he felt a surge of desire.

Everywhere, in every room, people were calling out, Fire! Fire! But instead of an alarm call it was a paean of triumph.

Martine drew in a sharp breath.

'He is here, He is here!' she exclaimed. 'Quick, bring her to the fire!'

She sprang from Arvid's lap and went to Sigurd, drawing her to her feet and bringing her over to the flames.

'Come, my lady, come,' she said.

Dazed, not even recognising Martine, Sigurd came to the hearth and stared uncomprehendingly at the fire.

Martine bowed to the hearth.

'My lord, my lord, be generous. You have stolen this woman's son and her reason with him. My lord, heal her, we pray you!'

'What are you doing?' Merroc snarled, and Arvid, for a moment, wanted to drag Martine away from the hearth, to shake her and berate her and even smash her to the ground for turning to Him.

But then Sigurd's eyes filled with tears and she reached out her hands to the flames.

'Osfrid!' she said. Astonished, Arvid saw Osfrid's form in the flames. It was clear. Unmistakable. Not the ghost they would have vaguely sensed at a quickening, but the man himself, carved from golden light. Even more handsome than he had been in life.

'Mother,' he said.

'I knew you would come back.' Her face showed a kind of idolatry, Arvid thought, and wondered if he had ever looked at Ember that way. He hoped not.

'I love you. Do not grieve for me. I am happy.'

Sigurd was sobbing. 'Osfrid, Osfrid,' but they were the clean tears of grief, untainted by madness.

'Goodbye until we meet again, Mother.'

He faded into red and vanished.

Sigurd turned to Merroc, her face alight with joy and grief.

'He came! I told you he would come!'

'Yes, Sigi,' Merroc said gently. 'He came.'

'I'm very tired,' Sigurd said in surprise. Her eyes were clear, with no sign of madness.

One of her women came up and took her by the arm.

'Come, my lady, come and rest.' She went with them willingly, Merroc staring after her in wonder. He turned to Martine.

'Was that my son?' he demanded.

She hesitated. 'In truth, I do not know. Perhaps Fire has the power to draw a spirit back from the darkness beyond death. Perhaps not. Does it matter?'

'Yes!' he exclaimed.

She bent her head and studied the floor. Arvid thought she was choosing her words very carefully.

'My lord, I asked Fire to heal her. He did so. He understands need, and how to answer it. Perhaps we should accept the end and not question the means.'

Merroc searched her face, which showed only its usual public calm.

'It was generous of you,' he said slowly, 'to – to do what you did.'

Her expression changed and she became the Martine Arvid knew behind closed doors, compassionate and wise and bearing many wounds from a difficult life.

'My lord, I weep with her, and with you,' was all she said, but Merroc's face crumpled and his eyes filled with tears. He turned aside to hide them, and stood for a moment, pretending to cough, harrumphing them away. When he turned back, he looked at Arvid.

'That promise I made,' he said. 'I think I may not keep it.' Running a hand through his greying red hair, he sighed. 'I'm tired, too. I may sleep a little, now.'

'We'll call you if anything else happens,' Arvid promised. His heart was light with relief. He would have gone to war with Merroc over Martine's life if he had to, but to have that threat lifted was almost enough to make him happy. If only they knew that Ember was safe.

After he had gone into the guest chamber and they were alone, Martine asked him, 'What promise?'

'To kill you, if I didn't,' he said, looking out the window. 'The wedding fire,' he added in surprise. 'It's gone out.'

FIRE MOUNTAIN

S he was going to marry Nyr.

There was not enough ice in the world to cool what she felt for Ash, but she was going to marry Nyr, and save two peoples, and bring peace, and no matter what happened, that was the way it had to be.

It was like out on the ice: ice pole, step, slide, ice pole, step. There was only one path to follow, and she would follow it to the end, although her heart broke inside her.

But here, now, the path hadn't yet begun.

She turned slowly to look at Ash, the dim light from the fire pool sending red and gold over his face, his hands. His felt coat was white and black and grey, and for a quick flash of a moment she wondered what Sight his Aunty Drema had, to give her a coat of red and gold and him one in a crane's colours, the colour of the air.

'Nyr,' he said, his shoulders hunched.

Ember's lips trembled. She was hot, too hot, suddenly. She took off her coat and let it fall, threw her hat into a corner, paced away from the fire pool's heat towards the passageway to the outside. Looked down it. Outside the sky was clouding over, and the passage was dim.

'How many people in Hidden Valley have the Ice King's people killed over the last thousand years?' she asked.

'Politics!' he said, scornfully, but she'd learned to know him better on this trip and she heard the pain underneath. He dragged his hat off and stood twisting it in both hands, the cool grey turning to a rag underneath his fingers. Ember went to him and put a hand on his arm and he stilled, like ice, as though he were afraid to move.

'If I could,' she said, searching for the words, the right words, that would bridge the pain. 'If I could I would fly with you.' A shiver went through him and he drew a long breath. 'If I could, I'd bear your children, and live with you year long, wherever you wanted. If I could, I'd warm your bed each night.' The shiver this time was more like a shudder. He was fighting for control, for strength to withstand her voice.

'My father could marry where he chose, but I cannot,' she went on. 'Not when I can bring Mountainside into the Domains. End a thousand-year war.' She was struggling for control herself, now. 'How can I *not*?' she cried, her voice breaking, tears welling over onto her cheeks. 'How can I not?' she whispered. 'Tell me, and I won't.'

His arm came around her; warm, comforting. And then not comforting, as his mouth found hers, his hands gripped her arms, the heat of his skin scorching through her dress.

Her lips parted under his and he tasted, at first, of dust – bitter, for a moment, until their tongues twined and found the sweetness underneath. They were suspended, mouth to mouth, as though that warm, soft, desperate contact was holding them up. As though all that was alive in her flowed through her lips to him, and back again.

Her hands went to his chest and slid beneath the coat; her fingers spread against the muscles, hard, strong, so *male* that she felt herself soften, her body curve towards him. He gasped for breath and then bent to her again, one hand sliding up into her hair, against the sensitive skin of her nape. She shivered, and his other hand slid down, pulling her hips against his.

She ached for him; a real, actual, physical ache she'd never felt before. Pushing her hips against him, against the tantalising soft hardness of his loins, made it worse, and she groaned.

He tore off his coat. His shirt went with it and he was no longer in bird's plumage, but human skin. Her mouth touched his chest; her lips clung and he made a small sound in his throat.

Fire filled her clean and thorough, sweet as mead, hot and liquid. She tasted him again, perfect as the dewgift which had lain in her palm. His breath was Air in her ear, on her skin, sighing through her nerves to quiver on her fingertips as she touched him.

Her head dropped back to bare her throat to him and he answered the invitation, kissing down, pushing her dress open, fingers fumbling with toggles and sash until she helped him, both frantic to feel skin against skin, flesh against flesh.

He curved his hand around her breast and bent his head to her nipple and the fire mounted up so high she thought she would faint. But it was awkward, he was so much taller, so he kicked the two coats together on the floor and they eased down onto the only wedding bed they would ever know.

Under her hips the earth cradled them, welcomed them, but although the part of her that knew Fire recognised it, she could spare no thought for it. She had no brain to think with, only a body, breath driven into gasps by his mouth on her breasts, his hands on her thighs.

She touched him back, sliding her fingers down until they

were frustrated by the waistband of his trousers. He pushed the trousers down and his body was bare beside hers. For a moment, one long moment, she simply looked at him. Ash. Not Osfrid, not Nyr, not any other male than this: the one she loved.

Tears scalded her eyes.

He looked startled, but then he leant forward and kissed her, gently.

'Princess,' he said, yearning, comforting. She kissed him back, not gently at all, and then the fire overtook them both, and she was crying as they kissed, and laughing, and gasping, flushed and alive.

She wriggled out of her own trousers, and her boots with them, wanting to be truly naked, truly just herself. She slid down and pulled Ash's pants and boots off, too, and he laughed and dragged her up until she lay full length, and then he half-rolled on top of her, his leg between hers so that she felt him against every inch of her skin on that side, nerves ablaze with his heat. The only fire she wanted.

Slowly, his eyes on hers, he slid his hand down over her belly and between her legs. She could tell that he was ready, even now, to stop, but all she wanted was for him to hurry, to touch her, take her, make the aching *stop*.

His skin was roughened, but she was so slippery it didn't matter after that first, searing touch. Her back arched as he stroked her with movements as delicate as a breeze, as teasing; she fought for enough control to touch him back, to make him moan in turn, and was deeply satisfied when he gasped.

'Ember,' he said, voice ragged, breathing fast, 'I—'

She stopped his mouth with hers and slid her legs fully apart, her hands on his firm buttocks, the muscles beneath her fingers bunching and coiling.

His penis was hotter than anything else, but so smooth, so

soft, so good it felt, rubbing, sliding, opening her, filling her … He paused, once again making sure of her intent, and in frustration she pulled hard on his buttocks, wrapping her legs around him.

'Ow!' she said in surprise.

He paled in horror. 'I didn't mean to hurt you,' he said, his hands gentling on her arm, her breast.

'Mam says it always hurts, the first time,' she said breathlessly, giddy. 'It's over now.'

That moment of pause allowed her to hear what was happening outside: the rising wind, and something else: a fine tremor in the mountain itself. Fire Mountain.

'We might not have to part after all,' she murmured, 'if the mountain eats us alive.'

He laughed – that irrepressible laugh that had irritated and cheered her so often.

'It'd be worth it,' he gasped, and moved within her, to be with her, to join in the glory of Fire and Air. Every movement they made sent streams and rivers of fire through her, through him, and back again, as the hot breeze fanned the fire pool into streams and ribbons of light.

Even naked, they were too hot. The mountain was moving continuously now, fine repeated tremors which cumulatively shook their bones and rattled their teeth.

Ember laid her hand flat across Ash's chest and kissed his skin, licked off the sweat, enjoying the shiver that went through him. He slid an arm around her waist and pulled her on top of him, breast to breast, nose to nose, and kissed her.

Warm and sweet and honeyed, his mouth was the whole world. She could stay here forever.

The mountain shook and the fire pit in the corner of the cave split open, the incandescent rock leaking across the floor towards them.

Ash leaped to his feet, pulling her with him, and together they dragged their clothes away from the deadly ribbon of fire.

There were sparks and smuts flying around the room. Ash put on his pants hurriedly. Ember sorted out her own clothing and followed suit, her heart achingly full of regret that it had all ended so soon. How soon was it? They had lost track of time.

'We'd better get out of here,' Ash said. He looked so young. So vulnerable, with his mouth red from hers and his eyes almost black in the dim light. He touched the back of his hand to her cheek. 'The world outside ...'

She closed her eyes for a moment and pressed her own hand against his, so she could feel his flesh firmly, warm and human and alive. Then she looked into his eyes.

'I love you,' she said.

'Not going to say it,' he answered, the stubborn look she knew well coming into his eyes. 'If I say it, I won't be able to let you go.'

Ember nodded understanding and rested her head against his shoulder as his arm came around her. Her eyes were full of tears, again. How much crying had she done lately? More than in her whole life before. She just wanted to stay here in his arms. Part of her thought it would be better to die now than live without him.

The air thickened and stank of brimstone. They both began to cough.

'Now, princess,' Ash said. They went down the passageway, which had rocks and shards of stones scattered along it where bits of the walls had broken off. Ash looked at them grimly. 'Time and past to leave,' he said.

It was dark outside; they had been longer than she had

thought. Perhaps they'd fallen asleep for a while, in that long moment of perfect peace after – her thoughts stumbled on the memory of Ash being part of her, fire and air and human flesh melding into a lightning strike of desire and satisfaction. She couldn't let herself think about that any more; not now, or she would never be able to let him go.

The slit of sky they could see as they stumbled down to the end of the passage in the meagre light from the fire pit behind them was swirling with wind, carrying aloft bits of – leaves, was it? When they got to the end, where the mountain fell away into its slope, Ash put out a hand and held her back.

It was not night. The swirling cloud wasn't leaves, but ash and embers, and the whole world was orange, even the air the colour of fire.

Hah! she thought. Ash and embers indeed. It's thanks to us this is happening.

All of them, when children, had heard stories about fire mountains down south on the islands near the Wind Cities. Mountains which vomited up fire and liquid rock, which bled flame. She had expected Fire's mountain to do the same; had expected to come out into a delta of fire. She couldn't see any ahead of them. But the smoke was like fog, and the ash – everywhere she looked, there was black ash lying thick on the ground. On the ice.

Red flared through the smoke. They twisted to look up at the cone of the mountain, where a long tongue of flame mounted and fell, climbed and retreated like a fountain as Fire and Air danced together. It was beautiful. Ember felt for Ash's hand, feeling her own desire for him return, climb with each burst of light. He slid an arm around her in response and kissed her temple; his lips were hot on her skin.

The sun showed a dim red circle through the smoke, but it

was still high; only just afternoon. Ember was surprised they could still breathe; then Ash looked up at the sky and said, 'Thank you,' and she realised that Air was sending tendrils of clean breath towards them from up high. To Ash, at least, and she got the benefit. But she said, 'Thank you,' all the same, and Ash squeezed her hand. It was a surprise that the cuts on her palm hadn't healed – it seemed so long ago, another life, that they had gone into the cave.

'I don't understand,' she said to him. 'I thought he wanted the mountain to explode so he could melt the ice.'

Ash was frowning, looking out over the blackened landscape. The fire above was fountaining ash, not flame. The ice, below, was covered with it. As they watched the wind took it farther, lifting great blankets of it up and laying them down on the ice field. What had been blindingly white was now deep black, the whole world sombrely shrouded, the land drinking in light instead of reflecting it back to their eyes. The only colour was the uncanny orange of the sky.

'It's summer,' he said. 'The summer sun will hit the blackened ice and melt it.'

'Not just here!'

'For miles,' Ash agreed. 'All the way north, it may be.'

'They're destroying Him completely. Why is She helping?'

Ash stood for a moment, a listening look on his face. 'He's been lying to Her, telling Her the ice hurt no one. But something – I don't know, something's been going on in the Last Domain that proved that was a lie.' He must have seen her face change, because he added hurriedly. 'It's all right now. They're safe.'

'So She takes revenge for a lie, after a thousand years,' Ember mused. 'Wipes Ice out completely.'

'He'll be back in winter,' Ash said grimly. 'But not like this—'

He gestured to the ice field. 'Not filling valleys and destroying everything. Ponds and lakes and small streams, that's what His allotment is and that's what He'll have to be satisfied with.'

For a moment, the wind dropped as though Air heard his words and was saddened by them. In the momentary pause, the sound of water dripping, trickling, flowing became clear. Ember became aware of how dry her throat was, how parched her mouth.

'Let's find ourselves a drink, then,' she said, and led the way down the mountain, trying hard, very hard, not to cry as she took the first step away from him.

ABOVE THE ICE

Cedar howled again, half for fun, half in hope that the wraiths would come back to him, and leave Ember and Ash alone.

He couldn't see them any more. Having led the wraiths on a long chase through winding mountain valleys, they were out of sight, although he could see the tall cone of Fire Mountain to his left. The smoke, darker in his wolf's sight, was getting thicker, and he hoped that was a sign they had reached their goal.

It was very cold. He half-regretted the human clothes he had stripped off just before he changed. Tongue lolling, he laughed at himself. Better go to Starkling, he thought, and change back there. They'd be used to naked men suddenly appearing where an animal had stood. No doubt Elgir would give him some new clothes. He was the heir, after all.

An astonishing thought.

His muzzle came up and he sniffed. The wind had changed. It was blowing from Fire Mountain, and it was warm, bringing with it a complex interlacing of scents: brimstone, grass, hot stone, smoke, ash. Surely that was a good sign?

His wolf mind seemed to work more simply, but the worry he

felt for Ash and Ember was no less. Or for the people left without fire, right across the Domains. Had they done enough? Had *he* done enough to help them?

He could feel strength coming up through his pads from Earth. Not a personage, as Fire was, but there, unmistakable in this form. A Power. His Power, presumably. Earth and Forest, Elgir had said. Perhaps he should go to the Forest before he headed back to Starkling, and see how different it was in his wolf's black-and-white Sight.

He should move. But as well as strength, he was receiving a sense of waiting from Earth. Of expectancy. So he stayed where he was, and watched.

There was a tremble in the ground beneath his feet. From the top of Fire Mountain, smoke began to pour as he had once seen mist rise from the altar stone, flowing out and up, roiling. Flashes of fire, like lightning reaching upwards, came from the cone, and he felt the wind rise, streaming towards the Mountain, and he knew somehow that Air was moving, as well as Fire.

They can't hope to melt it all, he thought in puzzlement. Then the fire and the wind began to dance on the mountaintop, a dance so joyous, so *alive* that he flung back his head and howled in delight. She's there! he realised. They've made it, and this is Fire's celebration.

High and wild, flame and wind climbed to the blue sky, seemed to climb right to the sun which stood above them, danced and clung and spun and flickered with joy.

The Mountain, in contrast, poured out black. Flakes of black, dancing like a stream of butterflies in the air.

The lower winds took it, flung it, spread it wide over the ice, and Cedar howled again, because he understood that each fleck of black was an arrow in Ice's heart.

EPILOGUE

After her daughter was born, the first living thing outside the birthing chamber that Ember saw was a duck. A duck. She had insisted on coming out to one of the stone houses for the birth, and insisted, too, that windows be made in its circular walls. Martine had pulled aside the curtains and set the door wide so she could see out as soon as the afterbirth had been delivered and the cord cut, and there above was a flight of migrating ducks, coming north to breed for the spring. They were flying low, coming in to land on the lake which had formed to the north of Mountainside now the ice was gone. Flashes of green and blue came from some of their heads as they angled into the setting sun.

Duck, she thought drowsily as she brushed her lips back and forth across the baby's downy brown hair. Not a good name for a princess. Her mind seemed to be working very slowly, and all she was conscious of was a deep joy and relief that the pain was over. Can't call her that, but they have another name ... Teal, that's it.

'Teal,' she said aloud.

Martine wiped her sweaty face with a cool cloth and smiled down at her. Ember had wanted no one with her during the labour except the two grandmothers. Halda had already gone to spread the good news to the men waiting outside.

'Nice,' Martine said. 'I'll tell Nyr. I'll bet Ari's already congratulating himself on the bargain he made with your father.'

Ember smiled wryly. 'Because he agreed the first child could rule the Last Domain and she's a girl?'

Martine laughed and looked out the window towards the fire pit, where Ember could hear the men were celebrating with drums and drink, near the saplings which had sprung up around the lake. There were trees again in the mountains. Ember wondered, not for the first time, if that was why the Forest had let them through.

'He's slapping Nyr on the back and poking fun at Arvid,' Martine said.

'Da won't mind,' Ember said sleepily. She gazed with adoration down at Teal, who was sucking on her tiny fist. 'She looks like her father, doesn't she?'

Martine slid a finger down Teal's soft cheek and the baby opened her eyes and blinked at them. Although she had the dark blue eyes of all newborns, Ember could tell that they would turn even darker. Hazel, although she might take a touch of real green from her mother.

'Yes, she does,' Martine agreed, 'though it wouldn't be wise to say it aloud too often. Where is he?'

Ember rested her head back on the pillow, and sighed.

'In Starkling,' she said. 'Learning to fly.'

extras

www.orbitbooks.net

about the author

Pamela Freeman's first novel for adults, *Blood Ties*, was released in 2007. It was followed a year later by the second book in The Castings Trilogy, *Deep Water*, and by *Full Circle* in 2009, the final book in the trilogy. Pamela is also an award-winning writer for young people, and is best known for the Floramonde children's fantasy series and *The Black Dress*, an inspired biography of Mary MacKillop's early years, which won the New South Wales Premier's History Award in 2006. She has a Doctorate of Creative Arts from the University of Technology, Sydney, where she has also lectured in creative writing. She lives in Sydney with her husband and their son. Visit her website at www.pamelafreemanbooks.com

Find out more about Pamela Freeman and other Orbit authors by registering for the free monthly newsletter at www.orbitbooks.net

if you enjoyed

EMBER AND ASH

look out for

BLOOD TIES

book one of The Castings Trilogy

also by

Pamela Freeman

THE STONECASTER'S STORY

The desire to know the future gnaws at our bones. That is where it started, and might have ended, years ago.

I had cast the stones, seeing their faces flick over and fall: Death, Love, Murder, Treachery, Hope. We are a treacherous people – half of our stones show betrayal and violence and death from those close, death from those far away. It is not so with other peoples. I have seen other sets of stones that show only natural disasters: death from sickness, from age, the pain of a broken heart, loss in childbirth. And those stones are more than half full with pleasure and joy and plain, solid warnings like 'You reap what you sow' and 'Victory is not the same as satisfaction'.

Of course, we live in a land taken by force, by battle and murder and invasion. It is not so surprising, perhaps, that our stones reflect our history.

So. I cast the stones again, wondering. How much of our future do we call to ourselves through this scrying? How much of it do we make happen because the stones give us a pattern to fulfil?

I have seen the stones cast too many times to doubt them.

When I see Murder in the stones, I know someone will die. But would they have died without my foretelling? Perhaps merely saying the word, even in a whisper, brings the thought to the surface of a mind, allows the mind to shape it, give it substance, when otherwise it might have remained nothing more than vague murmurings, easily ignored.

Death recurred again and again in my castings that night. I did not ask whose. Perhaps it was mine, perhaps not. I had no one left to lose, and therefore did not fear to lose myself.

There was someone at the door, breathing heavily outside, afraid to come in. But he did, as they always do, driven by love or fear or greed or pain, or simple curiosity, a desire to giggle with friends.

This one came in shyly: young, eighteen or nineteen, brown hair, green trousers and blue boots. He squatted across the cloth from me with the ease of near-childhood. I held out my left hand, searching his face. He had hazel eyes, but the shape of his face showed he had old blood, from the people who lived in this land before the landtaken, the invasion. There was old pain, too, old anger stoked up high.

He knew what to do. He spat in his own palm, a palm criss-crossed by scars, as though it had been cut many times, and clapped it to mine. I held him tightly and reached for the pouch with my right hand. He was strong enough to stay silent as I dug in the pouch for five stones and threw them across the cloth between us. He was even strong enough not to follow their fall with his eyes, to hold my gaze until I nodded at him and looked down.

He saw it in my face.

'Bad?'

I nodded. One by one I touched the stones lying face-up. 'Death. Bereavement. Chaos. This is the surface. This is what all will see.' Delicately I turned the other two stones over. 'Revenge and Rejoicing. This is what is hidden.' An odd mixture, one I had never before seen.

He brooded over them, not asking anything more. The stones did not speak to me as they often do; all I could tell him were their names. It seemed to be enough for him.

'You know what this refers to?' I asked.

He nodded, absently, staring at Rejoicing. He let go of my hand and slid smoothly to his feet, then tugged some coins out of a pocket and let them fall on the rug.

'My thanks, stonecaster.' Then he was gone.

Who was I to set Death on the march? I know my stones by their feel, even in the darkness of the pouch. I could have fumbled and selected him a happy dream: Love Requited, Troubles Over, Patience. I could have soothed the anger in his eyes, the pain in his heart.

But who am I to cheat the stones?

After he left, I cast them again. This time, Death did not appear. She had gone out the door with the young one and his scars.

SAKER

Saker remembered the first time he had tried to raise the dead. It was the night after Freite, the enchanter, had finally died. By then he had been her apprentice for thirteen long years, but only in the last two had she shared any real secrets with him, and only then because he had threatened to leave her if she withheld.

Freite had wept for her great age and his refusal to any longer give his power for her extended life. She had no more to offer him. He had learnt everything she had to teach of her Wind City magic, and it had not included pity, or generosity. So he refused to touch her in her extremity, knowing she would drain the power out of him to give herself another day, another week, a month if she were lucky ... She had died cursing him, but he was cursed already, so he disregarded it.

After she was buried, the Voice of Whitehaven had pronounced Freite's bequests and he had found that her house had passed into his hands, along with her savings, which were much greater than he had imagined. So there he was, rich but without a plan. He had gone to the stonecaster to find out what the gods wanted him to do next. And the stonecaster had sent him out the door with Revenge and Rejoicing awaiting him.

That first time, he hadn't even known he needed the actual bones for the spell to work. The enchanter had told him half-truths, half-spells, trying to hoard her knowledge as though it could ward off death. Saker knew, certain sure, nothing kept Death away for good. That Lady tapped everyone on the shoulder, sooner or later. But sometimes, just sometimes, she could be tricked.

He raised the black stone knife level with his palm, forcing his hand not to shake. *This must work.* Now, finally, he had the means, seven years since the stonecaster had set him on his path ...

'I am Saker, son of Alder and Linnet of the village of Cliffhaven. I seek justice.'

He began to shake with memory, with yearning, sorrow, righteous rage. There lay the strength of his spell. He touched the never-closing wound in his mind, drew on the pain and set it to work. The rest of the spell wasn't in words, but in memories, complex and distressing: colours, phrases of music, a particular scent, the sound of a scream ...

When he had gathered them all he looked down at his father's bones on the table, his father's skull staring emptily. He pressed the knife to his palm then drew it down hard. The blood surged out in time with his heart and splashed in gouts on the chalk-white bones.

'Alder,' he said. 'Arise.'

BRAMBLE

The blood trail was plain. Every few steps a splotch showed brilliantly red. There were tracks, too. In summer it would have been harder, but in this earliest part of spring the grasses and ferns were thin on the ground, and the ground was soft enough to show the wolf's spoor.

Even the warlord's man would have been able to track this much blood; for Bramble it was like following a clearly marked highway, through new fern fronds and old leaf mould, down past the granite rocks, through the stand of mountain ash, blood marking the trail at every step, so fresh she could smell it. The prints on the right were lighter; it was favouring the wounded side.

It wasn't sensible to go after a hurt wolf with just a boot knife in her hand. She'd be lucky to get home without serious injury. She'd be lucky to get home at all. But she couldn't leave a wounded animal to die in pain, even if she hadn't shot it.

The brown wolf had limped across the far end of the clearing where she had been collecting early spring sorrel at the edge of a small stream, too intent on its own pain to even notice Bramble.

The forest had seemed to hush the moment she saw the arrow, the wolf, the blood dripping from its side. The glade glowed in the afternoon sunlight. Rich and heady, the smell of awakening earth, that special smell that came after the snow-melt was over, rose in drifts around her. She heard chats quarrelling far overhead. The trickle of the stream. A squirrel leaping from branch to branch of an elm, rattling the still-bare twigs. It paused. The wolf stopped and looked back over his shoulder, seeing her for the first time. She waited, barely breathing, feeling as if the whole forest waited with her.

'There he is! See him? Don't lose him!'

'Quiet, idiot!'

The voices broke the moment. The wolf slipped into the shadow of some pine trees. The squirrel, scolding, skipped from elm to willow to alder and was gone. Bramble looked around quickly. The warlord's men were close. Nowhere to hide except up a tree. She dropped the sorrel and sprang for the lowest branch of a yew. Its dark branches would hide her, unlike the easier-to-climb willow next to it whose branches were still showing catkins, but no leaves.

She climbed fast, without worrying about scratches, so she was bleeding in a dozen places by the time she had reached a safe perch. She grabbed some of the yew leaves and crushed them in her hands, wringing them to release the bitter-smelling sap, then rubbed it on the trunk as far down as she could reach, to confuse the scent in case they had hounds, who would sniff out the blood for sure and certain.

She wondered who they were chasing. An actual criminal? Or just someone who'd looked at them the wrong way? Someone old Ceouf, the warlord, had taken against, maybe, or someone who had complained? Bramble smiled wryly. At least it wasn't a woman. Everyone knew what happened to a woman found alone by the warlord's men.

It angered her, as it always did. More than that, it enraged her. The warlords claimed that they protected the people in their Domain, from other warlords, of course, and in earlier days from invaders. Perhaps they had, once. But a couple of generations ago the warlords of the Eleven Domains had made peace, and there hadn't been more than a border skirmish since. The warlord's men weren't soldiers any more, just thugs and bullies. You stayed out of their way, didn't draw their attention, and spat in the dust of their footprints after they'd gone.

It's not meant to be like this, she thought. *No one should have to hide in fear of the people who are supposed to protect them.*

Today she had been happy, happier than she had been for months, since her sister had married and moved away to Carlion, the nearest free town. She had been out in her forest again, rejoicing in the returning spring, giving thanks for new life. And they had brought death and fear with them, as they did everywhere. Her chest burned with resentment. Some part of her had always refused to be sensible about it, as her parents demanded. 'The world's not going to change just because you don't like it,' they'd said, time after time. She knew they were right. Of course she knew it, she wasn't a child or a fool. And yet, some part of her insisted, *It's not meant to be like this.*

'This way!'

The voice came again. Bramble parted the needles in front of her until she could see the clearing below. There were two men, one blond, one red-haired, in warlord's gear, with a blue crest on their shoulders to show their allegiance to this, the South Domain. They were young, about her age. Their horses were tethered near the trail that led into the clearing. One was a thin dark bay, the other a well-muscled roan. The trail ended there, she knew, and the forest, even in early spring, was too dense from here in for mounted men to ride.

'I know I got it,' the blond said. 'I winged it, at least.'

'If you want to finish it off, you'll have to go on foot,' the red-head said. They looked at the undergrowth consideringly, and then the blond looked down at his shiny riding boots.

'I just bought these,' he complained. He had a sharp voice, as though it were the other man's fault that his boots were new.

'Leave it,' the red-head said, clearly bored now.

'I wanted the skin. I've always wanted a wolf skin.' The blond frowned, then shrugged. 'Another day.'

They turned and went back to their horses, mounted, and rode away without a backward glance.

Bramble sat appalled and even angrier. He had left a wounded animal to die in agony so he wouldn't get scratches on his boots! *Oh, isn't that typical!* she thought. *They're the animals, the greedy, heedless, bloody shagging bastards!*

She waited until she was sure they weren't coming back, then swung down from the tree, pulled her knife from her boot, and went to look for the wolf.

She followed the blood trail until it disappeared into the big holly thicket. She skirted the sharp leaves and picked up the trail on the other side. It finally came to an end near the stream in the centre of the forest.

The wolf had staggered down to drink and stood, legs shaking, near the water's edge. Then it saw Bramble, and froze with fear. But it was foaming at the mouth, desperate for water, and she stayed very still, as still as a wild creature in the presence of humans, until it took the last few steps to the water and drank. The black-fletched arrow, a warlord's man's arrow, stuck out from its side.

After drinking, it collapsed on the muddy edge of the stream and panted in pain, looking up at her with great brown eyes, pleading wordlessly.

Bramble came to it gently, making no sudden move that might startle it. 'There now, there now, everything's all right now ...' she crooned, as she did to the orphan kids she raised, or the nannies she helped give birth. She lowered her hand slowly, softly onto its forehead and the wolf whined like a pup. 'Not long now, not long,' she said softly, stroking back to grip its ears. She gazed into its eyes steadily until it looked away, as all wild animals will look away from the gaze of anything they do not wish to fight, and then she cut its throat, as quickly and painlessly as she could.

Bramble sat waiting, her hand still on its head, ignoring the tears on her cheeks, while the blood pulsed out into the stream, swirling red. There wasn't much blood. It had bled a lot already. Her fingers gentled its ears as though it could still feel, then she stood up.

She hesitated, looking at the caked blood on its side, then stripped off her jacket, shirt, skirt and leggings, so she wouldn't stain them. She had to hope that the warlord's men wouldn't change their minds and come back. She could just imagine *that* scene.

Her knife was only sharp enough to slit through the hide. She had to heave the carcase over to peel the skin off and it was much heavier than she thought. There was blood all over her. She wrinkled her nose, but kept going. It was a good, winter-thick pelt and besides, taking it gave the death of the wolf some purpose, instead of it being a complete waste of life. She cut the pelt off at the base of the skull. It was worth more with head attached, but Bramble had always felt that tanning the head of the animal was a kind of insult.

She would have left the carcase for the crows and the foxes, but she didn't want the warlord's men to find it, if they came looking for the hide later. Let him think that he had missed. She dragged it up the hill to a rock outcropping, and piled stones on it. At least it would make a meal for the ants and the worms.

She washed the blood off both her and the hide, put her clothes back on, tied up the hide and hoisted it over her shoulder. It weighed her down heavily, but she could manage it easily enough. She set off home.

The way was through the black elm and pine forest, and normally she would have lingered to admire the spring-green leaves that were beginning to bud, and listen to the white-backed woodpeckers frantically drilling for food after their long migration. She had been observing a red-breasted flycatcher pair build their nest, but today she passed it by without noticing, although she stopped to collect some wild thyme and sallet greens, and to empty one of her snares. She found a rabbit, thin after winter but good enough for a stew, and the pelt still winter-lush. Her hands did the work of resetting the snare but her mind was elsewhere.

The forest was ostensibly the warlord's domain, but was traditionally the hunting or grazing ground for a range of people, from foragers like Bramble to charcoal burners, coppicers, chair makers, withiers, pig farmers and woodcutters.

It was a rare day that Bramble didn't meet someone in the forest; depending on the season, sometimes she saw as many people there as in the village street. It was just her bad luck that today she had seen the warlord's men.

She came out of the forest near the crossroads just outside Wooding and realised that it hadn't been just bad luck. There had been an execution today.

Her village of Wooding saw a lot of executions, because it was on the direct road from Carlion to the warlord's fort at Thornhill. For centuries the South Domain warlords had used the crossroads just outside Wooding as the site for their punishments. There was a scaffold set up for when the warlord felt merciful. And for when he wasn't there was the rock press, a sturdy wooden box the size of a coffin, but deeper, where the condemned were piled with heavy stones until their bones broke and they suffocated, slowly.

Today they had used the rock press. There was blood seeping out of the box at the corners. The condemned often bled from the nose and mouth in the final stages of pressing. Bramble slowed as she walked past the punishment site. Did she want to know who they had killed this time? What was the point?

She went over to the box and looked in. No one she knew, thank the gods. Some stranger – the Domain was large, and criminals were brought to the warlord from miles away. Then she looked closer. A stranger, but just a boy. Fourteen, perhaps. A baby. Probably accused of something like 'disrespect to the warlord'. Her heart burned again, as it had in the woods. Anger, indignation, pity. She would have to make sure she was nowhere near the village the next morning, when the warlord's men rounded up the villagers to see the boy's corpse removed from the box and placed in the gibbet. She doubted she could applaud and cheer for the warlord over this execution, as the villagers were expected to do.

Some did so gladly. There were always a few who enjoyed a killing, like the crows that nested in the tree next to the scaffold and descended on the corpses with real enthusiasm. But the rest of the villagers had seen too many people die who looked just like them. Ordinary people. People who couldn't pay their taxes, or hadn't bowed low enough to the warlord. Or who had objected to their daughter being dragged away to the fort by the warlord's men. It was important to attend the executions, and to cheer loudly. The warlord's men were always watching. Bramble had cheered as loudly as anyone, in the past, and had been sick later, every time.

So the warlord's men would have done their job today and gone home as soon as the boy stopped breathing. The blond had probably taken the short cut through the woods and had seen the wolf by accident. He couldn't resist tracking it a little way. Couldn't resist killing again.

A hunter who didn't care if the animal he shot suffered deserved nothing but contempt. He certainly didn't deserve the hide of the animal he had abandoned to pain and slow death.

But the *sensible* thing to do would be to take the skin to the warlord's fort, say it had one of the warlord's arrows in it when she found it, and let the blond claim it. Let him have his prize for killing.

Bramble looked at the boy in the box, whose face was still contorted in pain. 'Well, no one ever said I was sensible,' she said.

She skirted the village and came to the back of her parents' house, through the alders that fringed the stream. She dumped the wolf skin behind the privy, then went the whole way back so she would be seen to come home through the main street with nothing in her hands but rabbit and greens.

Bramble passed the inn and ignored the stares of the old men who sat on the bench outside the door, tankards in hand, until one of them called out, 'Got your nose stuck in the air, I see! Too high and mighty to tell us how that sister of yours is doing off in Carlion!'

It was Swith, the leatherworker's father, both hands cramped around his mug. He was a terrible gossip, but that wasn't why he had called Bramble over. He wanted her to notice his hands. The arthritis that kept him sitting here in the mild sun had swelled his knuckles up like a goat's full udder.

'She's well, she says,' Bramble replied. 'They're building a new house, on the lot next to his parents'.'

'Ah, she's done well for herself, that Maryrose!' cackled Swith's crony, old Aden, the most lecherous man in the village in his day, and still not to be trusted within arm's reach. 'She wasn't an eye-catcher like you, lass. But he got a good hot bed to go to, I'll say that, her town clerk's son!'

The other men frowned. Maryrose had been liked by everyone in the village, and she was certainly no light-skirt.

'That's enough of that, Aden,' Swith said reprovingly. 'Your Mam and Da will be missing her,' he said with a cunning sideways look. 'She was their favourite, wasn't she?'

It was an old game of his, trying to get Bramble to give him back a short answer. It kept him amused, and it didn't do her any harm. Everyone knew that Maryrose was the favourite.

'They are missing her, of course, Swith,' Bramble said. Then, feeling she had given Aden and the others enough entertainment, she said, 'I notice your hands are bothering you. Could I be helping? Give them a rub, maybe?'

'If you want to help a man by rubbing something—'

'Close that dirty mouth, Aden!' Swith bellowed then glanced a bit shame-facedly at Bramble. 'Well, lass, now you mention it . . .'

She smiled at him. 'I'll come by after supper.'

It was a more or less regular thing she did, massaging goose grease and comfrey into the old people's hands and feet. Not all of them, of course. Just the cross-grained ones who couldn't find anyone else to help them. She was glad Aden didn't have arthritis; she wasn't about to get within groping distance of him.

She hefted the rabbit and greens in one hand. 'I have to get these to Mam.' None of them had mentioned the rabbit, though they had eyed it and no doubt would have liked to hear all the details on where she had trapped it and what kind of snare she had used, the kind of talk that kept them occupied for hours. To ask would have been against custom, since they all knew Swith had called her over to ask her a favour, which she was granting. If she wanted to tell them about her hunting, she would, in her own good time.

If she hadn't offered to help Swith, it would have been a different story, she thought with amusement as she walked up the street, exchanging greetings with Mill the charcoal burner, home at his grandparents' until after the snow-melt and spring rains, and ignoring the tribe of dogs that swirled around her heels as they always did. But she had made the offer, so the old men couldn't cross-question her without being unforgivably rude.

'I have a doe ready to drop twins, Bramble,' called Sigi, the new young brewster who had doubled the inn's clientele after she had married its owner, Eril. Sigi's three toddlers, who ran around her feet as she brought in her washing, were screaming with excitement about a maggot one of them had plucked from the rubbish pile. 'If she doesn't have enough milk for both, can I bring one to you?'

'Of course, and welcome,' Bramble called back. 'I've no orphans this season so far.'

When Sigi had first met Bramble, she had reacted as many people did, with suspicion at Bramble's dark hair and eyes. In this land of blonds and red-heads, a dark-haired person was assumed to be a Traveller, a descendant of the original inhabitants of the Domains, who had been invaded and dispossessed a thousand years ago. Old history. But no one trusted Travellers. They were thieves, liars, perverts, bad luck bringers. Bramble had heard all the insults over the years, mostly (though not always) by people who didn't know her, like ordinary travellers on the road through Wooding to Carlion.

Sigi had finally overcome her suspicion, and Bramble was trying hard to forget the insult. It would be nice to have a friend in the village, now Maryrose was gone, and Sigi was the best candidate. The other girls had long ago shut her out after she had made it clear that she didn't have any interest in the things that obsessed them, like boys and hair ribbons and sewing for their glory boxes. Not that boys weren't a pleasure, now and then.

Sigi's oldest child grabbed the maggot and dropped it down her brother's back and the resultant wailing distracted Sigi completely. Bramble laughed and went on to her own home, following Gred, the goose girl, as she shepherded her waddling, squabbling, hissing flock back to their night pasture outside the mill.

Bramble's family lived in an old cottage, a house really, bigger than it looked from the street, as it ran far back towards the stream. It was built of the local bluestone, all except for the chimney, which was rounded river stones in every shade of grey and brown and dark blue. It was thatched with the herringbone pattern you found on every roof around here, although in Carlion they thatched a fish-scale pattern, when they didn't tile in slate. The front garden caught the morning light, so it was full of early herbs just pushing through the soil. The vine over one corner was still a bare skeleton, but the house had a cheerful, open look with its shutters wide and its door ajar.

The door was ajar because her mother was in the road sweeping up the droppings the geese had left behind. The Widow Farli was doing the same thing outside her cottage a little farther down. Goose droppings were good fertiliser, and for someone like Widow Farli, who only kept a couple of scraggly hens, they were important. Bramble's mother, Summer, kept pigs, as well as goats and hens, and really didn't need them.

'No use wasting them,' her mam said as Bramble came up. She swept the droppings onto an old piece of bag. 'Here, go and give them to Widow Farli.' She held the bag out.

Bramble took the droppings and handed the wild thyme and the sallet greens and the rabbit carcase to her mother.

Farli had a face you could cut cheese with, and the tip of her nose was always white, as if with anger, but at what, Bramble had never figured out. She stared past Bramble and said snidely, 'Nice of your *mother* to take the trouble. *She's* not one to go off gallivanting and leave all her work to others.'

'Just as well,' Bramble said, smiling sweetly, 'or what would become of you?'

Farli's face flushed dark red. 'Your tongue'll get you into mischief one day, young lady, you mark my words! Mischief or worse!'

She turned on her heel and flounced towards her back garden, keeping a tight hold of the bag of droppings.

Bramble grinned and went home. She had a pelt to cure. She fetched it from behind the privy and went to the kitchen door to ask her mother for a loan of the good knife to scrape the skin down.

'A *wolf*?' her mam said, that note in her voice that meant 'What will the girl do next?' She had her frown on, too, the 'What have I done to deserve this?' frown.

Bramble had grown up knowing she'd never be the daughter her parents wanted – never be like her sister, Maryrose, who was a crafter born, responsible, hard-working, loving in the way they understood. Maryrose looked like her mother, tawny-haired and blue-eyed, clearly one of Acton's people, while Bramble looked like her granda, who had started life a Traveller. He looked like the people who'd lived here before Acton's people had come over the mountains. Along with her colouring – or perhaps due to the way people looked askance at her because of it – Bramble had inherited the Traveller restlessness, the hatred of being enclosed. Where Maryrose was positively happy to stay seated all day at the loom with her mother, or stand in the workshop shaping and smoothing a beech table with her father, Bramble yearned to be in the forest, for the green luxuriance of summer growth, the sharp tracery of bare branches in winter, the damp mould and mushroom smell of autumn.

She had spent all her free time there as a child, and a lot of time when she should have been learning a trade. While she never did learn to weave or carpenter, by the time she was old enough to marry, a good proportion of the family food came to the table from her hands, and a few luxuries as well. Their flock of goats came from Bramble's nursing of orphan kids or the runty twin of a dropping. If she raised a kid successfully, she got either half the meat if it were a billy, or the first kid if it were a nanny. She had a knack with sick animals, and sick people, too. In the forest, she set snares, gathered greens, fruits and nuts, herbs and bulbs. In early spring, the hard time, it was her sallets and snowberries that kept the family from the scurvy, her rabbit and squirrel that fed them when the bacon ran out and the cornmeal ran low. They could have bought extra supplies, of course, but the money they saved, then and all through the year, from Bramble's gathering, made the difference between survival and prosperity, between living from day to day and having a nest egg behind them. And her furs brought in silver, too, although they weren't the thick, expensive kind you got from the colder areas up north near Foreverfroze. And old Ceouf, the warlord, took a full half of what she made on them, for a 'luxury' tax.

There was always someone in the village ready to spy for the warlord. At Wooding's yearly Tax Day in autumn, it was amazing how the warlord's steward seemed to know everything that had been grown or raised or sold or bought in the last year. Bramble suspected Widow Farli of being an informer, but she couldn't blame her. A woman alone needed some way of buying the warlord's protection.

Bramble had never brought home a wolf skin before, but her mam thought poorly of it for one of those 'it isn't respectable' reasons that she could never quite follow.

'The gods alone know what'll become of you, my girl,' Mam said. That wasn't so bad; it was said with a kind of exasperated affection. But then she sighed and couldn't resist adding, 'If only you were more like your sister!'

When Bramble was six, and seven, and eight, that sigh and that sentence had made her stomach clench with anguish and bewilderment. At nineteen, she just raised an eyebrow at her mother and smiled. It did no good to let it hurt; neither she nor her parents were going to change. *Could* change. And if there was still a cold stone, an empty hollow, under her ribs left over from when she was little, it was so familiar she didn't even feel it any more.

'I'll make you a gorgeous coat out of it, Mam,' she said, and winked. 'Just think how impressed they'll be at the Winterfest dance.'